D1495370

OUT OF OUR LEAGUE

EDITED BY

Dahlia Adler
&
Jennifer Iacopelli

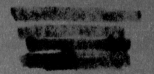

OUT OF OUR LEAGUE

16 STORIES OF GIRLS IN SPORTS

FEIWEL AND FRIENDS
NEW YORK

YAF
Adler, D

A Feiwel and Friends Book
An imprint of Macmillan Publishing Group, LLC
120 Broadway, New York, NY 10271 • fiercereads.com

Our books may be purchased in bulk for promotional, educational, or business
use. Please contact your local bookseller or the Macmillan Corporate and
Premium Sales Department at (800) 221-7945 ext. 5442 or by email at
MacmillanSpecialMarkets@macmillan.com.

Library of Congress Cataloging-in-Publication Data is available.

First edition, 2024
Book design by L. Whitt
Feiwel and Friends logo designed by Filomena Tuosto
Printed in the United States of America

ISBN 978-1-250-81071-7

7 6   4 3 2 1

TO ALL THE GIRLS OF THE MORASHA HOCKEY
TEAM THAT NEVER OFFICIALLY WAS, WITH
THANKS FOR THE MEMORIES
—D. A.

FOR MY LONG ISLAND HEAT GIRLS AND
EVERYONE WHO KNOWS DOTTIE DIDN'T DROP
THE BALL ON PURPOSE, THIS ONE'S FOR YOU
—J. I.

CONTENTS

SAFE AT HOME

JENNIFER IACOPELLI

My older sister has always been great. It's like a universal truth. The Earth revolves around the sun. What goes up must come down, because, you know, gravity. And Meredith Hancock is great.

Great at what?

Great at everything.

Great at school, near the top of her class since kindergarten; great at baseball, leading our town's All-Star team to the Little League World Series when she was twelve. She was the only middle school girl on varsity cross-country and basketball and, of course, softball, once she swapped over to play with the other girls. All-State as an eighth grader, All-Region as a freshman, and then All-American honors rolling in by her sophomore and junior years.

Like I said, great.

But I'm not sure I understood just how great until right now, playing against her in a national championship game at Hall of Fame Stadium in Oklahoma City, the capital of fastpitch softball. It's not even because of the home run she blasted off my best curve-ball last inning to put her team ahead. Though, yeah, my neck is still feeling the whiplash of watching the laser beam she rocketed disappear over the left field fence.

No, it's from where I'm standing in the on-deck circle while she's squatting behind home plate and she frames a pitch that's clearly outside so well even the umpire behind her is fooled into thinking it's a strike. The same way she's done the whole game. The whole tournament, really. She's the best player in this thing and it's not close. And that's saying something at the Amateur Softball Association's 18-Under Gold Nationals, the most elite club fastpitch softball tournament in the country.

"Strike three!" the ump yells, but no one is even listening to him because Meredith shifts her weight down, pivots on her knee, and fires a laser beam to third, where the runner, my teammate Kiera, drifted just a little too far away from the base. Kiera dives back, but way too late.

"Out!" the field umpire calls as the girl who caught the ball checks the other runner, Hayden, at first. She gets back to the base without a throw, but the damage is done.

The crowd in the stands explodes behind us. It's mostly our families and the players from the teams already eliminated and their families. And the college coaches here to scout. Not that I'm thinking about them. Or whether or not my parents are cheering.

I've always wondered who they'd root for if Meredith and I played against each other.

I'm absolutely never going to ask.

It's a pretty good life philosophy: Don't ask questions you don't want answers to.

That's not important now, though. What's important is what just happened, because ten seconds ago we had the upper hand.

We had runners on first and third, nobody out, and one of our best hitters up at the plate. We were a fly ball away from tying the game, an extra base hit away from scoring two runs—Hayden's superfast, she'll score on anything in the gap—and walking off this field National Champions.

But that was then.

Now?

We're down to our final out.

And I'm up to bat.

Tying run on first.

Winning run at the plate.

No pressure.

It's not like I'm the only rising sophomore on a team full of almost seniors, facing one of the best pitchers in the country, my sister's best friend, Nora.

"Hey, we got two down!" Meredith says from out in front of home plate, standing tall, nearly six feet in her cleats. Her catcher's mask is up, revealing her face to her teammates like the field general she's been since the first time she put on that equipment. She's holding a hand in the air, waving it to the outfielders, pointer and pinkie fingers raised. Her face is streaked with dirt. So is her uniform, the black material and maroon lettering of the famous California Diamond Queens—the oldest and most prestigious travel softball club in the country, the team I didn't make, thanks to Nora being completely dominant—almost disappearing under it. Her light brown hair, the same color as mine, is pasted against her forehead in the Oklahoma heat. It's been unforgiving this past week, but it's almost over now.

Bottom of the seventh.

Two outs.

Championship on the line.

I glance back at my dugout, my teammates lined up against the fence, fingers twined in the chain link, desperate to do something to change what just happened, but the only person who can do that is me.

And I'm just Molly. The other Hancock.

And yeah, maybe I'm good. Really good. But the SoCal Heat didn't pull me up from their 16-Under team for my bat. I'm not a bad hitter, but I'm mostly here because one of their pitchers got hurt right before the tournament. I half expected Coach to pinch-hit for me. But asking someone to come off the bench cold and face down a girl who'll play for UCLA next year? That's asking a lot of anyone.

Too much.

Meredith doesn't look at me when she backs up behind home plate, just replaces her mask over her face and squats down, waiting for me to get settled in the batter's box, like I'm any other batter. To her I probably am. Great players, they can separate everything else from the game.

That's what I need to do right now.

Okay, deep breath. I can do this. I take batting practice off Nora at home all the time. This is just like that, right?

Yeah, no, it's nothing like that.

I rest the bat against my shoulder and exhale, relaxing my entire body as Meredith puts down the sign. Nora, just forty-three feet away, nods, then rocks into motion, arm whipping around in a circle. I have less than a half second to react.

Hiss.

Yes—no. No! NO!

Too late. I swing and miss.

Pop!

The ball thwacks into Meredith's glove.

Strike one.

It was a riser, the bane of every fastpitch softball player's existence. Nora's has been tantalizingly good all game. It starts off looking like a fat, juicy fastball right down the middle, but then jumps just before it reaches home plate, out of reach of your bat before you can stop your swing.

And just like that, I'm down in the count.

Lay off it, a voice in my head screeches, one that actually sounds annoyingly like Meredith.

Okay, deep breath. Look for something to punch to right. Get on base. Get Hayden into scoring position. Keep the line moving. Keep us alive.

I feel Meredith shift behind me—I can't tell which way—just as Nora goes into her windup, and then the pitch is coming, my weight shifts, but way too early.

Changeup.

Shit.

I can't adjust, it's too slow and I swing, just before it crosses the plate, my feet tangling underneath me.

Strike two.

Meredith fires the ball back to Nora as I stumble out of the box trying to reset myself. Riser, then change, and now . . . what? A curveball like she threw me my last at bat? Another riser because of how silly I looked on the first one? Or a fastball, just to prove she can throw the thing by me after that incredible changeup?

No.

Don't think, just hit.

Don't think.

Just hit.

The crowd is back there somewhere, my parents in it, but that all fades to a distant buzz. I step into the box and breathe in and then out and focus.

Nora lets go of the ball.

Yes—yes. Yes! YES! It's a riser that doesn't rise. Contact, so solid and true I barely feel it as the ball launches into the right centerfield gap.

My feet grind through the dirt up the first baseline, wind whistling in the ear holes of my helmet. The outfielders converge on the ball in right center, but it bounces off the wall and then darts backward past them into no-man's-land. That's the last I see of it as I round second, my eyes lifting to our third base coach, who's waving Hayden home.

She's a flash of red, gold, and black uniform with her blond ponytail swinging out of the back of her helmet as she crosses the plate.

Tie game.

My foot hits third and Coach raises her hands to stop me, but I can't, I'm going too hard, too fast. Instinctively, I feel something in the field shift behind me. The ball is coming back in. I raise my head and there's Meredith looming ahead of me, out in front of home plate. There's my path. Hayden waves her arms violently to the outside and down, signaling to slide to the back of the plate, but I know I need to get as far away from the ball and the tag as I can, as far away from my sister as I can.

I take one last stride and dive just as Meredith lunges backward.

The ball, she, and I arrive in the same spot at the same time, and just as my hand brushes against the back corner of the plate, her shoulder blasts into mine.

We go sprawling, the momentum sending me flying into the hard-packed dirt. This might be softball, but there's nothing soft about it right now, with heavy brown dust rising around us into a cloud of confusion.

My breath goes out of me the same way the sound is sucked out of the stands, everyone falling silent around us as the air clears.

"Safe!" the umpire screams, and I've never heard a sweeter word in my life.

I'm still down on the ground and so is Meredith, but so is the ball, a few inches from her outstretched hand.

I'm safe.

I scored.

We win.

I win.

Waking up has a surreal, almost dreamy quality to it, back in my own bed after catching a late flight to San Diego last night.

But when I roll over on my shoulder, the aching bruise from that collision at home is very, very real. And so is the trophy sitting in the corner of my bedroom and the championship ring in its box on my nightstand.

Reality is so, so sweet, even if today is the first day of school and my body clock is still two hours ahead.

"Jet lag is the worst," I grumble, dragging myself into the kitchen and onto a stool at the island. "Do I really have to go to school today?"

My mom raises an eyebrow from her spot leaning against the counter, nursing a mug of steaming coffee. She doesn't even have to say it. This was part of our agreement. I can play with the 18-Under team as long as I don't give my parents a hard time about school.

But we *won* Nationals. That should count for something, shouldn't it?

"Morning," Meredith says, moving in behind me. She's already dressed. Not for the day, though, but for the run she's already back from. Her shoulder bruise matches mine, blue and purple, the same colors as the sports bra she ran in this morning. She grabs a banana from the bowl on the counter next to Mom. "I'm leaving at six forty-five sharp if you want a ride."

"Okay, fine," I mutter. She tosses me a banana and I catch it before sliding off the stool and heading back upstairs to get ready for school.

So yeah, I'm a little bit jet-lagged and I barely slept last night, but now I'm actually pumped. Today is gonna be awesome. None of our teammates go to Mitchell High School with us except for Nora, but *everyone* knows what happened. It's all over social media. My phone was so out of control when I got off the plane that I had to shut off my notifications.

I shower fast and pass Meredith in the hallway as she heads in for her own. She barely looks up at me, her eyes glued to her phone as she shuts the bathroom door.

She's probably texting Sawyer, her boyfriend. He's *almost* as annoyingly perfect as she is, but with his broad shoulders, bright smile, and purposefully messy hair, I'm willing to overlook it. He's headed to Harvard next year, probably, or Yale or whatever genius school people go to, to be a brain surgeon or president or whatever.

Meredith still hasn't decided where she wants to go and she's been really quiet about it all summer, despite all the college coaches drooling over her since she was like twelve. All the top schools—Oklahoma, UCLA, Alabama, Washington, Northwestern, Arizona, Stanford—they all want her.

Now it's my turn to get drooled on.

Wait . . . over, not on. Whatever. I'm definitely still jet-lagged.

We left Oklahoma with a stack of coaches' business cards that didn't even fit in Dad's wallet. And when I get home from school today I have a bunch of emails to send to Division 1 programs all around the country.

I throw on a T-shirt and shorts, pull my hair up into a wet, messy bun, tug on a pair of Chucks, and let myself stare at my trophy for a little while, but not too long. Meredith will actually leave without me if I'm not on time, and then I'll have to take the bus. I'm halfway down the stairs when a high-pitched murder shriek nearly sends me tumbling down them.

"What? Who died?" I yell, racing into the kitchen where Mom and Dad are squeezing the hell out of Meredith, tears running down her cheeks.

Shit, did someone *actually* die?

"Northwestern! Oh, honey, a full scholarship. It's amazing," Mom says, and Meredith laughs, gently pulling out of the hug and wiping away her tears.

Oh.

She's going to Northwestern. One of the best softball programs in the country. One of the best *schools* in the country, especially for journalism, and I know she wants to be like a female Steve Kornacki when she grows up.

And she decided today.

That's just . . . great.

"Congrats, Mere," I say when she sends me a watery smile.

"Thanks," she says, giving herself a little shake. "Okay, we should head to school. Still have to graduate."

Mom and Dad laugh and give her one last squeeze each before they hug me, too.

"Have a good first day, girls!" Dad calls behind us as we move through the front door and head for Meredith's car. Our car, technically, but I only have a permit, so until I pass my test, it's hers.

"You drive," she says, tossing me her keys. "I need to call Sawyer."

He picks up right away, clearly driving to school, too, because I can hear the engine in the background.

"Hey babe, what's up?"

"It's official!" Meredith squeaks, in a voice that's the exact opposite of her commands on the field. "Coach Hernandez sent me the offer last night. I didn't see it until this morning because I passed out after the flight, but I'm going to Northwestern."

"Congrats, superstar! No one deserves this more, M! I'm so proud of you."

"Thanks," she says, a smile playing across her mouth, her expression going soft. "I'm really proud of me, too."

Sawyer laughs. "I'm pulling in now. I'll see you in a minute, congratulate you properly."

Fair warning, then. I need to get out of the car and head straight inside if I don't want to watch them make out in the school parking lot.

We pull into our spot and it's already getting crowded, a mark of the first day of school. By tomorrow less than half the kids will be here at this time.

I take off for the building, passing a small crowd headed for Meredith getting out of the car, led by her boyfriend.

"Hey Molly," Sawyer and Nora chorus together, but that's it, before the group of seniors totally surround my sister, drawing an even bigger crowd from the arriving buses when the shouts of congratulations start to flow.

So much for my win, I guess.

"She just had to pick today, didn't she?" I complain, slamming my locker door shut. "She couldn't give me *one day* before it had to be about her again?"

"I mean, it's kind of a big deal," Carly, my best friend, says, her thumb scrolling through her phone. "Northwestern is amazing. I'd love to live in Chicago; a few of the girls from camp are from there."

"It snows ten months out of the year in Chicago. You start wearing sweaters when it drops below seventy."

Carly shrugs, not giving me the sympathy I'm craving because she's my best friend and knows as much as I do that I'm being ridiculous. "That way when I come back home I can appreciate eighty-five and sunny every day."

"Whatever. Maybe she can graduate early and go in January instead."

"Don't say that. You're gonna miss her. Who's gonna help you with Trig once she's gone?"

"You mean who is going to help *you* with Trig."

"Wow," Carly says. "Harsh, but fair. And maybe this will make you feel better. Someone grabbed a video of you scoring that last run and posted it. It's got like half a million views."

"What?" I squeak, as Carly shoves her phone under my nose.

"It's one of those highlight accounts."

I take the phone and stare at the screen. The video is good, taken from just behind home plate on the first base side. It's zoomed in on me rounding third, right through my coach's stop sign as the ball is fired home. It's just like I remember it. I can feel my shoulder hitting Meredith's, the air rushing out of my chest when I hit the ground, the umpire calling me safe, the crowd roaring a tidal wave of noise down to the field, my teammates piling on top of me and I'm happy to be suffocated by them. Ecstatic even.

This is almost as cool as living it.

Half a million people have watched me score a run to win a championship.

My eyes scan down to the comments and I start to scroll, pulling in a deep breath at all the verified accounts, actors, singers, athletes, and a few professional baseball teams at the top adding all-caps responses, thumbs-ups, and little notes.

GIRL POWER!

Third Base Coach: Molly, no! Molly: Molly, yes!

Nothing was stopping her. Look at her go. You can't teach hustle like that.

And it gets better . . . they're SISTERS!

It spreads through school almost as fast as it spreads online. My teachers have seen it. Everybody in my classes has seen it.

"Molly, someone set it to the song from *Titanic*!" Mimi, a very cute ice hockey player in my Chem class says, leaning over from her seat across the row to show me, just as Jake, the equally cute junior class president sitting in front of me, turns around to watch, too. There I am rounding third base in slow motion as the music swells, and just as Celine Dion's voice echoes through the tiny speaker, I collide with Meredith at home and actual goose bumps spread across my arms, making me shiver.

And that's when my eyes catch on the account that shared it.

Holy crap.

ESPN.

It's gone viral.

I've gone viral.

My notifications have been off since late last night and my DMs were a total mess even before the video blew up, so I haven't even been trying to keep up. It's not until I get to lunch when I have a chance to check my messages and when I do, I get goose bumps again, but this time not the good kind.

It's not winning if you cheat.

How nice, big sister let little sister win.

Her hand flexes on the ball before it falls out. She dropped it on purpose. Pathetic.

This is bullshit. Both of them should be banned.

And then, in my DMs, a bunch of media outlets sending long rambling messages about the video, asking for a comment, asking me to appear on their channels, asking if it's okay to come to our house for an interview.

I ignore them all.

Because I know they only want to ask me one thing right now: Did my sister, my annoyingly perfect, absolute beast-of-a-ballplayer big sister, let me win?

"It's crap," Carly says, as we move into the courtyard and sit at the table we claimed as our own last year, far enough away from the trash cans to avoid the smell, but close enough to the building to avoid being late to our next class when the bell rings.

I set my lunch tray down and sigh heavily. "Of course it's crap," I say flatly. "It's crap, right?"

"Total crap," Carly agrees, reaching out and squeezing my hand. "Meredith wouldn't do that."

"She wouldn't," I say, but the doubt is there now, spurred on by those stupid comments, talking about the way her hand hit the ground and how her fingers didn't lose grip right away and how she didn't let go as soon as it hit the ground and what if . . . what if she did let me win? What if she . . . what if she knew how much I wanted it, how desperate I was in that moment not just to win the game, but to beat *her*, and what if . . . what if my big sister, in a moment of absolute madness, just let her hand fall open and let the ball roll out of it? What if she let me win? What if the one thing I've ever felt like I earned all on my own is fake? The crowd, the college coaches, the viral video, what if it's all bullshit?

The rest of the day flies, and when the final bell rings, I head straight for the locker room. We have cross-country practice after school, but when I get there, Nora's waiting, holding out the car keys.

"Sawyer drove her home," is all my sister's best friend says to me, but it's enough. If Meredith's missing practice, even for her third-best sport, then she definitely saw the messages. Her DMs are probably even worse than mine. She's the one they're accusing of throwing the game. Something she'd never do.

And I know that, logically, but the doubt is still there, pulling at my chest.

I try to push it out of my head, but it's impossible. Practice today is just a long recovery run since I've missed the past week because of Nationals. So it's just me, by myself, setting my own pace, listening to the pounding of my feet on the pavement as a question I definitely don't want an answer to repeats over and over again in my mind.

What if it's true?

By the time I get home, after the slowest drive ever, terrified I'd get pulled over without a licensed driver in the car with me, Meredith's in her bedroom, the door shut. And when I sit down to dinner, freshly showered after running a quick 5K during practice, I can only stare across the table at my parents for a few seconds before breaking.

"How bad is it?"

Mom sends Dad a quick glance, but then sighs, putting down her fork. "The Northwestern coach called earlier wanting assurances that what they're saying online isn't true."

Anger prickles at the back of my neck. How *dare* that coach even suggest that my sister would . . . wait, but . . . isn't that what I've been doing? And then a terrible, god-awful thought occurs to me.

"Are they going to take her scholarship back?" I ask quietly, nudging my roasted carrots around my plate, circling the grilled salmon but not actually eating any of it. I'm not sure my stomach can handle food right now.

I expect a quick no, but Dad shrugs. "I'm not an expert, but I think they can withdraw it if . . . if something like this happens."

"They can't do that. It's all she's ever wanted. They can't just take it away from her. She earned the scholarship. She should tell them to shove it and go to Stanford instead."

Their silence speaks volumes.

That might not even be an option. Stanford won't want her if Northwestern doesn't. No one will.

Mom picks up a plate and leaves the kitchen, probably to try to get Meredith to eat something, so I pull out my phone and watch the video again. A reporter on one of those sports talk shows that fill up the day before actual sports are played at night has slowed it down and added commentary.

"She catches the ball clean and she's fundamentally sound," the dude says as the camera flashes to his unimpressed-looking co-host, Vera Nuñez from ESPN. "Her foot slides back, knee goes down to block the plate while she's moving to tag her sister. It happens so fast, there's no way for her to really secure the ball, and even though it's a clean play according to the rules, there's an actual collision, which complicates everything even more. There's no way to know if the ball got knocked loose or if she decided in that split second to give her little sister the win. The only person who knows is Meredith Hancock. If you had a little sister, wouldn't you let her win?"

Vera opens her mouth to respond, glaring daggers across the desk. "I *am* a little sister and I would be furious with my big sister if she let me win anything, let alone anything as important as a championship game. Who are we to be questioning this young woman's integrity?"

The jerk just shrugs, a smug grin on his face while the clip cuts out.

Mom comes back a minute later, the full plate still in her hand, shaking her head.

"I'm gonna try and talk to her," I say, pushing my own full plate away.

"Molly, that might not be—" Dad starts, but I don't hear whatever else he says as I move past Mom and out of the kitchen.

I knock on her door gently. I can't remember the last time I didn't just barge into Meredith's room, greeted by an annoyed, but affectionate eye roll as she stops whatever she's doing to ask me what I need.

"Mere?" I ask quietly. "Can I come in?"

For a second and then another, there's only silence, and I'm about to turn around and leave when she says, "It's open."

"Hey," I murmur as I push the door open just a crack and slip through, leaning back against it as I close it behind me.

She's sitting on her bed staring blankly down at her phone on the duvet as it lights up, the messages continuing to pour in, and she hugs a pillow to her chest, her knees drawn up against it. She looks so small. I've never seen her look this small before.

"You okay?"

It's a stupid question, but it's the only thing I can think of to say. Of course she's not okay. She lost a national championship and now she might lose everything she's ever worked for, everything she's ever wanted.

I'm such an idiot for doubting her.

"Sorry, I—"

"No, it's—" she says, and stops. "Well, it's not really fine, but you know that."

"Yeah," I say, hesitating, biting my lip and studying the floor, the brown wooden planks that lead to the soft cream-colored area rug under her bed, covered in a pink velvet duvet and an army of throw pillows. My sister is an incredible athlete, but she's a girly girl at heart. She must take my silence for something it's not, though, maybe judgment or, worse, anger.

"Just ask me, Mol," she says, her voice tight, and I look up to see her face, streaked with tears. Not the happy kind from this morning, the terrifying kind. Her eyes are bloodshot, her mascara and eyeliner staining the skin below them, her hair hanging limply around her shoulders; even the tan she's sported all summer seems faded. "Ask me if I let you win, if I deliberately lost a National Championship, letting down my coaches and my teammates, putting everything I've ever worked for at risk, just so my little sister could win a fucking game. *Ask me.*"

She says it all with an eerie calmness, her voice barely rising above a whisper.

"I don't have to ask," I say, all my doubt entirely gone, climbing up onto the bed and moving in beside her, putting my arm around her shoulders. I know my sister better than anyone, maybe better than I even know myself. "I know you'd never, ever do that."

"Do you?" she asks, laughing, a slightly hysterical note to it. I pull her in tighter. "No one else seems to."

"I bet Sawyer does," I say, trying to lighten the mood a little bit.

"Sawyer doesn't count," she says, pulling away, smiling. The smile stays for half a second before dropping again. "I talked to Coach Hernandez. She says she needs to know that her players will put the team first, no matter what. I told her that I'm that kind of player and she said she believes me, but I don't know. What am I supposed to do? What does she want me to do? How can I prove . . . I was just . . . I was so happy for you, Molly. I was sad we lost, but I was so happy you won and I'm so sorry everyone else ruined it. I'm sorry *I* ruined it and you have to deal with this instead of celebrating your win. You deserve to celebrate. I am so proud of you."

"You are?" I ask, flinching at how incredibly desperate the question sounds as her eyes brim with tears again.

Meredith laughs as the first one falls. "Of course I am. I don't know if I told you, after, but I am. I mean, I'm always proud of you, you're amazing, but you absolutely crushed that ball, Mol, and I tried, I really did, but you won, fair and square and now . . . now I don't know what to do. I'm so, so sorry, but I don't know how to fix this. I know I should. I've been trying to figure out how to do it all day, but I just don't know what to do. I'm the big sister. I'm *supposed* to know what to do."

"I do," I say, suddenly, pulling my phone out of my pocket.

"What?" she asks, leaning away and wiping her tears. "What are you doing?"

"Fixing it."

I know *exactly* what to do, and maybe it won't be the end of it, not entirely, but at the very least I know how to help her keep her scholarship.

I scroll through my DMs to find the account I'm looking for, sure it will be there. It's pretty buried, but when I find it, I just respond with my phone number and almost immediately a number based in New York lights up on my screen.

"Hi, this is Molly Hancock," I say, and grin at Meredith, who still looks incredibly confused. "Is this Vera Nuñez from ESPN? Great. My sister and I want to tell our story."

★

SAFE AT HOME
by Vera Nuñez

You may recognize the name Meredith Hancock. Six years ago, the San Diego native dominated from the mound in Williamsport, Pennsylvania, the first girl to pitch a no-hitter at the Little League World Series. Now she's one of the top softball recruits in the nation. But you might not know her younger sister, Molly, whose exploits at the fastpitch softball National Championships have put her in the spotlight alongside her history-making sister.

Only a day removed from her now-viral home-plate collision with Meredith to score the winning run, securing the National Championship for her team, the video has been shared over three million times in just twenty-four hours across ESPN's social media platforms alone. The play has sparked massive controversy, with some believing that Meredith allowed her younger sister to score that winning run, throwing the game and the championship, and earning herself a label that's kept some of the best ballplayers ever out of the Hall of Fame: *cheater*.

When asked whether she thought her sister dropped that ball on purpose, Molly laughed so hard that she couldn't answer my question for more than a full minute. Finally able to catch her breath, she said, "My sister wouldn't even let me win at Monopoly. Anyone who thinks she would deliberately lose knows nothing about softball or sisters, let alone *my* sister. And now, because some people hiding behind their keyboards with barely a fraction of her talent and drive and integrity decided she's a cheat, she just *is* and she has to figure out a way to prove she's not? She has to worry about her reputation as an athlete? About the full scholarship from Northwestern that she accepted this morning?"

It's common knowledge in fastpitch softball circles that Meredith

Hancock has scholarship offers from all the top NCAA programs, but she hadn't yet decided on where she would be taking her talents next year.

"Coach Hernandez has been so supportive through this whole mess," Meredith confirmed over the phone from the Hancock family home in San Diego. "I'm really grateful for her and I can't wait to join the Wildcat family." And as for the accusations? "Molly beat me. It happens. That's softball."

We reached out to Northwestern's head coach, Emilia Hernandez, who said, "We have no doubts about Meredith Hancock's integrity or her ability. She is everything a coach looks for in an athlete on and off the field and we're thrilled she's decided to join our program."

Why then, if anyone who knows Meredith Hancock is sure she would never do something like this, are people questioning the play?

Molly is pretty sure she knows.

"If we were brothers, would we even be having this conversation? If we were two boys who collided at home plate at the end of a championship, would you doubt for one second that I wanted with everything in me to score that run and Meredith wanted with everything in her to stop me? The answer is no and everyone knows that."

From one little sister to another: Well said, Molly, well said.

BETTER IN THE LONG RUN

SARAH HENNING

THE LAST MEET, LAST YEAR

Ella

I love running. I know that makes me weird. I know that running is literally the last thing most people want to do.

But I've loved running since I was five years old. Chasing Dad down at the track while he zoomed through 400-meter repeats in shorts that showed *way* too much leg. Bolting after Mom as she charged toward the finish line at one of her countless marathons. And, after, when they divorced and I was thirteen and pissed, running gave me time to breathe.

It doesn't hurt that I'm also really good at it. But I'd love it even if I sucked.

And, up until literally two seconds ago, running loved me back.

That was when I'd sprinted out of the covered-bridge portion of the 6A state girls' varsity cross-country race, hot on the heels of a Durango Bay senior I'd admired for the past two years. I was in step with her, a tall girl in softball cleats from Mitchell High drafting behind us. We had one mile left and a big hill to climb, and I was *alive*.

My lungs were crying out, blood in the back of my throat, legs flying. Every sense in my body was absolutely screaming for mercy at the same time as my brain was pushing to go harder, faster, to stay with the girl I wanted to be.

Which was when she tripped me. On purpose.

I stumbled forward, bumping into the senior's shoulder, my left leg lunging out ahead of me, trying to catch my weight.

But my left foot didn't plant squarely on the grass.

Instead, it rolled. My ankle rolled. My entire body rolled. I tumbled onto the slick course as the girl behind us tried to hurdle my body and totally misjudged. Her gassed attempt at a leap fell short and she stomped with the full brunt of her weight straight on the laid-out inside ridge of my left ankle.

I heard the crunch of bone on tendon on spiked sole as I belatedly threw my arms over my head to protect it from getting squashed, too.

Then the pain was there—hot and white and so very furious.

And I was alone with it. My competitors gone.

Cowbells were clanging. The crowd was cheering. And somewhere Coach Royce and Jenks were waiting to see me make it up that hill and to the finish line, a mile away.

I tried to stand.

My ankle couldn't do it. It was straight misery, bleeding and limp, and even the pressure of my shoe and sock against it was too much.

I couldn't go that last mile. I couldn't even go an inch.

I fell to my knees.

And as my parents' voices separated from the crowd, mixing

together in shared worry for the first time in a very long time, I knew my season was over.

My first time qualifying for varsity state. My first DNF.

My brain told me I had the next two years just as my body told me to give up and cry.

THE FIRST PRACTICE, THIS YEAR

Cade

Running is punishment.

No one can convince me otherwise. My entire athletic career, running has been a threat.

Not listening? Run a lap.

Talk back? Run five.

Embarrass the whole team by getting shit-faced at basketball camp and racking up a minor-in-possession charge?

Run an entire season of cross-country.

Just like in practice, one person screws up and the team is punished.

Okay, so Coach J didn't pitch it to the guys like that. Nah, all he did was *strongly* imply that if you wanted to be a varsity basketball player at Newburg High, you'd better get your ass signed up for the cross-country team, of which he's now the coach. Pre-season conditioning was the guise, but I knew that the player who needed to sign up most was me.

I can't fix the smudge on my permanent record. I can't fix the way Maizy dropped my ass the second I wasn't as perfect on paper as in prom photos. But I can fix this. Or at least give it an honest try.

Because basketball is my life.

And so here I am on the track infield, sweating it out under the afternoon sun of the first day of school, listening to Coach J fumble his way through running terminology like the basketball coach he is. We're clearly divided: basketball players on the right, actual runners on the left.

"I know y'all weren't expecting Coach Royce to hightail it to South Bear Prep, but I've got you." He sneaks a look at his phone, where I know he's jotted stats in a notes app. "This is the year that we make a State *run*—"

"That's not true."

Every muscle in my body tenses as a girl's voice cuts straight through Coach J's stated goal for the season. Coach J may give off Foghorn Leghorn vibes, but that Southern-fried accent and jolly nature is not something to be tested. Cut him off and you might as well chop off your own hand.

Yet the speaker keeps going.

"The team didn't qualify, but Jenks and I did, individually." She gestures to the boy next to her, all floppy hair and 5 percent body fat. "And he placed seventh."

She says that like it's a good thing.

In my world, placing seventh in a tournament is grounds for laps. Lots of them.

Coach J smiles and I know she's in trouble. "You must be Ella Curry."

The girl nods.

She's right up front, dark hair tied into twin French braids held back by a thick white headband. It makes her look like she couldn't decide between being all business or one of my sister's American Girl dolls.

Right now she's all business.

And she's about to get the business end of something, all right.

Coach J's motivation to say yes to this coaching gig may have been 90 percent getting his basketball players to run five days a week pre-season, and 10 percent the extra cash to maintain his Jordans collection, but he doesn't do anything without research. If Coach Royce didn't leave him with details on last year's team and incoming talent, he would've scoured the web himself and added it to that file on his phone.

He stares her down with that smile, his tone still cloying, but there's a razor blade hidden in all that honeyed sauce. "And remind me how you did at that race, Miss Curry?"

The girl shifts, and for a moment I can see her face. It's freckled and tan from what I assume was a summer in running shoes, but even that noise can't cover for the flush flooding her cheeks. "DNF."

I don't know what that means, but my bud Martinez clearly does, leaning over to whisper, "Did not finish."

Oh.

Coach J continues, his smile showing teeth now, as sharp as the cutting setup she stumbled into while challenging him.

"It's true that we had two individuals make it to State last year, with wildly different results. Jenks, man, congrats." He acknowledges the floppy-haired kid. "But I'm much more interested in what we can do together. Cross-country is a team sport that *looks* like an individual one. As a team, we collect a score. That score is based on the top individual times, but everyone who races contributes. Sometimes we win, sometimes we place, and sometimes we don't finish."

The girl's head dips at this, a braid sagging over her shoulder. I almost feel sorry for her, but she totally asked for it.

"As long as we work together, try our best, and"—here he glances at the basketball kids for the runners' benefit, but I swear he's looking straight at me—"take this seriously, we're going to have an excellent season and go to State *as a team*."

There's some tepid applause—it's not exactly enthusiastic, but it's enough for Coach J's ego to garner a smile. "All right, team, let's warm up. Jenks, show everyone how it's done."

The floppy-haired kid bounds up, clearly thrilled to be singled out even though this is absolutely Coach J not wanting to do it himself.

"Eight laps, Bulldogs!" He says it like that isn't two miles as our *warm-up*.

Punishment indeed.

THE FIRST MEET

Ella

This is bullshit. Absolute, unfiltered, full-strength cow DUNG.

That's all I can think as I stand at the last hill, cheering after placing fourth in the girls' varsity race—aka the first race of six on a Saturday morning doubling as our first meet of the season. They're medaling ten places out, and I've got a new, shiny piece of jewelry thudding against my sternum, my race bib crinkling under its weight each time I move to clap and cheer.

And despite medaling in the first race, at our first meet, my new, dumbass coach met me at the finish line with a "Not bad, DNF," before nearly spilling his coffee to collect on the doughnuts one of his basketball players offered him as penance for skipping the bus and then arriving an hour late. He's C team and races last, but still.

I didn't get my hopes up when Coach Royce abandoned us. Cross-country is basically invisible as a competitive sport. No one comes to our meets, or even really understands what we do. *Race on grass? Like, grass-grass?* Yet I still didn't expect the school to just hand the keys to the team over to the basketball coach with a smile and a wave. Even they have to know Coach Jackson—I refuse to call him Coach J—isn't doing this out of the kindness of his heart.

This is about basketball. Pure and simple.

There are plenty of rules about how many hours of pre-season conditioning a coach can mandate. But if his athletes sign up for a no-cut sport that is 100 percent the cardio training they won't do on their own? No rules against that.

Worse, the proof is in the pudding, because despite Coach Jackson's vocal exclamations that this is a team sport—including at my very embarrassing expense on the first day—and therefore is to be taken seriously by all participants, only five basketball players showed up this morning.

The scoring here is like golf, with the lowest total winning. Meaning, if you place first in a race, you get one point. The top six finishers from each team in each race score. So if your sixth runner sucks wind, it kills your overall score in both the race and the meet.

With the basketball kids in play, we'd have fifty people spread across the six races—divided into girl/boy and three categories: that is, varsity, junior varsity, and C team. But because they didn't show, our team is stretched so thin that *every* individual finish in each race counts toward our total.

And right now, because I'm stationed on bullshit mountain, I'm trying to clap home last year's junior prom king/forever Bulldog starting point guard Cade Brockton as he *walks* up the final hill.

He's been passed by three guys in the last ten seconds, but his hands are on his hips as he doesn't even attempt to run.

"Come on, Cade! Go, go, go!"

Cade does not go.

This, despite the enthusiasm in Jenks's voice that is way more than he should have the energy to give. He won the boys' varsity race—he should be pissed that we're witnessing one of the most popular boys in school tank our team score because he gave up.

Still, Cade's chin tips toward the call of his name. But instead of soaking up Jenks's unwarranted enthusiasm and using it to power his way up the hill, Cade looks like he wants to punch him. Like he's embarrassed anyone recognized him, doing this silly little sport in his silly little Bulldogs shorts and singlet. And now another runner is chugging up the incline with mechanical, staccato steps that pass Cade easily.

Maybe I have something to prove, but I don't want to see our chance at a team placement slip away, so I decide to poke at that flash of anger—if Cade's going to walk, he's going to have me in his pretty-boy face, *loudly informing* everyone in earshot exactly who this too-cool-for-this-shit asshat in the Bulldogs singlet truly is.

"Come on, *Cade Brockton*!" Cade's glare whips in my general direction. Walking backward, I smile about as nicely as Coach Jackson. "Do my eyes deceive me, or is big-shot varsity baller *Cade Brockton* walking this final hill? In a *JV race*?"

Another kid rounds the bend to the incline and starts charging up it. In T-minus ten seconds, he'll be the fifth to pass Cade on bullshit mountain.

"I must be hallucinating, because there's no way an All-City, All-State point guard would *walk*! He's too much of an athlete for that!" The fifth kid officially passes Cade. "GO GET HIM, *Cade Brockton*!"

Cade scowls, and at the top of the hill, with the finish line and Jackson *clearly* in view, starts *running*.

I hate him.

Either he conserved all his energy by walking, or Cade actually remembered that he has fast-twitch muscle fibers in his legs, because he turns on the jets. He chases down three of the kids who passed him, and finishes neck and neck with the fourth. He uses some sort of court-approved "hip check"' move to buy enough space to squeeze in front of that kid in the finisher's chute, which means in the end he made up four of the five places he'd lost.

Jackson gives him a high five for his trouble, and doughnut guy lobs an apple fritter at him like he deserves a prize. Cade snags it out of the air with the ease of an alley-oop, and they all laugh.

This boy who didn't even *try* gets praise and sugar while I'm shackled to a nickname I "earned" by trying so hard that I busted my ankle?

Bullshit.

Cade

"It's Ella, right?"

The words are out of my mouth before I realize I've chased her down, bobbling my water cup and the ridiculous baseball-size apple fritter Martinez chucked at me before I could say no. My voice is winded and I swallow, still breathing hard from my sprint to the finish, the taste of blood acrid in the back of my throat.

She whips around, scowl at the ready, probably knowing it would be me—her arms are wound defensively over her chest, the race bib still pinned to her singlet crinkling under the weight of the medal she won. I grin—I don't know why.

"Yep."

I'm not sure what I'd planned to say after I chased her down. I can't yell at her for yelling at me for walking. Even though I knew I'd catch those dudes at the end, I technically should've run the whole way. I gesture with the doughnut toward where the stragglers are struggling up that dumb hill. "What was that back there?"

Her lips flicker. It's not a smile, really. And it certainly doesn't meet her eyes—the same chocolate brown as her hair, which is yet again in French braids held back by a white headband. "I was cheering on a teammate. It's the polite thing to do."

I laugh and try to cover the scoff etched in it with a well-timed bite of my apple fritter. It helps the blood taste dissipate, but only a little. "Polite? You were being kind of rude."

"What?" She raises a brow, sharp and slicing, even as her tone remains light. "By detailing your athletic accomplishments as motivation?"

"That's not what you were doing and you know it." She rolls her eyes and pivots—toward where the girls' C team race is about to start. "Ella—"

"Look, I sort of just assumed varsity basketball players would appreciate their accomplishments touted anywhere they go. Like how they play 'God Save the King' whenever he steps over a threshold."

I snort. "I'm proud of my accomplishments, but not when they're weaponized."

"Only a boy with the title of prom king would have the audacity to whine about how his own accomplishments hurt him." Ella laughs, her quaking shoulders swinging her medal like a pendulum. "Thank you for gracing our little, boring, not-a-big-deal sport with your subpar performance today, Mr. Basketball."

I step closer until we're toe to toe—she's actually kind of tall for a girl. "Why is it that you know so much about me and my accomplishments, anyway?"

White teeth flash, the scent of mint gum wafting into the air between us. "Are you new to high school? Or can you just not see that well from your pedestal jacked all the way up to the eaves of Newburg High? When you're popular, everyone knows all about you. Even if they don't want to. When you're not, no one knows a thing about you—even your name."

Ouch. Not fair, not accurate, not going to stand for it.

"That's not true, *Ella Curry*," I say, making a point that I did know her name, I just didn't want to come off weird because I'd never said a syllable to her before. I'm not going to mention I remembered her last name because she shares it with my favorite NBA player. "I'm not new to high school, but I *am* new to this. After the way that went"—again I gesture with the fritter and add a shy smile—"I could use your advice—it's harder than I thought."

It's obvious that the whole tail-between-my-legs thing won't work on Ella. But I *do* want some tips—I should be better at this. And Coach knows it, too, showing it by insisting I do JV instead of C team.

After a second, Ella nods. "Sure, I have some advice."

I change my stance, ready to accept her runner's wisdom. She grins, full on, and it feels like the tide is turning—she sees I'm not a vapid ass—

"Maybe expend your energy actually giving a shit?"

"I—" I fumble as her punch lands.

"Based on your performance today, I'd say that apple fritter gives more of a shit than you did about that race."

On instinct, I pivot and shoot the pastry twenty feet in a perfect rainbow arc toward the closest trash can. When it swishes in, I know I should feel bad for literally throwing away two of Martinez's hard-earned dollars, but she's right—again.

She's also not done.

"You do realize that some of us care about cross-country, right? Like actually love it and enjoy it? I know that's impossible to believe because it's not big and flashy. I know you don't actually want to be here, but some of us do. *I do*." Her voice is breaking, and

I both can't look away and feel like I should. "If you're going to be my teammate, you have to at least *try*. And not just when Coach 'It's a team sport' Jackson has eyes on your sorry ass."

I don't know what just happened, but somehow, I've both tapped a vein and been stabbed in the back. Ella's angry. At me—at more. I raise my hands in surrender.

"Look, my performance *was* pathetic—I went out too hard, walked the last hill, and sprinted only when Coach J saw me. Guilty."

One of her long braids slides across the fine curve of her collarbone as she considers me, freckles gathering together as her mouth lilts.

"What can I do to be better?"

Her attention flits to the starting clock countdown—thirty-nine seconds until the C team girls' gun.

"Run fast."

I'm about to protest because that's the most annoying advice ever when she adds, "Run with me. At practice. No excuses, no complaints, no walking."

"Deal, Ella Curry."

I offer my hand. Another surprise—she humors me and takes it.

"Now," she says, terminating the briefest handshake ever, backpedaling, "if you'll excuse me, I'm going to go cheer on my teammates. It's the polite thing to do."

AFTER THE FIRST MEET

Cade

Coach J may have seemed chill Saturday, but I knew it was an act. Something he slipped on as a first impression for a new community of opposing coaches and the handful of nervous parents who huddled near our team tent, necks craning and eyes squinting to find their kids among the sea of runners.

For them, he put on a show.

For us, that show was over on Sunday morning.

Coach J: "From now on: Mandatory bus rides to meets. All basketball athletes will do an extra mile after XC practice for each team member who missed the meet. One mile a day until we have everyone accounted for. Miss this week's meet, and you'll add to that total for everyone. GO BULLDOGS!"

That last part is an automatic sign-off. It's also a challenge. And a fuck you.

Or at least that's how I read it.

TRAINING MONTAGE

Cade

"Brockton, DNF, looking good."

I do not look good.

I look gassed.

My shirt came off a mile in because I'm sweating so hard. It's in my eyes. Weighing down my shorts. Dripping into the insides of my ears, JFC. I must get this sweaty on the basketball court, but somehow it doesn't feel this way.

We're at the turnaround point in Monday's out-and-back 4-miler. It's a coffee shop parking lot, where Coach J idles with his pickup truck and three giant jugs of water.

I nearly sprint there, my hands trembling as I attempt to extract a paper cup off the top of a stack. The water is glorious, and I gulp it down so quickly it spills out the side of my mouth and dribbles onto the blacktop. Still, I inhale more, and attempt to fix my T-shirt, which is hanging out the back of my waistband like a really sexy tail.

I'm struggling with tightening the drawstring when Coach J chin checks toward the distance.

"Your ride's leaving, Brockton."

Shit.

Ella didn't stop for water. She didn't stop at all. The last thing I remember, actually, is her making an audible *UGH* when Coach greeted us.

I trash the cup. "Hey, wait up."

She doesn't.

I chase after Ella like she's a ball about to go out-of-bounds—leaping off the curb, onto the sidewalk, and into the grass. Down the street, I spot Jenks's bouncing form, high-fiving a three-pack of varsity girls as they approach the turnaround.

Maybe she wants to catch him. She could.

When I get to her, I'm breathing hard, and the liquid I just inhaled is sloshing more violently than I expected. "There's no harm in hydration, Ella Curry."

Ella peels her dark eyes away from where she's glaring at the cracks in the sidewalk like they'll jump up and get her. "No water during a race."

It's hot. Ninety-degrees-in-the-afternoon hot. And we're running a mile more than the 5K we race. Like an idiot, I double down. "Surely you're thirsty."

She snaps her gum. "Nope."

All the water in my stomach jumps. I'm going to cramp. I start to stare at the sidewalk, too. Maybe that's how she does it. Just concentrates so hard that she can't feel the struggle of her lungs, or the press of the heat, or the thirst that must nag her if she's even 10 percent human.

The varsity girls approach—and I plaster on a grin and give them high fives to go with Ella's automatic words of encouragement. After they pass, I clearly hear Maizy's name and accompanying giggles. I don't want to think about Maizy and everything else that fell apart after basketball camp, so I swallow and find my voice.

"How do you make this look so easy?" It's a compliment aimed at Ella, because despite every interaction I've ever had with her, I'm good at doling those out. I didn't win junior prom king by being an asshole.

Ella pauses at a stoplight, settling her hands on her slim hips. Finally, she actually looks at me. I kind of like that she doesn't have to crane her neck. "It's the same way you make a three-pointer look easy, I guess."

I smirk. "Well, I *do* hold the school record for most threes in a game."

Add that to your stats pile, Ella Curry.

The light changes and Ella checks her watch as she breaks into a run to cross. "We're on pace for a negative split. Let's pick it up."

I don't know what that means. I just know it's going to hurt.

It does. A lot.

But I survive my first practice at Ella Curry's pace.

I'm actually pretty fucking proud of myself for sticking with her—we did make a negative split, which means our last half was faster than the first—until I remember that for me, practice isn't over.

When the other kids are dismissed and gone, Coach J lays into us about personal responsibility, accountability, and "there's no *I* in *team*."

It's literally the PG version of the very heated, very private conversation Coach J and I had after my *incident*.

And even though I went to the race, even though I showed up and did the thing—though not well—it's hard not to feel like every single one of those words is aimed at me.

Ella

Cade stuck with me the whole time through negative splits on Monday.

Tuesday, he regretted it.

He didn't say that, though. No, too cool for that. But his stride shouted everything loud and clear.

Stiff and tentative. Shorter than usual. Less bouncy.

I know what it's like to push the pace—and how I feel the next day. Screaming quads, abbreviated steps, maybe a stifled groan when dropping into my seat at the start of each class.

Not to mention that when I left the locker room with Hannah and Sophia, the basketball kids were still on the track, doing laps. More proof Jackson's using our entire season as forced conditioning.

Still, because Cade's more stubborn than I'm probably giving him credit for, he ran with me the whole way Tuesday. After the turnaround—at which he did *not* guzzle water—his muscles started to warm up. His gait smoothed out, blood circulating to all the achy parts.

They ran laps Tuesday, too.

Wednesday, he finds me before warm-up, where I'm plastered to the stadium wall, taking extra effort to stretch my left ankle. I don't have to wrap it anymore, but it's been cranky for a year since I went down at State and it's always begging for special attention.

"What'll it be today, Ella Curry? Five-minute miles? A tempo run?" He leans in, conspiratorially. "Fartleks?"

Someone used Google.

I snap my gum and side-eye him. "I'm not related to Steph, you know. You don't have to say my whole name like it's important to acknowledge the Curry family line with each interaction."

Cade shoots me a disarming smile. It's the kind he can give as an all-star point guard, junior prom king, and a white male who totally 100 percent believes that flashing that grin will get him what he wants.

So when he says, "You act like I'm just an automaton in a letter jacket," I arch a brow.

"You're not?"

Another grin. "I happen to be a sentient being who knows plenty about the general population at Newburg High, Ella Curry."

I squint. "Really? Prove it."

"Fine. Bring it."

His whole body loosens—ready to react, execute, disseminate whatever I have coming. I blink up at him with an innocent expression. "What's Jenks's last name?"

He sputters. "I, uh, it's not Jenks?"

"That's his first name, Cade."

He's stumped. Then a little smile slides across his face. "Wait, are you guys a thing?"

I'm not even going to dignify that with an answer. He should know better than to pry, given all the rumors about him and Promise Ring Princess Maizy Abbot.

So instead, I answer his first question, pointing to where Jackson has arrived with a golf cart and the vestiges of a Newburg High home meet.

"Course marking."

Cade

"Jenks Vaughn."

I greet Ella with my new knowledge. Her eyebrows jump toward her headband. I saw her in the hall today with her hair down—it's actually pretty curly. There's no way to tell that when it's in braids.

We're walking with armfuls of flags—the kind the city uses to mark your yard before it's safe to dig. Only these are the same powder blue as our cross-country uniforms and plastered with a jowly Newburg Bulldog on each side. Apparently today we mark the course, tomorrow we run it, Friday we simulate a race. Saturday is the real thing.

Next I point to the crowd of varsity boys and girls spinning off in different directions across the sprawling Newburg campus and name them one by one. When I'm done, I turn to Ella and smirk. "*And* you give rides home to Hannah Chao and Sophia Zapata."

I don't know what I expect, but it's not Ella biting her lip as she sinks to place a flag in the grass. I jog ahead and plant the next flag twenty feet away—per our detailed instructions from Coach J. When she catches up, that little hint of approval has twisted to sarcasm. "Look at you, prom king, displaying interest in your team-mates. Can your basketball buddies do that trick, or is it exclusive to you?"

"I'm working on them."

Newburg is the only city school with a campus big enough to host its own meet on its grounds instead of at a park. We step into one of the treed sections—hedge apples and black walnuts are everywhere. We're supposed to clear this crap so we don't stumble.

Ella knocks a bright green hedge apple away with her foot. "Are you? Or is Coach? He's had you guys stay back two nights in a row."

She noticed that? Great.

"Punishment. For missing the meet."

I beat her to the next hedge apple, scoop it up, and with my best shooter's arc, send it rocketing toward the fence lining school property. The thing explodes on impact, blazing green matter splattering all over the grass. It's gross but satisfying.

"It's all punishment, actually."

Then, without judgment or expectation, Ella Curry's big brown eyes meet mine and she asks the one question no one has bothered to ask me before just yelling at me or breaking up with me or giving me the silent treatment along with the heavy-handed implication that I'm a major disappointment. "What happened?"

Then I tell her about basketball camp. All of it. Every last shitty detail.

It feels good. I don't know why.

Ella

I hate that Coach Jackson has made the sport I love into a monthslong punishment.

I'm not surprised. But I do hate it.

And most of all I hate that he's punishing Cade.

He made a mistake. He's got the blemish on his record and heaps of guilt to prove it.

And all that adds up to me lining up next to Cade Brockton, all-star point guard and actual real human being, for his post-practice punishment laps.

Cade cocks a brow at me, a little quirk to his mouth.

Then Jenks abandons his water bottle and comes bounding over. Hannah and Sophia and the other varsity kids, too. Cade watches all of them line up, that quirk splitting into a real grin as he takes us in, and then spots Jackson on the sidelines.

I expect Coach to yell at us. To send us to the locker room. He doesn't. Instead, Jackson just nods and revs the golf cart, pointing the remaining supplies toward the groundskeeper's shed behind the stadium.

I run with Cade in silence, behind Jenks, who's happily leading the whole pack—of course. He didn't ask me what I was doing. Maybe he will later. But right now, he's just happy to get in an extra mile. Always is. Just pleased as punch to put one foot in front of the other. Which is exactly what running should be.

On our last lap, I notice three of the JV basketball guys walking. Cade and I pass them and slow to a high-fiving stop after crossing the line. But then the JV kids stop, too. And something tender inside me snaps.

"You're not done."

The biggest kid, Kye Williams, smirks at me. "Mind your own business."

"Whoa, man—" Cade starts, but I don't let him finish, putting a hand on his arm and speaking for myself.

"If you're on this team, your business is my business."

Because it is.

"Is there a problem here?" Jackson is back, stepping onto the track. Out of the corner of my eye, I spot Jenks, frozen with his water bottle, watching as Coach turns to me, the troublemaker. "DNF?"

I can't help it—I cringe at the use of my dumbass nickname.

That anger of mine flares as I stare at the boys. If my favorite sport has been reduced to punishment, they're going to freaking take it.

"We lapped them—they're not done." I face Coach, not softening my fury. It's in my eyes, my stance, even in the way I'm winded after such an easy mile. "As you constantly point out, I know a thing or two about not finishing. And they didn't."

"*Shit*," I hear Cade mumble a half second before he steps in front of me, now the one holding me back as he snags my wrist. His hand is warm and protective and nearly knocks my breath away because I can't remember the last time someone touched me like this.

"Ella's right," he says, and I'm kind of shocked. So are the basketball boys, whose lips drop open in unison, betrayed. "They have one lap left."

Coach Jackson glances first to me, then to Cade, who nods—firm. Unwavering. With me.

I vaguely realize this is what a teammate does.

Jenks and I have run together forever—our parents are friends, or more accurately now, his parents are friends with my mom—but I guess I never thought of him as my teammate until it was a goal. And now Jenks is on the sidelines shifting his weight on nervous feet, and Cade is standing here. With me.

He *does* give a shit.

And apparently so does Coach Jackson, who sternly hands down another layer of punishment in the form of my favorite activity.

"It's two laps now." The boys' shoulders fall with a groan. "Give me lip, and it'll be three."

Cade

Thursday, as we line up to run the home course, Ella greets me with a little stick of gum. Trident Original.

"It'll help with your thirst."

And it did. For 3.1 miles, I didn't think once about my water bottle.

Ella Curry is a genius.

And thanks to training with her all week, I stay glued to her shoulder the whole way. Some of the course is single-track, and I let her go ahead, like the gentleman I am. And because she'd probably throw an elbow and bruise my kidneys without a second thought if I tried to pass her.

My time is minutes better than my first race. *Minutes.*

That night, as Martinez and I exit the locker room, showered, exhausted, and pointed toward my car and the ride home I promised him, a wily grin spreads across his face.

"You've spent a lot of time in the woods the past two days with DNF."

"Don't call her that."

He rounds my bumper. "Ooh, touchy. Does Maizy know?"

"Does Maizy know what?" I arch a brow. "That you're about to walk home?"

Big palms go up like he's expecting a chest pass. "Dude, okay."

Ella

On Friday, I arrive at practice to bad news.

Really, really, really bad news.

Jenks is sprawled on the infield, holding his right knee, writhing in pain. Varsity kids surround him, a cluster of basketball boys off to the side.

"Where's Coach? Somebody get Coach!"

But then I spot Jackson, sprinting over from the football practice fields, the athletic trainer they keep on-site barreling in with him, medical bag thumping against his belt.

"What happened?" For a moment, I think I ask the question in my head, but then I realize it's Cade, shouldering up to the basketball boys behind me.

The really tall doughnut kid—Ollie Martinez—answers. "He was warming up and, I don't know, his ankle rolled, he rolled, and then he came to a stop, clutching his knee."

Shit, I think.

"Shit," Cade says.

An hour after we learn that Jenks will be out three to four weeks with a sprained knee—which will totally screw up his chances of securing that scholarship to McArdle State as a junior—I'm shoving a forkful of pad thai into my mouth like it's going to make today disappear.

It doesn't.

Instead, I just manage to flick grease droplets onto my phone screen as a text comes through from a number I don't recognize.

Ella Curry, it's Cade.

How'd you get my number?

Popular people are magic.

Fuck you. What do you want? I'm trying to eat my feelings about Jenks.

There's a pause. The little typing dots dance, disappear, dance, disappear.

When the message finally pops through, I drop my chopsticks.

Coach put me on varsity tomorrow. To cover Jenks's spot. Promise to yell at me?

"Everything okay?" Mom asks from across the table. "Is it Jenks?"

I shake my head. My fingers hover a second before they finally beat out exactly what I need to say.

Fine. But the second I see you walking, I'm abandoning your ass and leaving you to suffer in silence.

I think that's it and I drop my phone, a little smile catching before I can stop it. I shove another wad of noodles in my mouth before Mom notices. My phone buzzes again.

What are you doing after you eat your feelings? Wanna meet me at the game?

The game—the football game. In the same stadium where Jenks went down. Football isn't my thing. I don't even know who we're playing. Instead of all that, I say: *Aren't you going with Maizy?*

I expect the typing dots to dance and disappear again as he types. Instead, the dots come and the message pops straight through, no careful rewording.

We're not together.

Then more.

Don't believe everything you know about the popular kids, Ella Curry.

THE HOME MEET

Cade

"GOOOO ELLA!"

Ella's whole face is flushed, her freckles crowding as she grits out an expression that might be a smile. Or a grimace. I'm not sure.

The finish line is in her sights, and she's like a bull, charging toward the cowbells ringing and the parents and teammates cheering as a girl from Grey Mountain tries to catch her. I don't know if Ella likes her own medicine, but I'm going to drown her in it.

"Ella Curry's gonna win this race!"

That definitely gets me a little smile. I jog along, picking up Martinez and the JV boys she roasted as I go. They're cheering, whatever they're saying getting lost in a general chant of "Go Bulldogs!" And just so the crowd knows it, I shout her name again. "GO ELLA! Sub-18!"

More people catch on, joining me, as she turns on the gas, the Grey Mountain runner too late with her finishing kick as Ella's lead only grows.

She hits the finish line, braids flying, shoulders reaching forward for the chute. Then Coach J's honey-and-corn-bread accent crackles over a loudspeaker. "Winning the girls' varsity race with a *course record* of 17:51, Ella Curry!"

Maybe now he'll stop calling her DNF.

I should've been C team. I was the last Bulldog to finish as JV. And now, a week later, I sneak one last glance at Coach J as I toe the line for the boys' varsity race, our conversation from Friday night ringing in my ears.

DNF hauled your carcass around this week, but I saw the effort, Brockton. Backhanded compliments are Coach J's specialty. *You're taking Jenks's spot this week. Prove to me you care when you're not chasing DNF's tail.*

Another challenge. Another test. But I miss it all together, stuck on something else.

Ella. Her name is Ella, Coach. And she's your team leader now with Jenks out.

I struck before I realized the iron was hot.

I know not to talk back. I've warned others not to do what I just did. But I'm already burned, so I strike again. *If you insist on calling her DNF, call me MIP. I deserve it way more than she does.*

Ella didn't choose to roll her ankle and limp off course at State—I looked up what happened. Coach J probably did, too. It was as much a fluke as Jenks's injury.

But I chose my mistake. I raided Dad's beer fridge, smuggled it into the camp dorm, got shit-faced. Me. I was the minor in possession. I earned the MIP. Me.

Coach stares. He leans down. I'm tall, but he's taller. My shoulders push back. *Worry about your choices, not mine, Brockton.*

The next choice I made was to ask Ella to the football game.

And when she says yes, when she meets me, I know that even if I place last in every race for the rest of the cross-country season, I'll have won the whole damn thing.

Here and now, the starting gun goes off.

Ella

Cade Brockton is a whole new runner. Or maybe this was how he always was, but now we understand each other.

His stride is strong. His steps are confident—he knows the course and it shows. He knows what he's doing.

The first hill's done. First mile, too. Two big, gradual climbs left, two miles, too.

From an incline, I spot him surrounded by a pack of boys. They're coming up on a single-track portion. We practiced this. We talked about it last night between sharing Twizzlers and popcorn and detailed explanations of what the hell we did to beat South Bear Prep 17–16. (Okay, Cade explained it, I only shared my ears.)

If he's going to get ahead, he needs to do it here.

I hold my breath, a whisper coming out on the last dregs. "Come on, Cade. *Now.*"

Cade cuts outside. He stomps over rough grass. His gait churns faster, eyes on the coming trees, encroaching on the course.

Faster. Faster.

Then he's a full stride's length ahead. He slips in front of the pack with fifteen feet to go, and sprints. Behind him, bodies jostle, curses and literal gobs of spit flying, as guys try to elbow their way into position.

"Yes! Go Cade go!" He can't hear me through the brush, but I yell anyway, my feet automatically moving so I can top the hill before he emerges.

Cade clears the trees and the second incline with it. Then we're both thundering down the back side. He's using its momentum to carry him into the final climb, just like I showed him.

"Cade Brockton! Mr. Basketball! Three-point school record holder! GOOOO!"

I'm running as fast as he is now, dodging around people on the sidelines. There's a good crowd—basketball groupies clutching Starbucks. They know his name, but I shout it anyway. "Hey, *Cade*! Beat me to the top!"

There's a knot of guys still behind him. He knows I'm thinking he'll get passed on the final hill. Cade's eyes lift to mine. Cheeks red, and sweat glistening, he smiles.

With that winner's spirit I knew he had, the same stuff he couldn't—wouldn't—tap into last week, Cade Brockton meets me stride for stride, churning up the incline at my pace. Though I've already raced, though I've got a medal hanging heavily around my neck, I sprint as fast as I can, knowing he can match it. My quads burn, the taste of blood licks at my throat, and air is a precious resource right now.

Then we're over it.

And suddenly Cade is charging toward the finish line, the cowbells, and *Jenks*, clapping so hard he loses a crutch to the line of rope meant to keep spectators clear of the last hundred meters or so. There's a guy in Durango Bay red in front of Cade, pounding toward the finish line and the clock that flashes 17:58.

"Get him, Cade!" I scream. "GO GO GO!"

He's sprinting—and then, just as he did in the first race, he draws up that basketball hip check and bounces the Durango Bay kid to the side to claim one more precious place.

My heart is in my throat, pounding with happiness and exertion and relief. And even after that, even after this week and last night, it jolts like it's been struck by lightning when Cade's eyes find mine beyond the finishers' area.

He squints, a smile in it. "It's Ella, right?"

I can't help it—I laugh. Everything about this moment is unexpected perfection.

My first varsity win. His first varsity race. And miles and miles to go.

And so, with a hopeful laugh, I give him the do-over he just offered me. "Wanna go cheer the JV girls with me?"

"Of course," he says, snapping the gum I gave him and falling into step beside me. "I hear it's the polite thing to do."

WOMAN LAND

MIRANDA KENNEALLY

DAY ONE

The very first time I set foot on this side of the gym, Josh McConnell smirks at me.

My physical therapist's office is attached to Xsport Alexandria, and it turns out a bunch of guys from school lift weights here. I spot Rafael Garcia from the baseball team doing biceps curls. Caleb Nelson balances a weighted barbell on his back, completing some complicated lunges.

Then there's Josh, a junior like me, and the football team's star defensive tackle. He's lying underneath a machine resembling a medieval torture device, using his legs to push it up and down, up and down. If he lost control, it would flatten him into a pancake. After he finishes his set, he slides out, adjusts his glasses, and locks his pretty gray eyes with mine.

That's when he smirks.

An embarrassed heat fills my cheeks. I feel totally out of my depth here on this side of the gym that Mom refers to as *Man Land*, but I can't let Josh know that.

I raise my eyebrows and look at him as if he's an ant I could squash under my sneaker.

The smirk melts from his face and his gaze sweeps toward the floor.

Good. That'll teach him to make fun of me.

Guys of all ages are lifting superheavy weights and breathing hard and grunting while staring at themselves in the mirror. It must take serious skill to do so many things and still have time to objectify yourself.

This one man with the Hulk's bulging muscles could probably rip a tree trunk in half. A gray-haired guy who looks Papa's age is squatting a bar full of weights. A shirtless man who has the physique of an Olympic swimmer is pressing a plate above his head. I reallillly want to tell him to put his shirt on.

As I peer around, I count at least twenty men and exactly one woman.

Frankly, I don't come to the gym much, other than using the treadmills when the sidewalks are too icy for running and that one ill-fated attempt at yoga with Mom.

"Are you sure I should be doing this?" I mutter to my physical therapist, Kayla, as we walk past a guy swinging a kettlebell the size of a watermelon.

"Definitely. This is the best way to get your arm back in shape."

I wrap a hand around my left wrist, squeezing it. The pain is still there. It's always there. Two months ago, I fell during track practice. As I hit the ground, I braced my fall with my hands, fracturing my wrist. The doctor surgically repaired it.

Now? It's always stiff. It always hurts. Some days I worry my hand and wrist will never be flexible again. When I was a kid, I thought there was nothing cooler than wearing a cast and having your friends sign it with a Sharpie. How wrong I was.

"Plus," Kayla says, "powerlifting is great for building all-over body strength, too. It'll help your running muscles activate faster."

I trust what she's saying. I mean, she has the fittest body I've ever seen in real life. She's Black, short, and made of hard muscle.

I follow Kayla over to the bench press area. There are four benches, all of which are occupied by men. One man has three plates on each side of the bar and is effortlessly pumping it toward the ceiling as if he's doing something simple, like lifting a pen to write a note.

"How much weight is that?" I murmur to Kayla.

She glances at the bar. "Three hundred and fifteen."

What! That's, like, three times my body weight. I imagine this guy lifting three of me above his head at once. If he were to lose control of that weight or suddenly didn't have the strength to push it up, I bet that bar could easily kill him.

I rub the side of my neck as we wait until one of the benches opens up.

"Okay," Kayla says. "Lie down on your back and brace your feet on the floor. I'm going to lift the bar to you."

"Wait. How heavy is this?"

"The bar is forty-five pounds."

This doesn't mean much. I haven't lifted weights before, unless you count Mom's little five-pound dumbbells she keeps next to her Peloton. But forty-five pounds seems like a lot, considering I find carrying groceries in from the car to be difficult, especially when the bags are filled with heavy things like milk or jars of spaghetti sauce.

As Kayla told me, I lie down on the bench. Bright lights on the ceiling make my vision spotty.

"Okay, grab the bar with both hands and squeeze tight."

She lifts the bar off to me, keeping a grip on it herself.

"Now bring it down to your chest and push up."

I lower the bar to my chest, but when I try to push it up, it doesn't budge. I kick a foot out, struggling under the weight. It's like a car is on my chest.

"C'mon, push," Kayla says in a calm tone.

I focus all my strength into my arms. The bar slowly begins to rise into the air, but only with the help of Kayla. She keeps her fingers beneath the bar to guide it up. *Her friggin' fingers are stronger than my arms.*

"Again," she says.

Blood rushes to my head and my vision blurs as I lower the bar to my chest and push it up three more times. The right side rises before the left, like a seesaw.

"Good," Kayla says.

I sit up, suddenly panting and out of breath. Shit. I can't even push up the bar. I study my puny arms. They always remind me of the time I tried to push someone away when it really mattered, and I couldn't do it.

I shake my head. "I don't think this is for me. I'm not strong enough."

Kayla touches my shoulder. "You can be. I started with the bar, too."

SIX MONTHS IN

Week by week I learn new things:

1. This side of the gym is not only for guys.
2. I suck at bench press, but I really enjoy squat and deadlift.
3. Whatever you do, do *not* make eye contact with the creepy old man who lives on the ski machine. He takes it as an invitation to talk.

4. People at the gym love to stand around
   gossiping between sets.

Seriously, gym bros chitchat more than old ladies at church.

People talk to me about everything from the best place to eat pizza to who is hooking up with who. Apparently gymcest is a total thing here.

The only person I don't talk to is Josh McConnell. Not since he smirked at me, as if I'm not supposed to be here.

That's why I'm so surprised when he comes over to watch me finish my squats. He observes me carefully as I move up and down, not in a leering way, but more like how a doctor examines an X-ray.

Kayla, spotting me from behind, pats my sides. "Focus, Emma. Eyes straight ahead."

How could she tell I was looking at him?

I take a deep breath to brace myself, then perform my final squat and rack the bar. The weight is so heavy, it makes a loud crashing sound like a garbage truck dropping a dumpster onto pavement.

I grin. "I did it! I'm alive!"

"Of course you're alive," Kayla says.

Josh steps forward and holds his fist out to me. I glance at his face before quickly fist-bumping him. "Your squats look really good, Emma."

I pause for a moment, to make sure he's not teasing me and my light weights. Well, light compared to his 450-pound squat. I'm very proud I just squatted 185 pounds. "Thanks, I think."

"Excuse me," Kayla says suddenly, and rushes to help lift a bar off a guy struggling on bench press. It's a pretty common occurrence here, that someone tries to lift too much weight and Kayla has to help. Some people are not as conscious about gym safety as they should be.

I expect Josh to turn back to his own workout or go talk to some of the guys, so it surprises me when he loiters. Before I started powerlifting, I always thought you were supposed to keep exercising without stopping. In running, it's all about endurance. You keep going and going and going.

With strength training, it's important to take breaks to give your muscles time to recuperate, but I always feel guilty standing around talking between sets. And there's always someone to talk to. A college girl, Salma, who works out in a hijab, waves and says hi. Caleb from school comes by and makes like he wants to give me a hug, but I sidestep him and put out my hand for a fist bump. I don't mind touching other people's hands or arms, but I'd prefer they didn't touch me. It's a thing I have.

I glance at Josh out of the corner of my eye, then walk over to my water bottle.

"Did I do something to piss you off or what?" Josh says.

"Huh?"

He waves a hand toward the gym. "You seem to have no problem hanging out with people here, except for me."

He thinks I'm avoiding *him*? "You never talk to me."

"You're the one who gave me the dirty look."

"You're the one who smirked at me! Acting like I'm not supposed to be here."

His mouth falls open. "What? What are you talking about?"

"When you first saw me here, you were making faces like I wasn't supposed to be on this side of the gym. Over here in Man Land."

"*Man Land*?" He shakes his head. "First of all, don't assume you know what I'm thinking. Second, I, uh, was just surprised to see you here, is all."

His voice is a little shaky. It's not confident like when he's sitting in the cafeteria at school, surrounded by kids listening to his stories, or when he's shouting into a megaphone at a pep rally, pumping up the crowds before one of his football games.

Dylan, this guy who graduated from college last year and now works at Target, wanders over to talk to us. He has a beard and a man bun, and he's chewing on a Twizzler. He is seemingly always at the gym—it's like he lives here.

Dylan fist-bumps me. "How's it going, Emma Emu?"

He assures me he gave me this nickname because it sounds cool, and not because he associates me with a giant bird with sticks for legs.

Josh drops a hand on Dylan's shoulder. "How about Emma? For the second spot?"

Dylan shrugs, ripping off another piece of Twizzler and gesturing at me with it. "You can ask her."

"What are you guys talking about?"

Josh clears his throat; his cheeks turn pink. "There's this team powerlifting meet next month. Me and some of the guys are in it."

"Yeah?"

"And, well, we need two women on the team. I think you'd be great."

"What, like, compete?" I watched weightlifting on TV during the Olympics. There's no way I can do that. "I don't lift very much compared to y'all."

As Dylan finishes his last bite of Twizzler, he adds another weight to his squat bar. "It's not about how many pounds you can lift compared to men—it's about how much you lift for your body weight."

"And you don't weigh a lot, but you can lift a ton!" Josh rushes to say.

"I didn't know you competed in this," I say, gesturing around the gym.

Josh shrugs. "I've done a couple competitions. It's fun. So how about it?"

"You're asking me because you need another girl, right? Not because I'm good."

He pauses to run a hand through his coppery hair. "I'm asking for both reasons. Because you're a girl, and because you're good."

"Who's the second girl?"

"Kayla."

She comes back over from saving that guy's life, and Josh tells her he invited me to be on the team.

"Don't you think Emma would be great in competition?" Josh asks Kayla.

"Emma's still learning how all this works." Part of me is relieved that Kayla says this, while the other half is disappointed. She knows I'm not cut out for this. I can barely bench-press ninety pounds, and she could probably lift a car off a person trapped under it.

My head is starting to droop when suddenly Kayla says, "But you're right, I think she would be good." She studies my eyes. "But you'll have to ask your parents."

IT'S ALL ABOUT ME

It takes a couple of days to find a chance to talk to both of my parents at the same time.

Dad is a lawyer for a health-care lobbyist downtown, and Mom works for the U.S. Patent Office. Both jobs require regularly working late, so we don't often get to eat dinner together with my younger sister, Ava.

But they make sure we go out every Friday evening. It's

something we make time for, even if we have something to do later. Like, tonight I'm going to my school's football game.

Dad lives for this steak place called Great Plains, and he never wants to go anywhere else, no matter how much Mom, Ava, and I beg to try something new. We're sitting at the table, with Dad happily eating the same ole chicken wings he always orders as an appetizer, while Mom digs into the dinner rolls she says she's sick and tired of but nevertheless manages to inhale anyway, when I gather the courage to bring up the competition.

"Mom, some people at the gym invited me to compete in a powerlifting competition."

Dad sets down his chicken wing to look at me. Mom lowers her glass of wine.

"You?" Ava finally says.

"Is that one of those competitions where men have to pull a semitruck by a rope, and carry trees on their backs?" Dad asks.

"No—"

"I don't think you should try to pull a semitruck," Dad says.

"It's not a strongman contest, Dad, it's only squat, deadlift, and bench press."

"Don't you have to have giant muscles the size of bowling balls?" Ava cuts back in.

I give her a look. "It's based on your body weight."

"Is it safe?" Mom's forehead crinkles up. "I saw that video you posted of you lifting two hundred twenty-five pounds off the floor and it worried me."

Dad shakes his head, with a far-off look in his eye. "Wow."

Mom gestures with her wineglass. "I understand you need physical therapy, but it seems like you're going way beyond that."

I like getting stronger and stronger. Kayla was right: Having stronger muscles has improved my speed on the track. Over the past six months, I've taken three seconds off my 400-meter hurdles.

And I feel a bit safer walking down empty corridors at school.

"Are you sure you want to keep doing this?" Mom asks.

"I mean, your butt's getting huge," Ava says.

"You're just jealous," I snap back, and Mom purses her lips while Dad is suddenly interested in Sarita Solís's boxing match on the bar TV that I know for a fact was on last night and is being replayed today. Dad clearly doesn't want to think about his daughters' butts.

"I don't want you to get bulked up," Mom says.

"I'm not! Kayla says I'm getting leaner *and* stronger."

Mom cradles her wineglass in her hands. "I just worry about you getting hurt." She is coming up with every excuse in the book.

I'd be lying if I said injury wasn't a low-grade worry at the back of my head. Josh texted me competition videos to watch. I'll have to wear a strange little singlet and lift weights in front of a big crowd. I looked up more clips on YouTube, finding some where people fail. In one particularly scary video, a girl faints while she's trying to squat a huge amount of weight, but luckily she's saved by the spotters who catch the bar and help hoist it back onto the rack.

"There's always a chance I could get hurt, sure, but Kayla spends a ton of time with me working on technique. Plus, you can get hurt doing anything. I broke my arm running hurdles! Look . . . They really want me to do it."

Dad points at me with a chicken wing. "The question is whether you want to."

My whole family looks at me. That's a really good question.

HOW TO DECIDE

On Saturday morning at the gym, I'm lying on the turf, stretching, when Josh appears. He looks comfortable, dressed in running tights and shorts and a baggy football sweatshirt.

"The worst thing ever just happened," he announces, plopping down next to me.

"Oh yeah?"

"I was in the locker room getting ready, when this guy came in and started doing lunges. Naked."

"Naked lunges."

"Yes, naked lunges."

"Nooooooo!"

He bursts out laughing. "The weirdest shit happens at this gym."

"Hey, good game last night," I tell him.

He looks at me sideways, a smile peeking out. "You saw it?"

"I never miss a home game."

I twist to the side to stretch my hip, letting out a groan.

"You all right?" Josh asks.

"Something is always sore, you know?"

"It gets better, I promise."

I shift to stretch my other side. "How long have you been power-lifting, anyway?"

"A few years now. My grandpa brought me here to work out, so I'd have more explosive power on the football field, but now I like it even more than football."

"Really?"

He kneels on one knee to stretch his quad. "Yeah, I'd totally put all my focus into this, but my dad and grandpa want me to get a football scholarship."

"Wow, I mean, I figured you loved football more."

"I do love it, but there's something about powerlifting that's perfect for me." He digs his thumb into his thigh, pushing at a muscle. "This is probably going to sound selfish, but I love that it's just me competing against myself and trying to become better."

I love it for those reasons, too.

Saturday mornings at the gym are quiet compared to weekday nights. On Saturdays, it's usually older people using the stationary bikes and free weights. Today, it's only Josh and me lying on the turf. Normally, I wouldn't stay this close to a boy. I'd find some excuse to vamoose.

It makes no sense that I don't feel that impulse to run, because it's been there since that one time at school between classes.

I shake my head to rid myself of the bad memory, then let out some air. It's almost relaxing, listening to the loudspeakers, even though they're strangely playing some old Taylor Swift ballad that in no way, shape, or form could pump someone up through a cardio workout.

My phone beeps with a text from Kayla: *Sorry Emma, my dog is sick and I can't make it today. See you Monday for bench?*

"Crap," I say.

Josh nods at my phone. "Everything okay?"

"Kayla isn't coming and I was counting on her to spot me. I'm supposed to do squats today."

Josh rubs his palms on his thighs. "I could, you know, spot you."

My skin flushes hot. Nobody but Kayla ever spots me. It's not because I don't trust other people—especially the strong ones—but most of the people who lift here are men, and I don't want them standing right behind me.

"I mean, if you're okay with that," Josh rushes to add.

I've known him for years because his name comes after mine in the alphabet. We're in the same homeroom. But he's always run in a different crowd from me. I'm the kid who stands at the side of the school dance making jokes with my friends, while he's out in the middle of the floor taking the lead. So it seems like I should be nervous or feeling weird about sitting here with him, but I don't.

Other than that time he smirked—which we are now past—he's been nothing but respectful. I look over at him and rub the side of my neck.

I was really looking forward to squatting today. Truth be told, I've been excited for it all week. I can't avoid the possibility of touching boys forever, can I?

My fear can screw off for a day. Josh can spot me for one workout session.

"Yeah, that would be good, if you could give me a spot."

As Josh and I carry our bags over to an empty squat rack, he waves at Sean, who's working on bench press. He has gray hair and always wears the exact same Nirvana T-shirt to work out. Everybody calls him "Gym Dad."

"Sean's going to compete with us next month," Josh says.

"Who else is on your team?"

"We can have up to seven people. So far it's me, Sean, Dylan, Kayla, Gael, and Theo . . . And we still need one more girl . . . Have you given more thought to competing?"

Not meeting his eyes, I sit down on a bench to put on my knee sleeves. "Yeah. I talked to my parents about it."

"And? Did they say yes?" he rushes to ask.

"They told me it's my decision."

Josh squeezes onto my bench to pull on his own knee sleeves. He doesn't say anything as he rolls the first one up over his leg. I get the feeling he's dying to push me for an answer about joining his team, but is also trying to seem nonchalant and give me my space.

Once I have my knee sleeves on, I step under the bar, secure it on my upper back, and lift off. I warm up with the bar, squatting as low to the floor as I can go. They call it *ass to grass*.

Next I move up to 135 pounds. This weight is relatively easy for me now, but the set after that at 175 pounds is where things get difficult, when I'll need a spotter.

Once I have a belt on, Josh steps behind me and braces under my arms. At first I gasp at his touch, but then I remember where I am, what I'm doing. *Focus, Emma.* After taking a huge breath to brace myself and the heavy weight, I squat low, my muscles on fire as I push up through my legs.

"C'mon, c'mon, push!" Josh says in my ear.

I push to the top and rack the bar, thanking the heavens I didn't hit him with my butt. It went okay. He touched me, and I didn't freak out.

"Really good," Josh says.

I help him add a bunch more weight to the bar for his set.

Finally he asks, "So what are you thinking? Will you do it?"

I do love lifting. It's something I do for me, because I like being strong. But competing is like performing a choir solo in front of other people. Track doesn't make me nervous, so why do I feel this way about powerlifting? Maybe it's because I feel like a poseur, as if I don't belong here?

"It just seems like powerlifting is something strong people should be doing," I say.

"You are strong." Josh drops a light, warm hand onto my shoulder and looks me in the eye, and I pull a deep breath. He's really close to me. I wait for a prickly sensation of warning, but there's nothing.

"It seems like there are an awful lot of rules." I bite my lower lip. "I've been watching the videos you sent, of how people bomb out of the competition because they don't make their lifts. I'd be embarrassed if that happened in front of a crowd."

Josh nods. "I'll help you learn all the rules."

I decide to trust my gut. "Okay, I'll do it."

"Woo-hoo!" Josh celebrates.

People from around the gym peer over at us, but Josh continues to whoop, so I whoop back at him, which is so unlike me, but I can't help it. His excitement is infectious.

Josh bumps my fist. "Let's do this!"

STUCK

During study hall on Monday, I'm sitting in the library typing on my laptop when Josh suddenly appears next to me.

"Emma Emu."

"You're calling me that now, too?"

Josh shrugs, and adjusts his glasses. "It's cute . . . Hey, I wanted to show you a few videos so you can learn more about the competition commands."

I shut my laptop cover. "Okay."

He sits down next to me, and leans his head toward mine, shifting his body to angle his cell phone where we can both see the screen. I'm acutely aware of how close he is. I can smell the cinnamon gum he's chewing.

Ashi Parker, the basketball player sitting at the next table, gives me a sour look.

I nudge Josh and nod at her. "What's up with that? Are you going out with her?"

"No," Josh blurts. He sits up straighter in his chair. "Uh, are *you* with anybody?"

I shake my head.

He pauses for a moment, then nods and drums his fingers on his table.

When I was younger, I couldn't wait to get to high school and find a boyfriend. But now that I'm in high school, I'm not ready for that. Not after what happened.

During sophomore year, I went to the restroom during class one day. A senior guy I didn't know cornered me in the empty hall and kissed me. I wasn't interested and put my chin down and looked at the floor to try to show him it wasn't happening and to get lost.

Still he pushed me up against the wall and ran his hands over my hips as he tried to kiss me again. He was so strong, and nearly a head taller than me, and I didn't think I could fight back. I snapped "No!" in his face, startling him, which allowed me to wriggle away and run as fast as I could down the hall to class.

Ever since, I've jumped away when boys have tried to get close to me.

I can't get stuck again.

THE BIG DAY

The night before the competition, I wake up at 2:00 a.m. with racing thoughts.

What if I squat and get stuck at the bottom? What if I go to deadlift and the plates don't budge from the floor? What if I pass out, like in those videos?

I have a poor night's sleep.

Luckily, by the time we pull into the parking lot at the Richmond gym where the meet is taking place, I'm wide-awake thanks to adrenaline and the giant latte Dad bought me.

My mind flashes back to the first day I learned how to bench-press. My body overheated, my hands turned clammy and slippery on the barbell.

Today as I walk into the gym, my body does the same thing, but it's a totally different type of nerves. It's like when you've studied and studied for a big test. You know all the material, but as you sit down at your desk, your mind goes blank. Suddenly you can't remember two plus two equals four.

Mom, Dad, and Ava stand with me as I gaze around. Loud music blares and lights flash.

"I feel like I'm at the 930 Club," Dad says.

"You haven't taken me there in years," Mom replies.

"We should go sometime." Dad scrolls on his phone. "I'll check the schedule to see who's playing."

Ava and I roll our eyes at each other. As if our parents would ever do anything besides go to Great Plains on a weekend night.

There's a stage set up in front of the chairs, with a big power-lifting logo in the background. My mind suddenly flashes back to first grade, when this boy in my class, David Kraft, locked his knees during a choir concert and fainted in front of everyone.

I take a deep breath, promising myself I won't fall off the stage in front of all these people.

"Emma," Ava says under her breath. "Is that really Josh Mc-Connell waving at you?"

I shrug. "Yeah, I guess we're friends now?"

"He is so cute," Ava says. "Just look at his glasses. And look how hot his ass looks in those shorts—"

"Ava, stop!" I lightly smack her arm. "He'll hear you."

He comes jogging over and gives me a quick side hug. I gasp, and pull away a little.

A hurt look crosses his face. Shit. I touch my cheek and bite my lips in embarrassment. Why can't I be normal?

Josh watches me carefully. "I'm sorry. I should've asked."

Before I can react, he's moved on to shake hands with my parents. As he glances back my way, I touch the place on my hip where his hand just sat. And I'm okay.

Ava raises her eyebrows.

Josh gestures for my family to follow him. "I'll show you where to sit so you can see. My parents are there, too."

My family finds seats in the second row off to the side. Mom keeps patting her neck and temples with a tissue, as if she's sweating profusely.

"Please be careful," Mom says, hugging me.

"I promise."

Josh takes me back to a weight room designated for warm-ups, where I discover so many other girls and women. One team, wearing T-shirts that say *Valkyries*, is mostly made up of girls and only has two men.

Kayla hugs me, and the men on our team give me fist bumps.

Kayla looks down at her clipboard. "All right, Emma. You're up first."

"What?" I touch my throat. "I thought I'd get a chance to watch, to figure out what's going on."

"It'll be okay," Sean the gym dad says. "You've practiced the commands and you'll know what to do. Let's get you warmed up!"

Before I know it, it's time for the meet to start. All of a sudden I can't catch my breath. Josh stays with me as I get in line for the stage. I tighten my belt.

The announcer yells "Emma Masterson!" into a microphone like I'm walking out onto the floor at an NBA game. "Emma's opening at one hundred ninety-five pounds."

When I step out in front of the crowd, I'm in a fishbowl. So many eyes peering at me. The spotlights are blinding, and I have to squint to see where I'm stepping on the stage. Three spotters stand by the rack: two college guys and one superbuff woman.

Having people watch makes me nervous, so I zone out and pretend no one is there. This is just for me.

I approach the squat bar. My team is yelling my name and clapping, reminding me I can do this.

I stand under the squat bar, grip it hard, lift it up with my upper back, and step backward. With a huge breath, I squat down as low as I can. At the bottom, I momentarily question whether my legs are strong enough—whether I've trained hard enough—and then all my hard work flashes before my eyes. Week after week of consistent training over eight months.

I push through my feet. It's so heavy my eyes go blurry and I worry it will never end, but then I'm standing at the top and my team is screaming.

The announcer says, "And Emma's lift is good."

It counts! I did it.

"Woohoo!" I hear Josh scream.

I throw my hands up in the air and jog off the stage to my waiting team. They pat my back. Josh, however, keeps his distance as he claps and smiles. He believed in me. He believed in me so much he invited me to join his team.

Taking a deep breath, I stride to him. Get up on tiptoes and give him a little smirk. "Can I hug you?" I ask quietly.

His gray eyes widen, then he folds his arms around me. Letting out a deep breath, I relax against his chest. When he pulls back and smiles, I expect to feel a sense of relief, and I do, but there's something else, too: I want to hug him again.

I have two more attempts to best my earlier squat score. I'm able to squat one time at two hundred pounds, which just about makes my dad's jaw hit the floor. Ava cheers my name. Even Mom stands up to clap for me, making my eyes tear up.

But on my third and final attempt, at 210 pounds, I do get stuck at the bottom like in my nightmares. I can't push through the squat. My legs aren't strong enough. I'm gonna fall forward. I'm tipping. The bar rolls up on my back. It'll hit my neck!

Then the spotters lift the bar and help me rack it.

"Good attempt," one of the spotters says with a nod. "You'll hit it next time."

I failed the lift, but everyone's still clapping, telling me I did a good job.

But I don't need their cheers to know it.

As I walk off the stage, unclipping my belt, Josh comes to congratulate me. I surprise him with the biggest bear hug. When he lets go, I reach down and squeeze his hand once. My heart beats one, two, and three times, as I make a decision. I decide to leave my hand in his, praying he doesn't drop it. A century passes as I wait.

Then he smiles at me, and squeezes my hand to hold on tight.

#GOALS

AMPARO ORTIZ

If you don't want to delete this post, you can archive it.

The Delete and Archive options hover over my latest selfie. I'd posted it on Instagram this morning—a sacred part of my daily routine. Ten hours later, it has around three thousand Likes. My highest yet! Everyone is praising the beaded embroidery dress I bought at T.J.Maxx. No one has mentioned my tongue—the thing Jeremy hates about this photo.

"You're not a camel, Rachelle. Sticking it out is classless. What if you lose a career opportunity or a seat at your top school because of embarrassing pictures? Take that shit down."

My boyfriend is right. I should be careful with my image, even though I'm not applying to Princeton like him. He's committed to getting a full ride playing soccer for them next year. But the Fashion Institute of Design and Merchandising might also have a problem with my tongue. I'll never forgive myself if I'm rejected from my dream fashion school over a silly pose. The other selfies with this outfit aren't as . . . effervescent? Is that the word I'm looking for? Jeremy's the one with a dictionary for a brain.

It *is* his birthday. Deleting the photo he hates is the least I can do.

If only he could see me do it. I've been sitting in Celestino's Pizzeria alone for the past hour. My calls keep going straight to voice mail. Soccer tryouts start next week, but as usual, Jeremy's already practicing by himself. He's following a rigorous training schedule modeled after his favorite player, Cristiano Ronaldo. Thankfully, Celestino's owner plays golf with Jeremy's dad, so our reservation in the private dining area has a never-ending extension.

I sigh. Sometimes I wish he didn't love soccer so much. Then I remember how selfish I sound. It's not like he *never* makes time for me. It's just that our dates are often very chill, and there isn't a lot of variety in his choices. We're regulars at Celestino's and other fine dining restaurants in Montecito, our sunny hometown. I've also spent a few weekends on his dad's yacht at the Santa Barbara harbor. Jeremy hates swimming, so we mostly eat, sunbathe, and take lots of pictures.

Well, *I* take lots of pictures. I used to post them on my personal account (@!/rachelle_amador/!), but now I upload them with my hashtag, #clearancestylevibes, which is the social media brainchild I launched ten months ago. It's where I post selfies with trendy outfits I've either bought or have tried on from the clearance racks at designer boutiques. I also make TikTok videos that help me show off how the pieces move and look in specific lighting. Waking up to comments praising my aesthetic and photo-editing skills . . . chef's kiss.

The server pours me a third glass of water. He smiles awkwardly at the teal-and-silver HAPPY BIRTHDAY balloons I've placed around the table. Then he's off to the elderly couple across the room. They're watching a cheerleading competition on their phones. Both women ask for more Cabernet. They clap as their favorite team finishes their performance. Then they stare deeply into each other's eyes. One even boops the other's nose! I wonder how long they've been together, how many adventures they've been on with the power of love guiding them.

That will be us one day, Jeremy.

A shadow swoops past me. The chair's legs screech as a boy pulls it back.

"Hey," says Jeremy.

"¡Mi amor!" I lunge at him like a feral cheetah. My arms wrap around his waist, and I bury my face into his cologne-drenched cotton polo. I don't recognize the scent; it's not one of the eleven fragrances I've bought him. "Happy birthday! It's so good to see you and—"

"Can we sit down? People are staring."

"Oh! Of course!" I release him and point to the balloons. "It's your favorite colors!"

Jeremy sits down without glancing at them. He's rubbing his forehead, his eyes firmly pressed shut. "Please sit. The faster I get this out of the way, the faster I can leave."

My shoulders drop. "We're . . . not having dinner?"

He scowls. In the seven months he's been my boyfriend, not once has he looked at me like I'm bothering him. I didn't even *know* I could bother him.

"I'm only doing this in person because I'm a firm believer in face-to-face conversations. Don't make this any more uncomfortable than it already is."

"Make *what* more uncomfortable? It's your eighteenth birthday. Why are you so upset?"

"If you sit down, I can—"

"I'm fine. Now tell me why you're an hour late with a scowl on that gorgeous face."

Okay, so the "gorgeous" part wasn't supposed to slip out. But even when he's angry, Jeremy Matthews is too handsome for my own good. The closest I've come to accurately describing him to my grandparents in Puerto Rico is if Tom Holland had a scar on his left brow and way more toned thighs. How could I ever be immune to his charms?

"You know why I was late. Practice is very important to me," he says.

"Yes, I understand, but—"

"Especially since I want to go pro. I have a few clubs from overseas coming to see me play this season, too. I need to stay focused on my future."

"I know, yes—"

"And that's what I wanted to talk about tonight. We've been together for seven whole months, Rachelle, and not once have you given me the same respect I give you."

My butt lands on the chair. First he treats me like I'm bothersome, and now he's acting like I've been the worst girlfriend ever? Jeremy doesn't do drugs, but I'm tempted to ask if he's high right now.

The selfie . . .

"Is this about my picture? Because I was going to delete it right before you showed up." I pull up Instagram on my phone and smash the Delete button. "There you go! All gone!"

"It's not just about that stupid selfie. I don't think we're a good match, after all."

My two older brothers have taken boxing classes. If I asked them to describe what it's like getting clocked in the face, I think it would be a similar sensation to what I'm experiencing in this exact moment—head shooting back from the whiplash; teary, disoriented gaze; throbbing bones; and choked attempts at breathing.

"We're not . . . what?" I whisper. "Are you *dumping* me?"

"You used to like soccer, too, remember? That's how we met."

"I . . . yes, we were . . . at the beach . . ."

Jeremy nods. "You were playing with your brothers, and you scored a goal despite being outnumbered. I thought you were outstanding. Still had some room for improvement, but I was impressed. Then I introduced myself. There was this . . . pull . . . toward you. I couldn't ignore it."

That day, he had looked at me like he was under a spell—eyes wide and shining, a smile that could light up the darkest maze at Halloween Horror Nights. I was in the middle of a kick when I saw him. Tripping in front of hot guys is the absolute worst, but Jeremy helped me up and asked if I wanted to join him for dinner.

"But you wouldn't practice with me," Jeremy continues. "Not seriously, anyway. It was just a fun activity for you—not a future. You have *so* much potential and you keep wasting it."

He says it like I've set a FIFA contract on fire. Like it pains him to realize I'm not whoever he thought I was on some random beach day with my family. I had a blast fooling around with a soccer ball in the sand because that's the closest thing to a water sport my brothers would ever agree to. And it's the only sport where I'm better than them! Of course I'm playing it in public!

"Are you dumping me?" I repeat even louder.

Jeremy sighs like he's spent the past week running uphill. It's a long, tired sound.

"All you *really* care about is makeup and clothes. Your dream to study Fashion Marketing is a distraction. I need to be with someone whose main motivations aren't lipsticks and high heels. Someone who isn't posting on social media all the damn time. And that person isn't you."

Pleas for him to stay, to change his mind, lodge in my tight throat.

I'm too weak to grab him as he walks away, muttering words that get lost in the bustle of Celestino's new patrons making a beeline toward their group table.

The birthday boy leaves me to bawl my eyes out alone.

"Rachelle Amador, open up right now or I'm eating your bistec encebollado."

Mami bangs on my bedroom door for the hundredth time.

"I told you I'm not hungry!" I shove a spoonful of Talenti's Mediterranean Mint Gelato into my mouth. This is my third pint of the day. Roberto—my oldest brother—stocked the fridge as soon as I came clean about Jeremy. While Mami and Edgardo—my second-oldest brother—wished ill upon the entire Matthews family tree, Roberto slipped out of the house to buy me a weekend's worth of breakup junk food. There's no need for me to exit this room until Monday.

When I'll be forced to face Jeremy in the halls of Monte Lindo High. I'll see him sitting with the friends we shared simply because I was his girlfriend, and who'll probably ice me out. I should've made friends of my own. Jeremy never told me *not* to spend time with people who shared my interests, but he also never encouraged me to do fun stuff without him. He always had plans for us ready to go, and he only canceled if last-minute soccer practices came up. It's like he wanted my world to revolve around him.

I let out a sob. Losing a boyfriend sucks, but it's so much worse when there's no one to wallow with. Family just isn't the same— they'll try to convince me this isn't a big deal. And I'd very much like to have someone treat this crapstorm like a big deal, thanks.

"You need to nourish yourself with *real food*. Nada de esas pendejadas." Mami heaves a loud sigh. "Jeremy did you a favor! Someone better will come along in the future."

There's that cursed word—*future*.

As much as Jeremy hurt me, he's still my first serious boyfriend. There's no way I'm healing from this heartbreak in the blink of an eye, and telling me to do so will only sink me into a deeper hole of complete suckage. But I guess a woman who raised three kids by herself, refuses to go on dates, and became the most sought-after plastic surgeon in town less than a year after opening up her clinic wouldn't understand that.

"Please leave me alone, Mami!" I can't even get through the sentence without wailing.

She keeps threatening to eat my bistec encebollado for a few more minutes, then stomps down the hall, probably headed to the kitchen to put my lunch in Tupperware.

I take another spoonful of gelato as I open Instagram. This is the first time since I launched the #clearancestylevibes hashtag that I've missed my posting schedule. I already have everything uploaded in drafts, but I can't bring myself to publish anything.

I need to be with someone whose main motivations aren't lipsticks and high heels.

How dare he belittle my passion? It's not like he's curing cancer by kicking a ball!

I scroll down my feed in search of mindless content that can help me forget Jeremy exists. There's the usual mix of celebrities, fashion stylists, designer brands, and classmates. My thumb gains even more speed whenever someone from Monte Lindo High pops up on-screen.

The feed falls into a steady stream of advertisements, then another classmate slides into view—Teresa Smith. She's a senior like me, a striker on the girls' soccer team, and our school's resident female athlete superstar. Her sandy-blond hair whips behind her as she poses in last year's finals match against Toreros High. She happily holds up the trophy for the camera.

I'm about to scroll past when I notice the first commenter's name: @jer:)matthews18.

That's Jeremy's Instagram handle. He's left Teresa two words: *Dream girl.*

The comment was posted on his eighteenth birthday.

I click on Teresa's profile and search every selfie she's ever posted. Her photo with Mimi, her cousin, has almost ten thousand Likes. Mimi plays ice hockey for the U.S. Under-18 Women's National Team. She's pretty popular and a pretty blonde, so it doesn't shock me. What does seem weird is Jeremy leaving red hearts and variations of his "dream girl" comment on almost every picture. They were all posted on the same day he dumped me surrounded by the balloons I bought him. Balloons I deflated with a kitchen knife as a coping mechanism.

Teresa hasn't pressed the heart next to his compliments yet, but his friends hit Like on his very blatant flirtations. Were he and Teresa talking behind my back all along? Did they plan for him to get rid of me so they could be soccer lovers together?

I throw my phone on the bed with a growl. How fucking *dare they*? Blaming me for being shallow and uninteresting when he's cheating on me and his soccer bros are okay with it? Ugh, why are boys??? That's it—that's the whole question. Why. Are. Boys. God, I hope they lose their first match. No, no . . . I hope they lose every match for the entire season! Or even better, I hope they don't make it past tryouts next week!!!!

Wait a second . . . Their teams for the school year haven't been formed yet . . .

A bolt of energy hits me harder than a ball to the face. Every position on the girls' team is up for grabs. Not even a star striker like Teresa automatically gets to keep her spot.

Jeremy's wasted no time in replacing me. He's riding high. Thriving in my lane isn't going to bring him down, but being better than his dream girl at the sport he loves . . . becoming the new star striker . . .

I wipe my tears as I fetch my phone again.

I have a tryout schedule to find.

As hopeful girls file onto Monte Lindo High's soccer field, my dog of an ex-boyfriend is already sitting in the stands. He hasn't yet seen me walking across the grass. He's been ignoring me in the hallways and during our few classes together, unaware of my plan to burn his world down.

I approach Teresa at a brisk pace. She's tying her hair in a poor excuse for a bun by the water cooler. Her back faces the stands, but Jeremy's loving eyes are glued to her.

Not for long.

"Good afternoon." I speak to Teresa like a British monarch arriving fashionably late to my own royal ball. "Could you please move aside? I'm parched."

Okay, I totally googled that word last night.

Teresa spins around, her fingers still lost in that messy bun.

"Hey . . ." she says, her brow furrowed.

"Hello, Teresa."

The last time we spoke was in ninth grade. I'd dropped my glittery butterfly stickers as I ran out of our History class. She'd handed them to me, which was nice, but she kept staring at them like she had no idea why anyone would need glittery butterfly stickers.

Teresa looks me up and down, carefully studying my matching pink sneakers and shorts. "Are you . . . here for . . . tryouts?" She backs away, as if she needs more space to fully take me in.

"Indeed. May I nourish myself before we begin?"

"Um . . . sure." She stands aside, scratching the back of her head. "Wow."

"Is something wrong, Teresa?"

"No, I just . . . didn't expect someone like you to be here."

"May I ask what you mean by *someone like me*?"

I start filling up my thermos, but I don't break eye contact. I think Roberto once told me about how staring straight into your opponent's eyes weakens their defenses or something.

Teresa finishes tying her bun. It's so lopsided the Leaning Tower of Pisa would be jealous.

"People who've never shown interest in our sport," she says. "But we all contain multitudes, right? Which position are you gunning for?"

She's supercalm—not like the snobby boyfriend stealer I hoped she'd be.

It could be an act. Our coaches are here. And people with camera phones. The last thing a prospective recruit to the top colleges in this country wants is her shot at glory to go up in smoke.

You're not fooling me . . .

I take a slow sip of water while holding eye contact. After I gulp down, I sigh. "Yours."

Teresa's eyes go wide.

I leave her behind with a spring in my step.

Jeremy's jaw is on the floor. He's leaning forward like an old man who's struggling to hear what those people in the television are mumbling about. He's too far away to listen in on our conversation, but seeing me in the last place he imagined must be melting his brain. The loser is even rubbing his eyes as if this is a hallucination. As if there's *no way* I could ever be here.

I blow him a kiss, then walk to where the first drill is about to start. This is *my* field. I want him and his dream girl to remember it for the rest of their embarrassing lives.

This is *definitely* not my field.

I've been huffing and puffing through these godforsaken drills for the past half hour. Why would anyone be good at—and even enjoy—repeatedly jumping over marker cones? What is the point of forcing us to pretend we're bunnies escaping a ravenous predator (yes, I googled *ravenous*, too)? And don't even get me started on the whole kicking-a-tennis-ball-back-at-the-coach-while-tapping-a-ladder-in-and-out! I may as well have signed my soul away to hell.

"You okay?" one of the midfielders asks. Chelsea Something . . . I can't remember.

"Yeah . . . I'm . . . great!"

I'm doubled over, fanning myself at full speed. Hopefully my smile and upbeat tone will fool everyone. Jeremy and Teresa won't get the satisfaction of seeing me fail.

A whistle blows.

At long last, it's time for striker drills! We'll be training near the touchlines on the right side of the pitch. I line up behind the dozens of girls trying out for spots on the team—one is known as the striker, which belonged to Teresa last season. Strikers are mostly responsible for scoring goals. I'll admit Teresa is pretty good at her job, but it's not like she's unbeatable. There can only be one striker on the team, right? She's gone after I outperform her, no? Ugh, I wish I'd actually paid attention to Jeremy's constant speeches about soccer positions! Either way, from what I've seen in YouTube videos of past matches, she's a fast dribbler, but I'm *way* faster.

Well, I'm faster in the sand without jumping around for a half hour beforehand.

Don't start losing steam now! You have a spot to secure!

Teresa goes first. She kicks the ball toward the metal bench that's been placed on the grass. When the ball bounces back to her, she leads it down the length of our assembled line, stops it with a flawless turn, then returns to the bench to start all over again. Her focus is sharper than the Japanese steel kitchen knives Mami bought recently. On her final run, Teresa goes a bit farther away with the ball, and kicks it with all her might toward the empty goal.

She scores.

"Good job!"

"That's right!"

"Go, Teresa!"

The other girls are clapping as if Megan Rapinoe herself is on the field.

Jeremy is clapping, too, but he's dead silent. And he's looking at me like I'm the hardest math problem he's ever had to solve. God knows what's running through his cheating mind, but after I have a go at this drill, I hope it's filled with my amazing performance.

"Thanks, guys," says Teresa.

I fold my arms and keep my gaze straight ahead. I'm not in the mood to watch her give these obnoxious groupies some high fives and fist bumps. Four girls later, it's finally my time to shine. I'm rested enough to kick the ball toward the bench without struggling for air, but I'm definitely lacking in strength. The ball *touches* the bench instead of fully slamming into it.

I pretend there's a picture of Jeremy and Teresa making out. The bench rattles with each grunt-fueled kick. It's like the shirtless Spartan army from that supermacho movie Edgardo loves so much has possessed my right leg. When it's time for the goal-scoring portion of my drill, I race past the line of girls, throwing Teresa a little side-eye. I sweep my foot forward.

It misses the ball.

Then flies high toward the sun, making me lose balance on my standing leg.

I'm launched onto the grass.

"Oof!"

My back and butt have never throbbed this much. I stay down as searing heat travels all over my lower body. The warmth on my cheeks is even hotter—I've just fallen on my ass in front of my ex-boyfriend and the girl he dumped me for!

"Whoa. Are you hurt?"

Teresa Smith stands over me, her hand outstretched.

There's no way I'm touching her. Is she trying to embarrass me further? Rubbing it in by pretending she's helping me up? She and Jeremy will surely roast me behind my back! This little act is simply another way to build up her spotless image, too. I refuse to be part of her schemes.

And I definitely refuse to be ridiculed.

"Get away from me!" I rise all by myself. It takes me a while to regain my balance, but at least I'm not depending on the fake girl in front of me.

"*What* is your problem? Please explain it to me like I'm five years old." Teresa blocks my path. Her smile is long gone. Now

she's full-blown glaring at me like I've scorched her precious trophies into ashes. "No offense, but you're acting like a total jerk for
no reason."

She might as well have kicked me in the gut. "For . . . no . . .
reason?" I whisper.

A whistle goes off behind me.

"Ladies, that's enough. We're moving on to partner drills,"
Coach says.

"You're kidding, right? You have to be," I tell Teresa. "How long
had you been talking to Jeremy before he left me for you? Did you
both plan for him to dump me last week?"

"Ladies!"

Teresa raises a hand to Coach. Her eyebrows are knitted
together in confusion. "This is because of Jeremy Matthews?"

"Does the guy clapping for you in the stands have another
name?"

Teresa's sigh is long. She lowers her hand, taking a firm step forward. "Your ex has been messaging me for the past three weeks, but
we're *not dating*. I'm not even interested in him. I haven't blocked
him because I planned on showing you his messages, but . . . I just
didn't know how to approach you. Whenever I saw the two of you
together, I could tell you were in deep, and I didn't want to hurt your
feelings. But I guess it's too late for that now. You can check my
DMs if you want. Everything is still there." She motions to Jeremy,
but doesn't break eye contact with me. "Boys like him only care
about themselves, and they make us believe we're the problem."

The whole team is gathered around us, hooked on her every
heartbreaking word. It's a miracle no one is filming this. All they
can do is nod along.

I almost nod, too. Jeremy treated me like trash back at the
restaurant, but he's probably dropped hints of his asshole-ness

throughout our relationship. I'd been too obsessed with him to notice. But to hear that he's been messaging Teresa during his time with me . . . that she's endured it only so she could have proof against him . . . that she's not into him at all and still he persists . . .

I shouldn't be ashamed of falling earlier.

The way I've behaved today is the real embarrassment.

Teresa is right—guys like Jeremy want us to think everything is either our fault or in our heads. They're never the source of our frustrations, and they're always allowed to feel frustrated when they're not the center of our universe. The faster my mind races with Teresa's confession, the heavier my limbs feel. I slowly squat until my butt finds its way to the grass again.

"Give her some space, okay? Let's back up," Teresa says.

The girls retreat a few paces. They're all staring at me like I'm a wounded bird.

"Can I get you some water?" one girl asks.

"Or an energy drink?" Another girl.

"How's that leg, by the way? The one you tripped on?" And another.

Soon they're all talking at the same time. They go from offering me tissues for my sweaty face to encouraging me to take deep, calming breaths.

I've never been part of a team, but this sure feels like it.

Tears spring to my eyes. I spent so much time wrapped around Jeremy's finger that I didn't make friends outside of his inner circle. That's exactly how he liked it, too—the less support for anything that didn't revolve around him, the better. But as kind as these amazing athletes are, I don't belong among them. It was a mistake to think I ever could.

"I came here to take your spot." I speak directly to Teresa. "Just to piss you and Jeremy off. And to prove him wrong about me. I've always been fairly good at soccer, but it's never been something I see myself doing for the rest of my life. I'm sorry for treating you the way I did, and for coming onto your field and acting like I have any claim to it."

Teresa shakes her head. "It's not *my* field. This is for everyone who works hard to be here. If you want to go, you're free to do so, but as high as your foot went after your fall . . . it's giving me major goalie vibes. I think we can ask Coach to test your skills in the net. What do you say, girls?"

"Yes!" they say in cheerful unison.

"Let's see what you got." Teresa winks at me.

I laugh. Maybe I'll suck even worse.

Or maybe I'll be good at it, but I won't know unless I try.

Is soccer my future? Probably not. Bonding with these girls, though . . . that definitely seems more promising. Besides, there's room in my walk-in closet for both high heels *and* sneakers.

And more important, this is a chance to build a life without the ex who never deserved me. Sure, I started on this path to spite him, but he doesn't get to dictate anything else again. For the first time in seven months, I'm not doing something for a boy. This is for *me*.

"The net it is." I reach out a hand to Teresa. "Help me up?"

She smiles. "Of course."

As she pulls me back to my feet, I hear Coach telling everyone to take their places. The girls offer me high fives first, then dart off toward their respective spots.

Teresa is about to turn away when I grab her by the arm.

"Feel free to delete those messages and block him," I say. "I don't need to see anything."

"Oh, thank God . . . I hate his sorry ass." Teresa looks right at him. Her scowl is intense enough to peel off his skin. "Next time he tries talking to me, I'm spitting in his ugly face."

Not too long ago, the thought of anyone calling Jeremy Matthews ugly would've been ridiculous, but now that I see past his looks, I can't find a single beautiful thing about him.

"Hey, Teresa? Can we take a quick picture?"

After she says yes, we sprint to my gym bag, fetch my phone, and do the exact pose I requested. After I apply my favorite filter, I post it on Instagram with a hashtag I've never used before: #GOALS. I also throw in my usual #clearancestylevibes and mention how I'll start searching for affordable sports-related items to include in my shoots.

Jeremy walks down the stands. He makes a beeline for the exit.

I smile down at my picture with Teresa, our heads leaning against each other and our tongues proudly hanging out.

SIDELINED

MAGGIE HALL

The first time I noticed Oliver O'Rourke, I snatched the football out of his hands and knocked him over. And then I stepped on him.

We were in peewee football. I was five. My mom made me apologize, but I wasn't really sorry.

In his defense, we were on the same team, so technically I wasn't supposed to do that. In my defense, he was just standing there, holding the ball, staring up at the sky as I screamed, "Throw it! *Throw it!*" He was about to get the flags pulled off his waist—the peewee equivalent of getting sacked—so . . . I took matters into my own hands. And I got the touchdown.

He maintains to this day that he heard a strange noise and got distracted. I think he was just watching a cloud that looked like a dinosaur or something. Anyway, we won the game. You gotta do what you gotta do.

After that, Ollie never let me run over him again. My twin brother, Austin, had been the star of the team, an already-talented offensive lineman at five years old, but suddenly Ollie was working harder, getting stronger, throwing a ball too big for his little hands more accurately every day. And since I was our best receiver, we spent every practice working together, me and Oliver, on the same team, but each of us determined to win.

NOW

I see the seconds ticking down in red: 0:09, 0:08, 0:07. There's a girl bearing down on me, her shoes squeaking on the freshly waxed court. She's tall and fast, with dark brown skin and an elastic in Braves's school colors, red and blue, wrapped around her topknot. Teanne Coleman. The best center in our district. She was all over the tape I watched of the Eagles this week.

She could not look less like smirking, blue-eyed Oliver O'Rourke, but I see the same calculations in her eyes I always see in his. She thinks she's faster than me. And she's probably right, but she doesn't know I've seen her do this trick before. As she tries to strip the ball, I dribble out of her reach, bound down the court, and make an easy layup.

The crowd screams. The buzzer sounds, drowning them out.

Halftime.

I jog to the bench and wipe my face with a Mountaintop Musketeers towel, dampening the forest-green and silver stripes with sweat.

"*That's* our college star. Miss Lexie Hawthorne, ladies and gentlemen." Jamila shoves me with her shoulder.

I smile back. Next week, I'm supposed to sign my letter of intent to play basketball at Western. I catch the water bottle Kelli tosses me, and join the team on the way to the locker room.

"You doing some kind of signing party?" Carmen asks.

I roll my eyes. "It's not the draft," I say, and bury my face in my towel so she won't ask any more. For some reason, I don't want to talk about it. Even before what Oliver said last night—and *way* more so now—every time someone asks me about college, I get this nervous, twitchy feeling in my stomach. I tell myself that's normal. It's a big decision.

Not that it was much of a decision. Western was the only school to offer me a basketball scholarship, and being a college athlete is what I've worked toward my whole life. So of course I'm going there, even if Western wouldn't have been my first-choice school otherwise. Even if they don't have the major I wanted. Even if—

I look ahead to the locker room. I'm captain, which means I'm doing the halftime pep talk and going over stats with Coach Lerner to make adjustments for the second half. But today captain duties are going to have to wait a few minutes.

"Gotta pee," I say. "Meet you guys in there."

I jog ahead. I swipe my phone out of my locker, take it into a bathroom stall, and pull up the Musketeer Minute, our school's student portal. It's where we keep track of our homework and our grades, and it also gives real-time scores of any games. First I see our score—Mountaintop Musketeers: 42, Braves High Eagles: 40. I feel a swell of pride over my last basket that put us in the lead.

I swipe to find the football team's score for tonight's district championship, which could send us into the state title game. The second quarter's just started.

At first, I'm not sure I'm seeing correctly.

Mountaintop Musketeers: 0, Valley Vikings: 21.

I blink at the screen.

The locker room door bursts open, and the space echoes with yelling and laughing and the metallic slam of locker doors. I click off my phone, flushing the toilet for good measure.

Was Ollie actually going to lose today? And for the first time ever, did I want him to win?

THEN

The year we turned six, Ollie's and my unspoken rivalry continued. Now I kept a silent score in my head: On any pass where we didn't connect, was it his fault, or was it mine? On the days when his passes hit the mark but I had butterfingers, I could see a smug smile on his face, and I was sure he was tallying up just like I was.

Then we were seven, and we started to compare real stats. How many passing yards for him, and receiving yards for me? How many yards after the catch did I rack up? How many rushing yards did he put on the board?

I tried as hard as I could not to gloat when I won almost every time.

That was also the first year I noticed that I was the only girl. Not only on our team, but on *any* of the teams. My mom tried to switch me to cheer—my cousin Hayley had been doing it since we were five, and by the time we were in 8 and Under, my friends Mari and Cat were, too. But when Hayley gave me cartwheel lessons, I fell on my face and busted open my right eyebrow. Three stitches. I have the scar to this day.

Sure, I could have gotten better at it, but I didn't *love* cheer. I loved football. I loved sizing up the other team before the game, picking out my marks. I loved catching a long, soaring pass the other team was not expecting, and seeing nothing but open field ahead of me as I sprinted to a touchdown. I loved that I knew the sevens times tables before I even learned how to add, from watching the scoreboard click up.

By the time we were in 9U, the other teams started complaining about a girl playing, pretending they were just "concerned" about my "safety." I think they were concerned because between me and Ollie, we kicked everyone's ass in the region.

That was when Ollie and I started the bets. If my stats were better, he had to bring me a mini bag of Cheetos to school on Monday. If he won, I had to sneak him whatever homemade treat my mom had made that weekend.

And it went on like that for third grade, fourth, fifth. I ate my weight in pilfered Cheetos. And if Ollie ever won two weeks in a row, it was a reminder to myself to work harder, get faster, be better.

The only problem was, he kept getting better, too.

By sixth grade, we were the best eleven-year-olds in the league. But after we won the 12U championship—on a forty-nine-yard Hail Mary pass I snatched from between the hands of two defenders—we had barely finished our celebratory pizza party when the hammer fell.

Turned out our league's commissioner had "suggested" to my dad that we were too old for a girl to be playing against the boys. My dad—even though he's Mountaintop's varsity football coach and had the league commissioner wrapped around his finger—didn't fight it.

The game we'd just played was going to be my last in football.

NOW

I look around at my teammates. Angie, our point guard, is wrapping her ankle. Hmm. Destiny is re-braiding her hair. Jamila's sitting on the floor against her locker, one earbud in, head bopping silently.

"J," I say. Her head snaps up and she turns off her music. "You're faster than the girl they have on you, but she's beating you to the line. You've gotta be more aggressive. Guys, the only one of them who's really fast is number twelve. I'm thinking we should switch—" I glance to Coach for confirmation, and she nods. "Let's switch to zone defense for the rest of the game."

I finish my pep talk and everyone's so hyped that the whole team bursts out of the locker room with a yell to start the second half.

I bring up the back, and before I hit the court, I pull my phone out of my sports bra to sneak another glance at the football score: 3–21. What is going on?

We are *on* in the second half. Jamila is hitting three-pointers like it's nothing. We sub in Carmen for Angie, and she puts six points on the board immediately.

I, however, am distracted. I keep seeing that football score in my head, and then the whiteboard of plays in my dad's office. I watched plenty of tape of Valley and helped my dad and the coaching staff refine almost every play. How did they have our number like this?

I miss a couple easy layups. I'm usually a robot about free throws—it's one of the stats I can consistently hammer Ollie in—but when I get fouled, two in a row bounce off the rim.

Lucky for me, it doesn't matter. As the clock counts down to two seconds, one, zero, Destiny hurls the ball toward the basket and collapses spread-eagle at center court. The scoreboard flashes as the buzzer rings out: 77–63.

The bench clears, and everybody dogpiles Destiny, all sweaty shirts and squeaking shoes, and Carmen's braids whip me in the face as Kelli throws herself into my arms.

I stare up into the lights of the gym. Forget about the football game, I tell myself. *This* is my sport now. I love being on a team. I love this feeling, this glee. I *love* winning. I love—okay. I *like* basketball. I like it fine.

Just like playing next year, in college, will be *fine*. It'll be good. Never mind that to be a college athlete, you have to be all in. You live and breathe your sport. Before classes, after classes, during meals, on weekends: Next year, my life will be all basketball, all the time.

I had started playing basketball in middle school. I had to stay in winning shape somehow, especially because I'd made Ollie a new bet: that I'd be back on the football team by high school. And after that, that I'd be the first female receiver ever to play in college.

First step: another sport to be good enough at that my dad would see the team needed me.

I had tried track. I was fast enough, but I hated the long runs. I twisted my knee my first week in soccer, and anyway, I'd have to catch up with all the girls who had been playing since elementary school. Softball should have been a natural fit, but the whole batting part just never came together for me.

The only thing that worked was basketball. At first, it was my height—I was still taller than everybody in eighth grade, and ninth. But I was good at it, too. And it was okay. It was something.

Carmen starts the *Musketeers, one for all* school chant. Everyone else jumps in the showers, but I pull out my phone again. The score is the same: 3–21. Middle of the third quarter.

I shake my head. As much as I tell myself otherwise, I just need to get to the football field before it drives me crazy. I yell out a rain check for post-game smoothies, pull a baseball cap over my two messy blond braids, and jog out of the gym toward the football field.

THEN

I'd gotten pretty good at basketball by the time I started at Mountaintop, and my dad noticed, just like I'd hoped. My next step was to worm my way back into the sport I *wanted* to be in. I started hanging around the athletic department. I scouted every team in the district, handing my dad dossiers every week.

One day I decided it was time. "So?" I said. "It's good info, right?"

"Better info than my entire coaching staff has given me in months."

I swelled with pride.

My dad closed the folder and looked up at me. "That still doesn't mean I can let you play."

"Come *on!*" I exploded, my whole rehearsed speech flying out of my head. Of *course* he had figured out what I was up to. "Are you really saying that Conner LaForce deserves to play football more than I do? He can barely *lift* a football. Or Jeremiah Garner? I saw him trip over his own shoe yesterday."

"It's not about who deserves—" my dad started, but when I huffed out a growl, he sighed. "Lexie, no one deserves to be part of this team more than you. You'd be just about the best football mind the Musketeers have ever seen, I can promise you that."

"And I'm *good*, Dad. I'm still good. I'm in great shape. I still throw the ball every—"

"I know."

"So let me play!"

My dad tapped his desk. "It's not like you're a kicker, Lex. Receivers get hit. Every time. Most of the cornerbacks are twice your weight, and only get stronger—"

"That's not fair!"

"It's not. But I'm not going to risk you getting hurt. You can't play football at this level, Lexie. Case closed."

After I left his office, I stood outside the door for a long time. I had really thought there was a chance. Looking back, I guess it had been naive. I just hadn't let myself imagine a world where I wasn't involved in football. But . . . here it was.

I had lost.

My favorite thing wasn't for me anymore.

NOW

As I leave the gym, the last thing I'm expecting is to run into my mom pacing the parking lot.

"Lex." She looks up from her phone, and her face is pinched.

My stomach knots. I swipe a strand of hair out of my face as I glance toward the lights of the football stadium. "What is it? Did something happen?"

"It's Austin. His knee."

My throat closes up. I forget about the football score, the basketball game, college, everything.

"ACL?" I croak out. Those are the scariest letters in the world to any athlete. If my brother tore his ACL—

"No," my mom says, and I can breathe again. "The trainer thought it might be, and Dad took him straight to the hospital. But it looks like it's just a sprain. He'll need to stay off it for a few weeks."

The whiplash from terror to relief is so heady it takes me a second to register the rest of what she said. "Dad took him? Who's coaching the team?"

Mom sighs. "Coach Walter."

Coach Walter is one of the assistants. He's at least eighty-five years old, and brings Dr Pepper and shrink-wrapped brownies to every game.

"Get in," my mom says, opening the door on her SUV. "We're meeting Dad and Austin at the hospital."

I glance at the stadium again. A steady stream of people is pouring out, in Musketeer green and silver. No real coach. Their star lineman out, injured. And fans deserting. The Musketeers could kiss the state championship goodbye.

"Tell Austin I'll see him at home," I say, and before my mom can stop me, I've thrown my duffel bag in the car and am running toward the stadium, dodging our fair-weather fans as I go.

I hop the turnstile and dash off a text to my brother: *You'd better be okay. I'm not doing all your chores for two months just because you're on crutches.*

Austin responds with a middle finger emoji, and I know he's going to be fine.

I stash the phone in the pocket of my hoodie and scan the stadium: 9–21. We'd managed two more field goals. My analytical mind switches on. Okay. So we're down only two possessions because our defense is holding them. There are over four minutes remaining, which normally would be a decent amount of time. But . . . we haven't made a touchdown all game. No way we're getting two in a couple minutes.

On the other side of the field, half the Musketeers are sitting on the bench, heads in their hands. Oliver is making a phantom throwing motion, over and over and over, to no one. It's his nervous tic. Mime falling back a couple steps, throw, repeat.

I don't know what my plan is, but I make my way around the stadium, my eyes on Oliver the whole time.

THEN

The day after the talk with my dad that closed the door on football for good, I'd brought Ollie a double-layer chocolate-raspberry cake from A Cake Above. He'd won the bet, fair and square. He didn't say a word to gloat, though. He just jogged to the cafeteria, came back with two plastic forks, and we dug in together.

It was only a one-day reprieve, though. The next day, the obnoxiousness that was Oliver O'Rourke came back in full force. He was real proud of himself for making varsity as a freshman, so he suggested there was no way my basketball stats could keep up with his football ones. I worked out an elaborate system of comparable stats for our bets, and now I had one new reason to work extra hard at basketball practice.

And a second new reason: I reminded him that though I had lost the first half of the bet I'd made, the second could still stand; I'd still play in college, just in a different sport. If I won, he had to do my bidding for a whole week. The fact that he agreed to that meant he didn't believe I could do it, which only made me want it more.

The summer between freshman and sophomore year, Ollie's family went to stay with his grandparents in Maine for two months. "I'm so glad he's gone," I sighed to my cousin Hayley. "He's just so annoying. It's *so* nice to have a couple months where he's not looking over my shoulder asking about my training."

Until, weirdly, I started to miss him. The person who would remind me if I did my weird flat-footed run that made my ankles hurt. The *only* person who was able to cure me when I'd gotten a bad case of the yips one time, because he understood what was going on before I did. And the only person who didn't think I'd break in half if I touched a football. Oliver never tried to stop our decade-long tradition of throwing the ball at the park on Saturday mornings, and even as he got stronger and his throws got harder, I could tell from the sting in my palms that he never held back to spare my poor fragile girl body. And in return, I never stopped giving him shit when he aired one so far over my head he could have killed a pigeon.

When, after months of being dark, the upstairs windows in his house lit up the night before school started, I told myself the weird little nauseous turn my stomach did was about proving myself this year, and nothing more.

The first day of sophomore year, I was standing at my locker when a voice behind me said, "What do you say we make this whole year double or nothing?"

I turned around and looked up. And up and up. Oliver O'Rourke, whose head used to barely reach my shoulder, had grown taller than me, and his blue eyes were sparkling, and for some reason, I could barely squeak out an answer.

NOW

I make my way to the home sideline. Even the cheerleaders look wilted, their pom-poms in green and silver piles at their feet. Hayley gives me a half-hearted wave. The players' families, at least, have stayed put on the bleachers, their painted faces anxious and pained.

A smattering of cheers breaks out when Valley has to punt. I climb to the edge of the bleachers to watch as Oliver and the offense take over.

It takes me all of three seconds to see the problem. Oliver is a scrambling quarterback, and there is no scrambling happening here. They're blitzing every play, and he's getting hammered. He gets sacked twice on this drive alone, and we turn it over on a three-and-out.

The crowd deflates further.

How is Coach Walter allowing this? The guy is nice, but I swear, he's a couple shoulder pads short of a full uniform. We are going to lose this game.

Oliver is going to lose this game.

Even if this weren't the district championship, it would be his last home game. And our last bet. Because in the fall, when I go to Western, he'll be starting at State, four hours away.

THEN

"I guess I'll have to find someone else to make bets with me next year," Oliver said, coming up behind me in line in the cafeteria a month ago. "You're not a good enough driver to bring me blueberry doughnuts long-distance every time I win."

"Screw that," I said, putting a fruit cup on my tray. "I am *definitely* making you drive to Western to clean my sneakers with a toothbrush when *I* win. Don't think you're getting off that easy."

He snorted out a laugh. But it was out there. We both knew it. Our stats at the district championship would be our last bet. A rivalry played out over thirteen-plus years, and this was the end. Sure, we could text insults back and forth. Sure, we could keep comparing stats. But it would never be the same. It would never be like this.

NOW

My foot is shaking so fast everyone on the bleachers must feel it. Oliver just got sacked *again*. I wish I could talk to him. He looks so overwhelmed, I don't know if he even sees the pattern. But I can't exactly waltz onto the field in the middle of the game.

And then I see it.

On the team bench, right by the Gatorade cooler. It's my dad's headset.

I take the bleacher steps two at a time, and whisper to Hayley. She jogs to the bench, pretending to get a drink, and swipes the headset as she does.

I leap back up the steps. As Valley's kicking team takes the field for a fourth down, I turn the headset on. There's a squeal, and I see Oliver grab his ear. Good. He still has the earpiece in.

"Your offensive line is Swiss cheese with Austin gone," I say. "You can't scramble like this."

Oliver's head whips up. "Lexie?"

"My dad left his headset. You have a new Coach Hawthorne now."

He's still looking for me. I raise a hand, and he clocks me, a smile breaking across his face. "Did you guys win?" he asks.

"Obviously."

"Is Austin—"

"It's not his ACL. He's going to be fine. Now come on. It's still a two-possession game, but you can do this. Remember Whitfield?"

Oliver turns back to the field when a cheer rises. Archer Akhil has gained a good thirty yards on the punt return before he's taken down, and for once, we're starting with decent field position.

"Yeah," Oliver says. "Okay. Yeah."

"What's the call?" I ask.

"Shovel pass to the sideline."

I'm already shaking my head. "No. They have DeSilva in double coverage. You won't get it off in time." I survey the field. "You have to go long."

Oliver hesitates. "Coach didn't trust my arm yet."

He tweaked his throwing shoulder six weeks ago. Even before the injury, Dad had been grooming him as a scrambling QB for years. It's been good for me—his stats never get as high when his passing yards stay in the double digits.

"Do *you* trust your arm?" I ask.

He's quiet for a second. "Yeah."

So do I. Maybe it's good for me in our rivalry, but I know Oliver. There's no way he hasn't been throwing every day anyway.

The offense takes the field. Oliver glances back at me, and a thrill runs through me. I might not be on the turf, but I'm in charge.

"Remember the 12U championship?" I ask.

I can hear the smile in his voice. "That Hail Mary."

"Nobody'll be expecting it on this play. Tell Sanchez to go long."

I can see his eyes widen behind his face mask. "Are you trying to sabotage me, Hawthorne? I know you'll do anything to win a bet."

I grin. "You never know. I guess you'd better not screw it up."

He huffs out a laugh. "Okay, Coach. Whatever you say."

THEN

Every day for the past month, we've traded ideas about the final bet.

"Breakfast every day for a week?" he'd yelled down the hallway between classes.

"Wow. You got really boring," I'd called back.

A few days later, I texted him. *How about you buy me a car? You're going to be rich and famous once you get to State, right?*

Sure. Start checking out the Matchbox lineup, he texted back.

He suggested I run drills with him all winter break if I lose. I reminded him that would just make him feel inadequate. I proposed a song-and-dance routine dedicated to me at the winter formal, which will conveniently be the night of the games. "If your date will let you," I added.

"I'm just going with the team," he said.

"Yeah," I answered, ignoring the little vibration in my chest. "Me too. With my team."

So then, we came to last night. We were setting up for the formal, since we're both on student council. As I went long and caught a roll of green streamers he lobbed across the gym, I yelled, "So the song-and-dance number it is? I hope you've been practicing."

I climbed up a ladder and taped my end to the wall. He brought me the silver streamers to tape up next to it. "Or," I said, climbing back down, "you shave your head."

He seemed to consider it. "Okay. I'd look good with a shaved head."

True. He would.

"So does that mean you'll shave *your* head if I win?" he asked. He mussed my ponytail. "Nah, I kinda like your hair as it is."

I looked up at him, and he cleared his throat and jogged across the gym to help Bryan Dao with the DJ table.

When we were done, Hayley and Mari and Cat went ahead, and I found Oliver leaning against the bleachers. "We have to choose the stakes before three tomorrow," I said. "Let me know if you have any ideas that are actually good."

He opened his mouth like he was going to say something, then closed it. "Yeah," he answered, and that was it.

An unexpected stab of disappointment ran through me. "Okay, well. Um. Night."

I was halfway out the door when he said, "Lexie." I turned back around. "If I win," he said quickly, "you don't go to Western. You come to State."

Before I could wrap my head around what he'd just said, he was jogging the other way. "G'night," he said over his shoulder.

I thought about it the whole way home, while Mari sang off-key and Cat painted her nails with green glitter in the back seat. The second I closed the door to my bedroom, I pulled up Oliver's number.

"State didn't give me a basketball scholarship," I said, before he could even say hello.

"I know." He paused. "Do you *want* to play basketball in college?"

I blinked at the wall behind my bed. It was covered in Musketeers pennants and pictures, newspaper articles about the NFL draft, and a whiteboard scrawled with football plays to propose to my dad. And one single photo of the basketball team.

"*What?*" I said.

No one had ever asked me whether I *wanted* to keep playing basketball. I'd been working toward getting recruited for years. Why, if they were giving me a scholarship, would I possibly not take it?

I hadn't even asked myself.

But as usual, it was like Oliver was in my head. Usually it's incredibly annoying. Now I'm shocked into silence.

"If you want the scholarship, if you want to play basketball, of course you go to Western," Oliver said quietly. "Night, Lex."

I kept staring at the phone long after he'd hung up.

NOW

Oliver huddles with the team. I can only imagine what they must be saying about the change in the play.

They line up. There's the snap.

Oliver drops back. Anthony Sanchez splits off and sprints down the field, so fast nobody notices.

Throw it, I think. It feels just like that very first game in peewees all over again. The blitz is bearing down. This time, I'm not there to snatch it out of Ollie's hand.

"Throw iiiit!" I scream.

This time he does.

The ball flies in a tight spiral down the field. There's not a Valley Viking in sight. The only person down the field is Anthony.

The ball hits him right in the numbers. Fifteen-yard line. Ten. Five. *Touchdown*.

Our fans erupt in screams. I jam the headset back on my head.

"You did it!" I yell, and on the field, I see Oliver wince and grab his ear, but he's smiling.

I can hear through the headset as he convinces Coach Walter that yes, in fact, that was the play that had been called. At that moment, I know the rest of the game is in my hands.

There is nowhere else I'd rather be.

Our defense holds them. Less than two minutes now. We have no timeouts, and Oliver is looking over his shoulder. To me. Waiting for me to call the play.

Ollie's arm looked so good I call a pass, then another—but they're on to us, and not leaving anybody open. One more pass, and Oliver connects with DeSilva—but only for eight yards. Fourth down.

Eighteen seconds on the clock. We're down by five.

A little doubt creeps in that I don't *actually* know what I'm doing, but Coach Walter calls the team over, and I know I'm their only hope.

I take a deep breath. "Quarterback sneak," I say in Oliver's ear. He glances up at me. "We have them confused. And as much as I hate to admit it, you are a good runner. I think it'll work."

"I trust you," comes the reply.

I watch, my knuckle between my teeth. I was right. They're defending against another Hail Mary. Oliver breaks a tackle, and he's got a first down—and more. He jukes past a final defender, who falls to the ground.

And . . . touchdown.

"Touchdown!" I scream, throwing my arms in the air.

The extra point sails through the uprights. Three seconds left. The kickoff. Fair catch. QB releases a long pass—and it's knocked out of the air.

We won.

WE WON.

My scream is drowned out by the rest of the stadium. I'm rushing onto the field. I scan the sea of sweaty guys in forest-green uniforms—and there he is, helmet dangling from one hand, hair tousled and wild.

Oliver's eyes meet mine through the crowd of jubilant bodies. He grins so wide I laugh out loud, and we push toward each other.

Oliver tosses the helmet aside and swoops me up in his arms.

I wrap my legs around his waist and bury my face in his sweaty neck and I'm laughing into his shoulder pads and he's holding me so tight I can't breathe.

"We did it," he murmurs, squeezing me even tighter.

"You did it," I say.

"There's no way I could have done it without you. *You* did it." He pulls back so we're face-to-face. "Lex, what I said last night, I'm sorry. I didn't mean—"

Just then, a waterfall of icy blue Gatorade dumps on my head.

I scream, Oliver yelps, and I fall from his arms, wheeling to face the grinning team, holding the now-empty cooler.

"I *may* have told them you called the last few drives." Oliver laughs.

"Nice win, Coach," says Sanchez, with a high five, and a few more of the guys clap me on the shoulder as they jog away.

Coach.

I'm freezing, and sticky, but my smile feels like it's going to break my face in half.

Maybe I can't play football anymore, but *this* is what I love, isn't it? The mental game. I love knowing how to get under our opponents' skin. I love seeing the whole game laid out in front of me like a chessboard, and envisioning the moves to get to checkmate.

And no, there are not many female head coaches, either, but no one can tell me I'm too small, or I'll get hurt, or I'm not qualified to do this.

I don't think coaching is a college major, but my first choice was always State's sports med program. I have the grades to get in. But then State didn't recruit me for basketball, and Western did, and that was that.

But if I went to State . . . I could do the program I want, and be a trainer for the football team. Maybe become a manager. Work under the coaches. For one of the top football teams in the conference.

This one thought makes me more excited than basketball *ever* has. And it's not like I'd have to stop playing. I'm sure there are intramural basketball teams. Basketball just wouldn't be my *life*.

Oliver is shaking hands with the other team's coach, and then he turns to me again. "What I was saying earlier—I'm sorry I said anything last night. Of course I didn't mean you should give up basketball. It was stupid. I'm sorry I—"

I stop him. "If you're trying to get out of bets next year, it's not going to work. I will expect a smoothie at my dorm room door before class every time I win. *And* I still expect you at my beck and call for a week, since technically I did get a scholarship, and therefore, I won that bet."

His eyes narrow. "Do you mean—"

"I think today has shown that you are nothing without my guidance, so me going to State is really the only way," I say.

Oliver is still just staring at me, blinking. I'll explain everything to him later. For now—

"We haven't calculated stats, but if you did win today it was only because of me, so it's really like *I* won," I say. "Which means I demand the song-and-dance number we talked about tonight."

I screech and dart away as he tries to grab me, and take off at a sprint toward the gym. I don't slow as he calls out behind me that a head start is no fair.

I'm going to win.

ALL FOR ONE

YAMILE SAIED MÉNDEZ

Some of the thematic material in this story involves disordered eating and bingeing/purging. For more information or help with eating disorders, please contact the National Eating Disorders Association.

The visitors' parking lot and a potential ticket, or the student lot and a half mile to Spanish?

By the time Alika Ferrer parks her mom's gray Camry and walks to the Spanish room, the class will be over, and she will have missed the test and, worst of all, failed the class. Her GPA is hovering just over the 3.0 mark. It's good enough to allow her to stay on the cheer squad for now, but her coach, Bobbie, is extra extra about grades. She checks them every week. Alika has never been in this situation before, and she doesn't want to find out what Bobbie will do if one of her senior team captains is anything less than perfect.

Alika is sweating, unsure of what to do. If she gets another parking ticket, she'll get a citation.

She makes her decision in a split second.

Don't you dare, stupid b—

"I have no other choice!"

There's always a choice and you always make the wrong one.

The voice doesn't lie, technically, but it doesn't tell the whole truth, either. Alika sighs. She's trying. She really is. Except no one notices.

She swerves the car and swiftly parks right in front of the entrance. "I'll be in and out within an hour. No one will notice. Everything will work out," she says in a cheerful voice.

She grabs her battered pink backpack with her name embroidered in turquoise and runs inside.

Her throat throbs. It hurts all the time now. It's not a virus, but she puts on a mask just in case.

You look psycho with the mask on. Now everyone is looking at you.

There's no one around, and besides, Alika loves the mask.

Sometimes.

Especially the kind that's pointy and leaves her a tiny space to breathe, to talk back to the teacher when they're rude and not get in trouble, to hide her chapped lips. Her mom bought a whole box of them in all colors, but the forest-green one is her favorite. It matches the school colors, meaning, it matches her cheer outfit.

Not for long . . . this is your last year as a Musketeer, and you're ruining everything.

Alika's throat clenches again.

"Should I get a tardy slip at the office?" she mumbles.

Before the voice replies, she adds, "Or should I just go to class?"

Just go in the class already!

"I'm one of Señora McAvoy's favorite students, after all."

I have no idea why. You suck!

"Maybe she'll let me help her clean her classroom in exchange for ignoring that I'm so late."

The voice scoffs.

Some teachers are cool, but others are vicious.

For the last couple of years with the whole corona thing, most teachers were chill about rules. They had no other choice, actually. Not with people missing class every other week. In junior year, Alika had to quarantine three times even though she never had symptoms (other than the sore throat, but the virus wasn't the cause of that). At least she could do remote, and her grades didn't suffer at all.

But when her dad . . .

Don't you dare think about Dad, the voice growls, and Alika shudders.

Well, the whole thing after Dad was definitely not easy, but she managed to keep her grades up.

But this year, it's all back to pretending things are normal.

Whatever.

When you mess this up and Mom finds out . . .

Her mom left for a mountain cabin getaway with her friends last Thursday. She only agreed to go because Alika pinkie promised she was okay.

And she had been.

But on Friday, when her alarm went off, she snoozed it by accident and by the time she actually woke up, it was lunch. She doesn't have a class for fourth on A days, so what was the point of going at all? She went online to triple-check the contact email wasn't really her mom's and went back to sleep.

Hours later, she went to cheer practice at the warehouse space two towns over. She'd breathed easier when, at 6:10, she got the absence notification. When Bobbie gave her the stink eye, the voice that had been a whisper for a couple of years turned into a roar.

We are the Musketeers! *CLAP* *CLAP* We are the Musketeers! Alika had sung, but she couldn't hear herself over the voice in her head that repeated, *No, you're not. You're a fraud. You're a liar. How can you smile like that when inside you're rotten and foul?*

After the game, instead of going out with Hayley and Tori, her best friends, and the other senior cheer squad captains, Alika went home with the darkness inside her.

The whole weekend, she fought the urge to give in. But she lost.

When her mom texted to ask how she was doing, what could she really say? That she was slipping? Again?

Mom seemed so happy and cute in her Insta stories with her friends for the first time since her dad died. Alika couldn't ruin it for her.

Contrary to what the voice said, she was not a bitch.

Yes you are. Yes you are, yes you ar—

This Monday morning couldn't have started worse.

Alika turns the corner into the hallway that leads to the language department when a voice stops her in her tracks.

"Ali! Is that you? Can I talk to you for a second?"

Bobbie's not wearing a mask, so Alika doesn't even have to wonder if her coach is pissed.

Alika takes a deep breath and turns on the charm.

"Oh, hey, Bobbie! I love your outfit!"

You're such a liar! You're never going to get out of this. You should've stayed home. You're never going to be like Bobbie.

Bobbie is like in her mid-thirties and has four little kids, but she looks freaking amazing for her age.

I love her.

I hate her.

She's perfect.

She's the whole package, blond and charming, and she has a big aura.

To look like her, lean and lithe, you'd have to be born again. With a new set of genes not built on empanadas and Argentine asados.

Besides being the cheer coach, Bobbie teaches E-commerce and Social Media. Today, she's rocking an impeccable white pant-suit and black four-inch stilettos. She's one of the many Utah Valley influencers. She looks the part.

Now her blue eyes are cold like Silver Lake up American Fork Canyon. But Alika holds her gaze.

"You're just getting in? Late again?"

"Again? I'm never late." *Don't scratch your head, you idiot! Your voice is too pitchy and defensive. Pull back a notch.* "I was on time at the game. And we did great! The team won."

She tries to conjure the feeling of euphoria of the boys beating the rival school. But she can't.

Bobbie's mouth quirks. "Babe, on time is late. You know the rules. You're never on time to warm up and . . . Today, for example."

Here it goes . . .

"Where were you for the freshman breakfast? It was at the middle school, and you never showed."

You forgot the freshman breakfast! Why did you silence the phone, you useless piece of shit!

Bobbie studies Alika's face in silence until her eyes soften.

See? You let her down.

"Have you been sick?"

Alika tries to swallow the knot in her throat, but it's like a fish bone is stabbing her.

ANSWER HER!

"No . . . Yes . . ."

If you say you're sick, she'll send you home.

"I just have a sore throat. Allergies, you know?"

She isn't buying it . . .

Bobbie puts a hand on Alika's arm and presses lightly.

Alika takes a step back and crosses her arms.

As if it were a dance, Bobbie steps forward and grabs Alika's hand.

Don't show her a thing. Bury all the evidence. Soften your face!

Bobbie says, "I know things have been hard. But I'm here if you need me. You know you can always talk to me, right?"

Lies, lies, lies.

No one wants to know the truth.

What can Bobbie do, after all?

The coach doubles down. "Everything good at home?"

The voice turns into an alarm. Alika lowers her gaze and sees the fresh scars on her knuckles.

Hide! Hide! She'll see. She'll know what they are.

Gently, she pulls her hand away and shoves it in her pocket.

Now tell her what she wants to hear.

"Yes, things are good. Considering . . . everything. It's just that it's hard to come back to school after two years. It's like a dream, you know?"

Good. Good.

Scarlett from the JV team passes by and sends them a curious look.

This is your chance! Get away! Get away! Get away!

"Hey, girl!" Bobbie says.

She and Scarlett talk for a few seconds.

Don't make Bobbie look bad in front of the younger girls. Never forget.

Alika laughs along with them and nods, but she has no idea what they're talking about. By the time Scarlett heads to the bathroom, Bobbie turns to her and says, "Well, it's too bad you missed the breakfast this morning. The freshman girls are adorable." Her eyes widen as if she has an idea.

Here it comes.

"In fact, to make up for that, I'll have you come to their trainings."

Alika makes her eyes crinkle so Bobbie can see she's smiling.

You can't. You can't. You can't let anyone see you more than necessary. They'll know . . .

"Tori is mentoring seventh, and Hayley is with the eighth-grade team."

Why didn't she ask you to mentor a team before you missed the breakfast? She doesn't think you're good enough. Same old, same old . . .

The middle school is seventh through ninth. The high school has two thousand students. In ninth grade, Alika had been so excited to finally leave the hellish middle school years behind and switch to the big building with the cool kids. Little had she known.

"What time do they practice?" Alika asks, going over her schedule.

You only have school. You can't handle anything! What are you so exhausted about?

Bobbie rattles off the info, which swirls in a vortex in Alika's mind.

"I'll be there," Alika says.

Sweat drips from her armpits and her heart booms in her ears.

Your breath stinks. Good thing you have a mask on.

Alika crinkles her eyes at Bobbie, shrugs her shoulders for emphasis.

Apparently satisfied and after a quick goodbye, the coach walks away.

Alika stands in the same spot.

You should go to class.

She knows everything.

No, she doesn't know. She doesn't even suspect.

We will start over tomorrow.

Mami will be home.

You can't make her even sadder.

What's the point of going to class? I told you not to even bother trying.

The clock on the wall marks almost the end of the period. She'll have to deal with that F.

Alika turns around and heads outside to her car to wait for the bell for second period.

And that's when she sees the boot on the car and the warning on the windshield.

When Guillermo Ferrer died of COVID, Alika and her mom held on to each other so they wouldn't die, too. They both felt responsible for his illness. Alika's mom thought she should've called 9-1-1 sooner.

Alika was convinced she'd been the one to make her parents sick. She'd snuck out one night to hang out with her friends and got sick with the virus. Now her dad was dead.

Of course it was silly of her to think it was her fault. The virus didn't walk around with a tag showing where it came from. It's been a year since his death, and hardly anyone talks about Guillermo anymore. Alika thinks about him every day. How funny he was. What a great dancer he was. What a supportive dad he was. How strong he was.

He was . . . he was . . . he was . . . Now he's gone because of you!

They didn't get to say goodbye, but before they put him on a ventilator, he texted Alika.

I love to see you cheer, mi gorda. Keep going. Go to college. Be happy doing what you love.

She took a screenshot of the text. She had it printed and laminated.

Nothing can ever fill the void he left behind.

Alika's mom put away most of the money from the life insurance for her college. In junior year, the coach at the university in Salt Lake (a friend of Bobbie's) said she'd let Alika join her team. Tori is going to California and Hayley to Southern Utah. But the thing is, Alika has no cheer inside her anymore.

How can you keep pretending and smiling when inside you're crumbling? When you have this double life? You're a liar.

The voice is right, so Alika keeps doing what the voice yells in her head. At the end of the school day, she uses her mom's card to pay the fee to get the boot off the car. She promises the office lady she won't ever park in the visitors' lot again.

Liar liar liar . . .

She heads home.

She blasts the music and sings along, trying to get into a better mood. To shake the dread of almost being discovered by Bobbie. But it doesn't work. Not when her hands on the steering wheel are the proof that she's a failure. She's had eczema since she was a baby, so that's what her mom thinks the scars are from. She buys all kinds of lotions that Alika slathers on to help her mom feel better.

Think of her. You can't let her know what a bad daughter you are.

There's no one in the driveway and the house looks empty.

Alika goes to the basement and runs three miles on the treadmill. She only stops when a cramp in her right calf makes her cry out.

You deserve it. If you didn't weigh so much, your legs wouldn't hurt.

Alika stretches through the pain, but stars fill her eyes and she gives up.

You stink! How can you stand yourself?

She showers again, and after, she tries to ignore the scale.

Really? Just see what the number is. It can't be that bad. You haven't eaten all day.

But the numbers are worse than ever.

How?

She cleans the hair that clogs the drain and the clumps in her brush.

The stupid vitamins aren't working.

By now it's seven o'clock, and her stomach growls so hard it's like it swallowed a bear.

You're delirious with hunger!

She laughs.

Right in that moment, her mom walks in.

Excellent timing!

Her mom is practically glowing. So happy to be back.

"Mami!" Alika runs and melts in her mom's arms.

She's so soft.

She's so fat!

Soft and smelling of her jasmine perfume. She kisses Alika's head. "I missed you!" she says.

"Did you have fun?"

"It was so great to see the girls again."

"See?" Alika says. "I told you it would be so good for you."

I needed you, though, Mami.

But Mami needed her friends more. Losing her high school sweetheart almost destroyed her. She looked so radiant, Alika's glad her mom didn't stay.

"I went grocery shopping. Come help me get the things from the car."

The sun is still high in the sky. The neighbor kids are running through the sprinklers with their dog although the air is definitely chilly. They moved next door only a few weeks ago. The girl is around fourteen or so. She laughs with her little brothers.

How lucky to have someone besides her parents.

She's wearing a hot-pink bikini and she's a curvy girl.

Look at her belly. How is she just so confident?

"She looks a little like you," her mom says with a chuckle.

You were never that radiant.

"Hi!" the girl greets them.

Alika waves in her direction and flashes the cheer smile. "Hi!"

I hope she doesn't come over to talk.

She grabs all the plastic bags and then hobbles inside.

While her mom tells her about her trip (all news about her mom's friends; nothing really about her), they put the groceries away. Lotion for Alika's hands. This one is cucumber scented. She can practically taste the chemical greenness of it.

Everything her mom brought home is healthy salads and veggies and fruits.

Nothing good to eat. Oh god, I'm so hungry!

She eats the cauliflower casserole and then tells her mom, "I have to run to Tori's to give her a book she lent me."

But instead she stops by the McDonald's and buys three burgers and fries and a shake. She eats alone in the canyon where no one can see her.

And when she goes home, her belly bulging, she takes her pills and runs another three miles on the treadmill.

She doesn't even need to gag herself for all of it to come out.

The ninth graders are a handful.

They're like caffeinated gremlins fed after midnight.

Alika lets them catch up and chat while they do the warm-up. And then the door opens and she shows up.

What's she doing here?

She even moves like you did. She smiles the same way, too.

"Daisy!" someone shrieks in adoration, and runs toward her.

They just saw each other at school, and they act like a thousand years have passed.

Remember? Tori, Hayley, and you were like that, too.

"I love your shorts!" one of the girls exclaims. "White? That's gutsy!"

Daisy smiles so brightly it's endearing, but she ties her jacket around her waist as if in her mind the words meant the opposite of what her friend said.

Alika claps once. "Okay, now that everyone's here, let's run the drill and see what we need to work on."

The girls form little groups of three and four.

"Judas" by Lady Gaga starts and they go about their routine. They're trying, really making an effort.

They're a mess.

The flyers are wobbly and the bases step on one another's toes. The back-spotters are always a second too late, which makes one of the bases have to work harder so the flyers don't fall.

When Alika mentions the issues, the girls send one another daggers with their eyes.

There it is. They're blaming each other.

"Actually," Alika says, trying to channel her inner Bobbie. The coach is watching from another section of the gym, after all. "It's not one person's fault. Remember, we're one. Cheer is a team sport. No shining stars."

But Daisy is a star. Look how she smiles.

"Well, the flyers are the stars," says one of the girls.

She's got a point . . .

Alika repeats what her coaches have told her before. "If the bases aren't strong enough to hold the flyers, and the back-spot isn't there to make sure the flyers are okay, then no routine can ever look nice."

The girls look at each other with doubt.

They don't believe you. You're losing them.

"Usually, the best tumblers are the bases." Alika doesn't mention anyone in particular, but she looks at Daisy.

They'll learn one way or another. If they stick at it long enough.

They practice over and over. Alika sings the cheer and claps until her palms are numb. But the voice is quiet for now.

At the end of class, everyone leaves in their carpools, but Daisy waits outside. She sees Alika heading to her car and she smiles shyly again.

Your job here is done. We need to get home. We need to run, lift some weights, then go to bed so you don't notice how hungry you are. After what you did last night, you can't eat anything at least until tomorrow.

But Alika can't leave Daisy by herself.

"Do you need a ride?"

Daisy swallows. She glances at her phone and her shoulders slump.

She doesn't want to be with you, loser!

"Really, it's not a big deal," Alika says. "We live next door, after all."

Daisy smiles big at that. She taps on her phone, and after a second, she nods. "My mom says thank you for driving me. My brother's still not out from his soccer practice." She shrugs and adds, "They always run late."

She's so little!

"Well, from now on you're more than welcome to ride with me." Alika gestures for Daisy to follow her.

"For real?"

"For real."

The seat fabric is uncomfortably hot, but not unbearable. When Alika turns the AC on, the sour whiff of vomit is a little too noticeable.

Gross!

"Sorry about the smell. I spilled a milkshake last summer and now I can't get the reek off."

Liar liar liar . . .

The truth is that last year, when she had another relapse, Alika didn't realize she'd spilled puke on her shoes and then got it all over the floor. She had stayed home for a solid week then, and the next time she got back in her car, the scent was like a sledgehammer to her teeth. She'd scrubbed every inch of the interior, but the stench lingered. That's why she never volunteered to drive when she went out with her friends. They would know immediately that she had relapsed, and Ali couldn't lie to Hayley and Tori.

"I don't smell anything," Daisy says. And then her face looks alarmed and she adds with a wink, "I don't have the virus, you know. I can smell the pineapple air freshener."

They drive past Alika's favorite milkshake place. "They're still making peach shakes. Do you want one?"

There's longing in Daisy's eyes, but she shakes her head. "I'm trying to cut sugar. My uniform won't fit."

She's started already.

Already.

She's started.

Just like you.

Alika started worrying about her weight in third grade. It was January. All the ads on TV, email, YouTube were about diets.

"Gordita, easy with the bread," her dad had said to her mom, jokingly.

Alika had felt the pain in her mom's face like her own.

Her dad always said they looked just the same.

That year for Halloween, as soon as she got home with Tori and Hayley, her dad had taken her candy away.

"You girls don't want to be like me when you grow up, do you?" her mom had said from the kitchen. Her voice had sounded "smiley," but Alika still saw the way her shoulders slumped, as if she'd been trying to make herself smaller.

The sun hits Alika right in the eyes, piercing through her sunglasses. Her hands sweat and at the red light, she puts them in front of the vent to dry.

"I wanted to move to Mountaintop High School because of you," Daisy says out of the blue.

Just like you. She's doomed.

Daisy speaks again, louder this time. "When my parents got divorced and we were looking for a new house, I asked my mom if we could move here so I could go to Mountaintop next year when I'm in tenth."

Alika's sore throat throbs. "Why?"

From the corner of her eye, Alika sees her shrug. "I saw your team at the winter showcase. I wanted to be a Musketeer like you. You looked so happy!"

You can't be anyone's example.

The day of that competition, Alika was in one of her lowest lows.

Luckily, they arrive at their neighborhood.

Daisy's mom pulls into their driveway at the same time Alika pulls into hers. She's young, but she looks gaunt, worried.

"Thank you for driving Daisy!" she hollers from her van. "You saved my life! I'll Venmo you money for gas!"

One of the little brothers is squishing his face on the window and the other one is chanting cheers.

"Bruh," Daisy whispers, embarrassed.

"Don't worry about it!" Alika says, smiling. "There's no point in both of us driving. I always come straight home after practice."

Because you're a loser.

Daisy beams at her again. Alika returns the smile.

Hours later, she realizes she didn't fake the smile.

She clings to the feeling, but it can't carry her through the night. She has mountains of homework and overdue assignments. She doesn't have a choice other than to run late at night. By the time she's done, it's too late to eat.

But her stomach growls.

If you're asleep, you won't be hungry.

But she's too wired to sleep. Her empty stomach roars all night long.

Don't think about food. Think of Daisy. Think of the ninth graders.

She goes over the routine time after time in her mind.

What if . . . ?

The voice is wordless, but Alika sees a vision of the exact routine the younger girls should do. How to tweak their moves to highlight each one of them and their abilities.

She jumps from her bed, switches her playlist from the weight-loss meditation to "That's My Girl," and starts moving things around, like a puzzle.

In her mind, Daisy and her friends are a constellation. Not cheering on anyone else but themselves.

Alika's dad had hated cheer at first because he said it was a waste of her skills, that cheering for the boys' teams instead of doing a sport was the most misogynist thing in the world.

Cheer is a demanding sport.

Cheerleader.

Leader of cheer. Sometimes there's anything but cheer inside Alika, but somehow she can give what she doesn't have.

The sun is peeking through the shutters in her window when she finishes the new routine, and it's time to get ready for school.

"That's the thing with light," her dad used to say. "It always finds the cracks."

The smell of coffee snakes all the way to her room from the kitchen. She heads down. Mom's music is soft and she's smiling as she nurses a mug and looks out the window. She looks so pretty, and Alika watches her in silence.

Perhaps she can tell her mom she needs help.

Don't ruin it for her.

"Ay! It's you, Ali!" her mom exclaims, startled by her presence. "You scared me!" But she's still smiling.

"Sorry. I didn't mean to. You looked really pretty."

The smile slides off her face and as an echo, Alika's heart falls to her feet.

Here it comes . . .

"Thank you, mi amor," Mom says. "I feel so frumpy lately. I've gained like . . . fifteen or twenty pounds with . . . everything." She makes a gesture with her hand.

"You still look pretty," Alika says.

Tell her. Tell her so she can see how she's hurting you every single time she hates on herself.

But no. Neither Alika nor her mom is ready for that conversation.

"I made you toast," Mom says. "Come sit here. The coffee is amazing."

At the sight of food, saliva pools in Alika's mouth. She sits at the table while her mom lovingly serves her the food.

Food has always been their love language. Their hate language.

Alika tries not to count the calories, but it's the only use she has for math.

Coffee with sugar and cream

plus

Toast, butter, and dulce de leche

plus

Orange juice

Equals way more calories than she wants in her body, but she craves them.

Alika chews slowly and the flavors almost make her sway. Her sleep-deprived swollen eyes fill with tears at the thought that she only has one bite left.

I could eat the whole loaf of bread.

Her hand shakes, but Mom doesn't notice as she talks about work at the salon and the problems of one of the girls who's apprenticing nails with her. Mom presses a hand on Alika's face and says, "You look lovely."

You don't. You look hideous . . .

They look the same.

How can you not see that, too, Mami?

"Thank you, Ma."

Mom looks at her for a few seconds. Alika's used to only showing a happy face. She pretends she's in front of judges, and when her mom finally smiles, relieved and unaware, the judges flash cards with the number 10.

Yes!

There are even pom-poms.

"Ferrer, are you okay?"

It's Señora McAvoy's voice, and with a bolt, Alika wakes up.

This has never happened to her before.

She sits up and looks around, dazed but alert at the same time. A couple of people are snickering behind their hands.

"Why don't you go to the nurse?" Señora McAvoy says in English, which is the scariest part of all. She's fanatical about only speaking Spanish in her class.

"No, no," Alika says, agitated, voice quivering.

Shut up! You just said that aloud! Fix your face!

"I'm okay."

But the blank test in front of her tells a different story.

"Go, Alika. You don't look well."

Finally Alika grabs her things and heads to the nurse. But halfway there, she detours to the bathroom.

Now you're going to have to redo that test, if she lets you. Your GPA is already at the bottom of the barrel. You won't be part of the squad for senior year. No college will take you.

Time is strange.

Three minutes onstage can feel like a lifetime.

The rest of the school day is gone in the blink of an eye.

Still in the bathroom, Alika gets a text.

Can we ride with you to practice? Hayley asks. *My car is in the shop and Tori doesn't have money for gas.*

It's one thing for Daisy to ride in her car, but this is completely different. Alika doesn't want them to get in her car. They'll know something's wrong.

But how do you tell them no?

Sure, she says.

In the car, neither mentions anything.

Perhaps the smell is in your imagination after all.

"Let's do a full out," Bobbie says after the warm-up.

You have no energy. You can't do it.

The music starts.

Five, six, seven, go!

Step back, lift your arms. Strong legs. Strong core.

Alika is like a puppet, but the strings are breaking.

I can't breathe!

Tori is in the top of the formation. Alika's leg seizes in a cramp. From the corner of her eye, she sees the ninth graders filing into the gym.

The white pain is searing.

Don't let Tori fall.

You told Daisy that the base is strong and vital, like the spine of the team.

You can't let Tori fall.

She's in so much pain. She's so nauseated.

There's no light at the end of the tunnel in her vision. Saliva makes her tongue prickle.

Don't throw up in front of the team and the young girls.

Don't hurt Tori.

"Ah!" Alika cries out, still holding on to her best friend.

The other girls on the base look at her with concern, but the music is too loud.

"I have a cramp!" she screams with all her might, tears streaming down her face.

Someone finally cuts the music.

Daisy. Sweet, shy, darling Daisy.

She looks just like you.

Alika's heart swells with love.

For Daisy.

For Tori.

For her mom.

For the little angry Alika inside her mind.

Carefully, she puts Tori down.

Bile rises in her throat, and she runs for the bathroom.

You're not going to make it.

The voice is right. She doesn't.

So she stays in the stall, knowing that the girls and Bobbie are waiting for her outside.

I can't face them. I can't tell them the truth.

You can't stay here forever.

When she comes out, the only one waiting is Bobbie. She doesn't look mad. There's only concern in her eyes. Alika wants to cry.

You're all covered in puke.

She wants to strip her skin away and leave it behind and start all over like a newborn snake.

"I relapsed," Alika says.

Shame! Shame! Shame!

Why are you not strong enough? How could you let my team down?

"Your knuckles, Ali. That's not eczema, is it?"

Tori and Hayley are waiting by the door. Quiet. Their tears are like daggers in Alika's heart.

I let all of them down. I'm sorry! I'm sorry!

Softly, she tells Bobbie everything. Halfway through her tale, her mom walks in, and Alika tries to steel herself. She has to look strong for her mom.

But Mom isn't crying. She looks concerned, but not sad. Not even angry.

Mama!

And this time, Alika, the one pretending to be happy and strong, and the little one, the little hurt girl, are one. She falls into her mom's embrace even though now both of them are going to smell like puke.

"Mami," she says, gasping. "I can't do it on my own."

And they rally. They surround her. Her team, uplifting her, encouraging her, motivating her, cheering for her because that's what Musketeers do.

It's the day of the showcase, and Alika has been attending a program for four weeks. She still drives Daisy back from practice, and she loves the conversations they have in the car.

And when the little girl inside her gets angry, Alika remembers she's only hurt and scared. She imagines Daisy, and she can't use that mean voice to talk to herself anymore.

She starts eating more, and running less, and treating her body more gently. She still has a long way to go. She's not as strong as she'd like to be, but strong is a spectrum, and it varies from day to day.

The ninth graders perform to "That's My Girl," and Daisy's smile is pure light, no fakeness there.

Alika's dad isn't there to see her perform, and she can't be a base yet, but she's there clapping and singing.

Her voice is coming back.

And in the end, the team surrounds her. Little by little, the emotion around her seeps through her skin and reaches her heart, all the way to the wounds that need real cheer to heal.

I love this. I love them. I love me.

"A-L-I-K-A! One for all, all for one!"

TWO GIRLS WALK INTO A WRESTLING MATCH

NAOMI KANAKIA

Okay, so here's the setup for a joke:

I'm sitting on a bench, at a wrestling meet, all alone. And it's the conference finals, and there's a decent amount of cheering and applause, which is rare for a meet, and a girl is up in the stands holding a giant sign with my name on it, and I know the girl, and I'm attracted to the girl, but she's the girlfriend of a teammate, so let's not think about her except to say her name is Shannon, and she's one of the most excellent people I know.

But there's another girl in the room, the only other girl who's competing, and she's sitting at the other end of the bleachers, with her mom and a clutch of friends, and all afternoon we've sort of ignored each other. I've wrestled this other girl maybe twice in my life—she's pinned me both times—and Denise is, like, a wrestling prodigy from this other school, Groveland Day. In our weight bracket, it's about a quarter girls, but the guys almost always win—except against her. When she won this final last year, it was only after three guys in a row forfeited their match instead of wrestling her, and it sucked, because *everyone* knew they would've lost.

Nobody has asked me, *How do you feel about being the only other girl here?*

I could imagine a lot of ways the conversation would go. Like maybe they'd say, *Isn't it great you short-circuited all the trans-in-sports stuff by competing in one of the extremely few sports where girls compete directly against guys?*

Or they could say, *Isn't it weird that after starting hormones, which usually hurt your muscle development and your ability to compete, you suddenly got way, way, way better at this sport? Like, what's up with that?*

Or they could say, *Do you feel weird that if you win, it won't be a girl beating a girl, it'll be a trans girl beating a girl? And that people won't know what to think?*

It's an absurd situation, I have to admit. Honestly, I admire trans girls who compete in girls' sports. I have no idea what that would be like: I hardly know any other girls—just Shannon, and even that's only because she's sort of adopted me, or something. Maybe I should be offended—I'm not a puppy! But actually I kind of like it.

What's nice about being the only trans girl at an all-boys Catholic school is that nobody ever talks to you. Like, ever. Not to laugh, not to tease, not to mock. You don't even get called on in class.

When I mention it to people who don't know Catholic schools, they're like wait, why did they let you stay at the school if you're a girl now? And I shrug and say, well, they're saying they're doing it for my benefit, to not disrupt my education, since I only have a year left. But really, in their hearts, they just don't think I'm actually a girl. It's not just Catholic schools that're like this—women's colleges are radical/progressive as hell, but lots of them still don't have a problem admitting trans boys (though they're pretty shy about trans girls. I thought about applying to Smith, but got embarrassed at them maybe being like, *Wait a second, you were a boy until like six months ago?*).

I'm here because St. Ignatius is so small that every high schooler *has* to take a sport. I chose wrestling because . . . it's the only sport where both girls and boys compete.

Of course, my parents won't believe that's true. They're like, *You had no idea, you didn't know, when you were eleven, and you started wrestling, that you were trans.*

And I guess that's true, but still, I also knew that if I had to do any other sport, I'd die. Like, fall into a pit and pass away.

The thing that's nice is nobody else knows I'm pretty sure I'm gonna win my weight class. And matches in our weight class are held kinda late, so we'll have a lot of other winners crowned by then to take away the spotlight. I'll pin my last guy, and then I'll run off, and get out before anyone notices what happened.

Another nice thing is there's only three other guys from my school who qualified. And unlike at a meet, they don't feel the need to sit with me.

So I'm sitting here alone, in the sweat and damp, watching people writhe on mats, slap the ground, trying not to look to my right. And then there's a hand on my back.

"Hey," Shannon says. "I was waving, why didn't you look?"

"Oh," I say. "Sorry. I'm focused."

"Are you excited?!"

She's a year younger, and she's on the bleacher next to me, with the sign awkwardly propped against her knee, and she came straight from school, so she's in plaid skirt and knee socks, and I can't look directly at her without shaking: It feels very Beauty and the Beast.

"Really, really, nervous."

"Why?!" she says.

"Err, because it's sports? People are nervous before sports."

"But you're already accepted to college! And you don't even need this. It's just extra!"

"Yeah," I said. "I just really want to win."

"You will!" she said. "Then you can wrestle in college, too, and maybe the Olympics and be superfamous!"

"Uhh no," I said. "I'm never gonna do this again."

"What? Why not? You're so good!"

"Because it's awkward. I just want to be a girl, and that can't ever happen if I play sports. Like, wrestling was my only chance, and even here it's weird."

"It's not weird!" she said. "You have a gift! You can't let that go. Come on! Promise, promise, promise me you won't stop!"

I imagine she's going to hug me, but she doesn't. Still, she's all smiles, and her hair shakes when she tosses her head. And now another voice pulls me up from my shoes.

"Hey." The voice is deep. It's her boyfriend, James, who also goes to my school. "What's going on?"

"Oh hey," she says. "Just hyping up Maya."

"Cool, cool," James says. "How's it going?"

"Uhh, good."

"I can't believe they gave you the bid," he says. "Have you had a match yet?"

"I have Denise up first, since she's the top seed."

"Huh, but she'll probably beat you, right?"

"Probably."

"Hey!" Shannon says. "Why're you trying to rattle her?"

"What? You've gotten pinned by a bunch of girls."

"That's not true," I say. "Or at least, none this year."

"Well, yeah, this year, but before that . . ."

The thing that people can't understand is the way coming out affects you psychologically. Like, my life is objectively terrible. My school is basically like, *We'll call you by your new name and pronouns, but otherwise we'll pretend you don't exist when we talk about how we educate fine young Christian gentlemen or begin every class with "Hello, gentlemen."* My existence was, essentially, a problem. I complicated every discussion at the school. The whole reason it existed was to educate young men. Most of my friends had stopped talking to me. My parents were afraid to ask how I was doing. But I was still happier than I'd ever been. It's like something from a cheesy movie: Embracing my true self was worth any cost. In a way, transphobia is a gift, because the moment I started going by a new name, wearing my new clothes, taking the hormones, I was like, I am happier than I've ever been, and there's no way this would be true—given all the other crap that fell down upon me—if I wasn't actually trans.

And over the summer, because nobody was talking to me, I just trained. It's that simple. Something changed inside of me. You know, true defeat is something most good wrestlers have never experienced: They've been winners all their lives. They've never known what it was like to be smaller, weaker, to be pinned over and over, to be on the team just to stop us from accumulating forfeits. And that experience with defeat, I think it actually helps you—it teaches you to fight with everything you have.

It sounds crazy, but it all just . . . came together. I got good, I caught fire. I expected people to notice, and I guess they did, but see above re: people never talking to me.

"No, he's right," I say. "From his perspective, I can see how he'd think . . ." I shrugged.

I'd gotten the wild-card spot in our conference championship, probably so they'd avoid a repeat of last year's embarrassing story, when a bunch of guys refused to compete against Denise. That'd been bad. It'd made national news.

"You gonna come see my match?" he says.

"Sure, sure," Shannon says. "Good luck, Maya."

"Thanks!"

I sneak a glance as she walks away, see the back of her knees, and then I freeze.

Because now I see the other girl: I see Denise. She's standing in the doorway, by herself, away from the usual group: She's short—which helps in wrestling—and has broad arms and legs, and even without a mouth guard, her chin and teeth jut out and she looks almost ancient, eternal. To be honest, I'd never thought much about her before today—she was just this girl who wrestled on the same circuit who'd beaten me once or twice.

"H-hey," I say, waving at her.

She looks at me, and stomps over. "Hey," she says.

"Uhh, hey."

"Hey."

"So we're gonna be, like, wrestling. Soon," I say.

"Yeah," she says. "You're Maya? From the boys' school?"

"But I was Raghav, before, I mean."

"So . . . ? What did you want?"

"Uhhh . . ." I gulp and take a breath. And she's on her phone, she's waving at the girls who've come along with her, and at her mom, and I'm looking at my feet, thinking, *Wow, I've been living in a fantasy land, thinking I'm gonna beat this person when I'm literally scared to even look at her.*

So I raise my voice a bit and I say, "H-hey, wh—sh-shouldn't you be more polite?"

Her eyes go up and down, across from my body, and for a second they're studying my knees. There's a big cheer from the stands, and she turns, grimacing. "I missed it," she said. "There's a thing Cowell does, when he pins someone . . . I came over here to look."

"Why do you care?" I say. "He's not in our weight class?"

Then her eyes narrow. "Why do I care? Uhh, why do you think? Because I want to get better. What're you even doing here?"

"Uhh . . . I got the wild-card spot," I say. "You're, like, obviously better than me. You've beaten me."

"Yeah, well," she says. "I've beaten guys before, whatever."

I smile at her. And this is what I signed up for, by choosing wrestling. I could've chosen another sport, or not played one at all— since my school doesn't have one for girls. But I chose this, just for that reason, so it wouldn't matter what hormones I took or what they did to my muscle mass. And the joke is, I still started winning, even against boys, and that, you know, theoretically, this ought to be really exciting for people. They ought to be like, holy crap, when trans girls do better after hormones, maybe—you know—maybe it means something. Maybe it's like they've had these lead weights strapped to them their whole lives, and the moment they get those weights off, they're like Superman under the yellow sun: suddenly superpowered in comparison to ordinary people.

"You won't beat me," I say.

"I've done it before," she says.

"Not this time."

"Keep telling yourself that," she says.

"You know, if you won—if you beat me—I wouldn't be a dick, like you're being."

"Well, pat yourself on the back, then."

And with that she goes back to the rest of her friends, and I get it. She's had tough times, she worked hard all through high school to become a champion. Her dad was a wrestling superstar, but even he thought it was a little weird for her to pick this sport. (I read the interviews she did last year, after she won.)

When I win, I wonder if there'll be interviews, if anyone will care, if even my parents or my friends—well, aside from Shannon—will notice. Whether it'll get announced at school, whether my parents will pat me on the back, or if instead everyone will be totally weird, will ignore it, just like they've ignored all my other wins this year.

And if I let myself think about it, then, sure, it sucked. I'd done so much to keep myself out of the way. I'd played this sport, where my gender didn't matter (theoretically). And I'd stayed at a school that barred people of my gender entirely, all so who I am and who I was wouldn't bother anybody—so they could see me as me, instead of as a gender identity. Just like my mom said: "The kids at St. Ignatius already know you—at any other school you'd just be the trans girl."

And none of it mattered. I'm still a problem. They still have no way of understanding me, of seeing me as a person, who might be good at something in her own right.

You'd think, you know, you'd think that I'd be depressed—I guess you're supposed to be, if everyone ignores you, and if walking into school each day with a bunch of boys, getting misgendered by your teachers, having them all say "Now, boys" or "Settle down, boys" or "All you boys are such a credit to this freaking school for boys," and then not even having anyone else look in your direction, not even having them notice, or think, wow, maybe there's something wrong with this. You'd think a girl would get depressed, if when she came out, her parents cut her a deal, saying you can go on hormones if, and only if, you don't switch schools (I guess they thought it was just a phase, and that I wasn't serious or something). You'd think a person would be depressed if they woke in silence, drove to school in silence, spent the day in silence, even when their hand was raised.

But I'm not. I'd be entitled to it, if I was. I'd be entitled to kick over things and cuss people out. I'd be entitled to a lot. But the weird thing is I'm happier than I've ever been.

Not that I forgive those people, of course. I'll remember it. I don't love my parents anymore, if I ever did. And I don't respect those teachers or those other kids. And Denise? I don't respect her either now. They've all done a terrible thing, and they might not ever realize it—they probably won't—they'll probably go home and say, *That competition was unfair. Something about hormones gave her superstrength. And . . . and . . . she just got the wild-card bid because she's trans.* My parents will look at where I got into college, and they'll look at how I'm doing, and they'll say, *Oh, so keeping her in that school turned out pretty well!* And my school will think, *Wow, we're so inclusive, I guess all-boys education is still relevant in this day.* And they'll all be wrong, though they'll never admit it.

So don't think I forgive them. But . . . I'm still happy as hell. Because before this year, I'd never done it before. I'd never worked hard, I'd never trained, I'd never won a single thing. And that's something no one can take away.

Okay, so if that was the setup, then here's the punch line: At the start of our match, I stood across the mat, nervous, my arms and legs tingling, my heart thumping, and with this crazy, desperate need to pee. Denise faced me, her face set, and her dad was off to the side, cheering for her, growling. It felt like the whole room was cheering for her, and I only had one girl high up in the stands waving her sign: LET'S GO MAYA. And even though my heart was going, and my head was buzzing, I started to smile.

She swarmed out, on me fast, and then I was on my back, flipped down and crumpled up. I arched my back instinctively, and she worked my body like a machine, pushing my limbs out of the way, sweeping my legs, almost like a math problem, subtracting each point of support so I'd fall. And I'd felt this a bunch of times before in my life, but there were new muscles now in my stomach and chest, so I tensed up, and I exploded, and I flipped, and then she was under me, and I grinned savagely. And I had her by the shoulders, her neck shuddering, her hair escaping from the headpiece, and she couldn't move. Her body was locked into place. And then the count was over, and it was done.

I stood on the mat, and I stamped my feet, and I waved my arms, and the stands for the first time noticed me—they booed. An opposing mom said I shouldn't be such a showboat.

But at that moment Shannon ran up to me and jumped into my arms, and I whirled her around, and then she danced around the gym.

None of the other guys forfeited for me, like they had last year for Denise, so I went through three more matches, but none of them even came close.

At school on Monday, they didn't announce the match—nobody else besides me had even placed—and when I looked up Denise online all I saw was a bunch of complaints from other Groveland Day kids about how the league had rigged things so she would lose. I emailed my college to say that I'd won the championship, and they wrote back: *That's impressive! Wrestling here has room for walk-ons, do you want to talk to our coach?*

And until that moment, I would've said, *No, never. I don't care a thing for sports.* But instead I wrote back: *Sure.*

POWER TEN IN TWO

LEAH HENDERSON

"Seriously?" Emersyn spun, running backward up Butcher's Pass. It got you up Nobel Hill in half the time, but some of the strongest runners at Travers Prep were on their hands and knees before they got there. "You all run slower than a loris!"

"A what?" Half her teammates scrunched up their faces.

"They're *superslow* nocturnal primates," Emersyn snapped.

"But they're also deadly . . . when they . . . strike," one of her teammates muttered, out of breath, stumbling up the hill every other team captain avoided.

"There won't be jokes when we lose Scholastics," Emersyn shouted back. "Stop complaining and move. We need to beat our time from this morning." The numbers zipping by on her watch said they were moving way too slow. She spun around again and took off, leaving her teammates behind.

"Emersyn, chill," Jordan, the team's best midfielder, yelled after her, stopping. The rest of their varsity lacrosse team stopped, too. "It's not that serious. Travers has won Scholastics in every sport you've played since our freshman year. I doubt you'll start a losing streak in *anything* now. Graduation's in like four months. Relax! Have you never heard of fun?"

A couple teammates chuckled, dropping to the dirt. Their arms spread wide, ready to make snow angels, even though the sun shone bright and not a speck of snow dotted the ground.

"Fun?" barked Emersyn. "We have to train harder and play harder than the practice before. Fun has nothing to do with it. Not if we want to win!" Emersyn didn't need to look back. She knew her teammates had quit. But she never did. She wasn't a quitter. She'd break their morning time by herself.

Twenty minutes later, she finished the loop at the top of Butcher's Pass, two minutes and fifty-seven seconds faster than she had that morning. Her heart slammed against her chest as she cut through the forest path to the Travers lacrosse fields in the distance. Her teammates were already there. Clearly, they'd gone back down the hill and taken the easy route—a half-mile run, instead of three. They hung around the benches laughing and spraying one another with water. Practice hadn't even started and they were already acting like a bunch of clowns. "Lorises for real," she grumbled.

"What's wrong with you?" she said when she got to the field. She flicked off her sneakers, pulling cleats out of the duffel slung over her shoulder. A mark of perspiration across her back. "The season hasn't even started and you're already taking breaks? You should be doing hill sprints with drags."

"Ugh," everyone groaned.

"Are you serious?" Jordan grumbled, her long brown ponytail swinging. "You just kicked our butt on Butcher's Pass for the second time today! I vote we take it easy."

Emersyn's jaw flexed. She didn't bother mentioning that they'd let Butcher's Pass *kick their butts* before they even tried. Instead, she stomped over to the bag of practice pinnies. Bright nylon mesh jerseys tumbled to the ground. Like they were torpedoes, she flung a knotted scrimmage vest to each of her teammates. No one said a thing.

Emersyn was like a sleeping bear. You didn't poke. Especially at the start of practice. As team captain, she could make the two-hour-long practice feel like a weekend in hell!

Coach Lawson stood to the side of the field, watching, letting Emersyn be boss. Everyone got paired up. Ready to sprint up the small hill at the side of their field, while their partner tugged their jersey for resistance. For everyone except Emersyn, hill sprints with drags were number two on their list of team torture exercises. Second only to Butcher's Pass.

"Emersyn, over here," Coach Lawson called.

Emersyn looked up the hill, her teammate low to the ground, ready to try to tug her back, but like everyone Emersyn was paired with, she'd probably only succeed in getting dragged. "We're about to start, Coach."

"It's fine. Jordan can start them off." Coach nodded toward the end of the hill. "Bronwyn, pair up with Jordan and Lacey."

Bronwyn dropped Emersyn's jersey and sprinted off, not trying in the least to disguise a smile full of teeth.

"What's up, Coach?" Emersyn said, stopping in front of her.

"Listen, Syn." Coach's feathered dark-blond bangs blew back. "I'm the last person to tell you to go easy. You know my motto. Outplay. Outwork. Outlast. Outshine."

"Nothing else matters," Emersyn finished, believing in the motto, too.

"Yeah, well, I'm coming to believe other things do matter," said Coach.

"Not sure I agree. Nothing matters more than winning."

"What about team bonding?" Coach asked. "It can make or break things sometimes."

"Bonding?" Emersyn's brow scrunched. "We're all about team-work. We don't win otherwise."

"That might be true," Coach agreed. "But I said team *bonding*. That's about more than barking orders and expecting others to fol-low. It's about wanting to dig deep for each other because of your bond. The feeling that you're in something together—for better or worse."

Emersyn could feel her teammates watching them, barely doing their hill sprints. She wanted to yell *Pick up the pace*, but something told her it wasn't the best time.

"Listen, Syn." Coach placed a hand on her shoulder. "You know as your coach I couldn't be prouder. I wish all my players were as dedicated—in any sport. I mean from day one, when I brought you up here in seventh grade to train with varsity soccer—everyone said it was a bad idea. That you were too young to compete with high school players. But you were fearless. Determined. Focused. You attacked every challenge. And come fall, you'll be headed to one of the best Division 1 soccer programs in the country."

"Sorry, but what does that have to do with lacrosse?" Emersyn wasn't about small talk, especially when training needed to hap-pen. Everyone would thank her when they had another champion-ship trophy in the medals case.

"It has everything to do with this season. And all the ones to come." Coach looked over at the rest of the team, everyone drag-ging up the hill. "Think we oughta give 'em a break? Let them do squats and burpees instead?"

Emersyn couldn't get why even Coach wanted to give her teammates a break. When she'd never given Emersyn one. And over the years, as much as it sucked sometimes, Emersyn was an All-American three-letter athlete—soccer, basketball, and lacrosse—because of it. No way she was slacking in her final season at Travers. Not happening! Besides, as a Black girl, you had to be more than better to even be considered okay.

"They can go a couple more rounds. They're only going half speed anyway."

Coach snorted. "You know squats and burpees aren't exactly a picnic."

"Yeah," Emersyn agreed. "But we're doing them next." She turned toward the field. "Is there anything else, Coach?"

Coach Lawson stared at Emersyn. Emersyn stared back.

You never look away.

Emersyn's insides twisted, though. Something about the expression on Coach's face wasn't exactly good.

"Emersyn, what's your favorite lacrosse memory?"

"Easy. That hatty in my first game," Emersyn said, quick.

"And basketball?"

"Come on, Coach. My half-court buzzer shot against Gable." Emersyn pretended to shoot, jumping back, arms lingering high in the air. "Nothin' but net."

"And soccer?"

"Man, there are so many. Beating out Teresa Smith for a spot on the U.S. U-18 Women's National Team was pretty sweet, though."

"Any memories with your teammates?"

Of course there were, weren't there? Favorite memories? Winning . . .

But every thought came back to what *she* did to win. Not her team. "Why?" she asked instead.

"I'm asking the questions," Coach said, sounding more like Coach. "When was the last time you had fun with everybody?"

Emersyn stared, as if Coach spoke Akkadian.

"Fun . . . you know the word, right?"

Emersyn's eyes shot over to her teammates, still running. "Did they come whining to you?"

"Nope," Coach Lawson said. "But I asked you a question. When have you had fun?"

"I'll have fun after we win. Right now, I need to get back on the field."

"That's just it, Syn, I don't think you will," Coach said.

"Will what?"

"Have fun." Coach looked around. "I know I've always acted like every second has to be intense, but it doesn't. You can try *and* laugh."

Emersyn shook her head. "No, you can't. Besides, why would you want to?"

"Listen, I need you to do something for me. You might not get why at first. And I know it won't be easy . . ."

"What, Coach? Anything." Emersyn stood taller. Ready.

"You're not going to like it," Coach warned. "But I hope it'll be good for you." She sighed. "Oh, maybe this isn't such a good idea."

Emersyn perked up. Never backing down from a challenge. "What is it? I can do it."

Coach exhaled. "I have another motto I want you to remember: A challenge met is the starting line for the challenge to come."

Emersyn nodded. She'd have to add it to her Wall of Power, Purpose, & Perseverance in her dorm room.

"I need you to go with them." Coach pointed down the hill.

Emersyn's gaze followed the direction of Coach's finger, confused. Two dark gray vans, with the school's maroon-and-white crest, waited outside the Mav, the Maverick T. Jacobson Aquatic Center. A state-of-the-art athletic facility for Travers Prep water sports.

"Now?" Emersyn asked.

"Yes, now." Coach nodded. "Coach Beckett and Sam are waiting for you."

"Coach Beckett?" Why were Coach's girlfriend and Sam waiting for her? "What about practice? Our first night game against Case Academy is in two weeks. Every second counts."

"Not that there are any guarantees. But don't worry, we'll be ready. You'll be ready." Coach laughed. "You've probably been ready since birth. Now, go. I know it's a bit unusual. But they won't wait forever."

Emersyn didn't move.

"Emersyn. Go! Now!"

Emersyn snapped out of her trance and dashed for her bag. Coach wanted action.

A minute later, she was jogging down the hill, away from her teammates.

"You're leaving?" Jordan called after her; both Lacey and Bronwyn tugged on Jordan's pinny. But judging from their laughter, they weren't tugging hard.

"Coach needs me to do something," she said, still clueless.

When she got to the parking lot, the boys' varsity crew stretched along a wall. They towered over a group of gangly boys she assumed were JV.

"Eh, Syn," her friend Niles said. "What are you doing down here? Don't tell me, you've finally come to see how real athletes train."

"Whatever." Emersyn rolled her eyes. "Work is always getting done up on the hill."

"Then what are you doing down here?" he asked, stretching.

"Beats me, actually. Coach wants me to find Coach Beckett and Sam." She looked around. "You seen them?"

"They're around here somewhere. Gotta go, though." He turned to his teammates. "All right, grunts. Let's pound some pavement!"

Seven guys from the varsity team fell in behind him, as his long strides immediately put distance between him and everyone else. The JV boys tried to keep up.

"Emersyn, there you are." Coach Beckett strolled around the side of one of the vans. Sam, a chestnut-colored Irish setter charged for Emersyn's legs. "Wasn't sure you were coming. Looks like someone's already excited you'll be joining us."

"Joining you?" Emersyn bent down to pet Sam as he leaped to greet her. "I think there's a mistake. I need to get back to practice."

"Of course," Coach Beckett grumbled. "She left telling you to me."

"Telling me what?" Sam pushed his wet nose against Emersyn's palm, wanting her to keep petting him.

"That you'll be with us for a bit."

"Us?" Emersyn looked around as girls crew streamed out of the Mav.

"What up, Syn." Riley, the captain of the girls' varsity eight, waved. "You finally ready to feel what a serious workout is all about?"

"Bring it." Always ready, Emersyn started running next to Riley even though she still had no clue what was going on.

"Um, Emersyn," Coach Beckett called. "Not so fast."

"Later, Syn," Riley said as she and her teammates took off in the same direction as the boys' rowing teams, toward Travers boat-house, three miles away.

"Why am I here, Coach? I really need to get back to practice."

"You *are* at practice. Or, at least I hope you are for the next two weeks, anyway. Sorry you're learning about it like this. Shar was supposed to tell you *before* you came down." Coach Beckett had worry lines creasing her forehead.

"Next two weeks? Is this a joke?" For the first time, Emersyn noticed students staring out at her from the van windows. *Travers Prep JV2 Boys' Crew* was written on a whiteboard in the window of the second van, while *Travers Prep JV2 Girls* was written on a board in the window of the first. With a green marker, someone had added *Plus Tariq*. "I can't. Our season opener's in two weeks. Plus, we need to focus for Scholastics."

"Syn, if I know anything, you'll have your team more than ready for both. You have four months before Scholastics. I'm only asking for two weeks," Coach Beckett said. Sam sniffed the grass at the edge of the parking lot. "Besides, a little birdie told me you've been campaigning for a double practice. Just think, this could kind of get you started? You start with lacrosse, then run down here."

"But two weeks?" Emersyn said again, trying to wrap her brain around everything. Were they seriously asking her to miss more than half of lacrosse practice? Then come train with what looked like a bunch of inexperienced first years? "Why me?"

Coach Beckett smiled. "Because if anyone can pitch in at crunch time, it's you."

A rush of adrenaline betrayed Emersyn.

Coach Beckett tapped the first van. The back doors opened wide. Eight faces watched Emersyn. "We're a rower short, so Shar and I hoped you could fill in."

"After two weeks, what happens?" Emersyn asked.

Coach shrugged.

That didn't make Emersyn feel any better. Besides . . .

"I, um, don't know anything about crew," she whispered, as Coach nodded for her to get in the back of the first van with the JV2 girls.

"No worries," Coach Beckett said, opening the passenger door and climbing in. "Most of them don't, either. Or not a lot, anyway."

She whistled for Sam to join them. He charged for Emersyn's legs again, scrambling over her into the middle like it was his designated spot. A kid wearing a Travers Crew cap backward pulled the doors closed. "Hi," he said quickly.

"Hi."

Coach Beckett turned in her seat. "Team, meet Emersyn. Emersyn, meet your new team."

Emersyn lifted her hand an inch, then let it fall. "Hey."

As they drove away, the lacrosse fields on the hill got smaller and smaller. Her *real* teammates, doing warm-up drills without her. She slumped in the seat, Sam sniffing around her ear. Her hand slid across his silky coat.

What in the world was happening? Every part of this was a nightmare.

A girl with floppy red curls and a face full of freckles leaned around Sam, smiling. "Hi, I'm Nova. I'm superglad we'll be able to row an eight now instead of taking turns in a quad. It's soooo boring sitting and watching from the launch. Besides, you freeze your butt off on those metal seats."

"I'm Chelsea."

"Quinn."

"Heya, I'm Mia and this is Kennedy." A girl decked out in a Travers Prep wind suit pointed to her chest, then nudged the girl next to her. "The one sleeping is Skylar, and that's Hailey with the headphones."

"And I'm Tariq. The only cox left," the boy who'd shut the doors said. "I think we're in AP Chemistry and English Lit together."

"Oh, yeah, hi," Emersyn said, trying to take in the names and faces. She didn't.

Reaching down, she pinched her thigh. This had to be a nightmare. They were like twelve!

A few minutes later the van slowed in front of the boathouse. Emersyn stared. When other teams rolled up on this place, it'd knock the confidence out of them, or at least make them falter. The building was intimidating and impressive as hell. Where wood met concrete and glass.

Sam barked, pushing against Emersyn. Ready to get out.

"Ahhh." The girl they called Skylar flung herself forward in her seat. Eyes wide. "What the heck. My dream was getting good and there weren't any dogs in it."

Sam dug his nails into Emersyn's thigh.

"Okay, okay. I'm getting out," Emersyn said, opening the doors.

Sam shoved off and was out of the van in no time. Everyone followed him.

"I don't know what the big rush is. The boathouse isn't going anywhere . . . unfortunately." Skylar said the last part under her breath. "Who are you?" She squinted, facing Emersyn.

"Your new stroke." Coach Beckett nudged Emersyn's shoulder. "Now you all have a place in the boat."

"Great." Skylar groaned. "So much for getting back to my dream."

"Your catnap days in the launch will have to wait. Today we're showing Emersyn the way of things on the water."

"Wait, what? Already?" said Emersyn. "I thought you start out on those rowing thingies. You know, on land."

"Sometimes we do. Sometimes we don't," Coach Beckett said. "Since I know you can handle it, what better way to get you up to speed than to drop you right in it. We have a regatta to prep for."

Emersyn stopped. Who said anything about racing?

"It'll be fine. You'll be fine."

Why did everybody keep saying that? Like if they put it out in the world, it'd be true. Emersyn wasn't sippin' that Kool-Aid.

Coach Beckett headed for the boathouse, everyone except Skylar rushing behind.

"So, you all been rowing long?" Emersyn asked, feeling queasy. She knew Niles and Riley rowed every semester.

"Not really," Mia said. "Nova started in the fall, but Kennedy, Hailey, and I joined winter season. Tariq, Chelsea, and Quinn only got out on the water last week. And, well, Skylar . . ." Mia trailed off, glancing back. Skylar had dropped farther behind. "She's been around crew her entire life."

"Then why—" Emersyn started but stopped herself.

"—Is she on the crappiest boat?" Nova finished for her.

"I, um, wasn't going to say it exactly like that, but yeah." Emersyn had no tolerance for mean just to be mean. But it was obvious she was getting stuck with beginners. She couldn't remember the last time that had happened. Even her first lacrosse season was as a varsity sub. Since Coach Lawson coached her in soccer and basketball, she had trusted Emersyn could pick up lacrosse fast. Plus, most of Coach's players followed her from sport to sport—soccer, basketball, lacrosse. So from the beginning, everyone assumed Emersyn would follow her, too. She'd never really started from the bottom. Or at least, she didn't remember when she had.

"Well, you'll stand by 'crappy' once you see the monstrosity we row," Mia added.

"It's called *Big Bear* for a reason." Tariq gulped, looking almost as nervous as Emersyn felt.

When they came around the corner of the boathouse, Emersyn stared. Large glass doors opened to boats stacked neatly to the ceiling. Behind the wall of glass on the second floor, Riley, Niles, and the other varsity rowers tugged handles on a line of ergs facing the water. They lurched forward and back as if they would shoot out the windows at any second.

"They have five a.m. practice," Tariq said. "So they work out in the gym afternoons."

"That's more working out than I ever want to do," Hailey shouted, her headphones still on.

Coach Beckett pulled them from her ears. "You say that now, but one day, I have a feeling that'll be you up there."

Hailey chuckled. "Never. I don't sign up for torture. No way."

"We'll see," Coach Beckett said, striding into the boathouse, Sam close by her side. "Crew has a way of grabbing hold." She clapped everyone to attention. "Okay, bags in cubbies. Four and four at pipes."

"Pipes?" Emersyn asked, not sure where to turn.

"Follow me," Nova said. "You'll have it down in no time."

"Thanks." It'd been a long time since Emersyn followed anyone. But for the next five minutes, she became Nova's shadow, trying hard to ignore snickers from the boys' team, pointing and laughing at Tariq as he passed them, leading the boat, which felt like a brick, down to the water.

"How does this thing not sink?" Emersyn whispered to Nova, mimicking her movements as they settled the shell in the water, careful not to damage the rigging.

"It better not," Nova whispered back. "This boat's got history. Barron Ahearn rowed it in the Olympics."

"Barron Ahearn?"

Nova nodded toward the silver letters across the boathouse: A-H-E-A-R-N B-O-A-T-H-O-U-S-E. "Skylar and Riley's grandma. Big shoes to fill. Riley wants to fill every bit of 'em, while Skylar whines about wanting to be forgettable or forgotten, I can't remember which."

Emersyn glanced over at Skylar, who didn't seem to want to be there at all. Emersyn's Black butt could never pull that crap. She couldn't do anything by halves!

"Hailey, you're our steadying bow," Coach Beckett said, stepping next to her. Then she tapped Skylar and the girl whose name Emersyn couldn't remember. "Skylar, two. Quinn, three."

Coach Beckett went down the line of girls, giving everyone their seat assignment. Emersyn was actually relieved Nova was next to her, but her stomach soon dropped. Nova was behind her, not in front of her. So much for having someone to shadow. As far as Emersyn could tell, the only seat left was that of the coxswain. And from what little she knew about rowing, she knew the coxswain didn't have an oar. And worse, they'd be shouting in her face. She was never one for having orders barked at her; she was always the one doing the barking, or at least most of the time.

"Okay, everyone," Coach Beckett said, "Let's relax and just have fun. No one's trying to win Head of the Charles today."

Pretty much everything said since Emersyn got to the boathouse was a foreign language.

"Tariq, get 'em in the shell."

"Yes, Coach." Tariq folded himself into the coxswain's seat. All arms and knobby ashy brown knees. "Oarlocks open. Blades in. Close gates." Tariq pointed to everything Emersyn needed to do.

So far so good.

"Extend water side," Tariq called into the mini-microphone strapped around his head. "Push your oar out," he whispered.

"Oh, right." Emersyn rushed to follow along. She wasn't going to mess up before she even started. Or she hoped not.

"One foot in . . . WAIT!" Tariq shouted.

Emersyn jerked back.

"Not there. There." Tariq pointed.

"You don't want to go through the bottom," Nova added. "'Specially not in this boat!"

"Um, nope. Don't want that." Emersyn moved her foot back a little to the thicker part of the shell.

"In!" Tariq ordered, and everyone sat on their seats, strapping into their shoes.

"Before you all shove off, let's do a little refresher." Coach Beckett knelt by Emersyn. "Finish position."

Everyone slid back, and for the next twenty minutes, Emersyn felt like a guinea pig being used to show every example of what not to do on the water. She gritted her teeth. She wanted to learn what she *was* supposed to do. She didn't like seeing things done the wrong way to start. Why not get it right the first time?

"Okay." Coach Beckett smiled at Emersyn. "I think you all are ready."

Wait, what?

Emersyn was being thrown into the deep end, not knowing which way was forward, let alone the difference between stern and bow, stroke and port, catch and recovery.

They were definitely going to sink!

"Emersyn . . . Syn," Coach Beckett called, clearly not for the first time. "You ready?"

Of course not!

"Always," Emersyn said, squeezing the oar grip tight as they pushed away from the dock.

Water lapped at the side of the boat.

They were definitely going to sink.

But to Emersyn's relief and surprise, they didn't.

The next hour went from something like *Okay, cool, I got this* to *Stop, stop, stop! Make it stop!*

Emersyn's oar knocked her in the gut, almost cleared out her teeth, and nearly chopped off her head when she did something called "catching a crab." Her oar went so deep in the water, it almost took her with it. But she wasn't the only one catching things and spinning the boat around. Nearly everyone else did, too, except Nova, Skylar, and Hailey. No one laughed or gave anyone a hard time, though.

So different from all of Emersyn's other practices. Colossal mistakes on the field meant you were down doing thirty push-ups with Emersyn usually the first screaming in your face. But out here, no one screamed—not yet, anyway.

They were in it together. Mistakes and all.

If one messed up, the boat didn't move, and Emersyn was one of the first messing up.

"Back six," Coach shouted as the launch motored alongside them.

The back-six rowers pushed and pulled. The riggings clicked like a revving engine as their oars sliced through the water. Emersyn hugged her oar to her chest as the shell did a jerky glide through the river.

Still irritated about missing her real practice, she couldn't remember the last time she'd been so anxious to want to try something and at the same time so freaked she'd mess it all up. It was awesome!

She'd even flown off her seat when she tried to show off and make the biggest puddle.

Crew was having none of it. And as frustrating as it was, she was kinda cool with it.

Then suddenly, around the bend, in a sleeker boat than their own, the group of boys from the second van raced superclose. The cox screaming. Water rocking.

"Whoa!" Emersyn reached out, steadying herself, as *Big Bear* shifted in their wake.

"Stroke and seven on two," Tariq called, snapping her back to their drill.

Chelsea's oar swept forward in the six seat.

Emersyn sat tall at finish. Or was it recovery? And was she supposed to go on two, or after?

"One," Tariq shouted, the boat jerking forward in the JV2 boys' wake. "Two."

Before her brain figured out what she should do, Emersyn's body moved. She slid forward, knees bent, her oar parallel to the water. Then she turned her wrist, squaring her blade seconds before it sliced into the river and feathered back out. She pushed with everyone. She pulled with everyone.

The boat surged forward.

Picking up speed, it was like they were sailing across air. The best feeling.

"One splash. One boat," Tariq called.

The oars hit the water and pushed through together. Tariq smirked as they moved. Emersyn dared smile, too. Her whole focus on getting her oar in the water at the same time each stroke.

"We're catching JV2 boys," someone shouted from the back of the boat. "We can take 'em."

The words raced up the shell and through Emersyn. Her competitive streak ignited.

"Eyes forward," Tariq warned.

Emersyn dared peek. *Big Bear*'s bow hovered neck and neck with the boys' cox seat. They *were* gaining, despite grunts and splashes that said the boys were pushing hard.

"Focus," sang Tariq.

"Come on," Hailey shouted. Her voice carried on the wind. "Let's have a little fun. Call a Power Ten."

Power Ten? What the heck was that?

Part of Emersyn didn't care. She heard *power* and wanted to do whatever it was, if it meant beating them.

"Yeah, let's do a Power Ten," Nova yelled. "We got this."

"Steady," Coach Beckett called, racing beside them, Sam sitting tall, his coat whipping back. The motorboat cut through the wake of the boys' boat.

"Power Ten, Tariq, come on. You know you want to beat 'em, too." Nova nudged her. "They talk way too much smack!"

It was only Emersyn's first practice, but when they took the shell out of the boathouse past the JV2 boys, she'd already heard a couple snickers about how Tariq couldn't make cuts—not even to row with girls.

She clenched her teeth. She hated mean. Mean was weak.

"What's a Power Ten?" she asked. "Let's do it, if it'll shut them up."

"It won't," Tariq said. "And who cares? Just keep the pace you're at. Only a couple strokes and practice is over."

"A Power Ten would get us there quicker," Skylar offered.

"But what is it?" Emersyn asked again.

"When you pick up speed for ten strokes, and push through the water like your life depends on it. Like an underwater monster is chasing you 'cause your legs are the turkey sausages it always wanted," Nova rambled.

It took all Emersyn's focus not to turn. "What?"

"It could happen," Nova added. "With the chemicals polluting waters these days, something like that could definitely live down there."

"Shut up!" Tariq shouted into the microphone. "I'm the only one talking in this boat!"

"Come on, T. Let's move this brick," Hailey taunted. "Show 'em where to shove it. And I'll shut up."

"Hailey, that's enough!" shouted Coach, but as she spoke, the voice of the boys' cox carried across the water.

"No way we're letting a boat of puny girls beat us with a kid who couldn't even make boys' alternates. Move it! Power Ten in two!"

Tariq stared at Emersyn. Emersyn stared at Tariq.

She knew that look.

Emersyn clutched the oar's grip tighter, ready to tug like an underwater monster *was* chasing them.

"On two," Tariq shouted almost at the same time as the boys' JV2 cox.

"Woohoo," Hailey screamed. "Let's get this puppy moving!"

"Let's go!" Tariq demanded two strokes later. "Show me some power."

Every part of Emersyn ignited. Her seat sprang forward to catch position and she surged back, muscles flexing as she pushed against her foot plates to the finish.

"Two . . . is this all you got?" Tariq gibed as they slid through recovery. "Where are your legs?"

Emersyn rocketed back with a fierce thrust.

"Three . . . that's it! Together. Four . . . quick and clean, together," Tariq shouted as the boat sprang forward.

"Five . . . halfway done! Six . . . give it all you got. Catch, send. Catch, send. I know you got more than this."

Emersyn's legs burned, her chest heaved, but as everyone's oars swept over the water, and their seats whooshed back, she knew she had more.

"Seven, we've gained a seat! Attack those catches together. Eight, Hailey can see the bow ball! Nine . . . dig in. Let's go. Let's go! Let's go!"

Emersyn nearly jumped when the stern of the boys' shell came into view. In one stroke her team could inch ahead.

Around them, other boats leisurely rowed to the dock for the end of practice. All eyes falling on their impromptu race.

Emersyn's flaunting brain took over. Leaving that boat in her dust, or spray, would be a perfect way to end her first day . . . and in a prized boat, no less . . .

Then, BANG!

The sun dropped from the sky!

Strobe lights ricocheted everywhere as Emersyn blinked.

"Emersyn!"

Someone shook her shoulders.

"You okay?"

"Agh!" someone else wailed.

Everything tipped.

Emersyn's body jerked sideways. Her hand slapped water.

Her eyes blinked faster.

"Syn, you still breathing?" Coach Beckett shouted, concerned.

Where the heck was she? White waves churned at the side of the boat. Emersyn's body stretched back in her seat. Her oar over her head.

The nightmare flashed back!

Nova held her own oar and Emersyn's so it didn't knock her out cold. "How many oars am I holding?" Nova asked. "Don't feel like an idiot—I mean, if you feel like one. It's happened to the best of us. No one *really* noticed."

Emersyn's oar had almost taken off her head as it swung over her, knocking her upside her skull, and no one noticed? Yeah, right!

"Mia!" someone else shouted.

"I can't get mine to turn, either," Mia cried, straining. Her oar clung, locked by the water like Emersyn's. One caught crab was bad, but two? And worse, it'd happened on the final stroke before they could overtake the other boat. And it was Emersyn's fault. She'd dug too deep, trying to show off. But the most mortifying part—everyone on the dock and boathouse had a front row seat.

"Tariq, straighten out!" Coach Beckett's voice shook through the megaphone. Her engine revved as Sam barked in warning.

Tariq moved his focus from Emersyn's and Mia's oars, but froze.

Before any of them could react, Coach Beckett's boat sped forward, moving around theirs. She released the throttle on her boat and actually dove into the water. She broke through the surface, arms up, catching the stern of the revered *Big Bear* seconds before it crashed into the dock. The motorboat puttered forward without her, bumping up against the shore. Sam barked before leaping out, too.

Silence stretched around them.

Every single person affiliated with Travers Crew stared.

Emersyn wanted to dive in the river, hoping to get swallowed by Nova's underwater monster.

"Well, Skylar," Hailey said a second later. "Looks like you won't get your wish."

"What?" Skylar grumbled.

"You definitely won't be forgettable *or* forgotten after this. Ever! None of us will."

No one made a peep, then laughter erupted from everyone in the boat.

Even Emersyn.

BUNKER BUDDIES

SARA FARIZAN

"I'm playing?!" I asked. This was not a part of the proposition that Millie Harding had pitched to me.

"You sure are," Coach O'Connell said with a grin. I couldn't tell if she thought I was happy about having a match or annoyed, but either way, the rest of the team seemed abuzz that I finally had someone to swing clubs with or whatever. I wasn't *supposed* to play.

It all started last winter when I didn't know much about Millie Harding other than she was a freshman with dirty-blond hair always up in a tight bun. I could tell she was nervous to talk to me when she was waiting for me at our school's parking lot reserved only for juniors and seniors.

"Um, Roya? Do you have a moment?" Millie asked, her green braces glinting in the January morning sun. She was shivering a little. It made me wonder how long she'd been waiting for me outside.

"Hey, Millie. What's up?" I asked, grabbing my backpack from the passenger seat and locking the doors on my dad's old Jeep, a beauty with all-wheel drive so I never sweat the snow. Her face smoothed out and relaxed, but she spoke a mile a minute.

"I didn't think you knew my name," Millie said, looking relieved.

"Of course I do." Our school wasn't that big, and even if I wasn't close pals with everybody, I made sure to get to know people. Unless they were assholes. There's a few in every class, but nobody has time for them, especially not me.

"Well, I was wondering if I could speak to you about an opportunity," Millie said, keeping pace with me as we walked toward the school entrance. "You see, I was recruited to play for the varsity golf team."

"Hey, good for you!" I said. I'd forgotten that we had a golf team. All their . . . I don't know, rounds of holes or games, were off campus and I thought they practiced on campus by the tennis courts. I didn't know anybody at school who was eager to go root for a bunch of rich boys at a country club where they may not be made to feel welcome. Our school, Groveland Day, was enough of a country club as it was.

"Yeah, it's great, but I won't, um, I won't get to play as much even if I rank higher than some of my teammates," she said. It didn't make sense to ask why. If she was on a team with all guys, I'm sure there was some teammate who wasn't as good as Millie, but whose daddy was a big mover and shaker and so the guy ranked ahead of her so he could go to the same college his dad had gone to. "So, I was hoping to start a girls' team."

"That's great. The administration has to let you because of Title IX, and don't you let them forget it. Your student class representatives, Amaya and Will, they're on the ball and can help you out with scheduling appointments with the athletic department. Or, if you need more noise to get things going, I'd get in touch with Sheetal on the school paper. She's the opinion editor this year," I said, completely clueless about why she was talking to me about it.

I wasn't on student government anymore after losing last spring's election to Tom Gardner and his speech about how voting for him would be like having your cake and getting to eat it, too. From his lack of effort and how boring and disorganized our social events were, I hoped our classmates were learning that the cake was stale and hard to digest.

"The thing is," Millie said, her voice getting louder as we joined the masses in the main hallway, "we need at least twelve players to be able to have a team. And I thought you'd be a great candidate."

I stopped in the middle of the hall and took a step to the side because I hate when people block the halls, especially when there are places to go and people to see.

"I'm sorry, you mean you want me to golf?" She nodded. "But I've never played before! I mean, mini-golf a handful of times, but I'm not good enough to be on varsity!" I watched *Caddyshack* once and I didn't laugh a whole lot. The groundhog was cute, I guess.

"You don't have to be excellent. At least, not this first season or until we get more players to join. We just need enough players to show interest and build the sport up," Millie said. "Most of the team won't even see playing time because the other schools' teams are small, too. And if you lose, it's okay. Most of the real competition happens at tournaments outside of school."

"Why me?" I asked. "I've never worn a visor in my life. Do I give off a golf vibe?"

"What exactly is a golf vibe?" Millie asked seriously.

"I don't know. Lots of plaid, maybe? Sweaters tied around shoulders? Hanging out with people called Muffy and Bunny and only consorting with snobs of the WASP variety?" My beautiful tan skin, ferociously fierce eyebrows, and black hair wouldn't exactly blend in with the Muffy and Bunny crowd. Not that I actually know a Muffy or Bunny, but hopefully Millie catches my drift.

"It's not all like that," Millie said. She blushed a little, which led me to believe it was a *little* like that. The history of country clubs gives me the creeps. "I play on a public course. And some of the best golfers in the world aren't white." A few juniors and seniors waved hello to me as they passed us by. "See? You know lots of people. That's like the twentieth person that's said hi to you since we started talking."

I hadn't noticed.

"Yeah, well, I used to throw a good party," I said. I hadn't felt much like partying since I didn't make the varsity field hockey team last fall and since my best-friend breakup with Alyssa. She was more interested in her corny boyfriend and his friends than me or any of her old pals. I also wasn't allowed to have more than three people over to the house anymore after my parents found booze in the basement from a theater cast party. I didn't provide the booze, but they didn't care and my social life went down the drain.

"What I mean is, I'm new here and I don't really, um . . . I'm not so popular," Millie said.

"You think I'm popular?" I asked, bewildered and a little touched. I was not a cool kid by any stretch of the imagination.

"You talk to lots of different students," she clarified. "I've seen you talk in assembly and I know you're in the play next month. You're not shy."

"That's true," I said. I sometimes didn't know when to listen and enjoyed the sound of my own voice when I talked over people. Or at least, that was a criticism I was given by my History teacher, my Drama director, and Alyssa during our big fight about how I didn't think she should give up time on her hobbies to accommodate her boyfriend Brendan's. She doesn't even like cross-country skiing and she'd been doing it every weekend because it was his favorite winter activity.

"I also know your schedule might be a little more open in the spring," Millie said.

"Are you stalking me or something?" I asked. Millie's blue eyes widened. I think maybe she kind of had been. Then again, it was a small school and word got around fast. "Let's say I get some teammates for you," I said, thinking I could maybe get a few students who I knew weren't that interested in the mandatory after-school activity they had to sign up for. "What if they don't have golf clubs?"

"That won't be a problem," Millie said. "I'll take care of that and I'll get the school to help. I just need some students to commit to playing by the end of February. I know I can get two freshmen, but that leaves eight students we'd need to join, not counting you."

"Who said I was interested in joining?" She looked deflated when I asked that.

"You'd have a varsity letter," she said, trying to sweeten the deal. "It would look good for college admissions."

"Only if you're good at the sport," I said with a laugh. But I did think about how my time on JV lacrosse had come to an end now that I was a junior. I was always on the bench and it wasn't really something I was passionate about. Still, for the first time in a long time, I had a lot of free time on my hands. I hated it. "Okay. I'm in. So long as you promise I don't make a fool of myself and I don't have to wear plaid."

Millie beamed at me. The deal was made.

I had pulled through by recruiting five seniors: Amanda Johansson, Imani Abimbola, Hannah Greenberg, and Jill O'Shea, none of whom were the most stellar of athletes, but who always tried out for varsity teams year after year only to be cut for younger and more promising jocks. The fifth senior, Denise Lavelle, is an incredible wrestler but needed a secondary low-impact sport. I also persuaded two of my friends from theater, Diane Bui and Adrine

Ohanyan, both of whom had no interest in musicals, which were always the spring production. I rounded out the recruits with a sophomore, Chelsea Boudin, who was very upper-crust and whose family donated a lot of money to the school, but who didn't really have any place she belonged to. She had a reputation for being stuck-up, but I figured she had a set of golf clubs lying around the house somewhere and maybe with her involvement in the team she could get the school to be more interested in the program.

Coach O'Connell was brought in from outside of school to teach us newbies what to do. She was a retired semipro golfer, well into her late sixties, and was excited to mold new golfers as a part-time gig. Our practices would alternate between campus and the club the boys used, but it seemed like they got to go there a lot more often than we did. I was planning on letting Sheetal know in case she needed an article for the paper. Coach would teach us putting and long drives on the soccer field. She had her work cut out for her, and let us know about it with a sassy sense of humor, but most of the team had improved a lot as the season went on. Everyone, that is, except for me. It was nice to have something to do in the afternoons, and I got along with my teammates, but mostly I felt like I was wasting time before senior year. I used to always have a plan: for weekends, for organizing club activities, for the future. Now I didn't know what I was good at or meant to do anymore.

"But I . . . I mean, I'm not ready," I said, facing the reality that I was going to have to play an official match.

"You'll be fine," Adrine said, but Diane laughed at that. They had both seen my swing.

"You're going to have to play sometime," Imani said with a smile, putting her glove on. She'd really improved a lot and was ranked fourth behind Chelsea. Imani was already sporting her visor and it looked good on her. She had the golf vibe I was sorely lacking.

"Yeah, Roya, it'll be fun," Millie said. The traitor. She promised me this day would never come! Usually when we hosted another school, I'd spend the time hanging out with Coach O'Connell at the snack bar area of the club that happily agreed to be our home base for matches once Chelsea's parents called both the school and the club. How quickly things were arranged after one little phone call.

"I was planning on enjoying a cup of cranberry ginger ale while watching a ton of videos of that girl from Virginia who can deadlift two hundred pounds," I said.

"Don't worry. I'll tell you all about it," Coach O'Connell said. "It's only nine holes, not the full eighteen. You know, you might surprise yourself and have some fun out there."

The team from Travers Prep approached us at the beginning of the course. They were dressed like us, khaki pants, cleats, team shirt from the school. Unlike us, they all had matching club bags that looked brand-new, and their faces were serious, like they meant business. Our equipment was a lot of hand-me-downs from family members or friends and old equipment the boys' team no longer used.

Millie paired off with their best player, and the two of them put their club bags on their backs and headed out for hole number one. We never had caddies to carry our bags or tell us what club to use and when. The biggest bummer of all was we didn't get to ride in golf carts. That I would have signed up for in a heartbeat.

The matchups kept being announced and players set off on their journeys while I waited to see who I would lose to. Eventually I was the only player left on either team.

"Hey, that's too bad! Not enough players yet again," I said with a giant smile. I put my hand on Coach O'Connell's shoulder. "Well, Coach, cranberry ginger ales on me while we wait for the troops to return."

"I'll take a rain check on that," Coach said, nodding her chin at a tiny blur that bounced toward us.

"Sorry!" the blur said, the giant bag of clubs overpowering them. "I was in the restroom."

"That's fine, Andretti," the Travers Prep coach said. "You and your opponent head over to the ninth hole."

"Hi!" the blur said from underneath a hat, extending a hand to me.

"Hey," I said, looking down when I shook hands. "I'm Roya. She/her pronouns. It's nice to meet you."

"Oh, I'm Jackie. I, um . . . I guess she/they," Jackie said with a bit of uneasiness. Jackie had short brown hair under a cap, freckles for days, and eyebrows as thick as mine but a lighter shade.

"Cool," I said. Jackie looked more relaxed after I said that. We strolled along the grass to get to the ninth-hole tee. I snuck a look at my opponent out of the corner of my eye. Jackie was shorter than me by about a foot, and had a baby face that couldn't be more than twelve years old. "So are you a freshman?"

"I'm in seventh grade," Jackie said. How beyond embarrassing. Not only was I going to lose my first match, I was going to lose to a middle schooler. "Travers Prep is seventh to twelfth grade. I'm the youngest on the team. My teammates call me Peanut, but I hate it."

"You should tell them," I said. "Nicknames are no fun if they suck."

Jackie shrugged and took their bag off their shoulders. I did the same, but my bag didn't have a cool kickstand like Jackie's, so I gently laid it on the grass.

"I don't know. It goes with the territory. I mean, I can't correct any of them. They already rank me lower because of seniority,"

Jackie said. Great. I'm really going to get slaughtered. "Besides, our school is kind of on the conservative side. Like, nobody really, um, introduces themselves with pronouns."

"Yeah, it's kind of split at ours, but I don't know, it's a habit I'm trying to get into," I said. "So who goes first?"

"Well, I guess we're ranked the same," Jackie said. "What do you shoot?"

"I don't know," I said, feeling like such a goof. "This is, uh—my first match."

"Ever?" Jackie's eyes bugged out of their cherubic face.

"Afraid so," I said, wishing I had worn a hat. I didn't even think to put on sunscreen since I was certain I was going to have it made in the shade watching TV, not burning in the hot sun while I failed miserably at a game I didn't know squat about. Jackie was still surprised, but didn't ask more questions and instead put a tee in the grass and picked up a club that I think was a nine iron. Jackie eyed the ball from behind, gripped their club, stood parallel to the ball, and swung a few practice swings before lining up and hitting the ball so far out onto the fairway my mouth dropped open. "Holy crap! You're really good!"

"Thanks," Jackie said as she picked up the tee. "Your turn."

I took out my heavy nine iron because that's the club Jackie used. My clubs were old and nowhere as light or fancy as some of the ones that belonged to the other players on my team. I put my tee into the grass and placed a ball on top. I also plucked out some grass, and when I stood up, I tossed it in the air to see what direction the wind was blowing. I couldn't figure it out as the grass fell.

"I don't feel a breeze?" Jackie asked. I cleared my throat and lined up my club behind the ball.

I focused on the ball, then looked at the fairway. I did this over and over again for a few minutes, but I knew I was stalling and would eventually have to do something. Jackie didn't rush me or say anything or cough, which I thought was classy. I mustered up the courage to take a swing and completely missed the ball.

"Second time's a charm," I said as I looked over my shoulder and smiled. I think Jackie smiled back, but it could have been a wince at how badly I whiffed. I positioned my club behind the ball again, took another swing, and missed yet again. On my third attempt, the club fell out of my hands and landed on the fairway, but at least the ball made it off the tee. Not very far from the tee, but enough so that we could move on.

"I think you might want to open up your wedge a little more," Jackie said as I struggled to get my ball out of a bunker on the fifth hole. Jackie had two birdies already while my score was well into the high double digits. There was no way I could win.

"Like this?" I asked, holding the club like I was playing hockey. Sweat dripped off my nose and I felt like the sand was full of sand-worms trying to gobble up me and the ball. Then I thought about how I didn't like *Dune* but it was Alyssa's boyfriend's favorite movie and all three of us watched it on TV when she and I were supposed to watch *Birds of Prey*. I hacked at the ball again. It rolled up and then dropped down even farther into the trap from where I had hit it.

Jackie walked into the sand trap and trudged toward me.

"May I?" Jackie asked, holding open their hands for the club.

"Have at it," I said with a laugh.

"Try gripping your club like this," Jackie said, showing me their hands while holding my club. "You want the momentum of your swing to impact your lower two fingers when you hold it like this." I held my fingers the way Jackie showed me to, around an invisible club. "And the best way to get your ball out of a sand trap is to have the wedge face open at a fifty-six-degree angle." Jackie put the wedge beside the ball to show me. "Give it a try."

I did as I was told and the ball still didn't get out of the trap, but it was close. I was about to try again when I heard a voice yell from behind.

"Keep pace!" the voice shouted. I turned around and it wasn't anyone from our schools. It was a group of three men, having an afternoon golf game, and we were in the way.

"WHAT'S THE RUSH? ENJOY THE SCENERY!" I yelled back at them. Jackie started to laugh. "What?"

"Nothing, it's just, it's good etiquette to let the golfers behind through if we're taking too long," Jackie said, still amused by my reaction.

"Well, they can wait a second," I said, and I meant it. "We have just as much right to golf as they do."

"That's true, but maybe not so slowly," Jackie said, looking back at the men. I held the club the way Jackie said and took a big swing from my hips. The ball finally popped out of the sand trap and landed on the grass. "You did it!"

"I did!" I jumped in excitement but then fell onto the sand. Jackie helped me up and we both waddled out of the trap. I turned back to the impatient men, their annoyed expressions giving me as much joy as getting the ball out of there had. "FEEL FREE TO PLAY THROUGH!"

I picked up my ball, knowing this hole was a wash. Jackie and I walked over to Jackie's ball on the green and I waited for them to putt the ball in the hole for yet another birdie, needing only three strokes to sink her ball when the par was four. Then we waited for the men to finish before we kept going. I watched them, the three of them decent but nowhere as good as Jackie.

"They're probably talking business over a game or something," I said.

"That's why my grandmother started playing," Jackie said. "She worked in finance in the eighties and found that a lot of clients played golf, so she learned in order to get face time with them. She had to be good, too, but knew when to lose if a male client was kind of sexist, so they wouldn't feel so bad about losing."

"That sucks," I said, but understood why someone back then might have had to do that.

"She's the one who got me into golf," Jackie explained.

"So that's how you got so good!"

"We used to go every Sunday in the spring and summer, but she recently had hip surgery, so it might be a few weeks before we can do that again."

"I'm sorry," I said. "I hope she feels better soon."

"Thanks. I hope so, too," Jackie said. "She's one of my best friends. I know that's dorky to say."

"It's not dorky. It's nice." The men finished and moved on to the next hole. "You could have taken those guys. You probably could have taken on our top player, Millie. Sorry you got stuck with me today."

"Actually, it's been kind of fun," Jackie said. "I mean, usually I get stressed out during a competition. At least, since I started playing for school. There's a lot of pressure to win, at like every-thing." I knew Travers Prep had a reputation for excellence, and sure, there was a lot of pressure I put on myself, but my school didn't seem to be as obsessed with discipline or being number one. Groveland didn't have sports teams that won tournaments, and our performing arts program never got very far in out-of-school competitions, but it didn't seem like the teachers were too hung up on that stuff. "I like that you didn't give up in the trap.

And this whole time you haven't asked for a mulligan, even though they're not technically allowed in competition."

Jackie was right. I wasn't a quitter. Even if things weren't going my way, that didn't mean I should stop trying, on the green or in life.

"What's a mulligan?"

Jackie shook their head and grinned.

"If you don't mind my asking, how did you get on varsity golf?"

"Ha! It's a long story," I said.

"We have a few more holes to play. You can tell me all about it," Jackie said. "But I think we need to hurry a little or the buses might leave without us."

"There they are," Coach O'Connell said as soon as she saw Jackie and me return to our starting point. "How'd you do?"

"Jackie eviscerated me," I said, my bag's shoulder strap digging into me. I passed my scorecard to Coach. She looked at it, her eyebrows rising higher and higher the longer she stared at it.

"Looks like there is room for improvement," Coach said. "That is, if you want to improve?"

I'm a Leo; I don't like to partake in activities I don't immediately excel at. But I thought about those guys on the course and how pissed I was when they told me to keep pace. I kind of wanted to show them—or someone like them—up one day.

"I would. You might have your work cut out for you, though," I said, repeating what Coach always said when we didn't listen or do what she told us.

"I should say so," Coach said as she held up the scorecard. "But I have a feeling it'll be worth it."

It was nice to hear I wasn't completely hopeless. I watched Jackie walk ahead of me toward her teammates.

"How'd you do, Peanut?" one of the upperclassmen on Jackie's team asked. I could see Jackie's shoulders slump.

"Hey," I said as I walked toward Jackie and addressed her team. "You should call Jackie Champ instead. You have an amazing player worthy of that title." From the way they were looking at me and my sand-stained pants, I had a feeling they weren't going to take up my suggestion, but I figured I'd give it a shot.

"Champ, huh?" Jackie asked me with a grin.

"I don't know. It sounded sporty," I said, extending my hand. "Thanks for your patience. It was nice spending the afternoon with you. I mean, the golf part wasn't so great, but I enjoyed the weather and the company."

Jackie took my hand and shook it wildly.

"I had a great time, too," Jackie said, before realizing they were shaking my hand a little too hard and letting go. "I'll send you that link to that web cartoon I was talking to you about. If you want."

Jackie's face suddenly looked worried like I might say no. It occurred to me that maybe Jackie didn't have too many friends to hang out with, especially if most of her time was spent with the serious bunch behind us boasting about their win.

"Send me all the cartoons. What's your email address?" I asked, pulling out my phone. We exchanged info and I got a message right away that read, *Hi! This is Jackie the Champ!*

"I hope you and Alyssa can be friends again," Jackie said, having heard about my friend breakup at holes seven to eight. "But if not, I think you've got plenty more." Jackie nodded at my teammates, who were calling me over.

"I don't know how friendly they'll be when they figure out I'm the reason for the team loss," I said.

"Want me to beat them up?" Jackie joked. We both laughed.

"Take care, Jackie. Good game."

"Good game, Roya." Jackie waved at me, then ran over to their coach to pass in the scorecard from our match.

I walked back to my team. Millie was the first to greet me.

"How did it go?" Millie asked, genuinely excited about my first foray into her favorite sport.

"I lost my ball in the stream on the sixth hole," I said. "I tried to look for it, but I didn't want to get my pants wet."

"That well, huh?" Millie asked, her face falling slightly, but not out of disappointment. More like she wished I liked the sport as much as she did.

"I'm sorry I let the team down," I said, "but I warned you I shouldn't play."

"You could never let the team down," Millie said, her voice so earnest I thought she was about to recite the Pledge of Allegiance. "There wouldn't be a team without you." I looked at our teammates joking around with one another, guzzling down water, enjoying the gorgeous afternoon in varsity shirts. Millie and I made that happen.

"Think you could remind everyone about that when they're razzing me on the bus?" I asked, putting my arm around Millie's shoulder.

"I wouldn't worry about that. Travers Prep beat almost all of us," Millie said as she patted me on my back.

"Except for you, I bet," I said.

"Who told you?"

★

From: jackieandretti12@traversprep.edu
To: royathedestroya@grovelandday.edu

Hi Roya! Congrats on winning the student government election! I knew you could do it and I'm glad you decided to run again. We should celebrate, but I'm sure you have lots of plans already. But if you don't, will Grandma and I see you on the course this Sunday? Let me know. She says you're improving a lot but I still say you're holding back and don't want me to look bad haha. Anyway, I've signed up for a big tournament this summer and Coach says I have a good shot at winning. Are you signing up for any tourneys?

    —The Champ

From: royathedestroya@grovelandday.edu
To: jackieandretti12@traversprep.edu

Hey Champ, Thank you! I wasn't sure I'd win, but I think I do make a decent class treasurer. It'll be nice to be back in the student government saddle. I don't know what that says about me, but hey, the heart wants what it wants. You tell Grandma Andretti that I've only improved because I have pointers from a master golfer like you. I don't think I'm quite ready to enter any tournaments, and I got a job this summer at a day camp that Adrine works at, which should be pretty fun. Anyway, I have no doubt you're going to win the whole thing. Did I tell you the team voted for me and Millie to be co-captains next season? I don't get it, either, but we can talk about it on the course. Let me know what tee time works for you. I'll bring the ginger ale.

    Your bunker buddy, Roya

THREE MINUTES

AMINAH MAE SAFI

02:59

"But the question on everyone's mind is—can Sarita Solís do it?"

It's the announcer on the TV, but it might as well have been me. *Can* I do it?

"The last time she was in the run-up to the Olympics, she failed her weigh-in before her first fight. A really disappointing start from the young superstar from California."

Ah, there it is. My missed opportunity. My defeat. I hadn't even gotten to fight two years ago. Hadn't even been allowed to get into the arena. I'd come all that way, jumped through all those hoops, only to be denied entry into the ring.

"And now she's back at the Americas qualifiers and fighting not one, but two weight classes above where she was before. Only eight fighters, one from each weight class, will continue on their journey to the Olympics. Eight fighters, not from the USA, but from the whole of the Americas. This is a level she's been on before, but in a whole class of fighters beyond her reach. What do you think, Dan? Has she even got a shot?"

The announcer asks this like it's the most normal question in the world. Like he had ever been sixteen, hungry, and dehydrated.

Rubbed down and oiled up to melt every last drop of extra fluid from his body. Like he had stripped behind a flimsy curtain in front of members of the international press holding audio equipment and cameras. Like he had been publicly weighed and measured.

And found to be, in fact, too much.

Like he had been there, through the months, weeks, hours of training and sparring. Like he had been the one who had given up a normal life for years, only to come up half a kilo over.

Like he knew what I'd given up for the privilege to step on that damn scale.

Then again, maybe he didn't have something to prove.

I do. I always have. Something I need to know about myself that I couldn't find anywhere else outside of that ring. I step into that arena to fight because I have to. Because if I didn't, then I'd never know the answer to the question that beats a rhythm through me, steady as a heartbeat.

It's not rage, though I've got plenty of that. I'm never angry when I fight.

It's not violence, either, though I'm not afraid to take a punch.

Even my ex-coach would tell you that the point of a fight was to *not* get hit. I still hate that he was right about that.

No, I push the ropes and swing my body into the ring, over and over and over again, because I need the fight.

The announcer doesn't know any of that. How could he? He doesn't step into an arena. He mouths off on TV for a living. At the end of the day, he's an entertainer, not a fighter.

He doesn't know what it is to put himself, his whole body, on the line. Not really.

Maybe he doesn't have anything he needs to prove.

I did. I still do.

I hadn't known then, before my first Olympics, what it was I'd been trying to prove.

Now I do.

When the shock had worn off, when the numbness from the weigh-in had faded, I knew three things:

1. I couldn't keep doing this to my body. Not like this.
2. I needed time. I didn't know how much, but I knew I needed time to recover, to think, and to heal if I ever wanted to get back into that ring again.
3. I needed to fire my coach.

I bet the pundit had never had to do that, either. Fire a coach and a mentor who had been working with him since he'd put on gloves. The man who had taught him how to throw a punch. The man who had taught him how to take that raw energy, that drive, and turn it into an art. A dance.

My ex-coach hadn't taken that well.

I should have known. Or maybe I shouldn't have.

He was, after all, the adult.

But he'd gone on a media tour. Calling me uncoachable. Calling me untrainable. A wild card.

I had watched the interview, the one on ESPN, live. I was so angry; I locked my boxing gloves in a closet. That was after I'd been talked down from setting them on fire. And I spent the better part of a month crying.

My dad hadn't known what to do. Nobody had. Least of all me.

But eventually the tears had run out. Eventually the anger had subsided.

The fight, though—that was still in here. It had gotten quiet. But that hunger, that need to prove myself—it hadn't died.

It had been a low hum in my life for so long, I'd forgotten it was there.

I'd forgotten what it was to listen to it.

So I stayed quiet. I listened.

It felt like, for as long as I could remember, I'd always wanted to know what I could do. I was the youngest. The only girl. I'd trailed behind everyone, trying to keep up.

I'd wanted to prove I was worthy of being among them.

I'd wanted to prove I was worthy of being in the ring.

But that wasn't something I could ever prove.

That was a phantom. A ghost. A figment of my own imagination.

So I went looking for a new coach. Someone who didn't believe in media tours. Someone who was too busy being in the gym and putting in the hours with her athletes to ever care what they were saying on ESPN. To ever pay attention to a highlight reel.

Because after a month of crying, I knew three more things:

1. I had no idea what I was capable of. Not really.
2. I wanted to find out.
3. I was going back to the damned Olympics. And I was making it into that ring. On my own terms this time.

No, the announcer on the TV, who was still rattling on and on about what it meant to be a smaller fighter in a heavier weight class, he didn't know any of that. He's just a pundit—a talking head—spouting nonsense.

He'd never had to step into that arena.

He'd never looked at his doubt in someone else's face.

And then fight it.

Not like I had.

So when there's a knock at the door—

"You ready?"

I look up at my new coach. She has a salt-and-pepper halo and a round face. She wears a faded burgundy tracksuit and wire-framed rectangular glasses.

She looks like she could barely run a mile, much less throw a punch.

Both of those assumptions, by the way, are untrue; if you were foolish enough, you'd find out both.

"Yeah," I say. And I mean it. Because I've got to mean it.

Because outside this room is a stadium full of people.

Outside of this room is the Americas qualifiers.

And I'd be my own kind of fool if I let the man on the TV tell me what I could do this time.

I push myself up from the bench. Hold up my hands.

Coach J checks my hand wraps. Checks the tape. She nods her approval, humming. Then she fits my gloves on my hands. Gives each a tap. "Good."

"Thanks," I say. I sound braver than I feel. I'm back where it all started the last time. Back in that place where I wanna prove myself all over again.

There's another knock at the door. A hollow, wooden sound echoes across the concrete-and-metal room. A tinny sound for such a slab of a door.

Coach J looks at me. "It's time."

I nod. Tap my gloves together.

The hum of the fight, buzzing through me, grows louder.

The arena calls.

My confidence evaporates as soon as I walk out of the tunnel.

The arena is full. The lights are glowing blue and red and white.

Coach J is behind me. In front of me is my official Olympic guide. She's holding a sign that says my name and my flag and my country.

The crowd boos as well as cheers when they call my name.

I'm the girl who didn't make her weigh-in. I took a valuable slot.

Eight slots from the whole of the Americas.

I took one and I didn't even fight.

I don't blame them for hating me. I wish I could, but I don't. I can see the world the way they see it. I used to only see the world that way, too.

Other fighters might resent me even more than the crowd. The ones who do know the sacrifice and know they made the cut. There's often contempt and pity in their eyes.

Every once in a while, though, they get it.

They know what it is to trust your coach when they look at you with some kind of alchemy and decide you're a flyweight or a lightweight. When they decide what you are, just by sizing you up.

No science, no data. Just gut instinct that you belong in a certain weight class.

That you belong in the box they put you in.

And all hell will break loose if you dare break out of it.

All hell did break loose, and I didn't even dare break out of it on purpose.

But when I was given the escape hatch, I took it.

I think that's why the crowd boos. They hate that I don't look contrite.

They hate that I didn't go on an apology tour. That I didn't take to my platforms and say, *I'm so sorry, please forgive me.*

The truth was, and the truth is, I'm not sorry.

Instead I said, *This is absolute crap. And I won't do it again.*

That's when I learned you had to turn off the comments.

That's when I learned that middle-aged men with internet connections and access to forums were always ready and willing to tell you what you could and couldn't do with your own body. They thought they had the power of alchemy, too.

That's when I learned people make up a thousand different stories for why you are the way you are. But they never wanted to hear the one you had to tell yourself.

There are a million different versions of you walking around all at once. Sometimes you're the hero. Sometimes you're the villain. And I don't have one of those stories about female empowerment. About coming from some culture that says I shouldn't do sports or I shouldn't box. I mean, deep down, I do. America hides below a friendly smile what is plain and obvious in other parts of the world.

But nobody stops me from boxing. Nobody bars me from the sport. My narrative is unspeakably mundane: I trailed after my older brothers, not wanting to be left out. Not wanting to be left behind. But as long as I could keep up, they didn't stop me. My dad was equal parts worry and pride that I was tough. My mom had that doubtful look on her face, watching me learn to box. But she didn't stop me, either. No, the truth is, I was allowed to play rough and I was allowed to fight my whole life.

And when push came to shove, when I didn't make weight—I

did the unthinkable. I didn't bow my head in an apologetic prayer. I didn't stand in the town square of public opinion and let them shame me.

Instead I told the truth: I don't want to play by anybody else's rules. I don't want to win just because somebody else decided who I was and what kind of fighter I am.

That's not the kind of story people like to tell on ESPN. It's certainly not the kind of story people like to tell in their own minds.

But you don't control any of those stories in other people's minds.

You only control the one in yours.

The spotlight finds me and tracks over me. It's all I can do to not squint into the glare.

I'm jumping back and forth on my feet. I'm rolling my neck back. Shaking out my arms. No matter how many times I've put on gloves, no matter how many times I've gone into a fight, my hands feel heavy and my arms feel incapable of lifting them when I walk around that ring.

It's as though my body conspires against me.

As though my whole frame, for that long minute, decides that I should go limp and play dead rather than get into that ring.

Across the way, I get a glimpse of my opponent.

She's tall, taller than me. She's got long arms and a better reach. I'm watching her as she dances on the balls of her feet. Keeping the blood pumping through her body. Keeping her body loose.

I know those things because I'm doing the same myself.

Back and forth; back and forth.

Left, right, left, right.

It's a dance. It's always been a dance. That's what they never tell you, as a girl, about boxing. They say it's violent and unfeminine.

They tell you you're not being ladylike. That you're too aggressive. Too assertive. Too violent.

Too much.

But what they never tell you is that a fight is about the rhythm. Set the rhythm; set the pace of the fight.

Change the rhythm and syncopate your punches—ah, well, that's when you catch your opponent off her guard.

That's how you win.

I know, because two weight classes down, I was undefeated.

That's why they're all asking: *Can she do it?*

Because I'm wild and ridiculous and out of line, going up in weight. I'm too short to be a lightweight. I don't have the reach. I don't have the frame. They look at me. They size me up. Everybody's got that alchemy in their eye. They say, *What good is her speed at that size? She'll get herself killed. She'll be eaten alive in there.*

They sounds like a conspiracy theory. But it's everyone with an opinion, really. It's my mom with the worry in her voice. It's strangers making comments on the internet. It's those talking heads on the TV.

For a while, it was my own ex-coach. He sowed the seeds of doubt in my mind long before I knew they were in his voice.

I catch myself wondering what she's thinking, my opponent on the other side of the ring. She's too young to have fought in the last qualifiers. But I wonder if she resents that I took that slot. If she thinks I wasted it. If she, too, thinks I'm some kind of a reckless jerk for throwing away my chance at the Olympics and then deciding to take on opponents who typically have five to seven kilos and at least three extra inches on me.

But that's not her thinking that, is it?

It's me. It's all me. All those thoughts, all those doubts. They're mine.

I've just placed them on some girl I don't know. Some girl I'm going to fight.

But I'm not fighting her. I'm fighting me.

I've always been fighting me.

That's the truest thing I know.

That's the thing I have to stop proving.

I look across the way. There's a girl in the stands. She's got on her Team USA warm-ups, though her sporty wheelchair is purple and gold. She's a riot of color and contrasts. I've passed her a few times coming in and out of the press room. Lotte Vogels. She's got those red-white-and-blue, girl-next-door looks that the sponsors just adore. The kind of looks that are a strange burden in this space, where what you want to be known for is your talent.

We lock eyes, Lotte and I. She gives me a nod. I nod back. Somehow, she knew: I needed that. That one piece of encouragement. That one piece of kindness, from one stranger to another.

And I know that she knows what it is to not fit yourself into a box that someone else made for you. I know she knows what it is to step into the ring and fight, even if she's never learned how to box. I know she knows what it is to have people look at you with that alchemy in their eye.

Coach J holds the ropes and I climb in.

Because no matter how afraid I am of what awaits me in that ring, I'm always more scared of who I'd be if I don't go in than who I am if I do.

00:27

The first time you climb in, you wonder how anyone ever does it efficiently. You wonder how everyone doesn't look like some kind of awkward, stumbling giraffe to get into that ring. But after fifty fights and a thousand times stepping in, you learn the rhythm and the grace of the movement. It's not something you think about. It's something your body knows.

My body knows how to swing through the ropes.

My body knows how to fight.

I wish my mind could remember that.

It's so loud. Doubt keeps rattling through my head, getting louder and louder to compensate for the lights and the cheers and the jeers and all of those eyes and cameras back on me again.

God, I pray I don't choke.

At least I made the weigh-in. I was more worried about not weighing enough this time. It was a welcome worry. I didn't go hungry trying to make weight. I didn't have special rubdowns and I didn't get in the sauna, sweating out all that fear and loathing. I didn't stop drinking water so I wouldn't bloat.

I stepped onto that scale and for the first time, I was free. I was enough.

Coach J reaches out, touches my shoulder. Brings me back to the here and now. Back to the present. "Kid?"

"Yeah?" I wish I could shut out the noise. I wish I could shut out the crowd. I try to look at Coach J and only Coach J.

"You can do this," she says. There's no doubt in her voice. No quaver. "You know what you're doing."

But what if I don't? I don't say it out loud, but sometimes, it's like she can hear me.

"You know what you're doing."

She's right. I know she's right. I just can't always believe her. I can't always find that switch inside myself where I know what I'm capable of. Where I just know what I can do.

"You're fast," says Coach J. "Faster than her."

I take a deep breath. My arms lighten. My feet begin to float. I'm amped up, vibrating with energy. But at least I'm not feeling that heaviness again. "I'm fast."

"Faster than her," Coach J repeats.

"Faster than her," I say.

"You dance like nobody I've ever seen," she says.

"I dance like nobody you've ever seen," I say.

She waits.

"I dance like nobody anybody's ever seen."

"Good," she says.

I breathe in. I breathe out. I'm so aware of every inhale through my nose. Every time my lungs fill. Every time I blow out a great puff of air through my mouth.

I close my eyes. Try to find that buzzing. The fight inside. The one that never went away. The one I couldn't lock in a closet with my gloves. The rhythm like a heartbeat. The one I couldn't cry out with a river of tears. The one that's been in me, probably since the day I was born.

That buzz that has nothing to do with a bad coach. Has nothing to do with trailing behind my older brothers. Has nothing to do with my father's worry or my mother's doubt. Has nothing to do with strange men on the internet or any other fighter across from me.

I know what I have to prove now.

What I prove every time.

"I belong in this ring. I always have." I say it unprompted. It's an embarrassing and earnest confession.

But Coach J just smiles. "I'm glad you see it now."

"I dance like nobody anybody's ever seen."

"That's right, kid," she says. She never calls me *honey* or *baby-girl*. She reminds me I'm a fighter every time she calls me *kid*. She reminds me that she's older, but not that I'm smaller or more docile.

"Now watch out for her left hook. She's got the reach and the hips to lay you out, do you hear?"

"Yeah," I say. I shake out my shoulders. I roll out my head. "She can't catch me. I'm faster than her."

"That's right." Coach J nods.

I nod back. She and I, we're finding a rhythm. But I have to break it.

I tap my gloves together, cut off the dance. "It's time."

And Coach J melts away into my corner. And I float forward into the center of the ring. The center that I'm gonna command. I don't care how many kilos this girl's got on me or how much longer her reach is than mine.

I know me. I got me. I'm fast. And I dance like nobody anybody's ever seen.

The ref talks us through a fair fight. We both nod. We tap gloves.

Three minutes. That's all a round is. I'll keep showing up, three minutes at a time. Until the fight is mine. Because in the end, I know who I am. I don't need to prove it. I just gotta go do what I can do.

I'm Sarita Solís. And I'm the comeback kid.

The bell rings.

NO LOVE LOST

KAYLA WHALEY

SEGMENT PITCH: After her breakthrough year, the Olympic Channel follows nineteen-year-old wheelchair tennis phenom LOTTE VOGELS as she revisits her high school tennis team.

INT. WILDWOOD HIGH SCHOOL CAFETERIA—MORNING

LOTTE VOGELS faces the camera. The cafeteria is empty. It's early. The first bell hasn't yet rung. Her sporty manual wheelchair is purple and gold, the school colors. She holds a Paralympic gold medal in her lap.

LOTTE VOGELS

Yeah, I'm a little nervous. I haven't been back here since graduation. Since before then, actually. I didn't go to the ceremony itself. The French, you know?

EXT. STADE ROLAND GARROS, PARIS—DAY

B-roll of the stadium from above. The clay courts are pristine, the start of the tournament.

CUT TO:

INT. COURT PHILIPPE-CHATRIER—DAY

Rapid-fire montage of highlights from LOTTE's wheelchair singles victory. She speeds across the court, tire tracks left in the red clay with every quick pivot and screeching halt. She attacks each ball with a loud *thwack* off her racket. We see ball after ball hit the opponent's lines, white chalk kicking up into the air, their own racket swinging at empty air, the point already won.

>   LOTTE VOGELS (V.O.)
>   It's only been a year, but so much has happened. It defi-
>   nitely feels weird to be back. But I mean, doesn't everyone
>   feel weird about going back to high school?

Slo-mo shot of LOTTE holding the French Open trophy aloft, crowd cheering in the stands.

CUT TO:

INT. WILDWOOD HIGH SCHOOL CAFETERIA—MORNING

LOTTE stares down at the medal in her lap.

LOTTE VOGELS

Do I think the team's excited to see me? (*pause*) I think this
is going to be a memorable homecoming, that's for sure.

CUT TO:

**EXT. WILDWOOD HIGH SCHOOL TENNIS COURTS—
MORNING**

A chilly early morning mid-March in suburban Atlanta. Lingering
fog high in the sky, only half burned away. Perfect conditions for
a pre-class workout. COACH SALINAS stands near the bleachers,
watching a handful of student athletes warm up.

COACH SALINAS

Lotte was always the first one out here. Always. She even
beat me most of the time. The whole school would still be
locked up, but she'd be here. Said, "Coach, I don't need a
roof to get some practice in." It could be raining buckets
and she'd be out here, swinging that racket, soaked to the
bone. Least till I told her she was gonna get me sued for
negligence if she came down with pneumonia. After that
she only came early on fair-weather days, bless her.

COACH SALINAS blows her whistle. The students stop their
motions and turn their attention to her.

COACH SALINAS

All right, folks, gather up. Y'all know today is a very special day, right? We've got these lovely film crew people
here to see how we do things at Wildwood.

Aren't they here for Lotte?

COACH SALINAS

They're here because I invited 'em. Now get to class and I'll see y'all for practice after school. Mikey and Rachel, I'll see you in just a few minutes. Do not make me wait on you for attendance again. (*to camera*) I teach Algebra. Mostly freshmen like those two rascals.

The students begin packing up their things and heading toward the school proper. One student hangs back, waiting to talk to COACH SALINAS.

COACH SALINAS

What is it, Jason?

JASON JOHNSON looks carefully at the camera, then back at COACH.

JASON JOHNSON

Have you seen Courtland today, ma'am?

COACH SALINAS

Not yet, why? (*to camera*) Dani Courtland, our team manager. She's a senior now. Been working with me and the team her whole high school career. Whip-smart, that one. (*to Jason*) She not answering her phone? Want me to check the office?

JASON waves his hands rapidly.

                         JASON JOHNSON

No, no! No worries. I was just curious is all. Have a good
day, Coach!

                                                    CUT TO:

INT. COACHING OFFICE—MORNING

LOTTE enters an empty, relatively small office, about a third the
size of a typical classroom. Five office desks are crammed in, two,
two, and one. The rightmost desk doesn't have an associated chair.
Overstuffed bookshelves line the room. LOTTE heads toward the
nearest one.

                         LOTTE VOGELS

Coach's not-so-little free library. She's got just about every
sports memoir and biography ever written.

She pulls a book from the shelf, a biography of Billie Jean King.

                         LOTTE VOGELS

All students are allowed to borrow from these shelves,
whether they're on the tennis team or not. Although
everyone on the team is required to read one per semester.
Coach always says, *It's one thing to know athletic technique,
it's another—*

                         COACH SALINAS

It's another to know athletic heart.

LOTTE startles and nearly drops the book.

LOTTE VOGELS

Coach! I thought you were in class! Don't you teach first period?

COACH SALINAS

I gave them free study time for today. Coach Jenny's with them if they have any questions.

LOTTE VOGELS

Coach Jenny? The Coach Jenny who thought a quadratic was a new leg workout?

Both laugh, trailing off to fond smiles.

COACH SALINAS

It's good to see you, Lotte. We've all missed you.

LOTTE VOGELS

Really? All of you?

LOTTE looks toward the desk with the missing chair. COACH SALINAS turns abruptly toward the cameraperson.

COACH SALINAS

So. Where would you fine folks like to start?

CUT TO:

INT./EXT. VARIOUS HOME FOOTAGE OF LOTTE VOGELS DURING HIGH SCHOOL

Most of the footage comes from taped practices on the Wildwood courts, videos used for training purposes. LOTTE practicing her serve; LOTTE returning balls; LOTTE during practice matches with other team members.

Sometimes, COACH SALINAS or other coaches talk to LOTTE, demonstrating some technique or correcting her form.

> LOTTE VOGELS (V.O.)
> High school was such a weird time for me, athletically. I was training constantly, but I rarely got to actually play in competition.

> INTERVIEWER (V.O.)
> Why not?

> LOTTE VOGELS (V.O.)
> There's not really a junior wheelchair tennis circuit, especially not through the school system.

At other times, we see LOTTE at rest. When not actively practicing, she's always surrounded by teammates. The center of attention. The other players (all ambulatory) are smiling and laughing with her.

In a few clips, LOTTE is the one coaching the younger team members. She offers tips about timing or their footing. When one athlete falls and starts crying, LOTTE slides out of her chair onto the hard court next to the girl, assessing the damage while other students call for help.

> LOTTE VOGELS (V.O.)
> When I *was* allowed to play in team competitions it was mostly against abled players. The rules for both disciplines are the same, except in wheelchair tennis you get

two bounces to return the ball. So as long as my opponent didn't mind, I could play anybody. And that worked for a while. Until I started winning.

Local news coverage of LOTTE's win against a rival high school. The chyron reads: *Disabled sophomore stuns in inspiring fashion at tennis tournament.* LOTTE's opponent glares in the background as LOTTE accepts her trophy.

LOTTE VOGELS (V.O.)

Suddenly the opposing coaches felt playing against abled athletes "wasn't fair" to me. So. That was that.

Often, in the background or on the sidelines, is another girl. She uses a power wheelchair and always holds a clipboard in her lap and a stopwatch in her hand. There's a whistle around her neck, identical to the ones the coaches use. She seems separate from the rest of the team. A part, but apart.

The final clip in the montage shows the end of a practice session. LOTTE, sweating, heads toward the other girl. LOTTE says something. The other girl laughs warmly before exiting the frame.

FADE TO BLACK.

INT. WILDWOOD HIGH SCHOOL GYM—AFTERNOON

TY TRASK

Oh man, Lotte was a superstar. Everyone knew she was gonna make it big. You could just tell, you know?

Two students stand off to the side during Gym class being interviewed by the film crew. Both boys wear Wildwood Tennis letter jackets. The gym is filled with the sound of sneakers squeaking on linoleum and basketballs bouncing off the backboard.

ANDY PARK

For sure. She just has this vibe. Like, this confidence or something. When she's playing, but even when she's not, too.

TY TRASK

Watching her play is just . . . She's *so good*, you know? I remember seeing her my freshman year, and just being in absolute awe. And she just got better every year! That's crazy. Plus she's smoking hot.

ANDY elbows TY in the side.

ANDY PARK

Dude, not cool.

TY TRASK

What? She is!

ANDY PARK

Yeah, but you can't just *say* that.

TY TRASK

All I mean is it isn't any surprise that she's already getting sponsorships and stuff. You can't be *that* talented and *that* . . . classically beautiful—

ANDY PARK

Thank you.

TY TRASK

—and not get a ton of endorsements. Like, come on. She's
a legend, is my point. Ask anyone.

ANDY PARK

Well, maybe not *anyone*. Remember when that freshman
pulled up Lotte's Super Bowl commercial on YouTube
right in front of Courtland? Of all things to show your
buddies with her there.

TY elbows ANDY this time before glancing purposefully at the
camera and shaking his head slightly.

CUT TO:

CLIPS FROM TOYOTA'S 2024 SUPER BOWL COMMERCIAL

LOTTE VOGELS blazes across the court, hitting winners left and
right. The camera focuses closely on her wheelchair. Tight shots
of her hands pumping the wheels. Close-ups of the ball smacking
the court in front of her footrests. Dynamic zooms in on the back
of her sleek chair. What little is visible of her body is in silhouette.

NARRATOR (V.O.)

We keep moving. No matter how difficult. We move forward.
We fight.

LOTTE sits on the side of the court. She breathes hard, sweating
profusely. She takes a big swig from a water bottle.

NARRATOR (CONT'D) (V.O.)

Lotte Vogels has never once let any obstacle stop her.

In the parking lot now. An adaptive Toyota SUV waits for LOTTE. She presses the key fob and a ramp unfolds from the side door. She drives into position behind the wheel, settling her hands confidently at two and ten o'clock.

> NARRATOR (CONT'D) (V.O.)
> The future is ours. We need only reach out and take it. No excuses. We keep moving. Together.

FADE TO:

INT. WILDWOOD HIGH SCHOOL CAFETERIA—DAY

> LOTTE VOGELS
> I couldn't believe it when I got my first brand deal. I mean, I hadn't even graduated yet! I'd won some bigger tournaments and I'd already qualified for the Paralympic team, but all of a sudden Toyota gets in touch and wants me? For a *Super Bowl* campaign? That's wild. It honestly doesn't make sense.

She's wearing the Paralympic gold medal around her neck now. The shine reflects the film crew's key light, sending a bright beam back toward the camera.

> LOTTE VOGELS
> It all happened so fast. By the time they contacted me two weeks before filming, they had already lined up the other athletes who were gonna be starring, so the schedule was set. But I didn't know exactly who else would be there until I showed up on set and there was freaking *Megan Rapinoe* standing in front of the buffet table holding a little Dixie cup of juice. I genuinely almost passed out.

INTERVIEWER (V.O.)

Why you? If they had a bunch of megastars already?

LOTTE VOGELS

(*laughs*) Right? The whole idea was a series of short spots, each building on the last throughout the broadcast. A passing of the baton. The legends would have the earlier slots and at the end of each commercial, the focus of that one would "hand off" to the next athlete. It was about celebrating the future of sports, I guess. The progression of talent into the younger generations or whatever. I was the last one to go. The representative of the next gen.

INTERVIEWER (V.O.)

Prescient. You won every match you played for the next year.

LOTTE picks up the medal and looks into its face. The light bounces up directly into her eyes, but she doesn't look away.

LOTTE VOGELS

Yeah. I won everything.

FADE TO:

EXT. WILDWOOD HIGH SCHOOL TENNIS COURTS— AFTERNOON

COACH SALINAS taps the microphone she's holding and clears her throat.

COACH SALINAS

All right, folks. Quiet down, please. Come on, that's right.

There are many more students here than early this morning. The ones standing on the court are dressed for practice: tanks, shorts, sweatbands on wrists or forehead, sturdy sneakers. Those in the stands are a mixture of athletes from other departments (some wearing basketball jerseys, some with lacrosse bats leaning next to them), teachers, and other students. The bleachers are nearly full.

COACH SALINAS

Thank you all for coming. As you know, today is a very special day. Our own Lotte Vogels is back after winning, oh, I don't know, just about *every* tennis championship on the planet! It's been a whirlwind of a year and I know we're all so proud of her. So let's give a proper Wildcat welcome to our queen of the courts, Lotte Vogels!

The crowd claps, a chorus of *whoops* ringing out.

LOTTE comes out from behind the bleachers where she's been waiting. She waves, smiling sheepishly, almost as if she's embarrassed, and heads over to COACH SALINAS. The older woman hands her the mic.

Just as LOTTE is about to speak, feedback rings out over the court. Everyone winces and covers their ears until it subsides. They turn toward the sound. At the top of the bleachers, DANI COURTLAND holds a megaphone. Beside her are JASON and a handful of other students carrying a large rolled-up banner. They unfurl it as COURTLAND reads the written message into the megaphone.

DANI COURTLAND

Welcome home, traitor.

INT. HALL OUTSIDE COACHING OFFICE—AFTERNOON

Chaos.

COACH SALINAS, COACH JENNY, and two assistant coaches are trying to calm the many students crammed into the small space. JASON and the other banner holders huddle around COURTLAND, shouting at the group opposite them. ANDY PARK, TY TRASK, and five other students stand behind LOTTE, yelling back.

At the center of the shouting, COURTLAND and LOTTE sit facing each other on either side of the door, both silent, the former glaring, the latter with her arms crossed.

COACH SALINAS stands between them in the open doorway. She blows sharply on her whistle. Silence follows.

> COACH SALINAS
>
> If your name isn't Dani Courtland or Lotte Vogels, please vacate this building immediately.

The students follow the order without much hesitation. Only JASON lingers, glancing at COURTLAND quickly. She gives a slight nod. He leaves.

COACH SALINAS looks at the coaches still standing in the hall.

> COACH JENNY
>
> Oh, you meant us, too? Right, okay, sure. Yeah. We'll go let everybody know to reconvene in a bit.

> COACH SALINAS
>
> Good plan.

COACH SALINAS turns toward the cameras. Or rather, toward the people holding the cameras. She stares pointedly.

> COACH SALINAS
> Was I not clear enough? *Out.*

> DANI COURTLAND
> I think they should stay. They're here to learn all about you, right, Lotte? So they should learn *all* about you.

> COACH SALINAS
> Dani, that's enough.

LOTTE sits forward in her chair and meets COURTLAND's hard gaze. LOTTE no longer looks chagrined; she looks mad.

> LOTTE VOGELS
> No, Coach. She's right. I've got nothing to hide. I did *nothing wrong.* Let them stay. (*to camera*) You wanna know what this petty high school drama is about?

> DANI COURTLAND
> *Petty?!*

> LOTTE VOGELS
> Then let's get into it, shall we?

COACH SALINAS sighs but heads into the office. Both girls follow.

CUT TO:

I/E. INTERVIEW CLIP MONTAGE

ANDY PARK

Those two were best friends. Like, *best* friends.

CUT TO:

TY TRASK

I always thought they'd end up dating, but no one else agreed with me. I guess they probably are too similar to make a relationship work.

CUT TO:

JASON JOHNSON

Courtland's okay with us talking to you? She said she's fine with it?

CUT TO:

COACH JENNY

Her freshman year, Courtland joined the team as manager. She knew she'd need sports on her résumé to get into the colleges she wanted, and she medically isn't allowed to do any sort of athletics. So she figured managing was a good substitute. I don't think she and Lotte knew each other before then, but after she joined, they were inseparable. At least until that last year.

NO LOVE LOST ★ **207**

CUT TO:

ANDY PARK

It was the Super Bowl commercial. Remember we told you about that? That's what caused the whole mess.

CUT TO:

TY TRASK

You can't deny there's chemistry there, though. I mean even when they're fighting it's just sparks everywhere! You saw it in there just now, right? The way they couldn't stop staring at each other? Major *Pride and Prejudice* vibes. (*pause*) This isn't actually helpful, is it?

CUT TO:

JASON JOHNSON

Look, Courtland's my best friend and Lotte was *her* best friend. I'm extremely protective. Lotte and Courtland worked for *months* trying to organize a high school wheelchair tennis competition for the state. It was gonna be the first ever. Courtland barely slept through that whole semester, I swear.

CUT TO:

COACH JENNY

When Lotte landed the Toyota gig, I honestly expected Courtland to rope us into throwing her a massive surprise party. That kind of deal is unheard-of for a teenager who's only won a handful of bigger trophies. But especially for an adaptive sport? Courtland's whole goal in life is taking wheelchair tennis mainstream. I figured she'd be even more excited than Lotte.

CUT TO:

ANDY PARK

I've never seen anyone as angry as Courtland when Lotte's commercial aired. She had been really upset that Lotte missed their wheelchair tournament, of course, but I figured it would blow over. I guess seeing the actual ad itself made Courtland snap. You know how sometimes Djokovic or Zverev just absolutely smash their rackets to pieces? Courtland can't exactly do that, but I was a little worried she might barrel straight through the school walls. Her chair's basically a tank. I mean, have you seen that thing? It could do some serious damage.

CUT TO:

TY TRASK

Everyone remembers that day Courtland blew up. She kept yelling at Lotte, like, *How fucking could you?! How could you betray us like that, you backstabbing bastard?* etc., etc. Coach stepping in is the only reason she didn't get suspended, honestly. But I mostly remember Lotte. I saw her coming out of the gym later that day and she looked . . . just . . . empty.

JASON JOHNSON

Did the tournament happen? Well, yeah. But Lotte was the face of the whole thing. Courtland's not an athlete, so she's fully behind-the-scenes. They were banking on Lotte being able to draw a crowd, get some of the money in ticket sales. Without her, well, the tournament lost money. Like, a lot of money. It'll be hard for Courtland to convince the state's athletic association to do it again, let alone formalize it into an annual event like she wanted. And like Lotte wanted, too! I still don't understand how she could just abandon something she worked so hard for. Even for something that big.

CUT TO:

COACH JENNY

I would never get involved in any student's interpersonal issues, so I can't comment on who was right or whatnot. But I will say that when Lotte popped up during the fourth quarter, sandwiched right between a Budweiser and an M&M's commercial, I'll admit I cried. I've never felt more proud in my life. Although maybe don't tell my kids that. (*laughs*)

CUT TO:

INT. COACHING OFFICE—AFTERNOON

Now that all the other students and coaches have left, the room is quiet. But the air still feels charged.

COACH SALINAS

How about we try talking this out, girls, huh? Y'all used to do nothing but talk!

LOTTE VOGELS

I know you're still mad, Dani. I do. But is all this really necessary?

DANI COURTLAND

Of course it's fucking necessary. What, did you think I'd have forgiven you?

COACH SALINAS looks to the camera and waves her hand, as if to say *Let them curse, it's fine.*

LOTTE VOGELS

I'm not gonna have this fight with you again. That money paid for my whole year on the circuit! I wouldn't have been able to get to the Australian, let alone every major *and* the Paralympics without it.

DANI COURTLAND

Yeah, but they were *using* you! And you were so caught up in the attention and the money and getting to meet Sarita Solís and Pilar Abiodun that you didn't notice. Or actually, you did notice and you just didn't care.

LOTTE VOGELS

That's what commercials and sponsorships *are*. They're companies using athletes to make money. That's the whole point!

DANI COURTLAND

You're right. Let me rephrase that. They weren't using you because they don't care about you. They were using your disability, and they knew exactly how to get the most bang for their dirty buck.

LOTTE VOGELS

Fine, I'll admit it wasn't the most tasteful commercial—

COURTLAND scoffs.

DANI COURTLAND

What a diplomatic way of putting it.

LOTTE VOGELS

But a lot of fucking good came from it, Dani. People got to see a wheelchair tennis player in action! They might have never even *heard* of the sport before, and now it shows up in the middle of the Super Bowl. Think of all the little kids out there who saw me and said, *Hey, maybe I can play tennis, too!*

DANI COURTLAND

(*softly*) And think of all the little kids who said, *I can't even play wheelchair tennis, maybe I really am worthless.*

LOTTE's eyes widen. COURTLAND blinks hard, seemingly surprised at her own words.

COACH SALINAS

Courtland. You know that's not—

LOTTE VOGELS

Don't put that on me, Dani. Don't you dare.

Gathering her composure again, COURTLAND squares her shoulders.

DANI COURTLAND

I'm not. It's just how it is. They hold you up as the standard, the good cripple, and the rest of us who can't measure up get told *No excuses, try harder, don't let your disability stop you.* It's not like we'd never talked about it. You knew. You know exactly how this shit plays out every single time. And you went along. For what? The exposure? The *money*? I didn't realize your principles were so cheap.

LOTTE takes a sharp breath. Sudden tears form and roll fatly down her cheeks. She doesn't reach up to wipe them off, her hands balled into fists on her thighs. Her voice is quiet and fierce when she speaks.

LOTTE VOGELS

Fuck you, Dani.

COACH SALINAS quickly walks around her desk, standing between the two of them.

COACH SALINAS

All right, girls. I think we're at a standstill. The day's almost over. Y'all think we can at least just get through Lotte's goodbye speech peacefully? For the rest of the team if not for yourselves.

The girls stare at each other. LOTTE seems as tensed as she is before a serve. A few long seconds pass. COURTLAND looks away first, the fight draining visibly out of her.

> DANI COURTLAND
>
> Sure thing, Coach.

CUT TO:

EXT. WILDWOOD HIGH SCHOOL TENNIS COURTS— AFTER SCHOOL

The stands are even fuller now. Word of COURTLAND's demonstration has spread during the unplanned intermission. The atmosphere is tense, no longer celebratory.

Down on the court, front and center among the tennis team members, is COURTLAND. Beside her, JASON leans over to say something, but she doesn't seem to be listening.

> COACH SALINAS
>
> Sorry about that, y'all. Let's try this again, shall we? Come on out, dear.

LOTTE returns to the mic. She smiles brightly, too brightly. The audience applauds, much more reserved this time. LOTTE clears her throat and looks to the little stack of index cards she's holding.

After a beat, she puts the cards away.

> LOTTE VOGELS
>
> I hope y'all don't mind if we go off-script here. I had this whole speech written out. Lots of *great-to-be-back*s and

*couldn't-have-done-it-without-you*s. The usual. And all of that is true, but it's not really what I want to talk about.

Tennis has not always been good to me. Honestly, it's been hostile more than it's been welcoming. I've had to fight not only for every point on the court but also for every chance to step out onto a court at all. It sucks, okay? It's not fun. It's not an exciting challenge to overcome or some triumph-over-adversity story line. It's bullshit. Just plain, simple bullshit. And it's even more bullshit that I have to always, *always* just sit and smile. I have to be oh-so-grateful for whatever scraps I manage to steal for myself.

The crowd grows uneasy. Lots of shifting in seats and murmuring to neighbors. A close-up shot on COURTLAND shows her watching LOTTE intently, hands clasped tightly in her lap.

LOTTE VOGELS

I've barely even started my career and I'm already exhausted. I keep thinking, if I just get big enough, if I can get enough people to care about me as an athlete, maybe I can get them to care about wheelchair tennis as a sport. And if I can do that . . . (*looks directly at COURTLAND*) maybe I can get them to care about disabled people in general.

It's not a good plan. It's a terrible one. A super-conceited one, too, and guaranteed to fail. But it's all I've got. The only thing I can control is how I perform—both on and off the court. I can't control how people see me, how they interpret my actions, what they project onto me.

LOTTE looks directly at the camera. Or rather, at the camerapeople.

LOTTE VOGELS

Even now, I have no idea how much of this speech will make it into the final cut. How they'll chop it up or edit it down. And that's fine. I signed up for all of this knowing that. (*sighs*) But I also need to remember that none of this affects just me. It's beyond me now. And I need to be more careful about that.

LOTTE finds COURTLAND's eyes and holds her gaze.

LOTTE VOGELS

I'm sorry I wasn't more careful. I don't regret my choices, but I wouldn't make the exact same ones in the exact same way again. And maybe I have more control than I think I do. If nothing else, I can be more open, more honest. I can call out the bullshit instead of taking it. I just hope I won't have to do it alone.

The camera zooms in again on COURTLAND's face. Her eyes are shining with tears. She gives the slightest of nods and LOTTE's relieved exhale whooshes through the mic and across the whole tennis court like a clean winner on match point.

KYLIE WITH AN I

CARRIE S. ALLEN

It smells like a candle store. Taylor Swift at full volume competes with a dozen chatty conversations, and there's a purple-thonged butt mere inches from my elbow. This is not how I pictured a hockey locker room.

After a decade of changing in the single-stall bathroom at Hawk Landing Ice Center, my first impression of a real locker room has me stress-sweating like a freshman on the power play. I hide my head in my hockey bag, pretending to search for an elbow pad while my face cools. I could climb in here, zip myself up, and let the whole camp continue on to practice without me.

Of course, then I'd have to go all the way home to North Dakota and explain to Dad and my boys' team and the whole town that I'll never play on the Under-18 team or the U22 or the big show—the U.S. Women's Hockey Team—because the changing room was too scary. Already, just for getting invited to this camp, I can't make it from my locker to homeroom without getting stopped and congratulated five times. Who knows how bad it'll be if I actually make the U18 team?

Who knows how bad it'll be if I don't?

It's this thought that pulls my head out of my ass—er, bag. As I'm tying my skates, my phone dings.

Purple Thong frowns. "If Coach catches you on your phone, you're done."

Another benefit of having been the only girl on my team: Phones were allowed in my changing room; coaches were not.

I debate for a split second, but it's Alex checking in, and I'm desperate for a pep talk.

In the locker room, can't talk, freaking out

St. Cloud's locker room???? Steal me some tape. Or gum. SEND PICTURES!!!!

Ew no we're changing, doofus. This place is loud and crowded. I can't focus.

Me either send pictures red tape not black

FREAKING OUT HERE

I stare at my phone, willing him to text magic words that will put me at ease.

GAME FACE, KYLE. You're our best skater. Fastest slapper. 2 years varsity against bigass dudes. Just try not to hurt anyone.

He's right. I've outskated eighteen-year-old boys and stood up tractor-size forwards. My D partner Ben is six foot three, 230 pounds. If I can hang with him in the corners, I can handle whatever a team of girls brings.

I'm breathing again. At least the bench will smell nicer, if this locker room is any indication.

Thanks, dude. I mute my phone, bury it in my bag, and pull my hair into my game ponytail. When we started checking, I learned to hide my hair under my helmet. Same year I "accidentally" forgot the *i* in *Kylie* when I helped Dad fill out the roster.

The girl next to me chuckles. "If anyone's going to check the ponytail, they'll have their choice to pick from."

Huh. Guess she's right. I drop my hair into a regular ponytail.

She holds out her hand. "I'm Dana."

I start to say *I'm Kyle*, but then I remember I can be Kylie here, so it comes out all funny, like I don't even know my own name.

"Nice bruise."

I glance at my biceps. "My brother Caleb got me with a puck yesterday."

"Hey, mine, too." She slides down her sock to show me a puck-shaped lump on her calf.

We're both wearing black jerseys, so Dana's also on D. Her fingernails are a bright fuchsia, but otherwise she's more like me than most of these girls. No makeup, zero-maintenance hair, muscles that make more of an impact than her curves.

The locker room silences like someone hit the Mute button. Four women in head-to-toe USA swag surround the massive position board on the wall.

"Welcome to camp!" Coach Chu says. "Hope everyone ate their Wheaties so you have something to puke during practice." When the nervous laughter ends, she continues. "Seven days here, and if you impress me, you'll move on to the U18 select camp next month. If you still impress me, you might make the National Festival in August. And if you survive that, the U18 Series against Canada.

"If you don't impress me, that's okay, too." She pulls a marker from her pocket and faces the whiteboard. "I have a hundred and forty-four women waiting to take your spot."

I gulp.

She scribbles *x*'s and *o*'s on the whiteboard, spewing plays like a coaching volcano at full eruption. None of it is anything like the drills Dad runs at our practices. I risk a peek at Dana. She's leaning forward, nodding as she tracks Coach's marker.

Good. I'll follow Dana.

Coach wraps up her pep-less talk and runs through the roster.

Remembering Alex's advice, I put on my game face to check out the seventeen other players on Gray team. The girl across from me is wearing silver eye shadow and has at least three rings on each hand. The forward next to her weighs as much as one of Ben's thighs. She daintily sneezes in a soprano range and everyone around her politely choruses, "Bless you!"

No one's ever been blessed at a Hawk Landing practice, I can guarantee that.

This is my competition. I'm not afraid.

I've never played in a real arena—my whole town could sit in the stands of St. Cloud State's Herb Brooks National Hockey Center and still have elbow room. Red banners, eerily still, hang from the metal scaffolding, reminding me that athletes who play in big arenas are supposed to win big games.

This is what every 5:00 a.m. practice was for. Every bruise from a guy who realized he got muscled out of the crease by a girl. This is for the Northwood coach who told me, after our game this year, *If you can play my boys, you'll have no problem against a bunch of girls*. This is for the mom who shoved a used pair of figure skates at me after our first Bantam practice because *the boys won't feel comfortable hitting a girl*. Like my brothers hadn't been playing full-check with Alex and me for years.

This is where I get to beat all the haters who said I couldn't or shouldn't. *I'm* the one in the USA jersey. Adrenaline pumping at full volume, I step onto the ice into a glide.

And belly-flop. Complete with a little shriek on contact.

I fucking forgot to take the guards off my skates.

Face hot enough to melt the ice, I wait for the laughter. At the very least, one of my teammates is going to spray my face with snow or sit on my helmet and fart.

But there's nothing. Dana steps over me like she's never met me and the rest avert their eyes.

Coach Chu is the only one who looks like she wants to laugh, but she presses her lips around her whistle instead, calling us to the center circle. I yank the cloth covers off my blades and fling them onto the bench before hustling to join the team.

Turns out Tiny Sneezer is the fastest skater I've ever been on the ice with, hands softer than a bunny's ears and eyes in the back of her helmet. Silver Sparkles crushes me into the boards on our first drill, giving me a view of next Christmas. Dana and I now have matching calf tats after I stood in front of one of her slap shots.

I'm three strides behind everyone on the drills. I completely whiff on a shot from the point. I'm lost in front of the net, unsure how much pressure I can put on these girls without getting slapped with a penalty. Without Ben's gruff, *Back door, Sammons!* and Liam's distinctive accent guiding me in front of his net, it's all a mess of girls' voices. I don't even recognize my own name when a teammate calls to me. Who the hell is Kylie?

I thought playing with boys was supposed to be harder, but I'm shaking from exhaustion, muscles burning and lungs raw, when we hit the locker room two hours later. I drop my helmet on the floor and spray my face with my water bottle. On either side of me, girls strip off their gear and head for the showers.

Showers. I've never had access to showers at the rink, so I didn't think to bring clean clothes. My sports bra is dripping sweat and my underwear has spent the last two hours wedged.

But even scarier, the showers are one large, tiled room with a bunch of faucets. No curtains, no stalls. I don't even know these girls' names. How am I supposed to soap my armpits (or worse) next to them?

Shrieking laughter comes from the showers. I can't do it. I throw my T-shirt over my sports bra, jam a hat on my sweaty hair, and hang up my jersey.

"The equipment manager will dry your gear and sharpen your skates," Dana says. She's got a towel on her head and is smoothing pink lotion onto her legs. She smells like fruity flowers. Or flowery fruit.

Dry gear, eh? Big-time here. But I hesitate. No one in the world besides Dad has ever sharpened my skates. I'll never get through the week without a cut, though. Not with practices this brutal. I squeeze my skates tight before setting them in my stall, like a toddler who's afraid the laundry will wash all the magic out of her blanket.

At lunch, I can smell myself even over the heavenly tomato sauce aroma of the cafeteria. My sports bra soaks boob outlines onto my gray T-shirt and my forehead tightens with dried sweat. When I'm pretty sure no one's looking, I dip a napkin in my water glass and dab at my face.

How'd it go? Alex wants to know.

I really don't want to tell him.

My roommate is a short blond forward named Naomi—*call me Mimi!*—from hockey hotbed San Diego—*only two hours from where Annie Pankowski grew up!*—and for a weeklong sports camp she brought an entire drugstore aisle of makeup, sprays, and hair power tools.

"You're welcome to borrow anything!" she chirps, as I unpack deo, ChapStick, and shampoo.

"You too," I say automatically. I'm sure she's drooling over my superchic store-brand shampoo.

"We have an hour before weights." Mimi opens her laptop. "*Dancing with the Stars?*"

I squirm uncomfortably from a combination of wet sports bra and the prospect of analyzing celebrity dancers. "I gotta shower."

I take my time, relishing the warm water on my worked muscles and my first quiet moment all day. Then I sit in the hallway to text Alex, who's supposed to be mowing the middle school field, but has sent me half a dozen versions of: *Who do you play for? USA!!*

Reluctantly, I relive the most humiliating moment of my life. *Forgot to take my guards off. Pancaked right in front of the coach.*

Fuuuuuuuuuck

Kill me now

Tell me you at least put the hurt on someone

Yeah. Myself.

My phone is silent for almost a minute and my hand is on the doorknob to reenter Salon Mimi when Alex texts again. *Weights next, right? You're a BEAST in the weight room. You got this, Ky. Hit 'em hard.*

If I can catch them.

St. Cloud's weight room is black and red and spotless. Nothing like Hawk Landing's dusty closet, with sixty years of sweat caked on the bars and the numbers completely worn off the plates so you have to guess their weights. I could get used to this.

I'm an ideal build for defense: five foot ten with the kind of muscles you get from sharing your childhood with two older brothers.

(Okay, five foot eight without skates, but who measures hockey players without skates?) Not only can I keep up in the weight room, I can spot Ben.

Coach Chu circles the room. I rack up a heavy bar for squats, hoping I'm still warm enough from my shower to jump right in. When Coach reaches my station, I shoulder the weight. Beast mode activated.

Coach frowns. "Going out for the O-line?"

I rack the bar before it plummets with my stomach. "Um, no."

She waves the workout sheet. "Did you read this?"

"Yeah. It says squats."

She points to the underlined heading at the top of the page: *Hypertrophy Phase*.

I wilt. "I don't know what that means."

"Then ask before you do something stupid." She pulls off plates, leaving me with a forty-pound bar and a tenner on each side. "We're building muscle, not training power, this time of year."

I complete my three sets of twelve, but the only place I feel the burn is my pride.

My whole career, I've relied on camouflage. Don't look good; make the team look good. Don't focus on lifting; focus on spotting. When you're the girl on a guys' team, you survive by blending in. Suddenly it's stand out or you're on a bus home tomorrow. But the second a spotlight hits me, I screw up. I'm not meant to be in the light.

I'm finally on a level playing field. But it's on top of a mountain.

I lag at the back of our group as we walk to the dorm for the night. Everyone's doing the hockey-is-a-small-world-you-know-her-too game. The only team I've ever played on is the same group of guys who came up from mites with me. I don't know who made triple-A or who's dating who.

Mimi pulls up next to me. "I'm making a snacks run while Kate sets up the Switch." She shakes her hips. "*Dance Dance Revolution,* baby!"

I dance like a hockey player. And I can't lose to these girls, even in a video game. I can't give them any edge over me. "I, uh . . . need to hit the bathroom."

She nods knowingly. "I stashed a team box of tampons in the all-gender."

My cheeks flame. For the last three years I've been hiding tampons in a box of the healthiest granola bars I could find, so none of the guys would be tempted to open it if it fell out of my bag.

Once inside, I hide in a bathroom stall, slumping onto the toilet, my legs finally giving out on me. Hypertrophy phase, my butt. My very sore butt.

My team has moved as a pack since preschool. Practices, road trips, watching NHL in the basement, hitting pucks on the river. I'm just supposed to swap them out for a new pack? One that, after today's practice, shouldn't even want me?

My team may be four hundred miles away, but I let them down today. It won't happen again. I grab my notes on Coach's drills and search for a room that doesn't come with a dance party. The housekeeping supply closet is perfect. Every non-male hockey player feels at home in a broom closet, since that's where we usually dress at the rink. I sit on the concrete floor, leaning against a tower of toilet paper rolls. Thank you, St. Cloud, for splurging on the two-ply.

Coach's drills are brilliant, if more complex than I'm used to. I thought women's hockey would just be hockey with no checking.

But not only did I get my world rocked multiple times today, the game was faster and more skilled than what I'm used to. I study the drills, trying to find spots where I can showcase my strengths.

"Sammons? Everything okay?" Coach. Shit. In the doorway of my hideout.

I jump to my feet, toppling the toilet paper. I hurry to pick up the rolls, so she knows I'm not the kind of person who leaves a mess behind.

She studies the situation with narrowed eyes. "Is this a prank?"

"Oh, gosh, no. No pranks." Although it's a shame to let all this toilet paper go to butt wiping when there's a perfectly good statue of Herb Brooks across campus. Alex would be disappointed in me.

To prove my innocence, I snatch up my notebook and wave it like a white flag. "Just needed a quiet place to study drills." Suddenly I realize this is my chance to explain all of my screwups. "Today was my first day playing girls' hockey. I'm used to playing against guys. It's a different game." And now I'm sport-splaining hockey to an Olympian. Poorly.

Coach meets my eyes. I sweat from every pore I've got. "It's not about who you're playing against, Kylie."

Dad would say the same thing. Keep your eyes on your own paper.

"I know."

"Then show me you know," she says. "And it's five minutes until curfew."

Crap. I drop to my knees, collecting toilet paper rolls. To my surprise, Coach helps restack them, before taking a sheaf of paper towels from a nearby shelf. "Coffee spill," she explains. "Get some rest, Kylie."

The end of her statement hangs out there unsaid. *You're going to need it.*

The defense is working on breaking the puck out of our zone—a perfect opportunity to show Coach Chu I'm focusing on me and not my opponents. Over the years, I've developed this sweet move where I draw the opposing forward in and, at the last second, avoid the check and clear the puck. I have to be quick because it takes me out of position and I can't risk a turnover. Or getting pancaked by a smelly buffalo.

Dana's up first. She demonstrates some sick puck-handling around the forward, then strides into the neutral zone before putting the puck right on her center's tape. Not one defenseman in my league handles the puck that well. Dana's name is gold-plated on the U18 roster.

Mine's in dry-erase marker.

I'm up. I dig the puck out, then pause, waiting for the forward to take the bait. As she nears, I tap the puck off the boards—and she traps it with her hip, drops it to her stick, and steps around me. If I wore a jock, it'd be back in last month where she left me. I'm now stuck standing still, out of position, while she skates in on my goalie.

Fuck fuck FUCK.

These girls are Aston Martins compared to the semitrucks I usually play against. Zero to sixty in mere seconds, lightning-fast reflexes. They're already in the next time zone. And they're not afraid of the spotlight. For ten years, I've made sure I don't stand out. Don't let them look long enough to realize I'm wearing a sports bra instead of a cup.

Desperate, I study Dana on her next turn. Guarding the puck with her body, she steers around the forward and makes the pass high in the zone. So I hunker down over the puck and shuffle through the forward. My center has to sprint to catch my ugly pass. But at least I clear the zone. Coach makes a mark on her clipboard. Most likely buying me a bus ticket home.

When we switch to small-ice games in front of the net, I'm paired with Dana on D, probably so she can cover my sorry ass. The forwards cycle so fast, I get whiplash trying to keep track. When the puck flies into the corner, I chase it down like a tornado is after me. I've got to do *something* right this practice. I've got to get noticed for something other than screwing up. And that something is going to be coming out of this corner with the puck. I dig hard, finally, *finally* victorious in getting the puck on my blade.

The black-jerseyed player battling me suddenly whacks my padded shins with her stick. "What the fuck are you doing?!" she yells into my face mask. I freeze.

It's Dana. I chased my own damn D partner into the corner. And now I've lost the puck to the Red team. I race back to the net, where two forwards are torturing my goalie.

"Body! Body!" Dana orders. I gently lean my shoulder into a forward, hoping it's not too much pressure.

It's not. She spins around me and puts the puck over the goalie's shoulder.

By the time we hit the locker room, I'm shaking so bad they'll feel the aftershocks back in North Dakota. Dana slams her helmet into her stall. I can't look at her. I totally let my D partner down. After this practice, I'd judge Coach if she kept me.

Laughter and thudding post-practice music rattle my nerves. My vision is suspiciously watery and it's not from the wafting hair products. Half-dressed in breezers and skates, I escape to the hallway and slump against the wall. With slow, even breaths of cool rink air, my tear ducts finally get their shit together.

I'm supposed to be focusing on my game, not my opponents.

But this is not my game and I completely suck at it. I don't have what it takes to be here. I should just play boys' hockey until I graduate, then hang up my skates. Retire at eighteen.

I hate my plan.

A crowd of girls exits the locker room and Mimi waves a pair of pink cat-eye sunglasses at me. "I need some sun, or I'm going to start camouflaging into the ice. Want to eat lunch outside?"

I jerk my head toward the locker room. "I gotta shower."

She gives me a smile, but it's brief and I don't think it was real. She disappears quickly with her crew.

In the empty hall, fuchsia toenails appear in front of me.

"It's a damn shame you're one of the best skaters I've played against, because you don't deserve to be here." Dana looks down at me with her arms crossed over her Shattuck hoodie. As if I needed another reminder of what I'm up against. Why would Coach take a kid from Nowhere, North Dakota, when she's got players from the best hockey school in the world?

"Sorry about that goal."

She shrugs. "Just made me look better than you."

She's not wrong.

"Did you bother training for this camp?" Dana asks.

"What the—of course I trained. Five a.m. sessions on the river. Weights. Film."

"You did *not* watch film."

"I did, but I guess North Dakota high school hockey is beneath whatever you watch at Shattuck." I lurch to my feet to avoid looking at her.

She snorts. "You prepped for camp by watching yourself avoid checks and throw away the puck?"

My fists clench, but she's right.

Dana shakes her head. "You've been playing boys' hockey for

what, a dozen varsity games, so playing *girls* should be easy, right? We're all so dainty compared to the pillars of masculinity *you* play against." She leans in. "You play like you have no clue what an elite women's game looks like."

Pretty sure that's an insult, but as she pointed out, I'm too clueless to know for sure.

"You hung me out to dry because you thought if you touched a girl, she'd break."

"I was trying to avoid a penalty!"

Dana shoves me, and I stumble, shocked. With all her weight concentrated into her shoulder, she slams me against the wall, even though I'm still in half pads and she's wearing flip-flops and denim shorts. Fully aware she's got me beat, she shoulders me into the wall one last time before pushing off, leaving me swaying.

"That's not a penalty, that's hockey," she says. "I'll show you a real penalty next practice."

I'm not looking forward to whatever Dana's planning on bringing at practice tomorrow, but at least she tossed me a life preserver while bruising me.

It was such an obvious tip, too. Watch the game you're playing. Duh.

I'm ready to give Mimi my usual brush-off after dinner, but she doesn't even bother to invite me to . . . whatever it is these girls do in our limited free time. I hope whatever Mimi's got planned takes a while, because I need our room to myself.

After making sure Mimi doesn't have any bras laying around, I FaceTime Alex. "Any luck finding game tape?"

"Yup. Worlds last spring. And I brought you an expert at breaking down film." Alex pans my living room so I can see Dad, flanked by my brothers, Connor and Caleb. Shame floods me from my helmet-smooshed hair all the way to my skate bite. My texts to Dad while at camp have been limited to a couple quick thumbs-up emojis between sessions. I'm guessing he wasn't fooled.

"Dad, I'm sorry. I'm totally screwing up, I should've told you."

He steps aside, revealing the TV behind him. There's a game paused, players in white-and-blue jerseys ready to face off against players in red and black. USA vs. Canada—and not the U18s, but the big show. The best players in the world. My brothers are setting up Dad's favorite posi board and his good dry-erase markers. Dad's prepared for battle.

"No. *I'm* sorry, Kyle. I did what worked for your brothers, but your path is different." He speaks to his Bauer sandals. "I kept you here longer than I should've. Didn't want to lose my best D to a girls' team. Guess I like coaching you, too."

I hate seeing him like this, when I'm the one who's messing up. He gave me the best teammates a girl could ask for. I loved every minute of being on his team. "You got me here," I remind him.

He straightens up and uncaps a marker. "Game's not over yet. You may be in sudden-death overtime, but you haven't lost." He gestures to the screen. "Not gonna lie, these women are impressive. But you are, too, kid. You've got all the right skills, we just have to transition you to a new way of using them."

"Can you see okay?" Alex asks, holding his phone up to the screen. It's small, but I can see.

One eye on the TV, one on his board, Dad keeps a running commentary, smearing blue and red ink on his hands as he draws and erases. He's so in the zone, he doesn't realize when he accidentally draws on the TV. Connor gently steers him back to the whiteboard, but Dad doesn't pause in his breakdown of the defensive positioning.

The game is next-level hockey. This is how Dana plays. I thought I needed to learn her moves, but it's deeper than that. I want to play fierce like these women. I want to play a game that *matters* as much as this one clearly does to these athletes.

"Dad," I interrupt. He startles mid-drawing, leaving a blue streak across the neutral zone. I gesture at the screen. "I can't get this good overnight."

He shakes his head. "You're not supposed to be 'this good' yet. You're supposed to *get* there. Coach Chu knows where you came from. She saw something she liked in you."

"Someone who tosses the puck away and avoids checks and doesn't listen—"

"She saw a team player," Alex says. "Someone who hates to leave her goalie out to dry. Someone who does too much in the weight room because she cares about her team and refuses to be the weak link."

"It's easy to be a team player with you guys," I say to Alex. "I don't fit in here."

"You could," he says. "Ky, you deserve a team where you can fully belong."

"Coach Chu saw you as part of this team." Dad jabs at the screen, leaving a red mark on the glass.

And I didn't. I saw me as part of *this* team. The one in Hawk Landing.

Dad motions Connor to hit Play again, but this time we're all silent, watching the game, appreciating it. Despite the long-ass day, adrenaline tingles, waking my body. *Game's not over yet.* I grab a stick from the row along our wall, needing to feel its grip in my hands and the blade grounding me to the floor.

On-screen, Jincy Dunne crashes into a Canadian player along the boards, coming out victorious with the puck. She fires a wicked pass to the tape of Abby Roque, who busts into the zone around a Canadian D. Her shot rebounds, but Hilary Knight somehow gets a miracle one-timer into the back of the net.

I scream, "YESSSSSSSSSSSSSS!" and fling my stick into the air. It lands on Mimi's crowded dresser, breaking a glass-something that hopefully isn't expensive, but I can't tear my eyes away from the replay.

For a split second, I swear I see a blond ponytail the exact shade of mine in the celebration on the ice.

I don't just want to do well at camp or make the U18 team.

I want to play for the United States.

Coach was right. It's not about your opponent. But she didn't mean it was about me, either. My guys will always be my family, but it's time to make new teammates. I take a deep breath, steadying my breakfast plate as I approach the table. Mimi looks up in surprise.

"Is it okay . . . ?" I eye the empty chair.

"That's Kate's," Mimi says, but she stands. "We can make room."

Breathing again, I set my plate down and squeeze a chair in.

I start with Mimi. "I'm sorry, I accidentally broke your perfume bottle last night. I'll replace it." Somehow, she came in and fell asleep while I was brushing my teeth. Or maybe she was faking sleep to avoid me.

"I wondered why the room smelled so nice! No worries."

"Perfume?" Dana looks at me like I wore my helmet to breakfast. Maybe I should have.

"Yeah, I threw a stick." Bracing for a hit, I take the shot. "Got too excited watching Worlds last night."

Dana's eyebrows hit the ceiling. "Reeeeally? Watching Worlds, you say."

"Someone suggested I might have a better appreciation of the game if I actually watched it." I let her enjoy that smug smile on her face. She deserves it. "It was good advice."

"Worlds, which year?" Mimi asks.

"Last year. Knight's rebound."

There's a collective sigh around the table. "Jincy's pass." Dana's eyes are dreamy. "That was so fucking hot."

"We should do a PyeongChang rewatch tonight," Mimi says, and the rest of the table nods enthusiastically. "We'll get the big screen in the common room." She elbows my side. "You in?"

I nod. I am all in.

Dana's roster spot is so locked in that Coach moved her to offense for today's game. Just for fun.

And she's playing against us.

But this isn't about competing against Dana. It's about USA finding the best U18 players in this country. Dana's the best, and I want her on that team. I want us both on that team.

Dana lines up against me. "Ready to go, Kyle?"

My helmet snaps up. "How'd you know they call me Kyle?"

She keeps her eye on the puck in the assistant coach's hand. "Because I was Danny till I got to Shattuck."

All my childhood, I kept my hair short. I disguised my name. I looked like the boys, talked like them, played like them. It's scary to step onto the ice as Kylie. Like playing without pads and a helmet. But there's a place for me in this game.

Dana whacks my shins. "Learn to Skate is in session."

I whack back. *Bring it.*

Coach drops the puck and we fly to the net, a tangled mess of sticks and skates, like fighting Caleb for the best seat on the couch.

"Don't look down, look for the puck," Dana growls. "We women multitask. And you got company, back door." She disappears like a ghost, cycling to another position. I spin to cover the open player in Kate's blind spot—why'd Dana let me know she was there? Coach clearly lined her up against me today; shouldn't she be trying to destroy me?

Coach Chu knows where you came from.

Coach sent Dana to push me.

Dana, who's living proof that a girl can transition from a boys' team to the highest level of women's hockey.

Coach wants me to know I can do it, too.

The next time we go into the corner after the puck, I don't hold back. I'm never holding back again, and if I get a penalty, so be it. Two minutes is better than playing timid. I keep my feet moving, accelerating even as I slam into Dana. The smash of the boards flexing is a satisfying sound, the glass waving in its stays.

There is no whistle. Coach wants to see how I match up against her best player.

The puck is in our feet. Dana digs in, leaning her full weight against me. I shoulder her up the boards, my legs drawing on every repetition I've given the weight room. Puck on my blade, I fight the urge to throw it away. If I lose it, I'll lose it with my feet moving.

How many times did Alex pretend to be our favorite NHLers on the river? *MacKinnon dekes, shoots . . . scores!* I couldn't dream like him back then, but now I know there were players for me to be, too. Channeling Jincy, I puck-handle until my center's feet are moving, and then hit her with the pass.

Breathing hard, Dana cuffs my helmet with her glove. "Just like that. Every shift from here on out."

I won't let her down. I don't let teammates down.

It takes every ounce of concentration I have to stay on Dana—and every bit of muscle glycogen. A downpour of sweat soaks my pads and my muscles burn by the end of the first period, but the ice is coming into sharp focus. I'm putting together all the pieces of hockey and I finally get what it's supposed to look like. What *I'm* supposed to look like out here.

After bonding with my goalie over the best oatmeal toppings at breakfast this morning, I can recognize her voice when she calls to me. The forwards still buzz, but now we're a team against them. I take more chances with the puck, knowing my team will back me up. I even risk a breakaway, trusting Mimi to cover for me. Of course she does—she's my teammate. Maybe I'll take her up on that conditioner offer later.

As I celebrate with my team, Coach nods her approval in my direction.

After the last game, after I brave the shower room, after the impromptu team dance party in the locker room, I pose for a picture with Mimi and Dana in front of Herb's statue. When Kate hands my phone back, the picture shocks me. I don't look out of place at all.

Mimi hugs me before getting into her parents' rental car, promising to call so we can coordinate our room next month. She thinks we need to explore festive lighting options. I'm indifferent on lamps, but I'm looking forward to our calls anyway.

Dana bumps fists with me. Coach wants to see how we play together next camp. Being Dana's D partner will make me the best hockey player I can be. If the twenty-page pre-camp training routine she emailed me doesn't kill me first.

Coach was right, of course. It's not about who you're playing against. It's who you're playing with.

ONE ON ONE

JULIANA GOODMAN

Asha's the kind of girl I normally don't hang out with. We run in different circles. My crew is small. It's just me, Teanne Coleman, known at Camp Arch for eating alone in the mess hall, and for being one of the top high school basketball centers in the state. There was also that time two summers ago when I lied and told everyone Candace Parker was my cousin. Asha's crew are the golden girls at camp. They're all popularity, varsity jackets, pulling girls, and only wearing the newest sneaker drops. Asha wants to go to UNC because that's where her dad used to play. She volunteers at the animal shelter scooping kitty litter and she's part of the Big Sis/Lil Sis program.

At a quarter to seven, I change into my shorts and a black Nike tee. I smooth my hair up into a bun. I look in the mirror and see nothing spectacular. I know I'm not ugly, but I never look as good as I want to when I see her.

When I get to the auxiliary gym, it's empty except for Asha at the far end of the court, doing layups. I watch her for a moment, mesmerized by her muscular legs, her toned arms, her long brown locs swinging from a low ponytail.

She's amazing.

She's rebounding a layup when she finally turns and sees me at the door. She waves me over and I jog awkwardly to her.

"Play me?" she asks, passing me the ball.

I catch it instinctively; these hands are always ready for the rock.

"I mean, shouldn't we talk first?" I ask.

"Talk after," she says, turning away from me.

We play one on one, like we used to do back at school in the early mornings before conditioning. When we're playing on the same team, it's like we have telepathic powers. I can just sense where Asha is on the court, even if I can't see her. I can tell when she's in pain, but too proud to sit out; I can tell when she's going to follow Coach's play or switch it up and try one of her own and get us all in trouble.

But playing against her is like trying to catch a phantom. Every time I think I have her she slips through my fingers, then body-checks me from behind somehow.

After we play, she tosses me a green Gatorade and we sit down on the bleachers. I'm a little annoyed at having lost, even though we only play for fun.

"So wassup with you and Omar?" Asha asks out of nowhere.

I roll my eyes. Omar's just this dude from the boys' camp who says hi to me sometimes in the mess hall. I don't think he actually likes me, just thinks I'm an easy target since nobody else at camp is checking for me. Or so he thinks.

"Why do you even notice stuff like that?" I want to hear Asha say it, just once.

She leans back against the bleachers and rubs her hand over her brown locs. "How could I not notice? Dude be practically drooling when he's looking at you."

"Whatever, he can look at me if he wants. What's the difference? It's not like anyone likes me," I say.

"That's not true," Asha says softly.

"That's how it feels."

"You know it wouldn't work, T. We're on the same team, " she says.

"Just for another year," I point out. I reel my feelings back in; I'm starting to sound like I need her.

"Are you hungry?" she asks.

"What?"

"Are you hungry?" Asha repeats. "If you're not, maybe we could take a walk instead?"

She turns to look at me and of course I nod yes, because it's Asha. With her, it's always yes.

Outside, the air is sweet and thick with the smell of barbecue sauce and something fried from the mess hall. Girls and guys walk by us, some in flip-flops with beach towels wrapped around their shoulders, the dark murky lake water dripping from their hair. A group of girls from the cabin across from mine are sweating and peeling off their scrimmage jerseys. They nod at us and we nod back.

It's not weird for me and Asha to be seen together at camp. Most people stick with the girls from their school, unless they're the only one from their team here, then I guess they just latch on where they can. We don't have to worry about looking like a couple, like my old bunkmate Stacy and her boyfriend Francis, who got kicked out of camp for making out in one of the outdoor showers. The coaches always say we're here to focus on our game, not to make a love connection. But me and Asha were already connected before we got here.

Nobody asks us why we're headed toward the trail in the opposite direction of the main campgrounds. As two of the top players here, everybody expects us to practice harder than normal. It's not unheard of for two insanely dedicated campers to spend dinner hour conditioning.

The soft dirt trail feels like home underneath my feet. Even though the coaches run us ragged every day and according to Daddy he's not working extra shifts at the warehouse for me to come here to have fun, I still do. It feels good to be outside my regular life, even if it's only for a month.

"Man, it's hot," Asha says, her curly sideburns sticking to the sweat on her face.

I kind of want to see if she'd let me hold her hand, but I'd die if she pulled away. My hands go right in the pockets of my shorts, where I know they'll be safe.

The forest of pine trees expands around us, sheltering whatever it is we have going on with their needles. Green lightning bugs flitter near the trees and big white stones line the worn path we follow. We walk in silence until the crash of the waves of Lake Silver echoes through the trees.

Asha and I stand side by side at the edge of the beach, which is mostly mud with aqua-colored pebbles embedded in it. The sun's completely set aside from a thin sliver of red at the horizon. Above us, the moon looks whiter and bigger than it ever does from my window back home.

"I don't want to be a secret anymore, Asha," I say, my eyes glued to the tops of my sneakers. "Either we're gonna be together or we're not. But I'm done doing whatever this is."

Never thought I'd be one to give someone ultimatums. But my older brother Xavier says this is what I have to do if I don't want to end up being just another girl to Asha.

She sucks her teeth. "Come on, you know how I feel about you, Teanne. But we can't be together here, it's against the rules."

"It's not against the rules at school, though. So why do we still have to be a secret there?" I ask.

"Because it just wouldn't work with us being on the same team at school. Like what if we got into it? How am I supposed to focus on the game with you next to me on the court?"

She has a point. But I don't care.

"We never get into it. It would be fine."

"Yet. We haven't gotten into it yet. But as soon as we start putting labels on things, that's when the arguments and the snooping and all the crazy shit comes into play."

"It wouldn't be like that with us. I don't like drama, either."

"Yes, it would. It always ends up like that eventually. I know, I've been in relationships before."

I kick at a stone in the path. "Well then, we may as well just end it now."

"I don't want it to end, though."

"Asha, I'm NOT doing the secret-gf thing—"

"—Wait. Last time we spent the whole hour arguing over bullshit. So before we argue about the same thing, can I kiss you?" Asha asks, moving closer to me.

My heart pounds against my chest and there's a tickle in my stomach. She smells like cocoa butter and bubble gum. She knows I can't resist her.

"Fine, but we're not done talking about this," I say, trying to sound stern but already slowly melting into her arms.

"Yeah, yeah, whatever you say," Asha whispers before pressing her mouth to mine.

"—Watch out!"

We both jump apart to opposite sides of the trail as Morgan Castillo comes barreling down past us. She gives us an irritated look as she passes, her curly black ponytail swinging violent as hell. She's another one of those insanely dedicated campers, but she's nowhere near me and Asha's level. I'm sure it pisses her off.

"Shoulda known she'd be skipping dinner for another workout.

She can run a million miles, but still can't shoot a three for shit," Asha jokes.

"So what do you want to do, Asha?" I ask.

"I want us to be cool. Like we are now."

I shrug. "You know what I mean."

She reaches for my hand and when my fingertips slide against her palm, I start to feel like someone new. Like who I'm supposed to be.

"I do. If we were talking about anything else, the answer would be yes, but we're talking about basketball. That's my career, Teanne. My life."

"It's not your whole life! You do other things! You have a family and friends!"

"They know that basketball is my whole life! They wouldn't ask me to do something they knew might mess it up!"

This . . . isn't how this was supposed to go. I turn away from her.

"Then this is it," I say.

"Okay, if that's what you want," she says. She walks me back to my cabin, but this time she leaves before I can hug her.

After breakfast the next morning, I head to conditioning, where Coach makes me run suicides for being late. Asha's there, too, of course, but I don't look at her. I can't.

All throughout the day, I go the extra mile. Not because I want to. Who the hell wants to run through a hot forest full of flying insects and wiry branches that stick out and scratch your arms? But I feel like I have to show Asha that I'm okay. I want her to believe that I'm fine even though I'm not.

After our evening plank contest around the campfire, I drag

myself inside my cabin and sit down on my bunk. It smells like evergreen and cheap detergent. I'm just about to take my sneakers off when one of my cabinmates hands me a folded-up piece of paper.

"What's this?" I ask, taking it from her.

She shrugs her shoulders like she couldn't care less. "Somebody told me to give it to you."

After she's disappeared into the bathroom, I unfold the note.

::Midnight Cabin 0, A::

It's from Asha. Maybe she's changed her mind after all. Maybe she still cares.

Sneaking out of my cabin that night turns out to be easy. Our cabin leader sleeps with her headphones on. And the other girls are so tired from back-to-back scrimmage games that they sleep so hard they might as well be dead to the world. There's no one awake to notice me as I tiptoe into the bathroom and climb out the frosted window.

Outside, it's dark except for the lights on the front door of each cabin. I duck down until I'm completely surrounded by forest. The trail is lined with the same fluorescent blue pebbles from the beach. They look like gravel during the daytime, but at night, the way they glow and weave in between the trees, it's like a river in the middle of the forest.

Cabin 0 is a run-down cabin that sits off farther into the woods than the other cabins. It's isolated, in its own cocoon of overgrown grass and vines. It's actually kind of pretty in the daylight, but now it looks like some creepy haunted house full of shadows.

Nobody knows what Cabin 0 was used for when it was originally built. Seems kind of weird to have a cabin in the middle of nowhere, like they wanted to punish kids. Some campers say it's where they kept the kids who got sick, or that the owner has a secret twin brother who was deranged and he kept him locked in there.

My sneakers crunch on leaves and twigs as I push my way through the brush. Why the hell would Asha want to meet here? I mean, I guess it's a place we can be alone together and not worry about anyone interrupting us again. But I've already decided I'm not kissing her until she decides she's ready to be official with me.

The door to the cabin is long gone. It's dark inside except for the light of a cell phone on the floor. I walk over to it and just as I'm about to pick it up, another hand reaches out from the shadows.

I look up, and it's not Asha standing in front of me. It's Morgan Castillo. And she's smiling.

"You know, for a minute, I almost thought you might not come," Morgan says. She sets her phone back down on the floor, the white light casting us both in a bright glow. The way it hits underneath Morgan's chin, she looks like Cruella de Vil.

"You wrote that note?" I should have known it wasn't from Asha. She's not the kind of girl to talk about things, she just likes to ignore a problem, which makes me feel even worse because now I know she's not even trying to fix it.

"I did. We have some things to discuss."

"Well, let the extortion begin. What do you want, Morgan?" I ask, already irritated.

"I want you to get Asha to sit out of the tournament. Say she sprained her ankle or something, I don't care."

"What? Why do you even want her to sit out? You guys are on the same team!"

"Everybody knows scouts are coming up for the game and I want them to see *me* play. Not Asha trying to run the show every play. I'll hardly get any time on the court since Coach has her favorites."

I cross my arms and lower my eyes at her. "Does she? Or does she just put the best players on the floor? I can't make Asha do anything. Why are you even asking me?"

"Because Asha's not the listening type. But you are. You can convince her it's the right thing to do." I take that as code that she's afraid Asha would kick her ass if she tried to pull this stunt to her face.

"So you're doing all this because you don't have any confidence in your own game?" I roll my eyes at her.

"Teanne, please. I don't want to have to say the ugly part."

"What's the ugly part?"

She clasps her hands together. "If you don't get Asha to sit out, I'll have to tell Coach what I saw last night near the lake."

"You didn't see anything because we weren't there." It's me and Asha's word against hers. Two against one, we win.

She smiles, and that makes me nervous.

"Remember last summer when Chrissy Matthews got sent home for smuggling beer into camp?"

Of course I remember, it was all everyone talked about last summer. We all heard how Chrissy cried and begged the coaches to believe it wasn't hers and she didn't know how it had gotten in her trunk.

"That was you?" I ask, realization hitting me. "But why? Chrissy wasn't exactly in line for MVP."

"No, but let's just say I had already warned her about messing with me. She didn't think I was serious, either, until that van showed up to take her to the airport. Not to mention, I have this."

She picks her phone up and holds it out to me as a video plays. It's her running with her AirPods and, in the background, a clear-ass view of me and Asha together, looking like two bewildered deer.

Morgan Castillo might be the most diabolical person I've ever spoken to.

"Morgan, come on! Even if I tried, how can I make Asha sit out of the game? Why can't the scouts just see us all? We're all good players!"

"Yeah, but only one point guard is going to play their best game that night and I want to make damn sure it's me. It's only fair, I mean, clearly Asha is more worried about being with you than her game."

I hate the way she says that: "with you," like I'm not somebody, too.

"Fuck you, Morgan."

"Oh yeah? Maybe I should just go and let Coach know right now," she says, walking toward the moss-covered entryway of the cabin.

I stick my arm out and grab on to her wrist.

"Wait! I can get my brother to send me some money," I say, literally pulling anything out of my ass. Because I already know Xavier's not gonna give me a dime.

Morgan sighs and flips her hair away from her collarbone. She's wearing one of those diamond nameplate necklaces everyone has, only hers are probably real diamonds.

"I don't want your money, Teanne."

"Why are you being like this? What did me and Asha ever do to you?" I ask.

"I'm just doing what anyone else would have done if they saw you two. This isn't friendship camp, it's basketball camp, and I plan to win by any means necessary."

"That's not true, everybody else has some fucking integrity and respect. If you worried about yourself as much as you worry about Asha—"

"—I'm NOT worried about Asha. Not this summer. Either she's going to sit out of the game or she'll be banned from Camp Arch. You'll be banned, too. Is that what you really want? Especially with how nuts your dad is. I still remember how he read you to filth after you missed that layup at last year's game."

My face starts to burn. I can still smell his cigarette breath, feel the uncomfortable stares from my coaches, who probably wanted to step in and rescue me, but know better than to interrupt an athlete and their parent, especially after a loss.

"Leave my dad out of this," I warn.

"What do you think he'll say if you get banned from camp? You really don't have a choice, when you think about it."

She's right. I know she is and I hate her for it.

"How am I supposed to get Asha to agree to this? What if she doesn't care if you tell, did you ever think about that?"

"If she won't sit out one little game for you, maybe she doesn't like you as much as you think she does."

"Or maybe you're just trying to break us up because . . . you're jealous!" That must be it, why else would she be this dead set on ruining my summer? Asha and basketball are the only things I have and now I might lose both.

Morgan shakes her head at me, the way people like to do when they know something you don't and want to make you feel stupid.

She turns her phone toward me again and pulls up an Instagram profile full of photos of herself draped around a tall and skinny blond dude.

"His name is Eric," she says, smiling down at her phone. "So nope, definitely not jealous of your . . . relationship, if that's what you like to call it."

Outside, the crunch of twigs and gravel makes us snap our heads up immediately. There's a pale stream of moonlight illuminating a group of boys walking together, the red glow of a joint in one of their hands.

Morgan and I both drop our shoulders and relax. If that had been a coach, we would have really been screwed. Although I'm already screwed, so I guess it wouldn't have made that big of a difference for me, but still.

I have to face reality here: Morgan holds all the cards. And Asha has to sit out.

"I'll talk to her tomorrow, okay?" I tell Morgan.

That night, I try to sleep but I'm too anxious. By the time my eyelids start to feel droopy, the morning trumpets are blaring through the PA system and my cabinmates are up and fighting one another for the bathroom.

I'm still in my clothes from last night, so I swish some Listerine in my mouth and walk over to Asha's cabin. When she comes out ten minutes later, trailing behind her cabinmates, I tiptoe up behind her and tap her on the shoulder.

She turns around and smiles. I nod toward the back of the cabins that face the brush. We're not completely hidden here, but everyone's tired and headed to breakfast in the mess hall.

"I was about to come find you. I thought about it last night and you're right, I was being an asshole. But I missed you," she says, her fingertips gently brushing against the inside of my wrist.

"It's only been a day," I say. No lie, I missed her, too, when I wasn't freaking out about Morgan.

"I know, right? Shit is mad weird." She presses her lips to mine and for one sweet moment, everything is fine. There's no Morgan, no coaches, no camp. Just us.

She pulls away and it's too soon. It's always too soon. But this isn't why I came here.

"Last night, I talked to Morgan. She said if you don't sit out of the game, she'll tell the coaches she saw us together. She caught us on video."

I know she's going to be mad at me. None of this would have happened if I wasn't always trying to get her to do what I want her to do. Our relationship, even in secret, doesn't seem so bad now that we won't be able to have that anymore.

"What?! What'd you say?"

"I didn't know what to say! I just told her I had to talk to you." I can tell that Asha's disappointed I didn't handle her myself. Another reason why I think she wants our relationship to be a secret. I'm not as strong as she is.

Asha starts pacing back and forth, rubbing her hand over her locs. It's what she does whenever she gets worried. Whenever she's trying to figure something out. But she needs to know there's only one solution.

"Hey." I grab on to her arm and she stops pacing. "I told her you wouldn't want to, but she was dead set on telling if you don't. Remember when Chrissy got kicked out last summer with that boy Cade? Morgan set her up. If you play, we'll either get kicked out or . . ."

"Or what?" Asha asks.

I don't want to give her the option. But it's her option. I have to let her choose.

"Or they'll make sure to keep us apart for the rest of the summer."

I close my eyes and wait for what I know is coming. The awful truth I keep trying to run around and forget. She might be okay with being apart for the rest of the summer because she might not really be into me.

The sound of steps on gravel enters my ears and I open my eyes. Asha's already headed back to the mess hall.

"Asha!" I shout, chasing after her. "Wait!"

"What is it now, Teanne?" She shrugs, like I'm annoying her.

"Hello, what are you gonna do about the game?"

"I'm gonna play, duh. Morgan doesn't run me," she says simply.

"But . . ." I can't tell her it's the wrong answer. If it's what she wants, then it's not. But maybe she doesn't get it. "If you play and Morgan tells, we won't be able to see each other like we've been doing."

Asha's eyes never meet mine the whole time I talk. All she says is, "We're here to play basketball. Maybe Morgan's just talking shit and she won't say anything."

"And if she does? Then what, Asha? You're just okay with not talking to me for the next month?"

"It's not up to me, is it? Who's to say that if I play the dummy and sit out, Morgan still won't run and tell? So I may as well do what I want to do. I'll talk to you later, Tea."

She leaves me standing there alone and confused as fuck. Was that the breakup? Can there even be a breakup if we weren't officially together? Maybe Asha's right and Morgan won't tell and none of this will matter. We can keep sneaking out and seeing each other in the forest. Only now I'm not sure I want that anymore. Not if she's willing to risk losing it.

The morning of the tournament, my team is eliminated first. Partly due to me spacing over Asha and freaking out about possibly being banned from camp.

It's not until after our coach has chewed us out for not *playing like we wanted it badly enough* that I see Asha again. Suited up in her green-and-white uniform and matching Foamposites. There's still another twenty minutes before her game starts, but I'm not even gonna hurt my own feelings trying to talk to her right now.

We don't even really have much to talk about at this point. She suited up, she's playing, Morgan's going to expose us to the coaches, and me and Asha will be over. But probably forever this time.

Tears start to burn my eyes and my throat tightens. But I fight the sobs dying to spill out of me, take three slow deep breaths. This isn't the kind of camp where crying is encouraged.

Overhead, gray clouds slide across the sky, covering the sun. The air smells like rain even though it hasn't started yet. I run back to my cabin for a jacket, the Braves High red-and-blue hoodie I borrowed from Asha one night a few weeks ago and never gave back.

I sit down on my bed for a minute. It's quiet in my cabin; everyone's at the tournament. My bed is soft and warm. I could turn out all the lights and just lie here and cry. I probably should do that.

But this might be the last time I get to see Asha before Morgan rats us out. Even if we're not talking, I want her to know I'm there. And after the game, I'll tell her she made the right choice. Even though we like each other, basketball is so much bigger. This is what we've been training at since before we even knew each other. We can't let Morgan win and mess it up for us.

Asha's on fire on the court. The first quarter, she gets fouled and hits both free throws. Then she hits an insane three-pointer. Morgan's sitting at the end of their team bench, seething and probably trying to kill Asha with her mind.

Ten seconds left of the second quarter and Asha suddenly starts limping. She calls a timeout and her teammates help her to the bench.

She doesn't play at all for the second half. Which is so not Asha. One time she played with a broken wrist. The only thing that could keep her off the court is her own death. And even then she'd probably come back as a poltergeist to finish the game.

Morgan steps in as point guard for the rest of the game and she doesn't play better than Asha, but they win the game all the same. After the game, Asha's teammates, minus Morgan, help her to the infirmary. I hang around outside and wait for them to leave and then I go inside the dimly lit cabin where the trainer is wrapping another girl's knee.

Asha's behind a curtain sitting up in a chair, her foot soaking in a bucket of ice water.

"Are you okay?" I ask.

She smiles. "Yeah, I'm fine," she whispers, eyeing the trainer across the room. "I talked to Morgan before the game. Told her I'd let her have the whole second half to herself. She knows half those scouts came to see me anyway."

"That's good, then. We'll get to stay at camp," I say.

But Asha shakes her head. "That's not the only reason why I did it," she whispers, reaching up and sliding her thumb across my bottom lip.

This is the most action we can get right now. Thumb kisses.

I don't press the issue about the girlfriend label. Not right now, when we can't afford to be a couple out in the open anyway.

"So," Asha says, "what are you doing tonight after curfew?"

I smile. "Whatever you're doing."

SAVE THE LEAD

CAM MONTGOMERY

PROFESSIONAL SPORT CLIMB COMMENTATORS

SPORTS NIGHT TONIGHT

That's Yeraldine Ruiz.

That's John Jackson.

And this . . . is Sports Night Tonight.

That's right. Tonight we're talking about the firecracker sport that
will be making its Olympic debut. And—oh! We see here we
have Pilar Abiodun prevailing and she is the winner. Great
times for both of these climbers, with Pilar Abiodun at 5.88 seconds. Beautiful! She gets nearer and nearer to the 15-meter
Speed climb record of 5.28 seconds. And she's really surprising
us here with her progress.

Do you think she'll make her Olympic debut this season?

As a climber who sticks to her style almost exclusively, John, I can't
say I'd place my bets on it. For Abiodun to come anywhere near
the Olympics as anything but a spectator, she'll need to place
at every stage of the World Cup. That's six competitive climbing
tourneys. After which time, she'll need to place in the Finals,
also known as the Qualifiers. All of that is going to require her

to be versatile in her climbing skill and it's going to force her to compete in something other than Lead climbing.

She's the best at what she does, though, we gotta give her that much.

Sure, when that's all she does, she'd better be the best at it.

I'm calling it now, this one's going to surprise us. The one to watch.

Bouldering is for the weak.

The climbers not quite disciplined enough to Lead climb or agile enough to Speed climb. That's my sweet spot, for sure. The Lead climb.

But now I'm out here in this stupid, wannabe-real-type-of-warm Washington sunshine, having my melanin roasted by global warming. And I'm pretty much over it. The new biker shorts are starting to chafe. Nike needs to get it together because some of us have thighs.

"Pilar," Alice snaps. "Are you listening at all?"

No. Not really, no. "I am! I'm just basically falling asleep over here because Bouldering is so dull."

"I'm a Boulderer," Alice deadpans.

"You are, but you *could be* a Leader."

"And deprive the Boulder community of all 'is?" She motions a hand down the length of her entire body, all Vanna White, gifting the world her café au lait. "I think *not*. Plus, you've got the lock on Lead climbing. Djojan doesn't need me."

Djojan. Our coach. He was the almost-very-nearly-great climber of decades past. At my age—eighteen—he'd already met what's now considered qualified status and would have been an Olympic climber if sport climbing had had a place back then.

Sometimes, when I look at him, I see me. I see me because the thing that brought him down was a simple yet faulty draw and even though he shattered nearly every bone in his body on the fall, he keeps going. He still climbs today—just not competitively.

I know I'll be like that. Gods forbid, not injured, but . . . when I am old, like forty, and have been out of the game, I know I'll still be chasing it. Climbing is in my blood. The calluses on my hands, the scrapes on my knees, all the cool muscles in weird places I didn't know climbing required when I first started as a kid—it's all seeped into my skin, my bones, and my marrow. My soul.

Alice turns to me. "Let's get this for the gram." So I turn and pose and smile and smirk in a way that always looks effortless once posted, but in reality never does feel great in the moment.

I know this photo will reach people because Alice and I have accrued followings as the "darlings" of sport climbing.

But on the other side of the follows and the Love reacts and the *STEP ON MY NECK QUEEN* comments (that one in particular usually comes from none other than my fave, Roya, aka @royathedestroya. We once spent an afternoon at the rock wall gym racing Speed climbs and have been friends ever since. She's a badass with a golf club, too.) are the ones that aim only to knock you down a peg. Which is ironic, because climbing is all about holding on.

But Roya's comments commonly go something like—

@royathedestroya: GET ITTT @ricepilar! LEGEND. You're rocking those boots! @JackieA You seen this, Champ? I NEED.

And so it must be said that those comments are worth a whole lot when your social media presence is the size of Texas.

Alice tucks her phone into her belt bag and as we're turning to get started, a group of five people just sort of rush by and between us like we're not even there.

"Fucking Boulderers," she says with an eye roll. It's not the word that's the insult; it's the disgust she layers into her very loud voice as she says it. Which is comical, to be honest. I mean, considering who she is as a climber.

Truth be told, Bouldering isn't the worst. Just close to it, for a Lead climber. It's just not our style. Bouldering is to Lead climbing as cliff diving is to skydiving. Bouldering is basically free climbing. Usually on rock formations that are smaller in size. Mostly, Alice does her Bouldering in the gym, where the artificial rock wall is. No ropes, no harnesses, just vibes.

The intruding group turns. Most of them, anyway.

I curse under my breath as they make their way back over to us.

"Thank you, Alice."

"You're welcome. They'll talk shit and then go. It's fine. Just be cool."

I cross my arms over my chest and Alice slaps at them and stage-whispers, "*I said be cool!*"

So I adjust and place my hands in the back pockets of my shorts, with a cocked hip.

Alice nods in approval just as the first of the Boulder jerks reaches us.

"Aw. This one's cute, Pav. Look at her two little French braids," he says just as Jerk Number Two deigns to acknowledge we exist.

Me. This is about me and I ain't even say anything.

"Go kiss your dusty rocks and leave it alone," I say with a can't-be-bothered swish of my wrist.

Jerk Number Two says, "Pavel," with an outstretched hand.

Alice laughs. "His name is Pavel. What the hell kind of name is Pavel for a Black kid?"

Jerk Number Two drops his hand and says calmly, "My mother is Russian. And it's they/them/their."

The mix of multiple cultures is all over their person. That

much is obvious. The gray eyes, the olive skin, the inky-black curls shoved back behind a headband.

"Okay, Russian Pavel. Well, we're gonna be on our way. Because we actually came here to climb. You know, because Bouldering is a leisurely sort of pastime."

"Definitely a senior citizen kind of activity," Alice adds helpfully. Even though I'm sure insulting her specialty goes against every moral code she's ever stood for.

Pavel nods. Smiles.

I die a little and it's almost like my brain has a mouth of its own, because I hear myself say, "I'm Pilar." And before I know it, I'm shaking hands with this stupid-attractive Boulderer.

"What kind of name is Pilar?" Jerk Number One says in his sad attempt at mocking Alice.

"That's LJ," Pavel says. They're still holding my hand.

"This is my friend Alice. She's a Boulderer, but I don't hold it against her."

Pavel lets go of my hand finally and . . . I die a little. "Let me guess, you're a Lead climber."

"That obvious?"

They shake their head. "No, not at all. You've barely said anything and your personality still seems to yell *Challenge me*, and if that's not a Lead climber's MO, I don't know what is."

"Guilty," I say, knowing full well if my skin wasn't so dark, I'd be blushing.

I preen in this moment. Just for a few seconds as I glance around at this tense little elitist-vs.-lowbrow climbers group. A bunch of skin colors, all of us some dope-ass shade of brown.

Climbing has not historically been open to people of color. It's nice to see that changing.

"Pilar is Spanish," I say. "My mom is from Spain. My dad's Jamaican."

"Explains the hair. The skin."

"The attitude!" LJ yells before Pavel elbows him in the stomach.

"Sorry about him," Pavel says. "Y'all down for a friendly little race?" The smirk in their voice is just . . . well. I die.

Just a little bit more.

WORLD CUP 1 OF 6
MEIRINGEN (SUI)
CLIMB(S): BOULDER, SPEED

Pilar Abiodun stumbles again in the middle section. That's really going to cost her. Abiodun is just one of those climbers people seem to love to critique, and that's primarily because her style is so unconventional when she's performing any climb except her specialty, the Lead climb.

I'll agree with you there, John—she Speed climbs in such a way that requires trust in skill, talent, and capability.

And confidence.

That, too, John. Confidence. And when you're a Lead climber, your focus is on stamina. Your goal is to make it up that wall at a steady pace, but within the allotted six minutes. That cannot be easy. It requires an incredible amount of endurance, strength, and, yes, confidence as well.

Though we do see these young athletes nowadays, and confidence is not at all an issue for them.

Oh, you're referencing Abiodun, specifically.

Yes.

And her "IG," as the youths like to say.

Yes. I'll send it back to Marion Greeley, our Culture and Pop correspondent for more.

PILAR'S JOURNAL

Things Pavel Smith-Borokov has said to me that Make Me Melt:

"Stop staring at me to distract me."

"Keep that sweater I lent you—I like you wearing it."

"The way you blink all chaotic like that and call it a wink—definitely on my long list of favorite things about you."

"I know it's seventy degrees out, but my hand is cold and you should absolutely hold it."

"You make me so nervous."

"You think you let me win that race? Self-delusion is a helluva drug, Abiodun."

WORLD CUP 2 OF 6

NAGANO (JP)

CLIMB(S): BOULDER

Watch the way Borokov climbs, Yeraldine, hands steady even on the Crimps; it's just such a sure hold that stems from raw talent and an amazing amount of practice.

You know, another climber I love to watch navigate holds is Pilar Abiodun.

They're calling her "the Juggernaut."

An appropriate title for one of the brightest and most skilled climbers we've seen in a while.

That's John Jackson.

That's Yeraldine Ruiz.

And this has been Sports Night Tonight, *sponsored by All Most Fresh Foods.*

The morning after I dominate Cup 2, I walk into the gym fresh at the ass-crack of 5:30 a.m.

I have fourteen days before Cup 3. The two-week period between each Cup competition always seems simultaneously way too quick and entirely too far apart. Most especially because the time zones and travel take their pound of flesh upon every departure and arrival.

But at the moment, I'm flying high on whatever drug the body gives off when you're crushing hard on someone.

Also, high on the recent competition win, but . . . priorities.

Now's the time to really get focused, though. Now's the time to prioritize *training*, to buckle down, eat more protein, embrace the utilization of my food scale—a kitchen tool meant to *literally* weigh my food.

A thoughtful gift from Alice two birthdays ago. Never let it be said my best friend doesn't give gifts with meaning. This one was a not-very-subtle finger pointed in my face.

So sweet.

The wall greets me the way it does every morning, a cool fifteen meters of wonder. Forty-five feet of gloriousness. Challenge, indeed.

I smile, not even noticing I'm not the only one in the gym.

"Somebody smiling, and I know it's not because of this new regimen I'm about to smash you with," Djojan says, walking out of his office.

"You know, I'm really not even smiling. This is more of a prolonged mouth twitch."

"Aha," he deadpans. "Who is she?"

"Who says it's a she? Maybe I'm just a happy person. Maybe I date *boys* now."

He chuckles. "So there is *someone*. And I know that last part is bull. So who is it?"

"Their name is Pavel."

With a nod that says everything that I will never be able to deduce, he says, "The Boulderer?"

"You know who they are?"

"I know their coach, yeah. Endy Flynn. Been working with him for about ten years now. I love this for you already. Even if they are a Boulderer."

I nod and file that bit of information away for later. "Me too. I've known them all of, what—four weeks? And I'm ready for marriage."

Djojan sings some song about white dresses and altars and meeting up there. He goes on for a few bars that are surprisingly on point, but he's only getting louder and louder the longer I let him go on and other people are starting to file into the gym now.

"Oh, my God. Shut up! Shut up, *please!*"

With a laugh, he says, "Go warm up, Little Miss Behold-My-Smirking-Wit. Ten laps."

I scoff as he's still humming the song's tune. "Ten? I thought Damian told you to be nicer to me."

"He did. But since when do either of us listen to Damian?"

Djojan's husband, Damian, is the team's PT.

"Get to warming, P."

"I'm going. I'm going. But stop singing."

He does not stop singing. He gets louder. He adds a falsetto.

I take off to stretch and I smile and I run my laps and I start to hum right along with him as I go.

WORLD CUP 3 OF 6
LOS ANGELES (USA)
CLIMB(S): SPEED

John and Yeraldine here today, and we've got both climbers on the way now, Pilar Abiodun absolutely flying. With Alice Wesley on the left, Abiodun on the right, it's all about speed now—both off to a blisteringly quick start. And while Speed climbing is one of Wesley's two specialties, it's not Abiodun's. And that much is obvious, John.

Yeah, we do see that quite clearly, but she's working hard for it today.

Here at the Climbers' World Cup series, both Abiodun and Wesley will need nigh perfect scores to advance to Cup 4 held next month.

The IFSC World Cup 4 of 6 will be sponsored by Retrograde Energy, the only energy drink that will have you floating into the universe.

Truly a fabulous beverage.

Chaotic in the best way.

Right. So that advancement will put both these young climbers one step closer to qualifying for their debut Olympic runs.

They'll have to score high all the way through Cup 6 first and then place, or "medal" for the final.

I'm on the edge of my seat, John.

I can see that! You're not alone there, Yeraldine.

"This blue is garish," I say as I slather the metallic nail polish onto Pavel's left hand. "Should have just stuck with all black."

"Except I'm not Pete freaking Wentz, so."

I giggle. I do a lot of that now, apparently. "Black nails are not exclusive to the emo populace. The gray could have been cool. Or the purple."

"Talk about garish."

"That's Alice's polish," I say.

With a solemn nod, they intone, with a *tsk-tsk*, "I know. She said she got it from the Land of the Great Unwashed."

"The swap meet and its shoppers are perfectly sanitary."

"Not the ones Alice goes to."

Fair enough. "Okay. There." I blow on their nails and then place a soft kiss on the back of Pav's hand.

As I lift my head, they surprise me and kiss me quick, the hard, now-familiar press of their lips to mine.

"Any word from your mom?" I say.

"Yeah, she's found a condo. One of the nicer neighborhoods in Moscow. It happened so fast, apparently she's really getting things off the ground over there."

We cap all the open bottles of nail polish, balanced precariously on uneven surfaces and the carpet in my bedroom. "That's good, right? That she found a place."

"Yeah. I hoped it might take a little longer, though. She'll get things set up over there and come back in a few weeks to pack up."

"We should FaceTime her so we can see it."

Pavel nods and it's the saddest droop of the neck. Their parents have finalized a long overdue divorce. But it means Pavel's mother, Mika, has decided to move home to Russia. Pav decided to stay here with their dad. To stay with me and their coach Endy and the climb.

I never bothered to dig deep on it. To excavate all their feelings, top to bottom. I'm happy, so I assume they'll tell me about it when they're ready. And I selfishly don't want to know their answer to the question. I know it could go either way. Climbing isn't a lifestyle for Pavel. They're good at it, naturally. For me, it's what I eat, sleep, and breathe.

I could never leave this behind. I think, for Pav, they might just.

WORLD CUP 4 OF 6
SEOUL (KOR)
CLIMB(S): BOULDER, LEAD

For Pilar Abiodun to have performed so well at this fourth install-
ment World Cup is not unexpected. We've seen her discuss her
training and it's clear she's the one to watch.

Well, at this point, who isn't watching the real-life romance be-
tween Pilar and Pavel? What do they call them—

P-Squared.

P-Squared. That's cute. Pavel Smith-Borokov keeps a much lower
profile and I wonder if that's why their performance remains
consistent while Abiodun has a series of massive highs and epic
lows on her record.

I'm trying not to laugh, but maybe she's more socialite than athlete.

I'm John Jackson and that's Yeraldine Ruiz—we're your All
Things Sports correspondents—and you're watching ATSN.
Now, let's throw it back to the studio, where our Culture and
Pop team will break down the styling and somewhat concerning
outfit choices Pilar Abiodun has made.

"You're supposed to twist left and under," I say. I'm right about this. I'm sure I am.

"No, because you did that the last time and we ended up right back to the beginning of the knot."

I hate TikTok sometimes. This trend of untangling two ropes that have been twined together. Without letting go of the ends of your rope. It's impossible.

Plus, the last video I got felt so bittersweet. One of me lip-synching Demi Lovato's "Give Your Heart a Break."

The video's caption is *Oh, so you're a competitive rock climber, you must be so good.* And the video is just a series of clips of me falling after some unsuccessful reaches.

The Likes are nice, but sometimes I feel the self-deprecation part of it is required. People, fans, supporters—they expect humility out of their female and femme athletes. Especially the ones of us with a bit of a tint to our skin.

At random, on a strike of inspiration, I shove my legs up and around one side of the knot, knee Pavel in the neck somehow, and . . . end up with our ropes even more tangled and my arms crisscrossed over each other.

There's no way this has a way. I have yet to watch any couple's TikTok show how they solved this.

"There's no way," Pavel says.

"I was about to say that! Do we . . . give up?"

I really don't want to give up.

"Let's try what you did one more time. With my neck not in your path of destruction."

I laugh and they mutter with a roll of their eyes, "Date a tall girl, they said. It'll be fun, they said."

But we do exactly what they proposed and we untangle it. And I can't help it: I scream and laugh and jump them.

We caption the video with *WE DID IT! <3 @PavSmiKov*

♥: 903.6K

COMMENTS: 9,624

SHARES: 4,807

"Hey TikTok, today I wanted to just share some climbing tools and terms with you guys. Today's climbing term is: *stick clip*. This can be used to clip your quickdraw and rope to a bolt outside. This'd help protect you from falls on rocky terrain, because outdoor bolts tend to be higher up and way farther apart than they are in a typical climbing gym. Just make sure you're putting your rope into the draw correctly so that you're not backclipped. Like and follow for part two!"

"I'm not even sure why you post those kinds of videos. Only like 8 percent of your followers actually like them," Alice says.

Her stats are probably off just a tiny bit, but she's not entirely wrong. The educational videos don't garner nearly as much attention as my climbing wipeouts or videos I do with Pav or the one I posted last night of me and Alice campusing at the Boulder walls. And then a few seconds of us using dynamic power moves here and there.

They seem to enjoy those, too. Probably because campusing in particular seems harder than it is. It requires a lot of upper body strength to climb with no feet to help your momentum, but when you work out six days a week, for two to three hours a day, you build that kind of strength pretty quickly. Really, it's no harder than goofing around on the monkey bars.

"I post those learn-a-term videos because I think there actually is a small amount of my followers who are beginners and need to learn them somewhere."

"They'll learn them the same way we did."

I throw my gym bag into Alice's back seat as she starts the car to drop me off home.

"How? You think they got a Djojan who's gonna beat them with a dictionary of climbers' terminology, too?"

"No one else has a Djojan," Alice says. The affection is there. We both have it. All of Djojan's athletes do. He's part of why we keep doing this climbing thing when the criticism gets a little too handsy with us.

He's a built-in support system with an affinity for any and every musical. Ever. Like, he saw the SpongeBob musical on Broadway. He collects Broadway experiences like he's collecting Pokémon.

Gotta catch 'em all!

WORLD CUP 5 OF 6
BALI (INA)
CLIMB(S): LEAD

Really nicely done there, a smooth grab by Abiodun. Very quick adjustments we see here, with her body positions. And now she just needs to do that pistol squat to get up there, nice heel hook with her right foot to get up top very quickly. An excellent run for Pilar Abiodun, all smiles as she makes her way down to her coach, famed ex-climber Djojan Tarlowe, and her partner, notably famous Boulderer, Pavel Smith-Borokov, who didn't quite make it to this round of the Cup.

They seem to be greatly supportive—ah, look, see there. Congratulations and total respect, one athlete to the other.

Pav: hey, can I come over tonight? Just for a little bit.

Pilar: yeah duh of course, but I just saw you this morning pav, I'm getting sick of you already

Pav: cute. I'm omw

I'm organizing and adding to a giant box made up of all the Leads I've ever owned. Even the broken ones. They're no good, not even worth finding someone to fix them. But I can't bring myself to throw them away. I can remember the day each of them broke and how, and the fall that came after or the competition I bombed because of it.

They all mean something and no one, not Djojan, not Alice, and not even Pavel, knows I keep them. And most especially, the internet doesn't know about them. Because how very dare I, a professional athlete, be sentimental—*emotional*—about anything.

Pavel walks through my bedroom door not long after I slide the box onto the very highest shelf in the very darkest corner of my closet.

My entire chest lights up—even as I joked about having seen them earlier in the day. The hug I give is tight and big like all of our hugs are, but the one they return isn't. Maybe they're sore from a long day of climbing. It happens. I let go of them sooner than I want to, not wanting to make the soreness worse, taking their hands into mine.

I smile. "Couldn't get enough, huh?"

"Cute."

"You may have mentioned that fact about me, yes."

As I turn and sit cross-legged on my bed, it occurs to me Pavel has barely passed the threshold of the door.

"What's up, Pav? Come here."

They do, but.

So far away still.

"What?" I ask. The feeling in my gut is heavy now, having totally eclipsed the lightness in my chest.

"Pav!" I say when, still, they say nothing. My outburst prompts them to move closer, but they don't sit on the bed with me.

They take a shuddering breath. "I'm leaving."

"I—wait, what? You . . . just got here."

"No, Pilar. I'm *leaving*."

And then it dawns on me. They're *leaving*. Their mom has been in the process of moving home to Russia, post-divorce. She was going to go alone, given she's already got family there. Pav was going to stay with their dad.

"You're—why?"

Don't cry, Pilar. Don't cry don't cry don't cry.

"It's been hard. For her. She was hiding it, I think. But she's having a hard time with the relocation and getting settled and now Moscow might not be a possibility, which means she might be headed farther away from the small bit of family that does still speak to her, to Saint Petersburg. I kind of thought our family in Russia was okay with my mom's choices. With my dad. And me. And they are. But not so much that they'll help Mom through this part. So. She needs me, P. My mom needs me and there's nothing I wouldn't do for her, you know that."

"Yeah," I whisper. I don't want to give them my voice. A whisper is all they get to have now. I want to be so selfish about all of this right now and I understand that's not supercool, but I feel exposed and gutted and wrong all over.

I want to beg them to stay. But this is not a decision Pavel has made lightly. Because of *all* the places to relocate as a Black nonbinary person . . . no. It's more likely they've been thinking about it for a while. Weighing the pros and cons.

I wonder which I am.

Pro: Get to stay with Pilar.

Con: Don't get to stay with Pilar.

They essentially mean the same thing, but they also kind of don't.

I cry anyway, despite the lockdown I tried to throw on these tears.

Angrily, I swipe one away. "I mean, there's not really anything I can say, is there. You decided you're leaving. And what kind of selfish asshole makes you choose between your girlfriend and your mom."

Me. I do.

"God, Pilar. I want to apologize, but I don't know if that would make things worse."

"Jesus, do *not* apologize to me."

They shove both hands into the pockets of their jeans. I love those jeans on them. I've said so, often. Black and well cut with a rip in the knee that happened, ironically, naturally.

"I want to. Because if it were me, I'd be demanding it, probably."

They wouldn't. They're too kind for that.

Pavel exhales long. "It's, um . . . it's not forever, okay? I'm not going to be there forever."

I laugh. "Okay. But it's not like you can give me a timeline, a calendar, and a Sharpie to draw an X through the days as they pass."

"Pilar," they say. It's their *be reasonable* voice. I love that voice on them, too. The quiet growl that happens so rarely.

I love everything on them.

I love them.

"When? When do you go?"

"Tomorrow night."

A ridiculous sob tumbles out of me and they finally move in quickly and hug me the way we should have done when they first got here.

I have a million emotions chewing on me.

After only the briefest hesitation, I hug them back, just as they move one hand up my back, the back of my neck, and then into my French braids.

I love those calluses on their hands.

"We'll talk all the time. Every day, all day. We'll FaceTime and I'll never stop DMing you TikToks. Not even death could stop that."

I laugh because . . . because it's Pavel.

But then they pull back. "I'm not asking you to wait. I would never ask you to do that."

Of course not. Because it's Pavel.

"I would," I say. "I will, if you'll let me."

"I . . . don't know. I don't know if that's fair to you."

I can't do this.

"So this is, like, what? The breakup talk?"

"This is the I'll-see-you-soon talk. This is the you'll-do-great talk. This is the I-love-you talk."

I die a little inside.

With their rough hands cupping my face, they bring us together for the softest press of lips. I shake, doing my best not to ruin this moment. What I know will be our last for a while.

Soon, the kiss turns from a mild rain to a tempest. The storm is all gnashing teeth on my insides and I pull Pavel as close as I can get them, breathing them in, memorizing every detail of this beautiful human who tumbled into my life like a rockslide.

Just before they pull back, I feel the sting of their bite on my bottom lip, then a soft suck to soothe.

And that is exactly my Pav.

BOULDERING WORLD CUP FINALS W1
WORLD CUP 6 OF 6
MOSCOW (RUS)
CLIMB(S): BOULDER, LEAD

I'm Yeraldine.

And I'm John.

And you're joining us for Sports Night Tonight *as we continue our coverage of the Climbers' World Cup.*

That's right. Now today we're joined by a celebrity power lifter known colloquially as "the Boulder."

A fitting guest host, considering the moniker.

Yes. Mr. Boulder—

You can just call me Gary.

Yeraldine, it seems I've an invitation to call him by his given name.
    Too, too kind, Gary. So, Gary, you're a power lifter. That's weights and strength training. And, though your name may be relevant, we're talking two different sports here, are we not?

Exactly—

Love that Jersey accent, John, don't you?

Mm-hmm.

Thank you, born and raised, y'know?

John, forgive me for asking, but, Gary—we must know, any interest in taking up rock climbing for yourself?

Rock climbing is a sport for skinny dudes who secretly wanna die 'cause they just can't get big. If I did thousands of pull-ups day

in, day out and had nothin' to show for it, except a hundred
fifty pounds of sinew, freakishly strong fingers, and the ability to
climb things that they invented stairs for, then I, too, would have
my go at this typa Russian roulette.

. . . Oh.

. . . Well, John, I think we're all going to need to sit with that one
for a while.

Speaking of—we're broadcasting here in Moscow and after this
plan to enjoy a nice tumbler of Ruble vodka from our friends
and sponsors at Ruble Vodka, Inc.

Ruble vodka, the system reset for you.

Well said, John. More from us and Mr. Gary Boulder in just a
moment as our climbers get prepared and chalked. First up,
Pilar Abiodun, USA. For now, back to you guys in the studio.

I exhale slowly and everything mutes. Everything slows. My heart
rate, the quivering muscles in my back, the static chatter of the
crowd. From where I'm looking, I've got about eighteen to twenty
more feet of wall to climb in maybe ninety seconds.

I wish I'd slept last night. I wish I'd not spent hours and hours
watching the ticking of my clock cued to Russian time zones go by,
like I have for weeks now. I wish I hadn't dropped my chalk bag
within the first minute of this stupid six-minute climb.

I wish I hadn't flubbed the Boulder piece by falling and then
crying as I walked to Djoj.

Forty-nine feet total. It's one of the bigger walls for competition. They don't exceed that, but what I'm used to—what my body
is used to—is about five to seven feet less than this.

Sweat drips off my nose and I wonder for a second what it will
look like as it hits the ground.

I can't do this.

I can't do this.

I cannot do this.

But I do it. By the skin of my teeth, I make it through the sixth World Cup Sport Climbing Competition, to the Qualifier, which is awaiting me three months from now, and it feels awful.

Pavel isn't here.

OLYMPIC QUALIFIERS
MOSCOW (RUS)
CLIMB(S): LEAD, SPEED, BOULDER

The first time, ever, in my life that I find myself mentioned in an actual print newspaper, one that's *kind of* a big deal—the *Seattle flippin' Times*, bruh—it's to talk about how sad I look while walking down the street.

A major publication! And they're not wrong.

"This picture," Alice says, pointing. "This picture isn't that bad."

"I am holding three chocolate chip cookies in one hand and a McDonald's ice cream cone in the other. The only piece of that they're seeing is that, supposedly, I don't care about my body."

"You don't."

"No, I do not. But that's not important. I made it to the Finals! To Qualifiers!"

This career high is essentially what I've been working toward.

This part right here was *The Goal.* Qualifiers. Because saying, *I almost made it to the Olympics* is vastly different from *I made it to the Olympics.*

And, as always, I keep in mind that this part does not define me. Winning here, qualifying . . . does not define me. But I can feel the nerves in my stomach. In my legs and my spine and my back, where most of a climber's power lies.

There is no guarantee I'll make it here. But I want to. Without

Pav, it rings . . . not quite *hollow*, but it does ring *different*. I guess the task at hand is figuring out how to be okay with any outcome.

Alice nods with every last ounce of authority she's got. "Precisely. You made it, P. That's not nothing."

It feels like nothing.

Climbing has never let me down before. It's always been the solution for me. I wish I could get back to the version of me that loved it with her whole chest.

I'm trying so hard to pick it up. To not be sad all the time, to not be this person. To be the athlete people *expect* me to be. One who is just fine so long as I have my sport.

I open the newspaper again and spot Roya kicking ass, too. She's smiling huge, a golf club in hand.

Love that for her.

"You are large," Alice says. "You contain multitudes."

It's like she's reading my mind. But honestly, she knows how this goes, too. Alice is fairly androgyne by choice, but the media doesn't make it a point to dismiss your gender unless you take them by the throat and make them do it.

Like Pav did. They've been an excellent advocate for nonbinary athletes since their start with such fierceness. Such adorable excitement and enjoyment.

And I do love where I'm at. I kicked ass and took names to get here. I worked hard *and I chose this* for me. With every reach and every step and every grab I made for the next rung on this ladder, I chose me. I chose this.

"We gotta get changed and get out there to warm up." Alice stands and reaches down to grab me by the hands and off the floor.

There's maybe thirty seconds where we execute this egregiously long and obnoxious secret handshake we made up years ago. It's tradition, though. It matters.

Sometimes, heartbreak makes scaling a forty-nine-foot wall *kiiiiinda* difficult.

I will never be able to get the crispness of the air, the static chatter of athletes milling around, the booming voice coming out of the overhead speaker in violent, vibrant Russian, out of my head.

This competition will decide whether or not I—Pilar Abiodun—am competing in the *fatherflippin' Olympics.*

I walk up to the wall, chalk my hands, and figure out how I'm gonna approach it, how I'm gonna need at least two power moves to start this Lead climb.

Good thing they're my specialty.

I don't falter even once as I begin. But then, instead of going calm and light, I get in my head. Thinking how great it would be if they were here. How they've gone all but silent even though they've only been gone for a month and some change. How our communication already feels like it's dying out. How, even though I'm here in Russia, they never promised they'd come see me compete.

And I'm so stuck, so stalled out, losing valuable seconds in this six-minute allotment of time I have to scale this massive bitch, that I find myself remembering one of Pav's last emails to me from two weeks ago.

You do this. And you do it well. You're excellent at what you do and you love to do it. Feel your feelings. Hold them inside you and use them to channel the power in your lats, the push in your forearms, the pull in your calves. You do this. You love it. You do it like no one else can.

One to watch.

The Juggernaut.

No one has a hand on this over you. No-goddamn-body.

FIRST ATTEMPT

Here is the first climb for the women. You can see here that Pilar Abiodun has already started her climb . . . a little bit harsher than the other girls where she has to put in more energy, and her elbow is a bit strained we can see there as she goes for that first dynamic movement—ah! And a miss. She was so close there and just barely misses.

SECOND ATTEMPT

Okay, we have Pilar Abiodun of Seattle, Washington, climbing her second attempt at this Problem today. Struggling with this first part again as she just did with her first attempt.

I'd say that's largely just confidence that hasn't set in for her.

Or maybe a bit of competitor's focus lost, given her personal life right now.

Well, we know Abiodun's strengths lie in Lead climbing.

Yes, and selfies, apparently.

Mm. She's a wildly technical climber, but her skill set is such that she's versatile. And that flag there—those seem to help her immensely.

They do, Yeraldine. And after this rough start, she seems to be moving well with almost no energy lost.

She's changed her strategy. A wise choice on her part.

Deciding to go for a toe hook while grabbing that volume, which has made this climb so much more stable for her.

Absolutely.

We've seen her struggle through similar Problems at previous competitions, where she just didn't seem to understand the Beta at the beginning and everything else is thrown off from there.

She's learned not to waste a ton of energy and that has saved her a few times. As it will here.

Another brilliant show—and more than a little awe-inspiring to watch—from Pilar Abiodun. Top: 1, Zone: 1, Top Attempts: 2.

He's John.

And she's Yeraldine.

And this is All Things Sports Network at the Climbers' National Qualifiers, sponsored by Retrograde Energy.

TIKTOK COMMENTS:

wonder if pilar was at a disadvantage because the other climbers discussed the problem in Russian

nah, she beats out angel varoquez in the end so I honestly think the first climb was just not her best send.

Pretty clear this problem is outside her comfort zone

Sure asf didn't stop her tho

idk how the hell i ended up on Bouldering tiktok

welcome to the dark and dusty side!

Love this video. I'm newer to climbing so it helps to see badass climbers like her struggle sometimes too.

Coming down off the second attempt is this whole roiling mix of swallowing Pop Rocks and Cool Whip you've left in the sun for too long at the cookout.

It's chaos. But in a good way until you pause, and then suddenly it loses some of its shine.

Why haven't they answered any of my messages?

Why did I get my hopes up that they might be here?

Why did *every day, all day* so quickly become *once every few days, maybe.*

After I meet with Djojan, hug him, high-five Damian, hip-bump Alice, and wave at my parents in the stands, I head into the section cordoned off to serve as something of a women's locker room. Which is what the sign above it says, even though I'm pretty sure it's just the remnants of a deconstructed preschool. The toilets are aggressively low.

I'm splashing water on my face, going over every way I could have attempted that Problem and not messed it up the first time, and the way some of my dynamic power moves made me feel like I was Miles Morales.

"What's so funny?" Pavel says.

"I was out there feeling like Spider-Ma—" Wait. What?

I'm in their arms before I've even fully turned around to face them. Shaking, crying, and I think laughing a little hysterically, I wrap my arms around them and squeeze and squeeze and hold tight as I can.

"You kicked ass out there," they whisper.

"I overthought that first attempt, what are you doing here, oh, my God."

With a rasping laugh, their lips pressed to my ear, they say, "I live here."

I pull back. Only just a little. "Russia is a big place. You do not live *here* in Moscow."

"This is true," they say.

"Pav!" I kiss their face, both eyes, their lips. "You live seven hours away from here."

"This is also true."

I breathe and admit slowly, "I thought I lost you." And I just have to laugh because it's so dramatic. But I love them. And they inspire me and encourage me and challenge me and I've decided I'd like to hold on to some of that. I've decided *it is okay if I want that*, but also that I can succeed and do big things without it, too.

My life feels so rich with the combination of Pavel and climbing and my family and Alice and Djoj's less-than-funny jokes.

My life feels full. Especially as I feel Pavel place a Lead in my hand. A broken Lead.

I know it as one of theirs. I also know, without a doubt, it is from the day we met.

"I'm sorry it's been radio silence. Getting settled in this country has been . . . a trip, to say the least. Things—time—it all kinda ran away from me. But Pilar, I saw. Today, I saw the moment you decided you were going to trust yourself and do things your way with that second attempt."

I nod. Because I did. Suddenly the voices and the gossip and the comments and Likes and ridiculous opinions about how sad I look with cookies—it all went away.

What I had left was me and the Problem in front of me.

What *is left* is me knowing even though Pav will always find me, through landslides and the dust and the dirt and the gravel, I alone get myself up that wall.

What's left is knowing I'm the One to Watch.

What's left is knowing I will always have the climb.

VOLLEY GIRL

DAHLIA ADLER

I can't believe I'm going to miss the smell of spicy fries. There are days I take two showers—one to wash off the sweat from a day spent teaching kids volleyball, and one to wash off the smell of grease from these very fries—and yet. When I am 120 years old and lying on my deathbed, I am either still going to smell like Camp Ilan canteen spicy fries or wish I did.

I mean, they *are* good, and by the time I hit up the canteen at night, I'm hungry enough to devour them even if they weren't. Camp Ilan is big on sports—bigger than pretty much all the other Modern Orthodox Jewish sleepaway camps—and between 9:00 a.m. and 5:00 p.m. I show almost a hundred kids how to serve, bump, set, and spike on a near-daily basis. (Well, except the youngest kids, who play Newcomb instead. There's not a lot to teach when the entire game is throwing and catching over a volleyball net, but *definitely* a lot of *Shira didn't hit you on purpose, Zoe*, and *We're gonna give Rachel one more chance, because the sun was in her eyes* on top of judgments about whether or not a ball hit the net, was in bounds, has enough air, was too wet from landing in that puddle, et-cet-er-a.)

The most important thing about spicy fries, and the accompanying smell, is that they mean that I am firmly among people my own age. The canteen only makes and serves them at night, which means strictly to staff, i.e., those of us recovering from a whole day of wrangling children all over the age and energy-level spectra.

When I enter tonight, the rest of the girls' sports staff is already there, crowded around a table dotted with bags of chips, paper boats of fries and mozzarella sticks, and bottles of water. I slide in, tapping Yael Ruben's hip with mine to nudge her over and getting a mouthful of long brown curls in the process. "We were just starting to worry about you, Azi Bean," she says as she sweeps her mass of hair over her other shoulder, promptly hitting Zeva Oppenheimer in the face and nearly knocking off her glasses. "Thought maybe you were still practicing that serve."

"Ha ha." Okay, so I've been a little hyperfocused on perfecting my jump serve. But in my defense, with high school now behind me and camp about to follow, my volleyball-playing days are numbered. If I don't nail it now, I don't know when I'll get another chance to try. Still, with four days left in the summer, I certainly wouldn't miss one of the last chances to hang out with my friends. "I went back to the courts to help Naomi clean up."

"You really don't need to kiss her butt," says Zeva, dragging a mozzarella stick through a blob of ketchup squeezed into the corner of one of those red-and-white paper boats. "It's not like she's going to replace you for next year."

"You're basically the one person she's *doesn't* have to replace," Michal Liebovitz adds, and it feels like she's rubbing spicy fries into my skinned knees.

I don't need a reminder that none of them are planning to return, that none of them want to come back from seminary or freshman year to still be making almost no money at a job that doesn't have a thing to do with any of our academic or professional futures. Even Michal, who runs basketball and is so in demand for private lessons that she's probably taking home five times what I am, has no plans to even try out in college.

Still, I can't let go. Not before I have to.

So why can everyone else?

"I'm not kissing her butt. I'm being helpful because the rest of you are deadbeats. Seriously, the courts were a mess."

"Don't look at me." Rachel Glaser runs her omnipresent Sharpie through her fingers at a speed that shouldn't be humanly possible. "My tweens begged to use the hopper to pick up all the tennis balls at the end of the day."

"This might shock you, Rach, but a bunch of eleven-year-olds did not do a stellar cleanup job. And just for that, I'm taking a mozzarella stick as commission." She doesn't stop me, but it's so greasy and good I may need to go get my own order of them anyway.

"I really don't think that's what commission is," says Yael. She takes a long, noisy drink from her can of Diet Dr Pepper, shakes it to confirm its emptiness, then fiddles back and forth with the top, muttering under her breath until she finally yanks it off.

"Lemme guess." Jordana Weissberg smirks. "An *R*? Again?"

"How'd you know?" Yael flutters her lashes, long and dark like the curls that hang almost down to her butt.

"I don't think you get to lecture me on things that make sense when you still play that ridiculous game," I point out as Yael slips the top into the pocket of her jeans. "I'm pretty sure you can't *actually* predict the name of your future husband by reciting the alphabet at a soda can, and if you could, I don't think cheating to make sure you land on *Ronen* would, you know, work."

"You find your bashert your way, and I'll find my bashert my way," she says coolly, patting her pocket. She plucks the marker from Rachel's fingers and uncaps it, all of us knowing what she's going to do before she even scrawls her fifty-millionth heart on the glossy wooden canteen table and puts her initials right over those of her crush of a million years.

There's nothing illicit about writing on this furniture; it's all absolutely covered in at least a decade's worth of similar hearts, song lyrics, idly drawn band logos, and stuff like *So-and-so was here in '16*. I have a little corner on one of the walls by the service window where I write *Azi Bean* followed by the year every single June, and at this point, it's quite the column—2013 right up through 2023, with a sad little gap for 2020, when the camp was closed for COVID.

I don't know what's worse—that next year will be my last time writing it, that no one who traditionally documents me doing it with a picture (usually Jordana or Zeva) will be there with camera phone in hand next year, or that it's a nickname everyone here recognizes instantly but will mean absolutely nothing to people in the future who have no idea a Camp Ilan lifer named Azriella Bienenfeld once existed.

Or maybe it's that none of that matters, because the only mark I'm leaving behind is one showing me all by myself.

Packing to come to camp is stressful—am I bringing the right stuff for everything from waking up at dawn to sing the national anthem at the flag to sweltering-hot days playing sports in the sun to Shabbos clothes for every Friday night and Saturday?—but packing to go home is so much worse. How many pairs of socks have I lost to the communal washing machines? Do I save every single Shabbatogram or just the ones that say more than the baseline *Have a great Shabbos! Love,* [insert name of friend who sends them to literally everyone every week, because the brightly colored paper greeting cards are three for a quarter so why not]? My mom, who was also a lifer at Camp Ilan, tells me I don't know how good I have it, because in her day they didn't have email or ebooks and they listened to music on CDs (which she's shown me, but I cannot believe are real), and blah-blah so many things taking up so much space. But I know for a fact she keeps a box of all those old handwritten letters in the attic, so I take her complaints with a grain of salt.

I wasn't planning on spending the morning packing, but it's raining outside—our third-to-last day and it's freaking *raining*—so there's not much else to do while the schedule shifts around to accommodate it, meaning all sports are cut for the first period of the day.

The phone rings as I'm trying to decide whether the T-shirt I just found behind my cubby is worth bringing home or bound for the trash. Naomi doesn't bother with opening pleasantries; no one else would be calling the sports staff room at this hour. "Azi and Michal, you've each got half the new gym for volleyball and basketball. Zeva, you're in the binyan for GaGa; Yael, you're in the old gym for BBK; and Rachel and Jordana, you're in the bayit for machanayim. Meet up in the lounge when you're done."

Michal and I groan simultaneously, both of us knowing full well that we're in for an annoying hour of balls flying everywhere. Yael's delighted; she's new to the world of Jewish summer camp, and still thinks that BBK—a mash-up of kickball and basketball—is the most hilarious sport (largely un)known to man. Zeva just shrugs and grabs a book; kids hitting balls at each other's feet doesn't exactly require a ton of supervision. Rachel and Jordana are probably in the worst position—a game that's basically dodgeball on steroids is a guarantee for a head injury, jammed fingers, or both—but they complain the least, so they get stuck with it the most. Secretly, I think Rachel lives for the potential of bloodshed.

I swap out the sweats I slept in for a new pair that look exactly the same, replace my Camp Ilan sleep shirt with a macaron-printed tee, slide on flip-flops so I won't destroy my sneakers in the muddy path to the gym, and pull on my poncho, using it to shield both me and a gym bag packed with socks and sneakers so I won't get reamed by Naomi for not wearing proper footwear. Then I weave my long brown hair into quick pigtail braids and Michal and I trudge outside, both of us grumbling about having to go out into the nasty weather despite both of us also knowing that the counselors have it way worse today. (And every day, tbh, but that's why they get tips at the end of the summer and we don't.)

As expected, we lose the entire first ten minutes to simply splitting the girls up into the two halves of the gym, but at least I end up with almost all of my favorites. Not that I have favorites, of course, but if I did, they might be Ayelet, the best athlete in her division of rising sixth graders and the only girl in it who can serve overhand; Kayla, who always compliments me on my pastry-print clothing; Liviya, who doesn't have the strongest athletic skills but tries her heart out anyway; and Ruchama, who . . . well, okay, who has a hot brother that she introduced me to on visiting day. I know that *really* shouldn't make me favor her, and yet.

With everyone divided into two sports when they'd ordinarily be split into three, there are way too many girls on the court for a six-on-six, so I squish in a middle row and pray they manage not to collide too often.

"Okay, everybody!" I clap my hands for attention, and get it from maybe half of them, but with the noise coming from Michal's half of the room and the rain pounding on the roof, I'll take what I can get. "We're gonna skip drills and go right to the game. Everyone, into position. Reichman, you're serving first."

I toss the ball to Ayelet, and smile when she catches it with ease between messy orange-painted fingertips. She didn't know a single thing about volleyball when she came this summer, and now her serve is a thing of beauty. Her loud grunt as she smacks the ball over the net with an open palm always cracks everyone up, but everyone also knows that if the yeshiva league had volleyball in junior high, she would absolutely be its star. I can't wait to see how good she's gonna get by high school, especially if she keeps growing like a weed.

And then it hits me with a pang that I won't see how good she's gonna get. I'll see her rock one more summer, but I'll be long gone from Ilan by the time she hits ninth grade.

The girls still struggle with returning serves, so Ayelet gets three aces before Kayla Fechter finally bumps it back over. The ball does skim the net, but Kayla's team erupts into so much joy that no one even notices, and I quietly let it go, even as I feel bad ending Ayelet's serving streak.

And then I gradually feel worse, because not a single other girl manages to get a successful serve off, even after I demonstrate an underhand for the millionth time that summer. Aliza Gutman gets close, and her twin sister, Nava, gets even closer, but after ten minutes of going back and forth to both teams, there's not a single other success.

Which means *I* am a failure.

"Okay," I say with a clap of my hands, trying to keep spirits up even though we can all tell that the basketball girls on Michal's side of the room are watching us and giggling, as if they're any better when I have them on Mondays. "Maybe we shouldn't have skipped the drills. Let's go over serves again. Nava, why don't you go first? Try again with that sidearm."

"Seriously?" One of the Lilys—there are no fewer than four—

huffs out a breath. "We can't do it. What's the point? Can we just play Newcomb?"

"Ooh, yes!" says the Lily next to her. "Newcomb!"

It quickly becomes a chant, and though I'm really not supposed to crack when they ask for Newcomb instead—which happens at least once a week—I look at the rain streaking the windows, realize that at this time three days from now, these kids will all be on a bus home, and I think *the hell with it*. "Fine." I toss the ball to Nava. "You still start."

Newcomb's a fairly autopilot game, so I grab one of the folding chairs from the corner of the room and drop my butt next to where Michal has already done the same, periodically yelling things about not dribbling out of bounds. "Please don't tell Naomi I let them play Newcomb," I say with a sigh, uncapping my water bottle and taking a long drink.

"Hell, I'm surprised you lasted until now." She jumps up, her blond ponytail nearly smacking me in the face. "Biller! You cannot just walk with the ball! If you're not dribbling, you're traveling!" Then she sinks back down. "God, I can't wait to be done with this," she mutters.

"But don't you feel bad? Like, look at these kids." I gesture to where Kayla is hurling a ball over her shoulder in an inelegant throw that smacks Lily #3 in the gut. "They've been with us for an entire summer and they've barely learned a thing. My kids can't even *play* the sport I've been teaching them all summer. At best, they can bump around in a circle and set for me to spike. I'm a total failure."

"Oh please, Azi. You're not a *failure*. Look at them." She gestures with her whistle at the girls in their colorful T-shirts and shorts, taking turns alternately hurling as far as they can and gently tossing it just over the net and forcing the front row to run. They're taking it *so* seriously for what's basically a game of catch, but it's clear they're enjoying it, and I'm glad I consented to it. "They're having a great time, and that's what they come for. My neighbor, Andi? She goes to freaking archery camp. Like, archery is all they do. I'm sure it feels like a ton of pressure to get it right, and yeah, if they come away from a whole summer not knowing what they're doing, someone is definitely failing. But here? It's not that deep, and that's okay. They're enjoying what they have while they have it, and sometimes, that's all it is."

"Is that all it is for you?" I ask, because the thing is, Michal is *really* good. And maybe she's just Jewish summer camp really good or maybe she's actually really good—I'm not sure I'd know the difference—but it does feel like it might be just a little deep, for her.

"I don't know," she says, fiddling with the whistle around her neck. "I hadn't really ever imagined playing it past high school, but if I went to Stern, I'd probably have a decent shot, and that's kinda cool. But I didn't wanna pick a school solely based on where I could maybe play basketball for a few extra years."

I watch as the ball slips right through Lily #2's hands and slams on the glossy wooden floor of the gym. She's the proudest of the Lilys, and I know that one's gotta hurt. She tosses the ball under the net to the other team with the kind of aggression that comes from feeling painfully embarrassed, and turns away even before Aliza scoops it up.

"Is that such a ridiculous thing to do?" I hedge. "If it were an option for me for volleyball, I'd probably do it. Being on the team was probably my favorite thing about school. I'd love to be able to hold on to it a little longer, if I could."

Her mouth quirks up in a teasing little smile. "Yes, Azi, we've met. We all know there's nothing you wouldn't hold on to a little longer if you could."

"Hey, I—"

"Kayla!" There's a slam of the ball on the ground, a wail as hands fly to nose, and then any response I might've had is drowned out by the fight that immediately erupts. I blow my whistle, jump up, and run over to make sure there's no blood.

I don't need to say it, but we both know that this part is something I would very, very happily let go of as soon as possible.

The rest of the day is rainy, slow, and full of girls who whine about wanting to hang out and be lazy in their bunks with snacks, magazines, and music rather than trudging through the mud to play volleyball in the gym. By the time the rain lets up around dinnertime, I'm so drained of energy and enthusiasm that I'm not sure even having barbecue for dinner can fix it.

It isn't just exhaustion, though. There's something more, nagging at the edges of my brain, and it has been ever since my conversation with Michal. It's making me feel restless, making my palms itch, but for *what?*

And then, sometime after we've had another night of spicy fries and doodling on tables and a Taylor Swift listening party and we're all lying in bed with our reading lights shining down on our bedtime books of choice, it hits me.

"We've gotta play."

Michal closes the Leigh Bardugo fantasy novel she's already read at least twice this summer over her finger to keep her place. "Play what?"

"Volleyball. Come on."

"What? Now?" Yael sits up and shines her light at me, forcing me to squint. "It's after midnight, Azi Bean."

"I know, but tomorrow night we'll have to pack and we'll be stressed and exhausted, and this is our last shot. Please?" I'm trying not to sound desperate, but I feel desperate. "It'll be fun."

"Or, you know, it'll be us getting our asses kicked for being out after midnight," says Zeva.

"It's the second-to-last night of camp and none of you are coming back next year anyway," I point out. "What are they gonna do? Send you home a whole day early?"

"The courts are probably still muddy," Jordana says. "It rained for hours today."

"And it also stopped hours ago, and was like eighty degrees afterward. They're dry." I have no idea if that's true, but it feels like it's probably true, and honestly, who cares if they're a little muddy?

"Aren't you tired?" Michal asks, yawning as if to illustrate her point.

"Do I sound tired?" Truthfully I've never felt less tired in my life, a serious 180 from the rest of my day. I realize I'm never going to get them out of bed if I don't lead by example, so I shine my reading light on my cubbies, grab a sweatshirt, and slip it over my head. "Come on. It's basically our last night together." I pull on socks and sneakers, knowing that even if they refuse to come with me—which they won't—I'm still heading down to the courts no matter what. "Don't you wanna go out on a sports high?"

"Oh, is that what we're gonna be getting?" Zeva asks with a snort, even as she pulls on her own sweatshirt.

"You know I suck at volleyball," Yael mutters, sweeping her long brown curls into a ponytail. "Somehow I don't think this is going to be equally joyous for everyone."

"Good news," I tell her with a bright smile, tweaking the long tail that streaks down her back. "I can teach you."

"Come on, Azi Bean! Woo!"

"Stop cheering on the other team!" Michal berates Emma, one of the lifeguards we dragged out of bed to give us an even four-on-four.

"She just got two aces," Emma reminds her, shaking out her hands. "I really don't think a cheer is gonna be the reason we lose tonight."

"Not the point!" She turns back to face me, her blond hair gleaming in the lights that loom over the court, the lights we absolutely do not have permission to turn on after midnight but did anyway. "The *point* is that she's not getting any more. Look alive, people!"

I'm feeling particularly smug about one of those aces being off a jump serve; clearly, all my practice has been paying off. But this time I go for a simple overhand, aiming straight for Michal. She smirks as she bumps it right back, midway between Jordana and Yael. I can already tell each one thinks the other one's going for it, and Maya, the lifeguard on our team, is too far away, so I dive for the dig, taking a face full of sand as I boost it just high enough to reach Yael. "Aw crap!" she yelps, but in all her flailing, she manages to unintentionally set for Maya, who slams it at Emma's feet with a "Spike, baby!"

Our team immediately starts whooping and victory dancing over the sound of Michal's groaning, and Jordana's trying to keep us quiet so we won't wake up the staff that sleeps in nearby cabins. "Rabbi Richton and his wife sleep *right there*," she reminds us in a fierce whisper, "and that woman can yell loud enough to shake the walls. Do not ask me how I know that."

We try to keep it down, but it's just impossible. We need to cheer when Yael gets her first kill. We need to scream "Ace!" every single time one happens. They need to ooh and aah every single time I nail a jump serve, and we need to crack one another up, howl at every near-miss, randomly break into Color War songs, and run victory laps around the court when we absolutely crush them.

In the cool summer night, with a blanket of stars twinkling overhead and the chirping of crickets in the air, the smells of damp sand and grass mingling together in the breeze, who could blame us?

Well, as it turns out, Rebbetzin Richton absolutely could, and the second we see the lights flick on in her cabin, we take off in a run to the sports shack, the room where we store our stuff and hang out in between periods.

"Oh, crap, I didn't bring my key," Michal says, her hand flying to her neck. Everyone else does the same; we're so used to having whistles and keys around our necks all day that I feel naked to realize I don't have my stuff with me, either, and it's clear everyone else feels the same.

"Well, we'll just hide here, then, until her light goes back off," Jordana suggests, and that's what we do, clustering behind the water fountain as if it'll protect all eight of us.

We all go silent but for the sound of our breathing and the familiar clicking sound of Rachel's Sharpie as she flicks it through her fingers.

Without thinking, I grab the pen from her and uncap it. There's enough light to see the new replacement wooden beam on the outer wall that still hasn't been painted, and I promptly write *Azi Bean '23* on it. Then I close up the pen and hand it back to Rachel.

She smiles, and instead of going back to flicking it, she uncaps it again and writes *Rachel Glaser '23* right next to my name. One by one the girls pass the pen around, adding their own names to the beam until we've officially left our mark. As Jordana leaves the final date, the funny feeling that'd been building in my chest crawls into my throat and sits there like a lump.

Afraid I might cry, I turn away from the group and promptly knock over a garbage can. It lands with a crash, and there's a shout from the direction of the Richtons' cabin, and I know we're screwed. I quickly right the can and then chase after my friends, who are all laughing and leaping back to the bunks we're calling home for the last time as the rebbetzin's holler carries on the air behind us.

"I still can't believe you risked getting into trouble tonight," Michal says when we're safely back inside and slipping off our sandy socks and sneakers. "You know if they figure out who was on the courts tonight, we're toast."

"I do know." I take a deep breath, unable to believe I'm about to say what I'm about to say. "I thought about it before I made the suggestion to go. What I would do if we got in trouble and they forbade me from coming back next year, I mean. And I think . . ." I smile, thinking of Yael's ducking away from the ball like an absolute coward, Jordana's *Go Bean!* when I blocked a spike from Emma, and my absolutely god-awful rendition of "We Are the Champions." "I think that if this were it for me, that'd be okay."

"Seriously?" Michal's jaw drops. "Since *when*?"

"Actually," I tell her as I rinse my hands of all the accumulated grit, "since you shared your wisdom with me this afternoon. You were right—you don't *always* have to make your mark, even with sports. It's okay to let fun be the endgame."

"So that's why you were so desperate to play in the middle of the night."

"That's why I was so desperate to play in the middle of the night," I confirm. "I wanted to leave on a note of fun, and now I am. That was the best night I've had the entire summer. And if that's what I remember about being here, well. That wouldn't be so bad."

"It wouldn't." She gives my hand a squeeze. "But I'm still pissed you won."

"Please, like there was ever any doubt I was gonna win *volleyball*?"

"Next time, basketball. I will absolutely destroy you," she says sweetly, a trash-talker until the very end.

"You won't, but it's okay if you do." We head into our shared room, which is filled with darkness and the sound of Yael's soft snoring, and slip into bed. "A friend once told me it's not that deep."

ANCHOR POINTS

MARIEKE NIJKAMP

Andi

This will be the summer when everything changes, but when I set up on the archery range of Camp Artemis, it occurs to me that some things will always remain the same.

One, I'm here a full day before everyone else. Perks of my dad being camp director.

Two, the grass is unwieldy, the targets look ragged, and despite its shabby appearance, this range is where I feel most at home.

Three, this is and always will be, the best feeling in the world. These heartbeats, right before I release the arrow. When I find my anchor point. When my drawing hand rests lightly against my jawbone and the bowstring barely touches my lips. My back muscles tense, my stance relaxes, and I remind myself for the thousandth time to keep my elbow from turning inward. The wind plays across the grass and the target comes into focus and I can feel my aim steady. And I know, I *know*, that this is the perfect shot.

I relax my grip.

The string slips over the pads of my fingers.

The arrow speeds toward the target.

I know it will hit the moment my hand slips back past my cheek and my bow tips forward.

If you've ever seen an arrow fly in slow motion, you'll know it ripples through the air. Its path is never entirely straight, and it's almost like the shaft weaves its way toward the target. Rationally I know that, too. But I can't see it. I can only see the direct path—the perfect path—to the center of the target.

The silence before it hits.

The oh-so-familiar *thud*.

When the arrow buries deep into the inner ring, I feel that rush of adrenaline. The rightness of my shot, of my being here. Without stopping to think, I nock the next arrow and repeat. With the third arrow, my hand trembles and the bow string swerves to the side, sending the arrow in a spin toward the next ring. Two tens and a seven.

Not good enough, a small voice in the back of my mind whispers. *Not good enough. You need to be consistent. Maybe—*

I scowl. *After this week, no one will care how I shoot anymore*, I remind my competitive self. *So shut up.*

Behind me, someone applauds, and when I turn and squint against the rising sun, my dad walks toward me, balancing a giant mug of coffee in one hand. "Your elbow is a bit high."

My stomach drops, the calm from the quiet range evaporating. "Good morning to you, too."

He opens his mouth, no doubt to repeat the same conversation we've had a thousand times already this summer, so I stall him by walking to the target to grab my arrows. The familiar pull and give eases my exasperation, but only a little.

Just enough to walk back to him, take a sip from his coffee, and tell him, as calmly as I can, "We've been over this. I'm not going to change my mind. Please let me enjoy this week, Dad. Okay?"

Maybe for once he'll leave it at that. Realize that I'm not going back on my decision. But stubbornness runs in the family—and I inherited mine straight from him.

He squares his jaw. "Andi, you should see how confident you look with that bow in your hand. Like you were *made* to do this. To waste a talent like yours is criminal. It's—"

"My choice," I interrupt him with more force than I intended.

Dad flinches and I wince, too. I know how much this matters to him. It's always been the two of us against the world, and it's always been archery that connected us. From the first bow he ever got me, to the first local tournament we went to together, to our Junior Olympic Archery Development club, summer camp, and our Olympics watch parties. From the start, he's been my coach and my biggest fan.

But I can't keep competing just for him.

I want to be something different, I want to *try* something different.

I steal another sip of coffee and try to smile. Try to find that same peace I felt when I was facing my target. Try to *explain*. Somehow, it gets harder every time we have this conversation. "There are other things I want to do when I get to college, Dad. I still love archery, you know that. But I don't want it to be my entire life. Isn't college a time when you're supposed to, like, figure out who you are? And try out new things and make mistakes and get no sleep and learn important life lessons? Only start your journalism assignments the night before they're due? I want that. All of it. And I need you to stop telling me I can't."

I wait for him to reply, to argue, to say anything. To my surprise, he doesn't.

He stands with his back to the camp buildings, one hand in his pocket, his eyes on the targets. The wind tousles his unruly hair. And he sighs.

So I do what I can: I take it as a tiny win. I collect my bow and gesture at the main building. "I'll see you when the campers arrive, okay?"

Without waiting to see if he responds, I turn and walk away. It's how all of our conversations have ended so far, with one of us strategically retreating. Maybe he'll think about it now. Maybe he'll come to understand me.

And once the campers arrive, I hope that my nemesis, my best archery rival, my best summer camp friend, will understand, too. Because archery also bound us together.

And if this is my final summer at Camp Artemis, I'm going to have to win the golden arrow one last time. No matter how hard she trained.

Rowan

I reach out to tuck a strand of hair behind my ear—a nervous tic I've had for as long as I can remember—but instead of finding purchase in the long brown hair I used to have, my fingers brush a freshly shaved buzz cut. I mask the mistake by adjusting my glasses and pretending that was what I intended to do all along. The ridiculous thing is, the first time I buzzed my hair was eight months ago. But somehow being here, in a place so familiar I could walk this path with my eyes closed, the past year is rushing back to me, the past *me* is rushing back to me, and I'm trying to figure out how to handle it. Because while everything has stayed exactly the same here, I have changed. And everyone around me notices it. I can see it in their furtive glances. The whispers when they think I'm not paying attention.

"Is that—?"

"I'm not sure—"

"What happened?"

I cut my hair, genius. It's really not that complicated.

Honestly, I know that for most of them, it's curiosity or genuine concern, but I already dealt with the pointed stares and loud whispers at school and at my job. I don't want to do this again.

I guess the only way is through, so I square my shoulders, raise my head, and stare them all down.

Deal with me or look away.

Until I see a pair of curious green eyes stare back at me, and my breath catches and my body tenses. All of a sudden my determination speeds away, like an arrow that misses its target. I don't know what to do with my face. Should I be smiling at her or scowling or looking mysteriously changed?

She isn't supposed to *be* here. Well, she's supposed to be here, of course. She isn't supposed to be standing *there*, right next to the entrance to the cabin we shared our very first summer together. I expected her to be next to her father, and I've been carefully avoiding eye contact with him so I could deal with the Andi problem later.

For some bizarre reason, she's found a vantage point on the other side of the gates to Camp Artemis. She's tugging at a perfectly curled strand of hair and her eyebrows are up near her hairline. Her mouth makes a perfect O, and then she smirks. Before I can say anything, she jumps between the other campers and makes her way toward me.

"Different, I like it." I can hear the smile in her voice—and the challenge, too. It's always been this way between us, ever since that first summer. Everyone here cares about archery, but most kids are also serious about downtime. Playing in the woods, singing songs around the campfire, telling scary stories at night. Not Andi. Not me. We spent extra hours at the range. We pored over videos of

Olympic athletes and the Lotte Vogel documentary. We were serious about learning. Improving. We were the best. We *are* the best. And we've been vying for the camp trophy every single year.

Every single year—or at least, the last three, once the older cadet archers graduated to junior—Andi has won. She knows exactly how much that bothers me.

She hooks her thumbs around her belt. "I'm glad you're here. I wasn't sure you'd—"

"It's Rowan now," I cut her off. I can feel my cheeks heat when she stops mid-sentence. I'd planned to casually drop my name. Or at the very least, wait for a moment when she wasn't in the middle of saying something. But it suddenly matters a great deal to me that she gets it right. That she knows it. That she knows *me*.

Andi closes her mouth. Considers. Then she nods. "Cool. Rowan. Nice to meet you. Pronouns?"

The ease with which she gets it takes me off guard. So I do the only thing I can. Cross my arms, let one shoulder drop, tilt my head, and play it cool. "She/her is fine for now. I'm still experimenting. If it changes, I'll let you know."

And she smiles for real, without trick or challenge. It's as bright as the sunrise crawling over the trees. "I'm happy for you."

"Thank you." I am, too. My name didn't fit anymore. The gendered words. The assumptions when people look at me. Cadet women. Junior women. The gender marker that hit me like a string slap at every competition. Every event. One step at a time, I may be able to leave that pain behind me.

But that's the crux, isn't it? Because archery is still a gendered sport and its binary options don't include me. I'm supposed to join the archery team at my college. I have a few small-but-essential scholarships waiting for me. And it's all for a person I'm not anymore. I don't know if any of it will still be there for me if it turns out I can't compete. This is everything I wanted once, and now I'm not sure if I can have it.

"Rowan?"

I start when Andi calls my name, and I realize too late that I zoned out completely, mulling over the same worries again and again. "Sorry, I was just . . ."

"Thinking about what it means to be back here?" Andi guesses. She glances in her father's direction, and something like a shadow flashes across her face. Then she laughs. "I'm glad you're here. Camp wouldn't be the same without you. I made sure we're in the same cabin again."

With that, she winks at me, turns around, and stalks toward one of the new campers.

And while I valiantly try to remember what to do next or how to keep walking forward, I do know one thing. No matter what happens after this summer, I have one year left at Camp Artemis.

One year when it's just me, my trusted bow, and all the nightly ghost stories we won't tell.

This will be the summer where I finally beat Andi and win the golden arrow.

Andi

Once camp officially starts, two things happen.

First, *briefly*, everything that happens outside of the borders of the camp disappears to the background. I still think about what life will be like once I get out of here, when I won't be practicing my form and cycling through arrows every weekend, but it feels different. Like when you're traveling, and home and school and daily life seem so far away.

I'd like to do more of that, maybe. Travel. See the world. Not because I'm competing anywhere, just because I want to.

Especially now that Rowan's here. I don't know what it is exactly. Every year, it sneaks up on me how at ease I feel when she's close. More than any of my friends back home, she challenges me and surprises me. Even if we haven't had much time to talk yet, I'm better for having her here. And that's especially true with this new sense of comfort and ease she exudes. I love this new Rowan—or maybe the Rowan she was all along, now here for the whole world to see.

Second, like it does every year, summer falls into a rhythm. We wake with the sun and watch the forest come to life around us, with the birds taking to the trees and serenading us with a morning cacophony, squirrels running around trying to steal our food, and deer coming to the edge of the lake to drink.

After breakfast, coaches take the campers out for different types of exercises. We have three coaches for three age groups—beginners, cadets, and juniors. Dad coaches whatever age group I'm in, and no one really makes a fuss about it. Occasionally people joke that I'm the only reason he started this place. They wouldn't be wrong.

But it means that when Coach Amira takes the beginners out to the field for 3D target practice, and Coach Thiago takes the cadets out for a run, there are only three of us left at the range. Dad. Me. And Rowan.

Rowan doesn't seem to notice the tension between Dad and me—or if she does, she's careful not to comment on it. She left our cabin before sunrise to go for a run along the lakeshore, and she's at the range bright and ready, her neon-blue recurve bow by her side, her new haircut as sharp as her arrows.

"Hey Coach Owen," she greets my dad.

He nods at her. "Rowan Stevens. Good to have you back. I heard congratulations are in order?"

Rowan tilts her head and furrows her brow. With her hair so short, the angles of her face are harder. The lines across her forehead. The sharp cheekbones. And the hesitation that plays around her mouth when she nibbles her lip. Before she can ask what he meant, Dad continues.

"Your coach told me about your scholarships. College archery, isn't it? You're a talented archer, and I always knew you'd go far."

I blink. Rowan hadn't mentioned that yet, and when Dad does, she looks less than thrilled about it. She's polite—she always is to coaches—but something of her untouchable confidence crumbles, and she pales. "Thanks, Coach." Her voice sounds flatter, too.

Before I can ask, Dad continues, "I do wish my daughter had some of that same determination. Instead she's just giving up."

I gasp. The ground shifts beneath my feet. It's one thing for *us* to be arguing about this, but for Dad to bring it up in front of Rowan, who's gone from pale to bright red, is deeply unfair. To her. To both of us.

"I'm *not* giving up, and I'm not giving in, either," I say. "And if you think that I would *ever* take the easy way out, that I wouldn't have thought about this long and hard because it's important to me, you really don't know me at all."

With that, I do something I've never done before.

I drop my bow. I unbuckle my quiver and let the arrows clatter to the ground.

And I walk off.

Rowan

Out of all the things I expected from my first days at camp, this was not a part of it. It explains why Andi and Coach Owen were keeping their distance from each other, but it's like a disturbance in the Force. The two of them have always been one team. Everyone knows that.

But in some strange kind of way, Andi and I have always been, too.

I find her at the foot of an abandoned tree hut that overlooks the lake. The steps that lead up to the wooden platform are dangling off the side of the tree, and the structure itself doesn't look any more stable. We used to climb in here when we were ten, when we came to camp the first time, and everything was still new and well maintained.

She sits with her back to the tree and doesn't look up when I approach. She's throwing small pebbles into the water, every movement jagged and frustrated.

I never quite know what to call her. We've known each other for seven years, but what we have is whatever the friendship equivalent of a summer fling is. We're closer than anyone here. We snark at each other and tease each other and enjoy the sport together. And when camp is over we don't text or call for the rest of the year. We don't see each other, outside of unplanned meetings at the occasional tournament. She's my favorite nemesis and the highlight of my summers, but I don't know if she's my *friend*, and I don't know if she would call me friend, either.

I don't really do friendship in general. Still, she's one of the people who's never judged me, and I know her well enough to see that she's hurting.

Unfortunately for her, I also don't really do subtlety. "So you're giving up on archery?"

Andi tosses another pebble into the lake before she turns to me, and her eyes are lost and lonely. "I'll never give up on archery, and if Dad would listen to me, he'd *know* that. I'm quitting shooting *competitively*."

I plop down next to her and wait for the sudden rush of anger and annoyance to pass, because she's so casually throwing away what I so desperately want, before I ask, "Why?"

She chuckles. "Do you know you're the first person to ask me that?"

I'm aching to be able to continue to shoot, and she's just giving it up? I can't wrap my mind around it. "You're so good at it. I don't understand." I wonder if she notices the tremble in my voice.

She glances at me sharply. "No one understands. I didn't, either, at first. But I don't enjoy it. Not anymore. I've always loved archery, and I love this weird world of ours." She gestures at the space around her, and I know exactly what she means. It often felt like Camp Artemis was its own small universe, away from everything else. This summer, for the first time, I can't stop thinking about everything beyond its borders, but for the other campers it must still feel the same. The beginners, who are walking around bright-eyed and with droopy smiles, as they fall in love with the very best sport of all. The cadets, who make lifelong friendships here, because some of them, at least, have the courage to keep up with each other outside of camp borders, bonding over superhero archers and video games and JOAD meets. I don't understand how that works. How people blend friends from school with work and family business, or friends from camp with real life.

Andi picks a blade of grass and rolls it between her fingers. "I always want to keep *this*. I'm tired of tournaments. I know I'm a good archer, and I love it, but I don't love that it's all that I have. Every time we travel it's because of events. Every bit of spare time, when I'm not in school or working at the pizza place, I'm training. Every birthday gift, every Christmas gift, it's archery equipment. And I know it's a luxury. So many kids come here on scholarships because their parents can't afford to support them.

I *know* I shouldn't just *squander my talent*. But what if I'm losing myself in the process? What if I don't love that it's all that I am? Do you know that feeling?"

I don't, at all. But before I can say anything, Andi continues. "That's the problem, you see? I don't know who I am without archery. It always used to be my anchor point, the thing that keeps me steady, but I'm worried that instead it's becoming the anchor that drags me down. And I wish Dad would get that."

I don't know what to say to that. I don't know who I'd be—who *we'd* be—without archery, either. If we'd be anything at all, or—

Oh.

I tilt my head. "Maybe that holds true for your dad, too."

Andi scoffs. "The anchor thing? I don't—"

"No," I interrupt her. "Maybe he doesn't know who the both of you are without archery, either."

Andi

Huh. I never thought of it that way. But with Rowan looking at me intently, something unspoken behind her piercing blue eyes, it makes sense. Archery was what first connected me and Dad after my mother walked out on us, and he was left trying to deal with a heartbroken and angry kid. It means as much to him as it does to me.

Except I don't intend to take that away from us. I want him to trust me on that.

"Ugh." I lean back against the tree. My head pounds.

"At least you'll keep competing, though," I mutter. "You can make him proud."

Rowan gets to her feet and walks to the edge of the lake, staring out. "Yeah."

Silence chills the air, and I swallow. It's like the boundaries between Camp Artemis and the rest of the world keep breaking down further. "Rowan?"

She shrugs. Her voice wavers when she says, "It's weird knowing this will be our last summer, isn't it? Part of me assumed this place would always be here. I know it doesn't work like that, of course, but . . ."

"We were so young and innocent once?"

Rowan snorts. "You were never innocent." She wraps her arms around her waist. "And I like who I am better now."

"I do, too," I say, before I can stop myself. I immediately rush on. "We could come back as coaches. Find ways to influence these young and malleable brains with cool trick shots and fancy arrows, and still see each other every year. That would be a solution, wouldn't it?"

The suggestion is equal parts jest and serious. It would solve a lot of problems.

Rowan's shoulders tense. "I guess . . ."

She keeps staring out like the weight of the world is pressing on her, and despite the fact that she came here to make sure I'm okay, I desperately need to make sure she is, too. "If this is our last time here together, you know what that means, right?"

Rowan turns to me, and her eyes are red. When she raises an eyebrow, I plaster on a smirk. "You've always wanted to beat me."

She scowls, but at least she relaxes. She recognizes the familiar pattern and follows the steps. "Don't you dare let me win, Andi Owen."

"Not in a million years." I laugh, relieved. "You can pry the golden arrow from my cold dead hands."

Andi

The campers gather around the fire on the third night. Tonight, our evening program consists of watching reruns of other sports, like

Lotte Vogel's French Open win or Pilar Abiodun's World Cup victories. Of discussing sportsmanship and goals and dreams.

When Coach Amira hits Play on her tablet, and the campers gather around her to watch, I see Dad staring at me, but he doesn't say a word. In fact, he hasn't said a word throughout our training sessions, either. I genuinely don't know what is worse. Fighting, or this.

Meanwhile, Rowan sits next to me, and I know there's something she isn't telling me. There are a lot of things I don't always notice. Like, according to my friends back home, when a cute girl flirts with me. Or when an opponent tries to intimidate me. But I notice that she isn't here fully, and I don't know how to broach that subject.

So instead I sit next to her and she sits next to me and the rest of the camp happens around us.

In other years, we would have had our questions ready. Not everyone got why studying other sports could help, but we did. I convinced Dad to let me try out martial arts so I could learn to improve my concentration and focus. I spent some time at the local shooting range to find other ways to experiment with my aim. I even attempted fencing, because I thought it might help with my hand-eye coordination, but that didn't last long. I prefer it when sharp and pointy things are *not* aimed at me.

Tonight, it's a girl and a boy who just moved into the cadets group, a pair of twins, who take turns peppering the coaches with questions. Until the various fragments have been shown and discussed half a dozen times. Until everyone around them starts talking, quietly at first, then louder. Coach Thiago walks to the main cabin and comes back with huge bags of popcorn and marshmallows. All that time, the two cadets keep asking questions, just like Rowan and I used to do.

I stretch my legs, and softly elbow Rowan, nudging her attention in the direction of the teens. "Is this what growing old feels like?"

She blinks owlishly, but I can see my comment doesn't register. I react before I can think the better of it. I grab her hand and drag her away from the fire, into the dark forest.

Rowan

In the shadows of the trees, Andi swings around and pins me with a stare. I can't see the color of her eyes—moss green by daylight—but I can see the campfire reflected in them, like burning embers. "I know you're struggling with something, too, and I want to know what it is. I want to know if I can help."

I cross my arms again, like I always do when I'm caught off guard. "Why?"

"You know, the last time you asked me that question there was a bit less venom to it. But you helped me then, and I want to help you now. If you'll let me. If you want that, I mean. I don't want to impose or make it sound like you have to tell, but just . . . you know." Andi trails off and even in the dim light, I can see that she's gone bright red. But she squares her shoulders and adds, "I like to think that we're friends, is all."

I can't help it. I laugh. "Are we?"

She looks chagrined and more than a little hurt. "You think I plan my summer camp weeks around the two of us just because you're a good shot?"

I start to shrug, but when Andi's face clouds over, I try to relax. "I wasn't sure."

"It's been *seven years*, Rowan," she says incredulously.

"And we never talked about it!" I shoot back.

She stares at me, and it makes me want to squirm. It's like we're ten years old all over again and meeting each other for the first time. I really don't do friendship well. "I thought maybe we bonded over both being precocious brats."

My words are followed by silence, broken only by the distant hooting of an owl and the rustling of undergrowth.

Then Andi laughs. She laughs so hard she doubles over, and it sounds like bells echoing against the trees. She wipes at her eyes and tries to speak, but she collapses again. "I love you, Rowan Stevens. You're even more obtuse than I am, and that's saying something."

My face *burns* at those words, and there's a quiet voice in the back of my mind that whispers to me, tells me to ask her what she meant by *that*. I clear my throat and reach for the nonexistent strand of hair again and say, "So friends, then?"

"Yes, friends," Andi says, sobering. Her cheeks are pink and her eyes are overbright. "So tell me what's up with you, and what I can do to help."

"You won't take no for an answer?"

She smirks. "No."

So I turn away. I can't look at her or I'll never find the right words. I'll trip over my tongue and I'll get flustered, or I'll clamp up completely. "Remember how we never told scary stories along with the other kids, because we decided it was important to *get enough sleep* and *be focused on our shooting*?"

Andi snorts. "We really were precocious brats."

I nod. We were. But I guess this year we're telling scary stories after all. "I only came out as nonbinary a few months ago, right before the end of senior year, and I haven't gone to any official events since. I didn't know how to register, and I didn't want to ask. I was terrified of finding out I'm not welcome anymore."

"Oh, Rowan . . ."

I push through, before I let Andi's compassion get to me. "I didn't have to gather more points for my ranking or my scholarships, either, so I just told my coach I was focused on graduation and surviving high school. But once I get to college, they're counting on me being part of the team. Excellent grades and excellent athletic results. Those are the requirements of all three scholarships. They won't pay for my entire education, but my grandparents set money aside as well, and between my own savings and this, it's just enough to get me started. But only if they'll have me." Once I get to the end of it, my voice is barely more than a whisper, and I don't know if Andi can still hear me. Hell, I don't know if she's still there at all. Or if she thinks I'm overreacting. Or. "I know I should ask, and maybe it won't be so bad, but—" I thought my school would get it, too and they didn't. "I read up on the rules a hundred times and it's like people like me just don't exist, you know? Those few articles I can find are all about people hating on trans athletes. Saying that we're lying cheaters who should not be allowed to compete at all. And it's not like there are archery tournaments with inclusive categories. Everything we do is gendered and I don't think they get how much that hurts sometimes. I just want to be able to be myself and still compete. That shouldn't be too much to ask."

"I'm sorry," Andi says, when I stop rambling. I brace myself for what comes next. Because I want her to understand. I think I need her to understand.

She walks up to stand next to me, and instead of trying to catch my eye, she simply joins me in staring out at the trees. "It shouldn't be too much to ask, and I'm sorry that it is. I'm sorry that I never even considered it might be. Not just for you, but for others here. We should do better." She breathes out hard. "But this is about you. When do classes start?"

I don't even need to check my phone for that. "Three weeks. And two days."

"And you haven't been in touch with them yet?" She keeps her voice neutral, nonjudgmental.

I think about it constantly. Several times a day. Whenever I wake up in the middle of the night. Every time I chicken out. Because: "What if they say they don't want me there?"

"Would you still want to go? If they didn't?" Andi asks quietly.

That's the hardest part. "I do. Bishop University has one of the best rehabilitation science programs in the country. I've wanted to be a physical therapist all my life. Should I go for the lesser option? Doesn't that mean I will let them win?"

"Are you willing to fight for it?"

"Of course." I don't want fighting to be necessary. But what's my alternative?

In my periphery, Andi hesitates before she places a hand on my shoulder. "Then you should at least email them to ask."

I swallow hard. "I don't . . ." I don't know if I can. If I want to. If I shouldn't just keep my head down and pretend for as long as I can, until archery is all that remains and there'll be nothing left of me. Truth is, I understand Andi far better than she could possibly know.

She squeezes. "I'll help. I'll be with you. I won't let you deal with this alone."

I don't know what to say to that. Or how to breathe.

But she leans in, and the pressure settles me. "Do you trust me?"

A small, scared part of me wants to say I don't even know her. But I do. And she knows me, even though we only see each other a few weeks a year. She gets me better than any other friend I've ever had. "Yeah."

I glance at her just in time to see her smile. "We'll write the email together. Tell them you're worried. Ask them what your options are. They may surprise you."

"Okay." I place my hand on top of hers, and squeeze, too, and another thought occurs to me. "But only if you try to talk to your dad before camp's over, all right?"

I can feel Andi tense. "I'm not sure he'll listen to me, but—"

"*Andi,*" I interrupt her. "This is important to me. But you and your dad, that is important to you."

The forest around us darkens further. Another owl hoots, the sound fainter and lighter. The laughter and songs that are drifting in from the campfire fade, too, before she nods. "Okay."

It makes everything feel a little bit more right again. The two of us together. The challenge. The smile.

The best.

Andi

It takes me another two days to pick up the courage to talk to Dad. In that time, Rowan has drafted a dozen emails to her future college counselor, and she's deleted all of them, too. But last night, after she beat me in practice sets for the second time in a row, we finally settled on the right words.

So today, when we're supposed to start the day with practice at the range again, Rowan is pretending to have cramps, and I'm cornering Dad. Because we have two days left at camp, and I don't want to remember my last summer here as the worst one. I don't think he wants that, either.

"Do you remember when we came here for the first time?" I start talking the moment he sets foot on the range, the same coffee mug in his hands as the first day. He frowns, and it's like I see my own scowl reflected to me. Is that what he felt like the first time I was angry with him? Every time since? Like looking in a slightly distorted mirror and hurting because the other side is, too?

"You and the other coaches didn't know if any of this would work. If it wouldn't just be a galactic waste of money and time to try to make a summer camp happen. But you brought me here anyway because you wanted me to see it. And the very first thing I told you was—"

"*Camp Artemis sounds like a portal to a magic world, and I don't understand why it looks so much like every other forest,*" Dad says, begrudgingly. "You were always reading those fantasy books and I think you had a very different idea of what camp would be."

"I probably did," I say softly. "But you told me, *We can make our own magic here. We can make our own small world where everyone can learn archery, and everyone gets to play, and everyone gets to be a hero.* And I knew right there and then that I would love it." I clear my throat and press on. "But I don't think I ever told you how true that turned out to be. It *is* what you, Amira, Thiago, and the past coaches created here, Dad. Every year, kids come here and fall in love with the sport—like Rowan and me. Like those twins in the cadet group. You know they'll be shooting at Nationals before long. Dozens of campers came through here and made friendships for life, or discovered their confidence, or had camp as a safe space to get away from the rest of life. To all of them, to all of *us*, Camp Artemis is a magical world we got to visit for a while."

Somewhere during that impromptu speech, Dad's placed his mug on the ground, and his eyes are suspiciously shiny, but he's shaking his head. "If this place is so special, then why are you so intent on leaving it behind?"

I sigh, but I don't rise to the bait. "I'm not, Dad. I'll keep coming back here as long as you'll have me. That's what I wanted to come here to tell you, so maybe you'll understand. I'm giving up on competing. I'm not giving up on Camp Artemis, even though I'm too old to be a camper. I'm not giving up on archery. And I'm never giving up on you."

When his shoulders drop and he unclenches his fists, I realize Rowan had a point. So obvious that I should've seen it.

"Going to events together is our thing," Dad protests weakly.

"Then we'll find another thing," I suggest with a careful smile. "Have you ever considered crocheting? Base diving? Do you want to tag along when I go to frat parties?"

"You are *not* going to frat parties," he shoots back immediately. Probably before he can think the better of it. But I know he means it when he adds, "You should probably rebel a little, though. If you want to learn those important life lessons."

I bite my lip. "Did you really believe I'd give up on us?"

Dad has the decency to look ashamed. He steps closer to me and holds out his arms. "I've never raised a teen daughter before, Andi. I'm making it up as I go along."

"Well, I've never grown up before, so I guess you're in good company." I let him pull me into a hug. "I know three things, though, Dad. Camp Artemis will always be here. Archery will always be important to us. And you and me? It will always be the two of us against the world."

He pulls me closer still and ruffles my hair. "You're a good kid, Andi. I'm proud of you."

"I'm proud of you, too, Dad," I mutter into his chest, though the words are muffled and my throat has closed up.

The feelings between us are so intense that I'm relieved when we hear a cough from the edge of the range.

A brown-haired girl—one of the youngest archers in the beginners' group—clears her throat. "'Scuse me, Coach Owen? Coach Amira wants to know if you and the juniors can demonstrate some trick shot techniques for our group." She has a bit of a lisp and a whole lot of determination.

"Does she now, Maddox?" Dad releases me and wipes surreptitiously at his eyes, while the girl pretends not to notice.

He glances my way. "What do you think, Miss Rebel? Are you up for some trick shots, even though you're nearly too old to be a camper?"

I pat my bow and grin—and definitely don't wipe at my eyes, either. "Sure, Coach. I can show the kids how it's done one last time."

Email from Bishop University

Dear Mx Stevens,
We haven't formally met yet. My name is Anne Pierce, captain of Bishop University's archery team. I understand that you have concerns about your eligibility to compete in archery events—and with that, your place on our team and here at Bishop University—on account of your gender. Please be assured that Bishop prides itself on being welcoming and LGBTQ+ friendly, and these values of inclusion and support hold true for its sports teams as well. While I can't promise you that we won't run into administrative red tape trying to place you for events, we are one team and we are committed to supporting you in this endeavor. Once classes start, I would like to meet with you and your counselor to discuss the best plan of attack. While I can't speak to the details and requirements of your scholarships, please know that your place here at Bishop University and on our prize-winning archery team is safe, and we look forward to welcoming you.

Andi

On the morning of the last full day at camp, everyone gathers for the traditional shoot-off for the golden arrow. Excited voices echo outside our cabin. Feet stomping through dewy grass. Challenges ringing back and forth.

I read through Bishop University's reply to Rowan's email once more, while she waxes her bow to get ready for our sets. She looks so relieved, and I'm pretty sure it makes her all the more dangerous. I'm looking forward to it. For the first time in a while, I'm looking forward to all the rest that comes next for us. Even if neither of us knows exactly what that will look like yet.

"What will happen to us? After camp is over, I mean," Rowan asks, as if she read my mind.

We've never asked that question before. *Before* there was always a *next year*.

"I wasn't entirely serious when I suggested we come back here as coaches, but we can do that," I say, tossing the phone back on her bed. I pick up my own bow to check the string and make sure all my arrows are in perfect condition. "Or we could plan to get drinks after your first event at Bishop. I'll come cheer you on. It's only like a seven-hour drive from me." I laugh, and Rowan blushes.

"You'd do that for me?"

"I promised you I wouldn't let you do this alone, didn't I? Besides, I also promised Dad to rebel a little at college. So I'll come to every one of your events until you get tired of me."

"Somehow, I don't think I will." She places the bow next to her and picks up the arrows. She glances at me sideways. "It's a date, then."

When, an hour later, we step onto the archery range of Camp

Artemis together, it occurs to me that some things will always remain the same.

One, time flies by, like an arrow speeding toward its target. I may not feel wiser or smarter than when I first came here seven years ago, but I do feel a bit more like me.

Two, the grass is unwieldy, the targets look ragged, but despite its shabby appearance, this range will always be where I first felt most at home. I can't wait to see what other homes are out there for me.

Three, and finally, this is and always will be the best feeling in the world. These heartbeats, right before we start our set. The rush of excitement. The celebrating campers. My anchor points. Dad, cheering me on one last time. And Rowan, next to me, ready to fight for everything she deserves and more.

May the best of us win.

ABOUT THE AUTHORS

Dahlia Adler (she/her) is an editor by day, a freelance writer by night, and an author and anthologist at every spare moment in between. She's the founder of LGBTQReads.com; her novels include Kids' Indie Next picks *Cool for the Summer*, *Home Field Advantage*, and *Going Bicoastal*; and she is the editor of the anthologies *His Hideous Heart*, *That Way Madness Lies*, *At Midnight*, and, with Jennifer Iacopelli, *Out of Our League*. Dahlia lives in New York with her family and an obscene number of books.

Carrie S. Allen (she/her) is the author of *Michigan vs. the Boys*, listed on YALSA's 2020 Best Fiction for Young Adults, the 2020 Quick Picks for Reluctant Readers, and the 2020 Bank Street College of Education's Best Children's Books of the Year. Retired from sports medicine, she writes about teen athletes who make a difference on and off the field. Carrie lives in Colorado and spends as much time outdoors as possible, usually chasing after kids, dogs, and chickens.

Sara Farizan (she/her) watches '90s cartoons and '80s commercials to relax, and loves pinball but is wary of certain games. She is the award-winning and critically acclaimed author of the young adult novels *Here to Stay*, *Tell Me Again How a Crush Should Feel*, and the Lambda Literary Award–winning *If You Could Be Mine*, which was named one of *TIME* magazine's 100 Best YA Books of All Time. Her novel *Dead Flip* is her favorite book she's written. She has short stories in the anthologies *Fresh Ink*, *All Out*, *The Radical Element*, *Hungry Hearts*, *Come On In*, and *Fools in Love*. She also had a dream come true in writing a DC Comics middle grade graphic novel, *My Buddy, Killer Croc*. She lives in Massachusetts and thanks you for reading her work. You can find out more about her at sarafarizan.com.

Juliana Goodman was born and raised in Blue Island, Illinois. She received her BA in English Literature from Western Illinois University in Macomb, Illinois, in 2014, and her MFA in Fiction Writing in 2017 from Purdue University in West Lafayette, Indiana. Juliana has received several awards and scholarships for her writing and was a fellow with the Tulsa Artist Fellowship for four years. She's had work published in Sigma Tau Delta's *Rectangle*, *Blackberry: A Magazine*, and *Fiyah Literary Magazine*. Her debut young adult novel, *The Black Girls Left Standing*, was a 2022 Junior Library Guild Gold Standard Selection. In her free time, she enjoys watching horror films, reading the latest young adult novels, and hanging out with her poodle, Darcy, and her cat, Pickle.

Maggie Hall indulges her obsession with distant lands and far-flung adventures as often as she can. She has played with baby tigers in Thailand, learned to make homemade pasta in Italy, and taken thousands of miles of trains through the vibrant countryside of India. In her past life, she was a bookstore events coordinator and marketing manager, and when she's not on the other side of the world, she lives with her husband and their cats in Albuquerque, New Mexico, where she watches USC football and does work in graphic design.

Leah Henderson is a national rowing champion, an All-New England soccer player, and a champion track-and-field athlete. When she isn't playing or cheering on her favorite teams or athletes, she can be found scribbling down stories. She is the author of a number of critically acclaimed books for young readers including *The Magic in Changing Your Stars, Together We March, A Day for Rememberin'*, and *The Courage of the Little Hummingbird*. Leah teaches in Spalding University's graduate writing program and lives in Washington, DC.

Sarah Henning is a former sports journalist and the author of several books for young adult and middle grade readers featuring headstrong girls, including two very sporty books, *Throw Like a Girl* and *It's All in How You Fall*. When not writing, she runs ultramarathons, hangs out with her husband and two kids, and takes the world's largest (and fluffiest) corgi for long walks. Sarah lives in Lawrence, Kansas, hometown of Langston Hughes, William S. Burroughs, and a really good basketball team. Visit her at sarahhenningwrites.com.

Jennifer Iacopelli was born in New York and has no plans to leave, ever. Growing up, she read everything she could get her hands on and now, as a high school librarian, she frolics all day with her students, books, and computers and writes at night while cheering on her beloved Yankees. Jennifer is the author of *Game. Set. Match.*, *Losing at Love*, *Break the Fall*, and *Finding Her Edge*, as well as the co-editor, with Dahlia Adler, of *Out of Our League*. Follow her @jennifercarolyn.

Naomi Kanakia is the author of *Just Happy to Be Here* and two other contemporary YA novels. She's also written *The Cynical Writer's Guide to the Publishing Industry*, and her short fiction, poetry, and literary criticism have been published, err, all over the place. She lives in San Francisco with her wife and daughter.

Growing up in Tennessee, **Miranda Kenneally** dreamed of becoming an Atlanta Brave, a country singer (cliché!), or a UN interpreter. Instead she writes and works for the State Department in Washington, D.C., where George W. Bush once used her shoulder as an armrest. Miranda is the author of many YA sports novels, including *Catching Jordan*, *Racing Savannah*, and *Breathe, Annie, Breathe*. Miranda loves Twitter, *Star Trek*, and her husband. Visit mirandakenneally.com.

Yamile (sha-MEE-lay) Saied Méndez is a sports-obsessed Argentine American Pura Belpré gold medal–winning author. She lives in Utah with her Puerto Rican husband and their five kids, two adorable dogs, and one majestic cat. An inaugural Walter Dean Myers Grant recipient, she's also a graduate of Voices of Our Nations (VONA) and the Vermont College of Fine Arts MFA Writing for Children and Young Adults program. She writes picture books, middle grade, young adult, and adult fiction. Yamile is a founding member of Las Musas, the first collective of women and nonbinary Latine MG and YA authors. She's represented by Linda Camacho at Gallt & Zacker Literary.

Cam Montgomery (nonbinary she/her) is a born-and-raised Angeleno. She is the author of YA novels *Home and Away* and *By Any Means Necessary*, and editor of *All Signs Point to Yes*, an anthology. When not off dreaming up some romance-y work in progress, you can find her on Instagram @camstagram.jpg or on TikTok @hey .itsCam. Having ditched L.A., she now resides in Seattle with her rescue pup Sébastien ("Bash").

Marieke Nijkamp (she/they) is a #1 *New York Times*–bestselling author of novels, graphic novels, and comics, including *This Is Where It Ends*, *At the End of Everything*, *Critical Role: Vox Machina— Kith & Kin*, *Hawkeye: Kate Bishop*, *The Oracle Code*, and *Unbroken: 13 Stories Starring Disabled Teens*. Marieke lives and writes in Small Town, the Netherlands.

Amparo Ortiz is a young adult and middle grade author from Puerto Rico. Her speculative work includes the Blazewrath Games duology, *Last Sunrise in Eterna*, and *Saving Chupie*. She's published short story comics in *Marvel's Voices: Comunidades #1* and in the Eisner Award–winning *Puerto Rico Strong*. She's also co-editor of *Our Shadows Have Claws*, a young adult horror anthology featuring myths and monsters from Latin America. Her story in *Out of Our League* marks her contemporary debut.

Aminah Mae Safi is the author of four novels, including *Tell Me How You Really Feel* and *Travelers Along the Way: A Robin Hood Remix*. She's an erstwhile art historian, a fan of Cholula on popcorn, and an unironic lover of the *Fast & Furious* franchise. Her writing has been featured on Bustle and *Salon*, and her award-winning short stories can be found in *Fresh Ink* and *First Year Orientation*. When not writing, she teaches at the low-residency MFA program at Antioch University as well as instructs new writers at the UCLA Extension Creative Writing program. She started training in aikido at age seven and nobody has managed to keep her out of the ring or the dojo since.

Kayla Whaley is the author of the chapter book series *A to Z Animal Mysteries*. Her essays and short fiction have appeared in numerous anthologies including *Unbroken*, *Vampires Never Get Old*, *Game On*, and *Allies*. She holds an MFA in creative nonfiction from the University of Tampa, and is a graduate of the Clarion Writers' Workshop. Kayla lives outside Atlanta, Georgia, where she drinks too much coffee and buys too many books.

ACKNOWLEDGMENTS

This project was a dream of ours for so long, and we're so grateful to everyone who got it off the ground and turned it into this baller collection. Thank you to Alice Sutherland-Hawes, Patricia Nelson, and Chloe Seager for finding it a home, and to our editor, Rachel Diebel, for making that home at Feiwel & Friends such a perfect one.

Of course this collection wouldn't be a collection without the incredible writers who gave us these stories—huge thanks to Carrie, Sara, Juliana, Maggie, Leah, Sarah, Naomi, Miranda, Yamile, Cam, Marieke, Amparo, Aminah, and Kayla for giving us these girls who kick so much ass.

Thank you so much to Andi Poretta and L. Whitt for this incredible cover (front and back!), and to Dawn Ryan, Arik Harden, Kim Waymer, Chandra Wohleber, Jennifer Sale, Kelly Markus, and Avia Perez for getting this book in tip-top shape. Huge thanks, too, to the whole sales team for all your work, including Natalia Becerra, Jennifer Edwards, and Rebecca Schmidt, and of course to Jennifer Besser and Jean Feiwel for welcoming our book into F&F.

And to our one-time teammates, fellow sports staff, the girls we've coached, and all the female athletes who've paved the way, this one's for you.

Thank you for reading this Feiwel & Friends book. The friends
who made **OUT OF OUR LEAGUE** possible are:

JEAN FEIWEL, Publisher

LIZ SZABLA, VP, Associate Publisher

RICH DEAS, Senior Creative Director

ANNA ROBERTO, Executive Editor

HOLLY WEST, Senior Editor

KAT BRZOZOWSKI, Senior Editor

DAWN RYAN, Executive Managing Editor

JIE YANG, Senior Production Manager

FOYINSI ADEGBONMIRE, Editor

RACHEL DIEBEL, Editor

EMILY SETTLE, Editor

BRITTANY GROVES, Assistant Editor

L. WHITT, Designer

AVIA PEREZ, Senior Production Editor

KELLY MARKUS, Production Editorial Assistant

Follow us on Facebook or visit us online at mackids.com.
Our books are friends for life.